Nothing Ventured

Stuart Bone

Copyrights

For all those taking a chance and embarking on a new venture.

Chapter 1

Lou had never been involved in an orgy before. She wasn't quite sure how she'd got here or when she had become naked but it seemed rude not to join in so she decided to try and make the best of it. That cute actor from the Jester's supermarkets commercial was here too. Granted he was at the far side of the pile of people and currently licking somebody else's nipple but Lou felt; if she somehow managed to get across to him; he'd want to lick hers too.

Her old Geography teacher, Mr Kendal, was also a participant for some reason; getting right into the action and wearing nothing but a smile. Fortunately the folds of his stomach were hiding the more unattractive parts from view. He caught her eye and winked lasciviously at her. He used to do that at school too, now Lou came to think about it.

She had to get across to Pete Crick. It wasn't going to be easy and that beeping sound wasn't helping her to concentrate either. Where was it coming from? Doing her best to ignore it, Lou concentrated on finding the easiest route through to Pete. She crouched down and parted a pair of legs in front of her. This looked to be the best way so she squeezed herself through the gap. That beeping seemed to be getting louder, even though Lou was now right in the centre of the throng. Perhaps it was just the noise of that woman's clitoral piercings clanging together.

She elbowed her way past a pair of very hairy buttocks. She was almost at the other side now. A big part of Pete Crick was almost at touching distance. Lou leant forwards and slowly extended her arm; her fingertips tantalisingly close to the prize.

1

The ground below her disappeared. As she began to fall, she reached out for something to grab hold of. Her Geography teacher groaned with pleasure. She screamed, let go and fell.

Opening her eyes Lou saw the familiar, dusty, old, pink lightshade, half hanging off the ceiling light. She stretched out her right hand and switched off the beeping alarm clock, knocking over bottles of perfume and lotion on the bedside table in the process. Silence entered the room.

God, she thought, I feel like shit; and not just because of that last image of Mr Kendal.

Had it been the drinks last night that had caused her to dream like that? They were certainly responsible for the pain in her head. Okay so she did often think about Pete Crick. If a man could still look hot wearing a jester's outfit while holding a bag of groceries then that's a guy Lou wanted to meet. And that might just be a possibility. Simon, her manager, had told all the staff at the supermarket yesterday that the actor was touring the country, visiting a number of stores in the Jester's chain as part of a promotional campaign.

Ah, who am I kidding, Lou thought, he's not going to come to a backwater like this.

She sat up in bed and groaned, her hands automatically reaching for her forehead. Last night had meant to be a few drinks in The Smugglers after work. Two days before, her five year old daughter, Maddie, had gone to stay with her dad and his wife in London for the last two weeks of the summer holiday and it seemed like a good idea to go out for a couple of swift ones; a belated celebration for finally dumping that arse wipe, Chris, a month ago. The fact that it was a Tuesday and they all had to get up for work today hadn't really entered into the equation. What time had she left the pub? Lou couldn't remember. What had they been drinking? Lou couldn't remember.

She swung her legs over the side of the bed and slowly got to her feet, farting rather loudly.

Jesus Christ, she thought, getting a flashback whilst wafting her hands in front of her, I've got to stop getting curry sauce on my kebab.

After a long, hot shower Lou didn't feel any better. Bits of last night kept reappearing in her mind and the back of her throat. As if her head didn't hurt enough she managed to catch her foot in yesterday's knickers as she returned from the en suite, which sent her crashing to the floor.

"Oh God," she said aloud, her eyes parallel with her bra; which was wrapped around the base of the bedpost, "So that's where I put the leftover lamb meat."

Fifteen minutes later, after throwing up, dressing, throwing up again and trying to apply a bit of make-up; Lou was looking at herself in the hallway mirror. Ten years ago she could have partied all night long and gone straight into work looking fabulous. Now it took a lot of effort to make the night before disappear from off her face. Those dark circles didn't exactly show off the green of her eyes. She didn't like scraping her long, brown hair back and up into a loose bun but she didn't have time to get the straighteners out. Even now frizzy bits were sticking out like she'd just pushed her finger into the light socket.

"Oh sod it," she sighed, "That will do." It was only the local supermarket she worked in after all, not some fashionable head office in a trendy city.

She opened the front door to her apartment. Directly opposite stood Diana Carlton, one of the founder members of

3

the Ryan Harbour coven as far as Lou was concerned. She was watering that hideous looking plant she kept by her own front door. Lou hated it and was sure that was the only reason Diana kept it there. Mind you, if she was honest, Lou had done a similar thing with Maddie's toys; leaving the bulkier items in an untidy pile outside her door for Diana to see every time she left her own apartment.

She was sure Diana was only standing there now because she knew it was the time Lou left for work. The woman didn't have a job, never had done, so why else was she up this early and immaculately dressed as always? There was probably going to be some comment about what time Lou had come home last night and how loud she'd been. Although she couldn't remember anything Lou was pretty sure a song would have been involved and perhaps a knock at Diana's door as she staggered past. Still, she was in no mood for an argument right now or to feel the full force of that withering, condescending stare Diana always gave that put her back up.

"Before you say anything, it was just one night out, okay," she called over, as she locked her door, "I had a good time but I'm not making a habit of it."

She headed towards the door to the stairwell, not making eye contact with her neighbour.

"It was just a one-off. There's no need to panic. It's not like anyone died."

Lou headed through the door before there was any response. If she had looked back she would have seen Diana take a handkerchief out of her sleeve and dab at her eyes.

*

Jamie had just come out from cleaning the Gents when he heard the rattle of the pub's main door. He unlocked it and

4

smiled as Gloria Turner walked in.

"I'm not talking to you," she said, sweeping past.

"Oh, why not?"

"I've just seen my daughter on her way to work."

Jamie grinned. "I bet she's feeling rough."

"And looked it, too. Honestly, a lady should always try and make an effort," Gloria said, removing her red, leather jacket and smoothing her zebra print top down around her ample bosom, "One never knows when one will bump into Mr Right."

"I'm sure 'one' won't meet him crossing the road to the supermarket at half past eight in the morning in Ryan Harbour," Jamie told her, disposing of the mop and bucket out the back.

When he returned Gloria was wiping down the bar counter. Her mind was still firmly on Lou.

"I don't know what she was doing coming in here last night anyway," she said, "I knew she was going to get on one. I saw that look in her eyes as I left after finishing my shift. Honestly that baby has only just been sent away to her dad's and she's already out on the town."

"That 'baby' is five years old," Jamie reminded her, "And it's been a long time since she's been at her dad's isn't it? He only sees her during school holidays."

"Well London is so far away just for weekend visits," Gloria said, "Not for him, he could make more of an effort to come up here; I mean for Maddie. She'd be too tired for school on the Monday with all that travelling."

"Exactly," Jamie replied, "Lou has to manage all on her own most of the time."

Gloria conceded the point with a small tip of the head.

"I think Lou was due a good night out," he continued, "It helped my profits along as well."

5

Gloria tutted. "I know you need all the help you can get," she said, "But I'd rather it not be at my daughter's expense."

"Oh come on, I meant the group she brought in with her, not just her drinks; I'm not that desperate."

Gloria raised her plucked to within an inch of their life eyebrows.

"Well, I'm not so desperate that I'd take advantage of someone like that. Lou's a mate."

Gloria smiled but the grin very quickly disappeared from her face.

"Are things that bad?" she asked.

Jamie sighed as he rubbed the back of his neck.

"I could do with a few more regulars than the handful I have," he admitted.

"Do you really think you have that many?"

"Yes," Jamie replied, sharply, "They may not all come in every day…"

"Or week."

"But they still come in. I mean, Mike the Wipe's visits are a bit sporadic these days, I'll grant you that."

"He really ought to get some professional help with that cleanliness obsession," Gloria admitted, "Sometimes he doesn't leave the house for weeks, so his poor wife told me."

She stopped her cleaning and shook her head, sadly.

"It can't be much of a sex life for her," she continued, "I mean, you only have to touch Mike with your hand and he's got his flannel out, wiping himself down. What happens when she puts her lips anywhere near his…?"

"Anyway," Jamie interrupted, "Mike still has his special glass here behind the bar, just for his use. Well, that's what I tell him; but it's a sign of a regular. Tricky Vince and the

6

Colonel come in more often than him. Okay so I haven't seen Doug the Bug in a long time…"

"Oh he's on another research trip," Gloria replied, coyly; leaning on the bar and going a bit doe-eyed, "He's studying moths in the Congo."

"Sounds pretty dull to me."

She sighed. "I bet he'll be hacking his way through scrub and vines in the jungle right now; all hot and sweaty and bare-chested."

"Do I need to turn the hose on you again," Jamie called over.

Gloria stood up straight, her face a little red.

"Anyway," she said, "I don't think you can call any of them, regulars; only Old Joe comes in each day. Even his shadow, Bill, has started drinking up at The Red Lion on the high street a lot more. Mind you, it's closer to his house and it is cheaper."

Gloria began wiping the bitter pumps.

"And let's face it," she continued, "Are those two old fossils really the sort of people you want as regulars anyway? They aren't exactly big spenders and Old Joe's suit that he wears day in, day out looks pre-war. I mean, a daily shave would help his appearance. I'm sure he only comes in because you keep giving him free beer. That's not exactly helping your profits either, is it?"

"It's just the occasional pint," Jamie reasoned, "And the odd cigar. I like the old guy. Quiet, no trouble; a whole life lived that's hidden from the rest of us. There's something almost mystical about him."

"He's not bloody Merlin. Mind you, a bit of magic is exactly what you need if you hope to keep this place going."

Gloria instantly regretted saying that when she saw Jamie's broad shoulders visibly slump; but it wasn't far from the mark and she was pretty sure Jamie knew it too. He was passionate about this old pub and those lovely dark blue eyes of his shone whenever he was serving customers, but that wasn't so often these days and then the light would dim and suddenly he'd look every inch his forty-eight years.

"Still," she encouraged, "The regatta is this Saturday. Perhaps that will draw a few people in."

"Perhaps," Jamie replied, wistfully.

He couldn't understand why the locals didn't like to come into his pub. The Smugglers Inn wasn't large but it was quite a wide building. The bar ran across the back of the room so that the majority of tables were along the windowed side, looking out onto the harbour. The interior was polished wood with all manner of boat-related memorabilia on the walls. It was a nice place; historic. It had been here for over three hundred years. Why wasn't it popular? Jamie couldn't get his head around it. Gloria guessed his thoughts.

"The locals gave up on this place when the tourists invaded," she said, "When I first lived in Ryan Harbour, before I got pregnant with Lou and moved up to Tenham, it was always a locals' pub and busy each night."

"So it can be again," Jamie whispered, more to himself.

"But this was the only pub around here back then. When I returned five years ago two others had opened up," Gloria continued, "This one was full of tourists. That's who this pub appeals to now. All of this décor is for them, really. It's too themed for the locals. They prefer the pub chains on the high street."

"But they're soulless."

"As long as there's a decent pint, competitively priced; that will do them. And the younger ones prefer the nightclub across town. That's why the last owner used to have strippers in here of an evening, to attract as many different people in as he could."

Jamie shook his head. "I still can't picture it," he said, "All this history on the walls and a woman taking off her clothes in the middle of the room."

"You should seriously think about getting them back. Only a few of the locals ever complained. It would fill this place."

"I'm not turning this pub into a strip joint."

"I think you're missing a trick. I was working here then and thought it was done rather well."

Jamie shot Gloria a look.

"I meant I worked behind the bar then, not out front."

He grinned.

"Hey! I could have worked out front if I'd wanted," Gloria told him, throwing down the bar towel she was using, "It may not all be quite in the place it should these days but that doesn't mean there isn't a market out there for it."

"I'm sure you'd be a wow if I turned this place into a strip bar," Jamie told her, trying to keep a straight face as he looked at the dumpy, fifty-five year old woman in front of him; all false eyelashes, thick red lips, and home-dyed, dark auburn hair.

"I'll audition for you now, if you like."

Gloria crossed her arms over in front of her and began to pull up her top.

"No!" Jamie yelled, "Thank you; but no."

Gloria winked.

"I'm going to go and see where that delivery guy has got to, he's late again," Jamie called over to her, as he walked out the front door of the pub, "Could you check the bread in the kitchen for me; it's yesterday's. I'm wondering if we can still use it."

Once outside Jamie sighed again. The harbour itself was a reminder of why his pub was failing. It formed a crescent shape and the road that led to the slipway came down from the high street right by The Smugglers, splitting the harbour in two. The right hand side, including the pub was the old part with clapboard buildings that were now mostly rundown arty type shops or empty guest houses. The left side had been redeveloped a number of years back with new apartments that had retail units on the ground floor. These had all once been busy bars and coffee shops and the harbour had been buzzing but last year the council had closed down the old smuggler tunnels due to health and safety issues. They were the main draw for the tourists. Without them the coaches no longer visited this part of Tenhamshire. The wine bars closed and the coffee shops moved up onto the High Street where they continued to make their big profits from the locals. That just left The Smugglers Inn and the shabby-looking tearoom next door down on the harbour front. Hardly anyone seemed prepared to walk down here just for them when they could get a beer or coffee in town. Even the boat owners brought their own refreshments with them and either took them out to sea or just enjoyed them, sat on their boats in the harbour.

No wonder the pub had been cheap to buy, Jamie thought.

The apartments on the newer side were all lived in but apart from Lou and Old Joe, not many of the residents ever ventured into The Smugglers. Out of the retail units on the ground floor only the larger one opposite the pub across the slipway was being used; having been taken over by Doctor Bryant for his new surgery. That brought locals into the vicinity but really; it wasn't like anyone went to the surgery and then thought, 'Ooh I'll just stop off for a quick pint; that will sit well with my antibiotics.'

Jamie looked up at the old, three storey building that he owned. The place really could do with some major restructuring to turn it into the sort of pub he wanted. A lick of paint wouldn't go amiss, or even just a new sign to replace the faded old one; but there weren't available funds at present; not that he'd tell Gloria that.

He wasn't giving up yet, though. Jamie was sure he could still make a go of things and without needing the 'magic' Gloria had referred to. He liked it around here. He just needed a few good ideas to get the locals using the place; something that wouldn't cost a lot to do. He had a plan forming already for the Regatta day this coming weekend. That event always brought the locals out. This year he was going to bring them into The Smugglers Inn.

Jamie spied the delivery van making its way down the high street. As it crossed the road by the supermarket towards him he looked at his watch and sighed. He'd have to have words with that driver; probably two.

*

Lou exhaled loudly as she walked up to the front entrance of the supermarket. Of all the people to bump into this morning it had to be her mother. Why was she getting to the pub so early and why did she have to spot her, just as Lou was attempting to pull her knickers out of her crack while leaning against the litter bin?

Still, she'd managed to avoid a lecture about the demon drink by telling her mum she was running late. She didn't feel Gloria was the best person to start preaching about living a moral life anyway. Lou's childhood consisted of many memories of Gloria being the wrong side of tipsy with

11

whichever man she was dating at the time.

Lou banged on the glass of the supermarket's main door.

"Morning," Simon said, as he opened it, "God, you look like shit."

Lou looked up at her boss with his thick mass of black hair that no comb could tame.

"I'm hung-over," she told him, "What's your excuse?"

He laughed as she walked past.

"So what happened to a couple after work?" he asked her, "I left at nine. What time did you leave?"

"Haven't got a clue," Lou called back, as she walked into the staffroom to take off her coat.

"Just so long as all the full timers are in on time," Simon continued, "I've got a couple of announcements to make before we open."

"Oh really," Lou replied, without much interest.

"Yes," Simon continued, "Head Office are really taking an interest in stores that can sell their new range of clothing."

"Right," Lou said, buttoning up her overall and coming back out onto the main floor, "But that doesn't concern us, does it."

Simon looked questioningly at her.

"Of course it does," he said, "This could be a big thing for us, put our little store on the map."

Lou sighed. "But isn't that the issue," she replied, "We're only a 'little' store."

"Size has got nothing to do with it," he said.

"I bet you say that to all the girls."

"You know what I mean," Simon told her, "Just because we're a small link in the Jester's supermarket chain it doesn't mean we can't compete with the big boys. In my last store, which was one of the biggest, I was always very much aware of

12

what the little ones could do."

"Fine," Lou told him, "But just where exactly are you going to display this range of clothing? We're packed up with foods because that's what the locals around here want to buy in their supermarket."

Simon shook his head, dislodging dandruff onto the lapels of his suit jacket.

"Selling isn't just about providing what people want," he told Lou, "It's also about selling customers things they hadn't realised they needed. In my last store we had a range of cosmetics that we priced right and displayed correctly. They practically flew off the shelves."

"I remember that range," Lou said, "Didn't it bring a lot of women out in a rash?"

"That's not the point," Simon replied, scratching at the grey stubble on his prominent chin, "We're only concerned with the selling side."

Lou sighed resignedly. "Fine," she said, "I still say good luck in finding a place to display clothes in here."

Her manager winked.

"Oh God, you want me to do it, don't you?"

"It's all good experience for you, Lou. I've been watching you very closely in the six months that I have been running this store."

"That's been you on my balcony? Thank God, I thought it was the bogeyman."

"I'm serious," Simon said, "You're more than capable of running your own store."

"Yeah, right."

"Honestly. Jester's can provide opportunities for you to move on to bigger and better things."

Then why were you moved here to this backwater, is what Lou wanted to ask but instead she smiled and walked out to the rear of the store to pick up the milk delivery. By the time she wheeled it back in to put onto the shelves the other two full-time members of staff had arrived. Precious looked very much the worse for wear after her night out with Lou. She had a bag of frozen peas pressed to her forehead and was groaning quietly. She didn't look quite with it. The water from the defrosting packet was sliding down her elbow and dripping onto the head of Terry, the newest recruit. He was too young to be able to go drinking with them in the pub but he too didn't look quite with it either...he never did.

"Right, I'm glad you've all made it in," Simon told them, "Now then, just a couple of announcements before we begin a fresh new day."

He repeated what he had told Lou about the clothing section.

"So, are there any questions?"

Lou raised her hand.

"Aside from, 'why are we bothering?'" Simon said.

She put her hand back down again. Terry raised his.

"So these clothes are the supermarkets'?"

"Yes," Simon replied, "Jester's own range."

Terry was obviously thinking hard. He pushed his tongue out and screwed his eyes up tight before saying,

"Why would anyone want to buy these?"

He indicated his overall. Lou sniggered.

"We're not selling our uniforms," Simon told him, "Who would want to buy these?"

"That's what I just said," Terry replied.

"He's right, he did," Lou grinned.

Simon sighed and shook his head again.

14

"Where are we putting them?" Precious asked, swapping over her packet of peas for a colder one.

"I'm leaving that in Lou's capable hands."

Precious laughed; a deep booming sound that bounced off of the walls.

"Good luck with that one, darling," she called over, to Lou.

Lou rolled her eyes. "Right," she said, "Is that it?"

"Er, no; I have one final piece of news for you," Simon shifted uncomfortably on the spot, "I've now filled the post of security guard for the store."

He waved his hand over Lou's shoulder at someone in the office, indicating for them to come over.

Lou was still facing in the other direction and saw Precious drop her bag of peas onto Terry's head as she recognised the person who had just emerged.

"Some of you may already know Chris," Simon said.

Lou's stomach somersaulted. She slowly turned round and came face to face with her ex; the man she'd only recently got out of her life. He was grinning at her, that smile that showed too much gum. She felt physically repulsed. He was still wearing his biker jacket and his very black hair was either full of gel or hadn't been washed for a number of days, it was hard to tell. His dark eyes were on Lou.

"Surprise babes," he said.

*

Lou's headache was still with her in the afternoon, although she wasn't sure whether it was hangover related or due to her brain working overtime on planning a layout for the new clothing range. She was certain Chris was to blame for some of it. He was a permanent headache. She could see him across the store now, throwing himself up against the side of shelving displays and peeping around corners, searching for shoplifters. She'd confronted Simon about him as soon as she could that morning.

"I'm sorry, Lou," he'd told her, "But I had to give the job to the best applicant."

"Best? Who were the other candidates, Tweedle Dum and Tweedle Dee?" Lou was pacing the floor of Simon's office, "Chris hasn't worked in security before. I doubt he could spell the word."

"I had a glowing recommendation from his last employer, the art gallery over in Tenham," Simon told her.

"Of course you did," Lou replied, "They couldn't wait to get rid of him could they; especially after the fiasco with the local Masonic Lodge exhibition."

"What fiasco?"

"The lodge was celebrating its fiftieth anniversary and the gallery was going to display photographs of lodge members past and present. They thought that was easy enough for Chris to handle; putting a few photographs up on the wall."

"And?"

"Well they said that they wanted him to arrange a display of male members. He got confused and the Mayoress fainted on opening night when confronted with a room full of fifty photographs of Chris's willy. The only reason he wasn't sacked was because his work should have been checked by the manager before the exhibition opened. No, they were looking for the chance to move him on and now he's here."

"Oh well," Simon mumbled, "I'm sure that was a mistake any of us could have made."

"You think so? Honestly I thought it was bad enough when you employed Terry instead of that other guy."

Simon looked up sharply from his notes.

"I told you about that in strictest confidence," he whispered, "I thought it was the other candidate that was called Terry. I was as shocked as you when this one showed up on his first day. Anyway, he's improving."

"Is he? I asked him to fill up the lemons this morning. He said, 'Are they the yellow round things or the green round things.' In my mood I almost kneed him in his round things."

Simon stood up.

"Look Lou," he said, "I've employed Chris and I'm afraid you'll just have to deal with that. He's on a probationary period so any problems with his work he'll be asked to leave. Staffing issues are never easy; you'll find that out one day. Back at my last store I had a large number of employees and it took a lot of effort to keep them all happy."

Lou doubted Simon put much effort into anything work related. She'd spent the rest of the morning seething, spending as much time as she could in the stockroom so that she didn't take her mood out on the customers. Only Terry got a taste of her wrath when he came in and asked if the store sold loaves of toast. Fortunately Simon walked in before Lou did much damage with the packet of spaghetti.

She'd spent her lunch hour going through the stocklist of clothes that Simon had neglected to tell her that he'd already ordered and now she was looking for the best area in the store for the display to go. Along the wall behind the check-outs was a possibility. Precious was working on the till. She always had a small queue of customers but Lou knew from experience that even if she opened up the other till, no one would come over to her; preferring the wait to enjoy the personal service Precious always gave.

"Hello darling, you back again today? Love the new hairstyle Mrs Roberts. Hey Mr Peters, is that a pepperoni in your basket or are you just happy to see me, darling."

During a quiet lull Precious spun her stool round to speak to Lou.

"Oh my God, how did that arsehole ever get a job here?"

Lou looked across to where Chris was crouching down behind the chiller cabinet and beyond that to where Simon was talking Terry through the public address system.

"You're going to have to narrow that one down, Precious," she said, "Which arsehole are you talking about?"

"Chris. My God; security? If anything I feel less secure with him being here."

"I still can't believe Simon got funding for a security guard in a store this size anyway. I'm not convinced he actually knows how small this shop is."

"Makes you think about why he ended up here," Precious said, twisting the end of one of her curly, copper-coloured hair extensions around her finger, "I spoke to Linda over at the Tenham store and she reckons his area manager caught him in one of the storage fridges at his previous place, demonstrating to a young trainee all the things you can do with a parsnip and a jar of horseradish."

"Oh my God, who told her that?"

Precious shrugged.

"I don't know how these rumours start," Lou said, "I mean; his last store wasn't even in Tenhamshire."

"You know what they say, darling," Precious replied, "There's no smoke without fire."

Lou shook her head. How long would it take for that rumour to be all round Ryan Harbour? It was such a small town and

18

there were plenty of old gossips in the coven. If it wasn't Diana's friend, Joyce, it would be one of the others. Lou was aware of what they said about her; 'Like mother, like daughter.' And she knew full well what Gloria's reputation was. Not that it was deserved…well, not completely. She returned to her task of finding the right spot for the clothing range but got distracted by Chris.

"Look at the prat now," she said, to Precious.

As they watched, Chris jumped across one of the freezers and threw himself into a forward roll. Unfortunately he lost his balance halfway through and fell to the side; right into the huge pile of tinned peas that were currently on sale. As the room fell silent after the crash so Terry's first public address announcement came through the speakers.

"Jester's tinned peas are two pence off a can. That's fucking cheap, man."

Simon wrestled the microphone from his fingers and sent Terry across to pile the tins up again. Chris grinned at the two women and sidled over to them.

"Have you stolen anything?" he leered at Precious, "Do you want to stand up against the wall and spread 'em for me?"

Precious made a noise of disgust and returned to her till. Chris turned his full gaze onto Lou.

"She wants me," he said, "It's only a matter of time. The tall, Kenyan ones always do."

"Her family come from Nigeria," Lou corrected, "And anyway, Precious was born here in Ryan Harbour."

Chris sniffed. "You know what I mean," he said, gazing at the back of Precious' head, "I'd love her long legs wrapped round my waist."

"You've more chance of her long fingers wrapped round

19

your throat."

Chris chuckled.

"So," he said, placing one hand on the wall above Lou's head and leaning in close, "Can you check if I've got a hernia, babes? Hold this and I'll cough."

Even though she was against the wall Lou still automatically recoiled.

"You're such an arse," she told him.

Chris grinned again; that big, gummy grin.

"That line worked on you the first time we met."

"Don't remind me. Look, what are you doing here?"

"Securiting," he replied.

"I mean how did you get the job?"

"Interviewed for it, babes. I wanted a new challenge, a fresh start; a taste of success."

"The gallery wanted to fire you, didn't they?"

Chris shrugged his shoulders.

"I wouldn't put it quite like that, babes."

Lou nodded, knowingly.

"I still don't know how you were hired. You've got no experience in Security."

The grin returned.

"Well it must have been my animal magnetism in the interview. I guess your boss Simon must be...well, you know."

"What?"

"You know," Chris repeated, raising his eyebrows at her, "He must like to go beachcombing for chocolate starfish...down at poo bay."

Lou made the same noise of disgust that Precious had made earlier.

"Let me get this straight," she said, "You think Simon must

be gay and he fancies you?"

Chris nodded. "Stands to reason, don't it? All you ladies can't get enough of me; why not the happy fellas too? I could probably turn a lesbian."

"Her stomach, maybe," Lou told him, "Look, I think you got the job here because Simon couldn't be bothered to check out your references. I don't think it's because the entire population of women and gay men fancy you."

Chris pulled his collar up.

"Well, if you've got it," he said.

Lou rolled her eyes again.

"You know; if I called you a scum-sucking, ignorant pig it would still be a compliment."

Chris winked at her.

"Cheers babes," he replied, "But don't you start feeling jealous; I've always got a place for you; and that place is right between my legs."

There was only a two word response to that but as customers were nearby Lou had to stifle it.

"You'll come running soon," he continued, "It won't be long until I'm parking my bike at your place."

"You don't have a bike," Lou sighed, "You only have the jacket."

"Who says I was talking about an actual bike?" Chris said, looking her up and down, "It was one of them euphoniums, weren't it."

Lou opened her mouth to tell him the word was euphemism but Chris held up his hand to silence her.

"Hang on," he whispered, "Shoplifter at large."

Before she could respond Chris rushed off. She and Precious watched as he rugby-tackled old Mrs Robson to the ground, just

21

as she was leaving the shop.

"He's keen, I'll give him that, darling," Precious said.

Lou nodded. "But he's going to have to improve his self-defence technique. Mrs Robson is kicking his arse."

"Dr Bryant said she would soon get used to using that stick."

The two women continued to watch as Simon came over to sort out the commotion.

"Did he really think she was shoplifting that roll of wallpaper?" Precious asked, "Doesn't he realise we don't sell that sort of thing here?"

Lou sighed. "The amount Chris doesn't realise in life could fill the Amazon basin," she said, "Anyway, how's your hangover; headache gone?"

"Getting there," Precious told her, "But I'm glad church choir practice has been cancelled this evening."

Simon took Mrs Robson into his office. Chris limped over to the tills, trying to look cool.

"She'll think twice next time," he said.

Lou ignored him and continued on with her conversation.

"Why's it been cancelled?" she asked Precious.

"I think there's something wrong with my pastor."

"You're probably over cooking it," Chris told her.

Lou shook her head.

"Haven't you got somewhere else to go?" she asked.

Chris rubbed his shoulder.

"I might just go and check out the staffroom sofa for half an hour," he said, and limped off.

Lou returned to her clothing plan. Behind the tills wasn't really the best place for a new display, she decided, and headed up the main aisle to the back of the store where any display would be seen as soon as a customer entered the shop. This looked to be the better place. Just as she began to take down a couple of old advertising posters she heard a, "Hello dear" beside her.

"Hello Grace, how are you?"

"I've just popped in to get some chops for Robert's dinner."

"Of course, it's Wednesday isn't it."

"Have you seen Diana today, dear?" Grace asked.

Lou's smile disappeared from her face.

"Very briefly, this morning," she said.

"Oh, so you'll have heard all about it then."

"Heard about what?"

"Well, her sister," Grace told her.

Lou shrugged her shoulders. "I'm not with you," she said.

"I saw her as I left the apartment just now. She did seem upset so I asked her what was wrong."

"And?"

"And she told me."

Lou was exasperated. For a chatterer Grace took a hell of a long time to tell you something.

"What about her sister?"

"Well she's dead, isn't she?"

"Is she?"

"Yes. Poor Diana got a call during the night. Quite sudden it was, apparently and quite a shock by all accounts."

Lou's mind returned to when she left her apartment for work this morning. What was it she had said to Diana; 'There's no need to panic? It's not like anyone died?'

Shit; Lou had an apology to make.

Chapter 2

Robert Keane parked his car in the car park behind The
Smugglers Inn and walked across the slipway towards the block
of apartments opposite. It was six thirty, the time he always got
home from work. Grace, his wife, would be cooking dinner. It
was Wednesday so that meant lamb chops. It was always lamb
chops on a Wednesday evening. Even then he knew Grace
would have forgotten to buy them and made a second hasty trip
over to the supermarket in the afternoon. Robert sighed.

His neighbour, Lou Turner, crossed the road in front of him
with what looked like a bottle of wine in a Jester's carrier bag.
They smiled and nodded at one another.

She's planning a good night, he thought as he watched her
walk round to the entrance of the pub.

Robert sighed again as he entered the gate that led to his
apartment block, although this time it was more to do with the
sight of builders' rubble and lorries, than boredom. A new
block of apartments was being added up at the far end where a
parade of amusement arcades had once stood. They hadn't been
very popular and had looked rather shabby so he wasn't too
concerned about their demolition. However, as the only access
to the site for the builders was through the residents' car park,
Robert and all his neighbours had been told to park elsewhere.
Fortunately the landlord of The Smugglers had kindly made the
pub car park available. It wasn't a busy place and Robert
always managed to get a space. He really must pop in there
sometime for a drink to show his appreciation.

He entered the communal hallway to his block and took the
lift up to the second floor. Robert knew that when he opened

the front door Grace would call out, "Hello love; had a good day?" He would respond in the affirmative, no matter what his day had been like. Grace would then proceed to give him a blow by blow account of her day while he washed up and got changed, not really listening and then the two of them would sit down to dinner with a glass of Chablis each. He put his key in the lock, sighed again and opened the door.

"Hello love; had a good day?" Grace called, from the kitchen.

"Ye-es," Robert replied.

"That's good. You'll never guess what I forgot today."

"The bloody chops," he whispered under his breath, frowning so tightly his black, bushy eyebrows almost united as one.

"Only the lamb chops for dinner. I had to run over to the supermarket again. I spoke to Lou. Oh that reminds me, poor Diana has…"

Robert walked into their bedroom and through into the en suite. He washed up and got changed into his baggy jogging bottoms and a t-shirt that he felt must have shrunk in the tumble dryer as it had become a rather snug fit. When he walked back out to the hallway and down to the living room, Grace was still in full flow.

"And after I finally got off the phone with Linda, who isn't going to make the regatta this year, I put the chops under the grill."

All of the apartments had the same layout. From the front door the room directly opposite was the master bedroom with en suite. Beside that was the second bedroom with the main bathroom on the opposite side of the hallway beside the storage cupboard. The main open–plan room consisted of a dining area with a large, square kitchen behind it. To the side of this, facing out onto the balcony, was the living room. It was a very modern apartment, especially compared to the previous house Robert and Grace had lived in but neither of them regretted the move. It was something different in Robert's monotonous life and Grace loved the large kitchen space. Dinner and a chilled glass of Chablis were waiting on the dining table.

Robert remained very quiet throughout dinner, not that Grace really noticed, continuing to chatter between mouthfuls of food. She only stopped when he went to the fridge and got out the bottle of white wine.

"A second glass?" she questioned, "We don't usually."

"I feel like it tonight," he replied, sitting back down before filling his glass and topping up his wife's.

Robert took a long sip before speaking.

"Grace," he said, "Do you ever feel bored?"

She thought for a second before replying,

"Not especially."

"But don't you ever get fed up with the same routine? We never do anything different."

"I've never really given it much thought," Grace said, "It's just life, isn't it. You get on and live it."

"What about excitement? Don't you crave it?"

"Robert, we're both coming up for sixty-five; excitement can be dangerous."

He sighed again.

"I'm bored, Grace."

"What's brought this on, love?" she asked, placing a hand on top of her husband's.

"I don't know, really," he said, getting up from his chair and pacing the room; wine glass in hand, "It's nothing specific, I

26

just think we could do more."

Grace was eyeing him, warily, as he paced. As soon as she'd put her hand on his, Robert had moved away.

"Are you bored with me?" she asked, "Is that what this is all about?"

Robert stopped walking and smiled down at his wife. Even though she was looking at him in fear, making those few wrinkles around her brown eyes crease even more deeply; he could still see the young woman he had fallen in love with all those years ago.

"Of course I'm not," he told her, "It isn't you. I'm talking about both of us. We should do more together."

"That's a relief."

Robert took a large gulp of wine before forming his next sentence.

"I thought we could start off in the bedroom," he said.

"Start what off?"

"Well, I thought that's where we could maybe be a bit more adventurous."

Grace smiled.

"It's funny you should mention that," she said, "I was thinking the same thing, just the other day."

"Really?" Robert's heart pounded a little faster in his chest.

She nodded. "Oh yes. I was thinking of a feature wall; perhaps a stripe or a bold print."

"I didn't mean decorating," he snapped, "I was talking…you know…sex."

"Sex?" Grace questioned, "But we do that regularly."

"It's once a month Grace, unless it's my birthday; and then we always do it the same way."

Grace was confused. She scratched her head through the

light curls of her brown hair.

"Do you think you're coming down with something," she asked, "Should I make an appointment with Dr Bryant for you?"

Robert sat back down again. He took his wife's hand in his.

"I'm not ill, love. I just want to explore the possibility of adding a little bit of excitement to our life, bedroom-wise."

"Like what?"

"Well, there are lots of things," he said, reddening a little, "Different positions, toys, adult films; maybe even a threesome."

"A threesome? What; get someone else involved? Like who? No one we know surely? I'm not sure there is anyone I'd want involved. Unless of course you meant..."

Grace began thinking. Robert watched but became rather alarmed when she began counting on her fingers. When she got to three he cut in.

"It doesn't have to be anyone we know," he told her, "I believe you can advertise for someone."

Grace looked incredulous.

"I'm not putting an ad on the supermarket noticeboard for something like that. What would people think?" she shuddered, "Besides, how would you word an advert like that? It would take some explaining and there's a charge for any advert larger than postcard size."

"We wouldn't use the supermarket noticeboard," Robert said, wearily, "There are magazines for that sort of thing."

"Well I'm not having another person in this house anyway," Grace told him, firmly, "Not without the spare room being decorated first."

"What has that got to do with it?"

"Well you don't think I'd let this happen in the master suite, do you? Diana's bedroom is the other side of that wall. What would she think if she heard a strange man's voice?"

"She wouldn't."

"The walls aren't that thick," Grace pointed out.

"No, I mean it wouldn't be another man would it; in bed with us?"

"Why not?"

Robert gave a nervous laugh.

"Well, it would be a woman."

"Why?"

"Well, you know," he could feel himself blushing again and the top of his bald head was sweating, "You two...both with me...you know."

Grace shook her head, firmly.

"Well what were you thinking?" he asked.

"I assumed you wanted another man," Grace told him, matter-of-factly, "Help you out a bit. You're not as young as you used to be and you do tire easily these days. I really ought to get you on a proper diet."

Robert pulled surreptitiously at the front of his t-shirt.

"Look, we're getting ahead of ourselves," he said, "It doesn't have to be a threesome anyway; perhaps just a change of room."

"A change of room?" Grace looked disgusted.

"Why not?" Robert asked, "We could do it in here, on the sofa; or I could throw you across this dining table."

"But I've just had it French polished," Grace said, looking down at it, "I'd shoot off the other side."

"Well we haven't got to decide anything yet," Robert interjected, "Let's just talk it through and see what we can come up with; okay?"

Grace fell silent while she had a think. She took a healthy swig of wine and then emptied the remainder of the bottle into both of their glasses.

"Ok," she said, finally, "We'll talk about it some more. I'm not promising anything mind and we must keep it between ourselves."

Robert smiled.

"That's fine, love," he said, "It'll be fun. You just wait and see."

Mind you, he thought, as he lifted his glass; if Grace imagined another man was getting into their bed she had another thing coming.

*

Jamie was bored. He'd last got off the barstool forty-five minutes ago to pull a pint for Tricky Vince, who was now stood outside the front of The Smugglers, talking loudly into his mobile phone and smoking a cigarette. He hadn't stopped talking for ages and half of the lager remained in the glass. Gloria came out from the small kitchen area with two jacket potatoes and some cutlery.

"Right, I'll just have this before I head off," she said, "Which one do you want; cheese or sweetcorn?"

Jamie took the sweetcorn filled potato. At that moment Vince walked back in, swinging his shoulders as he swaggered up to the bar.

"Here you go," he said, placing his half-filled lager on the counter, "It's gone a little flat."

"Do you want another?" Jamie asked.

Vince shook his head.

"No, I've got to head off; bit of business to attend to."

He tapped the side of his nose with his index finger.

"By the way," he said, eyeing the two plates, "Where do you buy your potatoes? I've got a mate who can get you…"

"No thanks."

"Straight up," Vince continued, "It's all kosher. My mate's got a field…"

Jamie held up his hand. "It's fine," he said.

Vince grinned. "I'm off then. Stay lucky."

He turned and left.

"That guy is such a conman," Gloria confided, watching him go, "He once tried to sell me some 'luxury winter legwear.' It turned out to be surgical stockings."

"I thought you used to go out with him," Jamie said.

"It was one date," Gloria replied, "I don't usually go for short men but he had a certain appeal. He was very confident in himself. Not cocky, just confident. Anyway he said he had a table booked at that posh French bistro in Tenham. He said he'd done a favour for the owner once and was owed."

"And it was a lie, was it?"

"Oh no, it was true. He was owed. Manager came out and punched him. Apparently the mushrooms he'd supplied were a bit on the poisonous side. I spent the evening with him up at Tenham General while his lip was stitched."

"How romantic."

Gloria had just popped a forkful of potato into her mouth but quickly swallowed it as she remembered something else she wanted to say.

"He told everyone the scar was the result of him breaking up a gang fight. What a liar. Honestly; I saw him scream at a moth once."

Lou walked in through the door.

"I hope that's not for tonight," Gloria said, spotting the bottle

31

of wine in the Jester's carrier bag.

"Calm down, it's not for me," Lou said, sitting up on a barstool and placing the bag carefully onto the counter, "It's an apology gift."

Gloria sighed. "Due to last night I suppose."

"No; well not directly. It's…why am I defending myself? My God, you were always out getting drunk when I was growing up."

"I was not," Gloria said, indignantly, "It was only ever a weekend when I got a little bit, well; light-headed; and even then I always left you with someone you knew."

"Putting the word 'auntie' or 'uncle' in front of their name didn't make me automatically know them," Lou responded, "My God; I remember being looked after by Uncle Milkman once."

Gloria grabbed Jamie's plate and stormed off into the kitchen. He felt it wasn't the right time to say he hadn't actually finished with it.

"Your mum's a good person," he said, to Lou.

She sighed. "I know. I shouldn't keep bringing up the past but, well; she's left it a bit late to start telling me what to do. I'm thirty, not thirteen."

Jamie stood up. "Can I get you a drink?"

"No thanks," Lou said, "I think I had enough yesterday."

"It's on the house."

"Great," Gloria had just returned to the bar, "Why don't you just pour it down her throat?"

"I've already refused it, mum," Lou said, "I'm sorry I snapped at you."

Gloria waved her hand dismissively.

"I know I go on at times but I just don't want you to…"

32

"Turn into you?"

"Oi, that's not what I was going to say."

Lou winked at Jamie.

"I was going to say that I don't want you to get hurt," Gloria said, firmly, "I worry about you. I can't help it; you're my daughter. Perhaps I wasn't always there for you but I'm here now and I always will be. I'm not going anywhere. I'll be here for you every day from now on."

Lou pulled a face.

"I think I've changed my mind about that drink, Jamie," she said.

They all laughed and any remaining hostile atmosphere evaporated.

"You're not exactly busy are you," Lou said, looking around the room.

"You've just missed Tricky Vince," Jamie told her.

"Good. I couldn't face another chat about him supplying the supermarket with meat. I don't think it's a coincidence that the last time he did was just after that stray dog disappeared from the car park out back."

"Old Joe was in earlier, as usual."

"Wow, two of mum's exes."

Gloria looked up from where she was wiping down the already spotless bar.

"Hey," she said, "I've already explained once tonight that it was only the one date."

"Yeah and you spent all of his pension money."

Jamie got a whack on the arm.

"Not Old Joe," Gloria told him.

Lou laughed and picked up her carrier bag.

"I'm going. I just came in to tell you that you might see

Chris about."

"Oh no," Gloria said, "You're not dating that shit again are you?"

"No, but he's managed to wangle himself the security job at the supermarket."

"How?"

Lou sighed as she got off the barstool.

"Let's just say I don't think my manager did a lot of interviewing for the position. I can't believe he'll be there for long anyway, but I just wanted to warn you, in case you see him. And we're definitely not getting back together. He's a complete slime bucket."

"It took you long enough to work that out," Gloria said.

Lou opened her mouth to respond with a comment about her mum's love life but managed to stop herself. Gloria smiled, knowingly.

"It's not always easy to root out the losers," she conceded, "I still have trouble at my age."

"Anyway," Lou said, "The bright side is that he'll probably spend a few quid in here; help your profits, Jamie."

"I'm not that destitute," he replied, "Why does everyone think I am?"

Lou and Gloria looked at each other, both sharing the same opinion.

"Things will pick up," he said, "Once those new apartments at the end of the harbour are finished."

"Come off it," Lou told him, "You can't even attract the guys building it in here at the end of the day."

"Well, they're not local. Besides, they've got their cars with them so they can't drink."

"And what success has come from letting us residents use

your car park?"

"I'll admit I did hope that would bring in a few people."

"Yes," Lou told him, "But you should have still charged the building firm some kind of rent. That would have brought in some money."

Jamie didn't respond; realising Lou was right. Why hadn't he thought of that?

"I heard," Gloria interjected, "That the council are considering allowing those empty shops below your apartment block Lou, to be converted into some ground floor retirement apartments; a sheltered housing type thing."

"Well that's good," Jamie said, his mood brightening again, "They'll have all the time in the world to come in here for a drink."

"You'll need more than a few geriatrics to get this place turning a good profit," Gloria told him, "Anyway, the sort of people that get put in those places probably won't even be able to walk as far as here; or remember where the pub is, bless them. They'll be a lot of sad, old, lonely individuals."

"But a feast of dating opportunities for you," Jamie said, ducking to avoid a swipe from the bar towel.

"Oi, cheeky. I'm not at the stage yet where I need to start raiding the local nursing homes for a date. Back me up here, Lou."

Lou shrugged her shoulders.

"Never look a gift horse," she said.

Jamie sniggered. Gloria put her hands on her hips.

"Isn't it time you were leaving?"

Lou smiled at her mother and then winked again at Jamie before leaving. He watched her go, grinning. As soon as the door closed the smile left his face. When Lou left a room, he

35

thought, the place always seemed so much emptier than before.

*

Dr's Case Notes – Wednesday 26 August

It was definitely the right decision to move the surgery out of my house and down here into these new premises right on the harbour front. It's so peaceful and has a great view from the reception area across the harbour and out to sea. I think it must help patients with their recovery. Not that everyone is pleased. That Joyce Pendleton complains every time she comes in. Okay, so the old surgery used to be in the next road along from her house but it's still only a five minute walk down the hill for her now. The facilities are so much better but she moans at me each time she comes in for an appointment about her haemorrhoids. I mean, most people will do a little moaning while I've got a finger up their back passage but she spends the whole time complaining about the state of the world today.

I guess it's not just her. Mrs Andrews, my receptionist, does her fair share of complaining, telling me she's overworked now that there are two doctors here. You wouldn't know it to look at her sat behind the reception desk, glaring at anyone who dares to be sick over her half-moon glasses on a chain. I've tried my best to get her to be more courteous to the patients; to say, 'Good morning' rather than, 'What have you got?' but she's not one of life's gentle souls.

I think on the whole most people are happy with the new premises. It's certainly benefitted Mrs Bryant now that I've moved the surgery out of our two front rooms and down to here. She gets her dining room back and the other one she wants to use for her hobbies. I find that a little worrying as most recently she's been into Taekwondo and welding.

But it is nice to finally have two consulting rooms and get

36

some help with all of my patients. My new locum, Dr Moore, is very easy on the eye. What the hell, let's just say it; Dr Moore is a beauty. Blonde hair, dark-brown eyes and a bottom so beautiful the good Lord must have made it on the sixth day so that He could rest and admire it Himself on the seventh. It's a shame Mrs Bryant didn't stick with Pilates. Maybe her bottom could look like that now, rather than resembling two giant cauliflowers gone to seed.

Old Mrs Robson came in earlier on for her check-up. She told me she'd been attacked at the supermarket by a security guard. I find that a little hard to believe. Still, she really seems to be getting on well with that stick. I just wish she wouldn't start stripping off before I've even got the consulting room door closed. I only needed to check her knee for goodness sake and didn't really want to see her in vest and pants. She has the physique of a pre-pubescent choirboy. Not like Dr Moore. Dr Moore has curves and bumps in all the right places. I'm shocked at how strong my feelings are. I've never felt this sort of thing before, it's scary…but rather exciting.

I've had to come up with a cunning password to hide these 'case notes.' I'd hate for anyone to see them. Mrs Andrews is a nosy, gossipy, old cow. You can usually see her ginger, tightly permed hairdo in the middle of a group, telling them all the latest scandals. I'm just glad she's not that great with a computer. I still don't know how she managed to mix up those appointments last week or how it only came to light once Mr Giles was already in the stirrups at the hospital, waiting for a smear test.

But what if Mrs Andrews got lucky and found these diary entries? This town isn't so big that everyone doesn't know what everyone else's business is. And if they don't know, they'll make it up. What about that time Mrs Bryant got her body moisturiser mixed up with my hair restorer treatment? We ended up with a film crew down from the BBC; doing a feature on the recent sightings of, 'The Beast of Ryan Harbour.' It was cruel that rumour. I still have to shave Mrs Bryant's back for her every Friday evening.

Dr Moore has just left for the night. We don't have a surgery Wednesday evenings but I pretended we needed to do a stock take of our equipment and boy has Dr Moore got some fantastic equipment. Those dulcet tones just sang out, 'Good Night' to me. I ran to my door and watched that luscious form amble through reception and out into the night. Oh my God, I think I'm in love.

*

Lou took a deep breath and knocked on the door. She looked at the vile plant beside her while she waited. A part of her wanted to rip it out of its pot but that act would just end up in another apology.

Diana was taking a long time to answer. Lou wondered if she'd seen who it was through the spyhole and ignored the knocking. They'd never really got on, even before they'd both wound up living opposite each other; Diana having sold her big house up on the hill to buy her apartment overlooking the harbour, while Lou was offered her place by the Housing Association; overlooking the car park. She was just about to return to her apartment when she heard the latch turn.

Diana didn't say anything when the door opened. It looked to Lou like she had recently been crying.

"Oh, erm; hello," Lou said, "I, er...well I was just pass...no, that's stupid."

Why was she so tongue-tied?

"Look, I'm sorry for what I said this morning. I didn't know you'd had some bad news at the time. Not that that excuses me but…"

Lou held up the bottle of red wine she'd bought at the supermarket.

"Here," she said, "A small peace offering."

Diana looked at the bottle that Lou was holding.

"Why don't you bring it in with you?" she said, and disappeared back down her hallway.

Lou really hadn't expected that. She'd never been inside Diana's apartment before and tentatively followed her. Although the layout was the same as in hers it couldn't have looked more different. In the main living area there was a large, mahogany dining table with a matching, glass-fronted unit, full of porcelain figurines of ladies in big, flowing dresses. The sofa and two winged-back chairs had mahogany armrests and the green-striped cushions matched the fabric of the curtains that hung at the French doors leading onto the balcony. Diana had obviously brought the furniture with her from that large, Victorian house on the hill and although it looked a little odd in this modern apartment, it practically screamed the words 'class' and 'elegance;' and was a complete contrast to Lou's eclectic mix of old furniture she'd been given over the years and which was now all falling apart.

Diana was rooting through a drawer in the kitchen.

"Found it," she said, producing a corkscrew.

"Oh," Lou replied, placing the bottle on the counter, "No need, this is a screw cap."

Diana smiled. Lou realised she'd never noticed how attractive Diana was before. Her slim figure still showed gentle curves. Her grey hair was, perhaps, a little too long and aging,

39

but it was neat and tidy and the shade complimented the blue of her eyes. The smile lit up her whole face. In her lilac skirt-suit Diana, like her furniture, screamed, 'class' and 'elegance'.

"Take a seat," she said, indicating the sofa.

Lou felt some newspaper ought to be put down before she dared place her bottom anywhere near Diana's furniture. The room was so tidy but then Diana didn't have a five year old girl's mountain of toys to contend with. Lou glanced at the photos on the wall behind the sofa before she sat down; old, black and white photographs of family and a wedding photo of a young Diana marrying her husband. Lou had never known him.

She eyed the full glass of red wine Diana brought over warily. My God, she thought, I hope I don't spill any.

"I could just do with this," Diana said, sitting herself down in one of the winged-back chairs.

She held her glass up to Lou in a cheers gesture and took a sip. Lou did the same, memories of this morning's hangover passing through her mind.

"I know it must seem like I'm acting a little strangely," Diana said.

"Well, you've had some bad news."

"Yes; but it's not like my sister and I were that close," Diana continued, "It wasn't that we didn't get on, we just moved in different worlds."

Lou leaned forwards and very carefully placed her wine glass onto a coaster on the coffee table.

"I must say, I was a bit shocked when you invited me in. We've not exactly exchanged pleasantries before; far from it."

"That's my fault," Diana admitted.

"Not entirely."

Both ladies exchanged a smile.

"The wine's a nice gesture, though," Diana said.

By the time a second glass was poured Lou felt a lot more relaxed.

"So where did your sister live?"

"Oh, all over the place," Diana replied, "Uganda was her latest project; working at an orphanage somewhere."

"Had she always done that sort of thing?"

"No, she started out as a journalist. That didn't go down too well with my parents. They were, shall we say, of a certain class and rather old-fashioned. They expected their daughters to marry well and produce lots of grandchildren. Frances was never going to do that but I think my parents always thought she'd 'settle down' one day. Bless them; they tried to help her in their own muddled way. They said; if she wanted to work then they would pay for a secretarial course but Frances didn't want to do that. She wanted university and freedom. Mum and dad thought it such a waste as she'd have to give it all up when she married and had children. That sounds so funny now, in this day and age, doesn't it; but for them, being a wife and mother was the most suitable career a woman could have."

Lou sniffed. "I wasn't exactly given good career advice when I was at school," she said, "Mrs Bridges was the designated career's officer and told me, 'You won't go far in this world Louise Turner.'"

Diana laughed.

"I don't really know how a teacher can give career's advice," Lou continued, "I mean, they've never left school really have they, all they know about is education. There's a whole world of jobs out there but you're never told about them; you're just given a few pamphlets."

"Well Frances never needed careers advice. She knew exactly what she wanted to do," Diana smiled to herself as she remembered the past, "She was always a tomboy, climbing trees and generally getting into scrapes. When she became a journalist my parents at least hoped she would work for a local newspaper or for a nice magazine but Frances became a war correspondent, travelling the world. Wherever there was fighting and danger, Frances would be there."

"Was she well known?" Lou asked.

"No, not really. She never did it for fame but it wasn't long into her career that she began to notice the plight of the children in all of the war zones and soon she'd left journalism behind to concentrate on helping them; still travelling the world as before. It's funny really when I think about it all now. My parents were right in a way. Frances did give up her career for children."

Diana fell silent. Lou couldn't think of anything to say and had a gulp of her wine.

"Do you know, if I'm honest," Diana eventually confessed, "I think I'm more upset about me than my sister?"

She looked across at Lou, a tear in her eye.

"Does that sound terrible?" she asked.

Lou shook her head, not really knowing why.

"My little sister went out into the world and did what she wanted. She may have only been sixty-two when she died but she packed so much into those years. What have I done? I tried to be the dutiful daughter and do what was expected of me, but even that I couldn't get right. I married well but wasn't able to supply the grandchildren."

"Did you ever..." Lou wasn't sure how to phrase her sentence.

"Several miscarriages," Diana said, "I can't tell you how

disappointed my parents were, let alone my husband; but then I had one last pregnancy in my early forties. The baby died inside me and I almost followed him. After that Richard finally realised what I'd been going through and we settled down to a very happy life together up until his death."

Lou drained her glass. She could feel a headache coming on; mostly due to the wine but also, she felt, a little to listening to Diana's life story. Lou wasn't always that open with her own friends. Still, if talking had helped Diana to feel better, that was good. Perhaps she'd be able to leave now. Before she could say anything Diana looked over, noticed the glass and gave her a top up.

"I've never really done anything with my life," she continued, "I mean; I did have a wonderful marriage. We obviously had our ups and downs; who doesn't; but we did love each other. I have friends, a bit of money in the bank but when I look back over my life, I haven't done anything."

"Don't you help out at the charity shop each week?"

Diana huffed. "A few hours every Thursday afternoon isn't exactly saving orphaned children," she said, "Besides I started helping out because I was bored, not because I thought I was making a difference."

"Do you want to be like your sister?" Lou asked her, taking another swig of the wine and realising she'd probably had more than enough.

"That's just it; no. The thought of travelling the world like she did, living out of a bag in dangerous places where there's filth and disease; that makes me shiver. I don't even want to get onto a crowded plane to Spain. The bus into Tenham is the longest journey I do and even that can be a nightmare when the kids are coming out of school."

43

"I've always fancied a nice cruise abroad somewhere," Lou said; a faraway look in her eye, "A bit of pampering and a lot of luxury."

"I just don't know what it is I want to do," Diana continued, "I really don't. All I know is that I've missed out."

"It's never too late to change," Lou told her, sitting up in her seat, "You've just said yourself; you have no ties and a bit of money in the bank. You've got the opportunity now to do whatever you want."

"And that scares me."

"Well that's a good thing," Lou said, warming to her theme, "They say you should do something each day that scares you."

"Who says that?" Diana asked, "That's just stupid. Being mugged in the street scares me, doesn't mean I should go out and let it happen."

"They don't mean that sort of thing."

"Who's this they?"

Lou scratched her head. That wine had really kicked in now.

"It doesn't matter," she said, "All you need to know is that you can do anything you want. I mean, this place was a big change wasn't it? You used to live up the hill."

"That old house was far too big for me on my own," Diana said.

"And so you sold up the family home and moved."

"Not very far."

"But that's not the point," Lou said, "It was still a big change for you wasn't it. I bet it wasn't an easy decision to make."

"It certainly wasn't."

"Exactly. Okay, maybe compared to your sister's life that wasn't a big deal but to you, that was a huge step. Do you see what I mean? Changes can be subtle; they don't have to be big.

44

Why don't you make a list of all the things you'd like to do? Don't compare them to your sister or her life; just write your list and do the items on it. I'll help you, if you like."

"I can't do that."

"Why not?"

"Well…" Diana thought for a couple of seconds, "It's my day at the charity shop tomorrow, I won't have time."

"You just told me you only do a few hours."

"Well yes, but I'm also meeting my friends Joyce and Muriel for lunch. We always meet for lunch first and then go on to our stint together in the shop."

Lou sighed. "You're making excuses," she said.

"No, it's just that we always meet on a Thursday for lunch. It's too late to cancel; that's all."

"Okay," Lou said, "Let's start with that."

"What do you mean?"

"You want to do something different; let's start with something small. Where are you going for lunch?"

"Harbour Tearoom, next to The Smugglers. It's run by my friend, Celia. Mind you, it's closing soon so…"

"Change it."

"Pardon?"

"Change it. Tell your friends you want to meet in one of the coffee shops on the high street."

"Why?"

"It's something different."

"But we're going to meet at the tearoom."

"No you're not. You're going to be spontaneous and meet somewhere else. Make a new start, Diana."

Diana thought for a second and then smiled.

"I'll do it," she said.

"Great," Lou nodded, "The first of many new changes. We'll build them up gradually. Tomorrow a new lunch experience and by the end of the week we'll be flashing our tits at the fishermen in the harbour."

"Sorry?"

Yep, that wine had definitely kicked in.

Chapter 3

"I can't say I enjoyed that lunch experience."

Diana took a deep breath and sighed.

"We know," she said, slowly and quietly, "You've made that quite plain, Joyce."

Joyce placed a box onto the counter beside where Diana was going through a list of addresses.

"I'm just saying I don't know why we couldn't have gone to Celia's as usual while she is still open. That tea was very expensive in that coffee place you selected and had about as much flavour as one of Moo's dropped scones."

The maker of the said cakes was currently up a ladder in the window display but she turned and grinned at Diana.

"I quite liked it myself," she called over, "Very modern. It made a nice change."

"We should be supporting Celia," Joyce said, firmly, "In her last weeks of being open."

"I thought we were supporting Diana in her hour of need today," Muriel replied, stepping down off the ladder.

"Really, I'm okay."

"You didn't have to come in today you know," Joyce told her, "Moo and I could have managed on our own."

"Yes I can see that," Diana replied, looking around the empty charity shop.

Muriel slowly dragged the ladder, which was twice the size she was, across to the counter.

"Right," she said, "That's the lights in the window fixed. Shall I put the kettle on?"

Joyce looked at her watch and tutted.

"Yes," she told her, "It's about time, Moo."

Muriel staggered through to the back of the store with the ladder. Diana returned to her list of addresses but became aware that Joyce wasn't unpacking the box she'd just brought out from the back. She looked up to see her friend staring down at her through her large, black-framed glasses. From this angle, with her rather crooked nose, Joyce resembled an emaciated vulture, about to bear down onto a dead carcass.

"So," she said, "How are you doing, really? You were pretty quiet over lunch; the shock I suppose."

"No, honestly," Diana replied, "I'm fine. I was thinking over a list of things I'm going to write."

Joyce nodded, knowingly.

"Yes, there'll be a lot to do what with bringing your sister home and arranging the funeral."

"No, that's already happened," Diana told her, "Over in Uganda."

Joyce was shocked.

"You mean you're not bringing her home?"

"She was home. Frances hadn't set foot in England for fifteen years; and even then it was only a fleeting visit. Why would I bring her back here?"

"So you could mourn; have a grave to visit."

"I don't need a grave to mourn," Diana said, "It's becoming a chore visiting and looking after Richard's to be honest with you. After all it is twelve years now since his accident."

Joyce couldn't believe what Diana was saying? What had happened to her friend to make her talk this way? She'd always been so reserved. She must be more upset about her sister's death than she was letting on.

"But it's your husband's grave," she pushed, "Surely you like to go and visit. There's a duty too. That's how I feel about my Norman."

"Your husband's still alive."

"I'm aware of that," Joyce said, "I just mean that I'd go visit him each week as and when anything happens. He's fine now; always at home; forever getting under my feet."

"He'll be more under your feet in the cemetery."

"Diana!"

The door opened and a customer walked in. All conversation stopped while they both watched the young woman. It wasn't a very big shop. The storage area out the back was always cluttered with new stock as Joyce never turned anything away. Out front the counter was set along the back wall with a floor to ceiling bookcase beside it, mostly full of well-thumbed paperbacks. The majority of the stock was placed down the sides of the shop. On the left, rows of shelves ran along the wall from the counter down to the window display and were crammed full of ornaments. The right-hand side had a long rail that was practically groaning under the weight of all the clothing hung on it. In front of this, by the window, were a few small pieces of furniture. A large, round table in the centre was used to display the better quality items.

The customer was walking around that table now. As she picked up a pair of small, crystal vases she looked across at the counter. Two sets of eyes were staring back, watching her every move. Diana realised what she was doing, smiled and returned to her list. Joyce continued with her stance. The lady came over to the counter.

"I'll give you two pounds for these," she said, putting the vases down on the counter.

"The ticket says six pounds for the pair," Joyce told her.

"I know, but they're not worth that," the woman replied, "I'll give you two pounds."

"Then I will let you have one of the vases."

The woman stared at Joyce.

"This is a charity shop, not a car boot sale," Joyce continued, looking the woman up and down; "Perhaps that would be more your sort of thing."

"Stuff it then!" the woman said, and left.

"Was that wise, Joyce?" Diana asked, "We haven't had a sale all afternoon."

"I'm not selling to her," Joyce said, carefully picking up the vases, "I've heard she sells a lot of stuff on one of those internet sites. She's not making profit out of us. These must be worth more if she's interested in them. I'll put them out the back to get them valued."

"She may have just wanted them for herself."

"Her?" Joyce stopped in the doorway, "Diana she lives on the council estate. Why on earth would she want crystal vases for herself?"

She walked out the back.

"Careful Moo, you almost knocked me over!" Diana heard her say.

Muriel walked gingerly through to the front holding two mugs of tea in one hand, a cup and saucer for Joyce in the other and with a packet of biscuits under her arm.

"Thanks Muriel," Diana helped her friend put all of the drinks down on the counter.

"What's Joyce doing with those vases?"

"Probably getting them valued at Christie's," Diana told her, taking a biscuit.

Muriel giggled. Whenever she did her whole body seemed to shake, as if every part of her wanted to join in on the laugh.

Joyce returned to the counter.

"That ladder's a bit skewwhiff out there, Moo," she said, looking down her nose at her friend.

"I can't push it in anymore, it's too heavy."

Joyce tutted. "Well I'm sorry but I can only give you manual jobs to do," she said, "If you could see over the counter I'd let you serve."

She picked up her cup and saucer and took a sip.

"I must say this tastes better than the one at lunch."

Diana pulled a shocked face at Muriel for this tea complement. Her friend giggled again.

"That place was heaving," Joyce continued, "At least at Celia's there are always plenty of empty tables."

"Which is probably why she's closing it down and retiring," Diana replied.

"I don't know why more people don't use it."

"Be reasonable, Joyce," Diana said, "It's a bit out of the way for most of the locals and her cakes and bread aren't always the freshest. It's only out of loyalty to Celia that we keep going."

"I once saw that assistant of hers mop her armpits with the oven gloves on a hot day," Muriel chipped in, "Just before she used them to carry two breakfast plates over to an elderly couple at a table by the window."

"She's never looked the most hygienic of women, that one," Diana agreed, "I heard she put used chip fat in her hair to keep it out of her eyes."

"Oh come on now," Joyce said.

"No she told me that herself," Muriel interrupted, "She says she feels it's better for the environment than using hairspray. Mind you the seagulls always attack her as soon as she leaves the premises."

"Come on ladies," Joyce cut in, "This is just idle gossip."
They room became quiet as the ladies sipped their teas. Muriel eventually broke the silence.

"Oh look," she said, "There's that neighbour of yours, Diana; Old Joe."

They all looked up and watched the grey-haired old man shuffle passed the shopfront, a single carrier bag in his hand.

"Off home I suppose," Muriel continued.

Joyce huffed. "Off to that pub more likely."

"Not with his shopping surely. I always feel sorry for him. Never has more than one carrier bag of groceries."

"It's not food, Moo," Joyce informed her, "It's beer."

"You don't know that," Diana said, "The man's got to eat. Besides he always goes to the pub each day for his couple of pints. I doubt he drinks at home. He has a routine; a walk along the harbour front up to where the new apartments are being built and then back to the pub."

"I don't know how he can afford it," Joyce said, "He must be living on benefits."

Diana tutted. "And how would you know that?"

"Well he can't own that apartment he lives in on your floor. It's got to be Housing Association, like your other neighbour. Honestly, I don't know why you stayed there after Louise Turner was given her place."

Diana sighed. "I only moved in just before she did. I didn't want to go through all the stresses of moving again. Besides, Lou isn't so bad once you make the effort to get to know her. She's actually very knowledgeable and kind. Only yesterday we had a chat and…"

Joyce snorted. "So that's it," she said, "This overnight change in you. It's Louise Turner's doing."

52

"What change?" Diana asked, "I've not changed. But I'm willing to admit that I've not ever given Lou a proper chance."

"Don't you remember what she was like when she came to live here; when Moo let out one of her rooms to her?" Joyce glared accusingly at her friend, "Always out drinking, being loud and obnoxious. We're not like that up on the hill. Honestly Moo; I don't know how you stood her."

Muriel smiled. "Oh I've always found her rather fun," she said, "She was always very polite to me and paid her rent on time. She worked really hard at that supermarket job; still does. I don't begrudge her wanting to enjoy herself after a hard day."

Joyce tutted again. "She's just like her mother. Both of them single mothers at twenty-five; what does that tell you? I'm not surprised. She still thinks she can pull the men, that Gloria. When she moved back here I couldn't believe how much she'd aged. She's no svelte thing now either but still acts the same way she always did all those years ago. It's disgusting. Doesn't she realise how old she is? And as for those cheap clothes she wears. I doubt those breasts of hers have ever felt a good quality wool across them; or any other material for that matter. They're always on display."

"Must get cold in the winter months," Muriel mused, picking up her empty mug.

"The likes of her have their own ways of keeping warm."

Muriel looked puzzled. "What do you mean?"

Joyce let out a long sigh. "Oh Moo," she said.

Diana drained her cup and passed it to Muriel, who took them outside. Perhaps she should have defended Lou more but she realised, up until last night, she had pretty much shared Joyce's view. Diana felt terrible. Was she that much of a snob? Lou may have been a bit on the loud and rude side when she

53

first moved here but that was twelve years ago. Well, it was never too late to change. Perhaps 'Stop being a snob' could be one of the items on her list.

"Are you coming along to the old folks' luncheon at the hall after the regatta on Saturday?" Joyce asked Diana, "I need to know numbers for who's helping out. Moo's making four sponges, two coffee and walnut cakes and a tray bake; (no dropped scones, thank goodness); and on the actual day she's doing the sandwiches and setting out the tables."

"And what are you doing?" Diana asked.

"I'll be organising everyone as always," Joyce replied, "Now, can I at least put you down for helping the pensioners get back from the harbour to the church hall? I need someone reliable. Mrs Whittaker did it last year and one of the old dears was missing for two days."

"Oh, well I'm not sure I'm quite ready to be around a lot of people yet. You know, feeling a bit down and all that, after my sister."

Joyce nodded knowingly and Diana felt guilty. It wasn't right, lying to her friend like that and using her sister's death to do so, but she helped out with the old folks' luncheon every year. This year, she wanted to do something different.

Muriel came back out into the shop and began to help Joyce empty the box on the counter.

"I meant to say, Moo," Joyce said, "I'm getting a committee together to tackle the youth problem. They've been hanging around the church hall doing nothing again. I think we can arrange to sort something else out for them. Can you phone round the usual crowd and start getting dates for when they're free to come to my house?"

"Another committee," Diana questioned, "What happened to

54

the other one, regarding the weekly bin collections going fortnightly?"

"That disbanded two weeks ago," Joyce told her, "Didn't you know? Afraid we lost that battle. Anyway Moo, get some dates off of people and we'll get the first meeting organised for the week after next."

"The week beginning the seventh," Diana asked, "Wasn't your son coming down to stay with you then?"

Joyce busied herself with the box of clothes.

"Change of plan," she said, quietly, "William can't get the time off of work. He's got a promotion coming up and doesn't want to jeopardise it."

"Oh, that's a shame," Diana replied, "You were so looking forward to the visit. When was it he and the family were last down?"

"Anytime that week, except Thursday afternoon, Moo; obviously," Joyce said, ignoring Diana, "Now, where shall I display these?"

She picked up a couple of cardigans and walked over to the heaving clothes rail. Diana watched her go. Joyce doted on her son and it was a shame she and Norman didn't see much of him. Mind you, Diana mused, maybe her friend had been a little too doting during William's childhood; stifling even. Were all these committees just a distraction for her? Hadn't they started as soon as William headed off to university? Diana had never been involved in them. Richard hadn't wanted her joining, what he called, 'A group of meddling, old women,' and Diana always felt she had nothing worthwhile to bring to the meetings anyway. Maybe it was time to change that and join up. She wasn't sure what she could do to help the youth of the area but perhaps Lou would have a few ideas.

Jamie finished pouring the pint of bitter and handed it to Old Joe who gave Jamie his money in silver and coppers.

"Hang on, Joe," he said, as the old man turned to go back to his seat, "Here, have this; for later."

Jamie handed over a small cigar. Old Joe smiled at him and then returned to his seat.

"Think of your profits," Gloria whispered, over Jamie's shoulder.

"There's more to life than money."

"Not where this place is concerned. I've just had to throw out the sandwiches from lunch because no one came in."

"It's a Thursday," Jamie reasoned, "We're never going to sell many."

"One would have been nice," Gloria told him.

Jamie bit his lip. He liked Gloria but she was always on at him lately about his profits. He was aware of the state of them and didn't need reminding every five minutes. Still, he couldn't run the place without her help; especially since it was now just the two of them working here after he'd had to let Adam go last month.

"Saturday is going to be a great success in here, remember that," he told her, "I've got an advert on the community website detailing our regatta-themed day. I picked up my outfit this morning; I'll show it to you."

Jamie headed upstairs and brought down the pirate costume.

"Here you go," he said, holding up the hanger in front of him, "How do you think I'll look in this?"

"You arsehole!"

That wasn't quite the reaction Jamie had expected. He lowered the hanger and looked at Gloria but saw her gaze was concentrated on the main entrance. Chris was standing in the doorway, grinning at Gloria with that smile that displayed so much of his gum line.

"Surprised to see me, doll?" he said, walking up to the bar, "And how's my Glorious Gloria? You haven't changed a bit."

"That's because you haven't been gone long enough," Gloria told him, "Why don't you piss off for ten years and then come see me."

Chris laughed as he sat up on a barstool.

"I'm going to be around for a while," he said, "Got a new job; lots of responsibility."

"I heard," Gloria told him, "Shouldn't you be there now?"

"I'm on surveillance," he replied, "Checking out the local area for trouble spots. Thought I'd start in here."

"Are you having a drink?" Jamie asked.

"Well, I'm on duty; so just a pint."

Gloria pulled the lager and Jamie watched to make sure she didn't spit in it. Chris looked about the bar.

"Not exactly packed is it," he said, "I see Joe's still with us. Alright Joe?"

Joe held up his glass in a cheers gesture.

"Thought the old bugger would have kicked the bucket by now," Chris added, none too quietly.

"So," Jamie said, "Security eh?"

Gloria stood holding the pint until Chris had handed over the money; then she slopped it down onto the bar in front of him.

"Cheers doll. Yeah, Security. I reckon this is going to be my kind of job. I was looking into a few other careers too; but this will do me for now."

"What other careers could you manage?" Gloria asked, returning from the till.

"Well, I did look into becoming a porn actor, obviously."

Gloria's expression didn't change.

"Really?" she said, matter-of-factly, "And how did that go for you? Did you get a part in a movie?"

"I've got a contact who managed to get me an interview with a producer, but honestly; it's harder than you think."

"Is that what you had to tell them in the interview?"

"Eh?"

"Because if it is," Gloria continued, "That's probably the reason why you're a security guard now."

Chris looked confused.

"I meant it's hard to get a foot into the industry."

"It's not your foot you need to worry about."

Jamie grinned.

"What about a porn name?" he asked, "Did you have one of those lined up, because Christopher Collins probably wouldn't cut it."

Chris's gummy grin returned. He held up his hands in front of him as if he was seeing his name in lights.

"Girth Schlong."

"Oh," said Gloria, "Not Dick Splat then?"

Chris gave it some thought.

"That's not bad either," he told her.

Jamie stifled a laugh.

"Anyway," Chris continued, "That interview didn't go too well, but never say never. What I really need is an audition; show them what I can do."

He winked at Gloria.

"I'm guessing you'll be the tunnel and the other guy the train," she told him.

"Eh?"

Before Gloria could offer an explanation, Tricky Vince walked in through the door. His mobile was stuck to his ear and he was shouting down it.

"I'll bet there's no one on the other end," Gloria whispered.

Jamie pulled a pint and set it down on the bar just as Vince hung up.

"Just what the doctor ordered," he called out, before taking a large swig, "So what's all this about?"

He indicated the costume that Jamie had hung up behind the bar.

"It's my pirate outfit for Saturday. We're having a themed day in here for the regatta," Jamie told him, "Gloria and I will be in costume and a friend of mine who does amateur dramatics is coming in too, to be a pirate character and mess about with the customers. There'll be a free drink for everyone and my salty nuts will be complementary."

Chris sniggered. Gloria rolled her eyes.

"So where did you get the costume from?" Vince asked.

"Fancy dress shop," Jamie replied.

Vince sucked breath in through his teeth.

"You shouldn't have done that," he said, "I could have laid my hands on an outfit for you."

He turned to Gloria.

"How about you Spangles; are you all sorted?"

Chris laughed.

"What's wrong with you?" Gloria asked.

"Salty nuts," he said.

She sighed. "I'm fine for a costume, thank you."

"And are you a pirate too?" Vince winked, "How about a walk on my plank to make me go, 'aaargh'?"

Gloria giggled coquettishly. Jamie shook his head.

59

"I'm not a pirate," she said, "Just an old-fashioned barmaid."

"A wench," Chris said, and received a smack around the head with the bar towel.

Vince took a long sip of his beer.

"Well," he said, "I must come in to see that. Anything else you need Jamie? What about your friend?"

"No he's fine; he says he can borrow a costume from the theatre. I told him I wanted an old seadog. He says that's not a problem. But actually, I was trying to borrow a parrot off of someone; a tame one that will sit quietly on its perch. I thought it would add to the atmosphere."

"I can get you one," Vince offered, "It won't be cheap though."

Chris sniggered again.

"Parrot going cheap," he said, "I like it. Salty nuts."

Jamie shook his head at Vince's request.

"I haven't really got a lot of cash to splash out," he told him.

"Don't worry," Chris piped up, "My mum's got a parrot. She's had it years."

Vince's face took on a startled expression. He shook his head.

"No," he said to Jamie, "You really need something that's been trained for what you want. That's why there's a bit of expense to it."

"My mum's just sits there," Chris continued, "She hates the bloody thing. Keeps it in the box room next to her bedroom so no one else sees it," he looked across at Jamie, "She'll let you borrow it for nothing; no problem."

"Really?"

Both Vince and Gloria looked aghast that Jamie appeared to consider this a good idea. He ignored them.

"If you're sure she won't mind."

"I think that's a bad idea," Vince whispered.

"No probs," Chris said, "I'll tell her tonight."

Vince downed the rest of his pint.

"Right, I've got to go and make a phone call."

He muttered a quick 'goodnight' and left the pub. Jamie hoped he wasn't too upset at being done out of a deal by Chris. He couldn't afford to lose a regular. He turned round and saw Gloria checking out her cleavage in the mirrored splashback behind the bar and relaxed. There was nothing to worry about. He was sure Vince would be back in on Saturday.

*

Lou sighed to herself as she filled up a shelf with jars of various sandwich pastes. Her lunchtime phone call to daughter, Maddie, had unnerved her a little. Maddie had mentioned how 'Mummy Cheryl' had bought her a princess dress.

"It's not 'Mummy Cheryl,'" Lou had corrected, "It's just Cheryl. I'm mummy."

Maddie had then continued to talk about 'Just Cheryl' which Lou found amusing but the conversation about her went on far longer than she felt comfortable with. Apparently, Just Cheryl had taken the week off from her job in London to look after Maddie. They had done lots of things but, because she had a very important job in an office, she kept getting phone calls from her team as they couldn't manage without her.

Lou looked about her now. Her role in this tiny supermarket hadn't changed in twelve years. What had happened to all of her plans? Actually, if she thought about it truthfully, Lou realised she'd never really had any. She'd left school as soon as she could at sixteen and managed to go fulltime at the shop she'd been working in on Saturdays. After the big fallout with her mum she'd left Tenham and headed here to Ryan Harbour to be closer to the nightclub she and her friends always used. Lou got the job at this supermarket the same day she arrived. Aside from Maddie and a few house moves, from renting at Muriel's through to the apartment she was in now, her life hadn't really changed much. Friends had come and gone. No one her age seemed to want to stay in Ryan Harbour. Lou actually quite liked it but was she missing out? Would her life have been better if she'd moved away? What if she had gone to London with Maddie's father, Tony? Would she be in Cheryl's position now?

Lou became aware of a figure standing beside her and she jumped. It was Terry. He was staring at the shelf she was currently filling up with a puzzled look on his face. Mind you, that was his usual expression.

"Did you want something, Terry?"

He picked up a jar and said,

"I didn't know we sold crab paste here. My gran loves this stuff. She's always talking about picking some up when she goes shopping."

"Why don't you take her home one of these? You can get it on staff discount."

Terry pulled a face.

"I don't know whether she'll like this brand," he told her, "She usually buys her crab paste at the pharmacy."

Lou gently took the jar out of his hand and placed it back onto the shelf.

"Perhaps it's best to leave your gran to do her own shopping," she said, "Was there anything else you wanted?"

"Simon wants a word while it's quiet," Terry told her, picking up a jar of curried crab paste which made Lou wince.

"Right," she said, "Shall we go over to him then?"

Terry nodded. They both walked over to where Simon was standing with Precious by the checkouts.

"Ah, good," he said, "Right then; oh, where's Chris; still out? It doesn't matter. I wanted a quick word about Saturday."

Lou's heart sank. Was he about to ask for extra hours? She normally only worked weekdays due to Maddie and was actually looking forward to having an entire responsibility-free weekend.

"I'm just wondering if we're not missing a trick with this regatta business," Simon continued, "I mean it sounds like quite a big thing for the area. I don't know; I wasn't here last year. Is it?"

"Not really," Lou said, "I mean people talk a lot about it, but it doesn't take place around here."

"Doesn't it?"

Lou shook her head. "There's a big procession further up the coast."

"Then why do I keep hearing about it?" Simon asked.

"Because there's nothing else that happens around here," Precious chipped in, "It's the most excitement the oldies of this town get, bless them."

Simon looked disappointed.

"That's not to say nothing happens," Lou said, "I mean most of the boat owners in the harbour take part and so there's a mini procession when they leave there. That's what everyone is referring to really when they mention the regatta. A lot of people go down to watch as the boats are all decorated with banners and bunting, that type of thing. It brings most of the town out."

Simon nodded. "So we should maybe try and involve the

supermarket in some way," he said, "Use it as a way to advertise our wares. It's a shame out clothing range isn't here yet; we could have done something nautical with it. Perhaps a staff fashion show."

Lou caught Precious's eye and knew she was as relieved as she was that the clothes weren't here yet.

"Well," Simon said, "We haven't got long then. Has anyone got any ideas about what we could do for Saturday?"

There was silence.

"Anyone?"

"We could go and watch," Terry suggested.

Precious laughed. "That's an idea, darling."

Terry beamed.

"Hmm, that's not quite what I had in mind," Simon told him.

"We could close early," Precious threw in.

Simon sighed. "Lou, how about you?" he asked, "You must have an idea."

All eyes turned to her.

"Erm, well; it's a bit short notice to just come up with something on the spot," she said, feeling her face redden, "But, keeping to the nautical theme, how about a deal on some of our fish dishes. We could have some fish recipe cards printed; oh we're probably too late for that. Erm…"

Simon was smiling. "There you are," he said to the group, "Someone who's thinking along the right lines."

Lou blushed even more.

"What we need is a gimmick. Maybe we could dress the Saturday staff up in costume and offer some free drinks to get the customers in."

"Oh don't do that," Lou said, "Jamie's got a theme like that going for The Smugglers. I'd hate for us to take away any of his customers."

"Business is business," Simon said, "We've got to think of ourselves."

"And we also need to think of all the local businesses too," Lou shot back, "We're a small community around here and need to watch out for each other and help. This isn't your big store now; we don't tread on other people's toes here."

Silence resumed again. Lou wasn't sure where that little outburst had come from but she really wanted Jamie's themed day to be a success. Precious's mouth had dropped open but Simon seemed unfazed.

"No, you're absolutely right, Lou. It's a community and we should be working together. It's a shame I didn't think of this earlier, we could have combined resources with other businesses."

He sighed. "Oh well, maybe we've left it too late for this year. Perhaps we should just open as normal. Most of the town will have to pass us to get to the harbour anyway; I'm sure we can tempt them to pop in. Perhaps I'll get a couple of the Saturday staff to stand outside and tell them about our latest money-off deals. Lou, maybe you could think of any other upcoming events in Ryan Harbour's calendar and let me know your ideas for what to do for them. Let's be better prepared for the next one."

Simon returned to his office and Terry disappeared off down one of the aisles. Lou sighed.

"Why me?" she said, to Precious, "I've got enough to do. I've still not worked out the whole plan for this clothing range and now he wants a list of Ryan Harbour events."

"Let's face it, that won't take long," Precious reasoned, "What goes on around here anyway?"

"I suppose so," Lou replied, "Aside from the regatta there's really only the pensioners' party that the church organises in April of each year."

"Yes and the vicar's Wrinkly Balls are nothing to get excited about, darling."

Lou nodded her head in agreement.

"Maybe once Simon realises that we're just a small backwater store he'll stop trying to get us to compete with the big ones."

"That reminds me," Precious said, "Natalie at the Harper Street metro store in Cunden Lingus heard that he left his previous store because he arranged a hold-up. Apparently it went wrong and a security guard was shot dead."

"I wonder if he could arrange a similar thing here," Lou replied, thinking of Chris, "Besides, if he'd stolen from the store they'd have sent him to prison, not Ryan Harbour."

"I'm not so sure about that, darling," Precious told her, "This place feels like a prison sometimes. And have you noticed that no one ever seems to die anymore."

Lou smiled. "That's true," she said, "We should have a caption on our community website, 'Come to Ryan Harbour and live forever.'"

Precious laughed. "The last death that got the town buzzing was that old woman who ran that God-awful arcade where those apartments are going up."

"Oh, her!" Lou said, "Yes, Selina Johnson; I couldn't stand that woman. She fitted right in with the local coven; Joyce Pendleton, Tess Andrews the doctor's receptionist and that Celia from the teashop."

"And Diana whatsername," Precious added, "Lives near you. She's a right cow, you said."

"Oh, well; I may have been a bit…she's actually not so bad," Lou stammered.

"You always said she was a snobby bitch," Precious continued.

"I know but; well…people can change."

"Can they? I don't think they do, not really."

Lou wondered if Precious was right. Diana had said herself last night that she knew she was acting strangely. Perhaps today she regretted ever letting Lou into her apartment. But that wasn't what Lou was bothered about right now. She was more worried about her own life. If people didn't change, was this all there was for her? For the first time in her life, Lou realised, she wanted more.

Chapter 4

Robert was excited. His talk with Grace had gone better than he'd hoped on Wednesday. They'd even reached a decision on what they were going to try. Sexy nightwear wasn't exactly whips and chains but it was enough to give Robert a thrill and he'd been grinning ever since.

Grace didn't appear to quite share his enthusiasm and had been appalled when he'd suggested wearing the outfits on Saturday afternoon.

"Not the day of the regatta, surely," she'd told him.

"There'll be plenty of time, love," Robert had responded, "You can still watch it go off from the balcony afterwards."

"But why the afternoon," she'd asked, "What will the neighbours think?"

"Well I hadn't planned on asking them over to watch," Robert had told her, "Besides, they'll all be outside watching the regatta. We'll probably have the whole block to ourselves. We could do it up against the wall on the landing and no one would know."

"Robert!"

Saturday afternoon was finally here and Robert was almost panting with excitement as he sat at the dining table after lunch. He'd felt exhilarated all morning but Grace had been moody and snappy. It was probably more embarrassment than anything; not that there was anything to be embarrassed about really, Robert felt. They were only wearing underwear for each other in their own home; no one else was going to see.

They'd lunched earlier than usual, at twelve o'clock, not that either of them ate much. Alongside his excitement Robert did have a fear that Grace was going to change her mind at the last minute.

"Hadn't you better start getting ready?" he asked her, tentatively, after she'd stacked their plates in the dishwasher.

"Not yet," Grace told him, "I want to watch my cooking show first. They're stuffing a red snapper this afternoon."

"Just like me."

"Robert! You're being coarse again."

"Sorry love. Let's record your programme and watch it later."

Grace sighed. "Fine," she said, "You set the recorder and I'll go and get ready."

"Great," Robert smiled.

"You'd better be grateful for this. I can't tell you how embarrassed I was shopping in Tenham yesterday. I was so worried someone would see me buying a see-through negligee. And then I had to fetch it home on the bus! I bought a big gammon joint and the Tenham Herald, just to make sure I could keep it hidden from view in my bag. Guess what you've got in your sandwiches all next week."

Probably the Tenham Herald, Robert thought.

"I appreciate it love, honestly," he said, "Now, go and get ready."

Robert was desperately trying to hold onto his feelings of eagerness and anticipation but Grace obviously wasn't experiencing the same emotions. She sighed again and slowly made her way into the spare room where she was going to get ready. Robert gave her a few minutes and then walked into the master bedroom to change into his purchase. He hadn't told Grace, but he'd been deeply embarrassed when buying his choice as well.

Robert stripped off and retrieved a carrier bag from under the

69

bed. He pulled on the PVC, see-through underpants. He had to admit, it wasn't the most comfortable thing to wear. Grace had insisted that all the windows remained closed so that there was no chance of anyone hearing them make love and the apartment was stifling. PVC really wasn't the ideal material to wear in heat. Robert could already feel himself sweating down in that area.

He caught a glimpse of himself, sideways on, in the mirror and tried to pull his stomach right in; holding his breath for as long as he could. When he exhaled Robert watched, dismayed as his belly shot out again...and down. When was the actual moment that his body had changed into; well, this? He could still remember when Grace had admired his physique but now the stomach resembled a large, hairy beach ball. Robert could only wish that the hair on top of his head would still grow that thickly.

Grace walked into the room while he was still looking melancholically at his reflection in the mirror and wondering why the aging process was so cruel.

"I'd love to have gone over this whole thing with an iron first," she said.

Robert sighed. "You can't change how you're made love," he told her, kindly, "None of us can."

Grace's head whipped up from where she was fiddling with the hem of her outfit.

"I was referring to the negligee!"

Well that wasn't a great start to the afternoon festivities. He turned round to face her.

"I'm sorry. I didn't mean...you really do look beautiful."

Grace couldn't help a shy smile escaping onto her face.

"Thanks, love," she said.

"Can I ask one question though?" Robert added, looking her up and down.

She giggled. "Of course you can."

"Why have you got your cardigan on over the top of it?"

Grace sat down on the end of the bed.

"Because I might get cold," she told him.

"You're kidding, it's stifling in here."

"Well I'm not taking any chances in this stupid, wispy, little thing. Don't you remember that cold I caught over Christmas? It took weeks to get over."

"But you're ruining the mood," Robert said, exasperated.

"Me? What do you think you're doing to my mood wearing that?"

Robert looked down at his PVC pants. The heat of the room had misted them over. He turned round and grabbed a handkerchief.

"If I'd been allowed to have a window open this morning they wouldn't be doing this," he said, frantically trying to wipe up the moisture."

"Don't blame me, this was all your idea," Grace said, "I'm doing this for you."

"Then make an effort love, please," he told her, turning round to face her again.

Grace looked at him and began to laugh.

"That's not helping!"

"Sorry love," she said, "It's just that it looks like you're wearing my plastic rain hood."

Grace laughed again but abruptly stopped.

"You're not are you?" she asked.

"Of course not," Robert snapped, "This outfit cost me forty-five pounds."

"Forty-five pounds; for something that looks like a pair of plastic incontinence pants! My God, Robert, do we really have that sort of money to throw away? I mean, I know we'll both be wearing those someday but..."

"They're not incontinence pants! Oh, what's the point now," Robert said, pulling them off and sitting down on the bed, "You've ruined the mood."

"Don't lay all this at my door," Grace told him, standing up, "I was doing this for you, remember that."

She walked over to the window while Robert began pulling on his boxer shorts, muttering under his breath. Grace opened the window a crack and straightened the net curtain.

"Oh, I think the boats are leaving for the regatta already," she said, "If I grab my dressing gown I could pop out onto the balcony and watch them go."

She made her way across to the doorway into the hall.

"The decorations are so colourful, particularly on the fishing boats. They're displaying their tackle beautifully."

"Well that's all I was trying to do," Robert moaned, before getting up and stomping into the en suite.

Grace sighed and left the room.

*

"Here it is, all finished this morning," Diana said, waving a piece of paper.

"It took you long enough," Lou told her, sitting down at Diana's dining table.

"Well, there was a lot to go through."

Lou had felt rather pleased when Diana knocked at her door earlier to ask if she wanted to come and watch the boats leave for the regatta from her balcony. She'd begun to think their chat the other night had perhaps been a one-time thing; but here

72

she was again in Diana's apartment. She was due over at The Smugglers later to support Jamie and her mum on their themed day. Perhaps Diana would like to come too.

Diana brought the list she had written over to the table and sat down beside Lou, taking a sip from her glass of white wine.

"There are nine things on it," she said, "They're not necessarily specific things. I don't want to jump out of a plane or swim the English Channel, nothing like that. If I jumped out of a plane, I'd still have to return to my normal life once I'd landed. What I want this list to do is change things in subtle ways. Does that make sense?"

"Of course," Lou replied, "You want to make some permanent changes, not just have an occasional adrenalin rush."

"Yes. Is that a bit...well; wimpish?"

Lou shook her head. "I don't think so. Let's have a look," she picked up the piece of paper and read aloud, "Number one, 'Do something liberating.'"

Diana nodded. "Like I said, it's not very specific. With this one I want to do something that's totally different from anything I've done before; something that would shock people if they saw me."

"Something wild and crazy," Lou added.

"Well, kind of; yes; but within reason. I mean, it should be legal."

Lou laughed. "Don't worry, I've an idea for that," she said, and winked; leaving Diana with an ominous feeling.

"Right, what's next? 'Learn a new skill.'"

"I was toying with the idea of driving lessons, what do you think?" Diana asked.

"I think that's a great idea," Lou replied, "You could then avoid those bus journeys to Tenham with the school kids you were talking about the other night. If you pass your test you could even drive over to the Continent."

"Let's not run before we can walk."

Lou looked at number three.

"'Improve an old skill.'"

"In case the new one proves too tricky," Diana told her, "I thought I could improve on something I already do."

"Like what?"

"I'm not sure at the moment. I had a think last night but couldn't come up with anything I was already good at, and that just depressed me."

"Moving on then. Number four, 'Keep Fit.' Oh God that's something I really should do too."

Diana's face brightened.

"That's great," she said, "We could do a class together. It would be so much better to do these things with someone else."

Lou was quite surprised to realise she liked the sound of that idea.

"Number five, 'Face a Fear.' I guess you did that inviting me in the other night."

Diana laughed. "Not at all."

"So what is it then?" Lou asked, "What fear do you have; is it spiders?"

"Oh no, I'm not bothered by them."

"Are you not?" Lou shivered, "I should get you over to mine the next time I have one. I'm a bit worried it's wrong to let my five year old pick them up while I'm screaming."

"Is that why you scream?" Diana asked, "I always wondered."

"Oh God, could you hear me?"

Diana nodded. "Sometimes, yes. I'd hear a scream followed

by, 'Get that thing away from me.' I always thought it was some kind of sexual role play."

"What?"

Diana shrugged her shoulders.

"You know, playing hard to get or something."

Lou was taken aback but couldn't stop her lips twitching into a smile. Diana noticed and the two of them burst out laughing.

"My God, I'm not sure if that says more about you or me," Lou said.

Diana pulled a tissue out of her sleeve and dabbed at her eyes.

"I've led a very sheltered life," she joked.

Lou was shaking her head.

"Honestly, with all the spiders I find in my apartment; you must think I'm very sexually active."

"Don't; you'll start me off again."

Diana stepped into the kitchen and grabbed another couple of tissues.

"Mind you," Lou called over to her, "If I ever found Chris in my bed again I'd certainly be screaming."

"So that's all finished then," Diana asked, "I've noticed him around this area again."

"That's nothing to do with me. It's definitely over."

"Good. I think you can do much better."

The two ladies both smiled and then Lou returned to the list.

"Right then, number six, 'Change Appearance."

"New hairstyle, that kind of thing," Diana told her, sitting down again.

Lou pulled a face.

"That one may err on the side of wimpish," she said, "I mean, how often do you go and have your hair done?"

"I go every week," Diana told her, "To the same hairdresser that I first went to when I moved here over thirty years ago. I've had the same look for the past fifteen years."

Lou whistled. "Okay," she said, "I guess that one isn't wimpish after all. What's number seven; new shoes? Oh, 'Find Companionship.' Is that another way of saying you want a man?"

Diana blushed.

"Are there going to be a lot of spiders in your bedroom?" Lou teased.

Diana's face reddened even more.

"Don't," she said, "Besides it's not all about sex. I just miss having that closeness; do you know what I mean? It's something a friend can't give, no matter how dear they are to you."

Lou made a huffing sound.

"A boyfriend doesn't necessarily give you that either," she said.

"I'm sorry," Diana replied, "I probably shouldn't be talking about this when you've so recently split up with someone."

Lou shook her head. "No, it's fine. I'm totally over Chris. I just feel like I've wasted two years of my life being with him, that's all. We never shared that closeness."

"Not ever?"

"No. We just…well we just muddled along really. I suppose at the beginning I must have wanted more…actually no, I think it was more of a convenience for both of us. It was someone who was there if you needed a date or just wanted a fuck buddy."

Diana winced at the expression but didn't say anything.

"It's only recently I've realised that I want more and with

hindsight, that's probably why I ended it with him. I suppose I'm craving that closeness you're talking about."

"Have you never had that before?" Diana asked, tentatively.

Lou took a moment before admitting,

"I'm not sure. I guess I had that with Tony, Maddie's father; but we were both young. It was a first proper relationship for both of us, but even then I think we were just playing at it."

"Playing at it?"

"Yes. We'd always call it a serious relationship but it was only when I got pregnant with Maddie that we suddenly understood what serious meant. We'd already begun to grow apart by then. We tried to make it work but in the end I had to let him go. At least we remained friends, for Maddie's sake."

Lou remained lost in thought for a moment before looking over at Diana. She smiled.

"You're surprised aren't you?" she said.

Diana frowned. "How do you mean?"

"That I've only spoken about two relationships; Tony and Chris. You thought there'd been a lot more hadn't you."

"Well I…" Diana became flustered.

"I know what people think of me. I've heard the phrase, 'Like mother, like daughter' enough times around here."

"I'm sorry," Diana said.

Lou sighed. "I suppose I can understand why. I wasn't exactly the best behaved person in the world when I moved here at eighteen but I wasn't a delinquent either. I enjoyed a drink and was trying to stick my middle finger up at parental authority. I used to get chatted up a lot but, after growing up with my mum and having so many 'uncles,' I knew which guys wanted to date me and which ones just wanted to get inside my knickers. I'd lead those guys on and then tell them no. Stupid of me, really. Some of them would get pretty angry."

"I remember witnessing a few of the arguments when you still lived at Muriel's," Diana said.

Lou nodded. "I guess I can't blame you for what you thought of me."

She returned to the list again.

"Right, number eight, 'Work with Animals.'"

"Yes, that's something I'd love to do. I've always liked animals. I'm not so keen on birds but cats and dogs I like and I enjoy watching nature programmes. There aren't many pets one's allowed in an apartment which is why I've just got Charlie over there."

Diana indicated the goldfish bowl.

"Yes, Maddie wants an animal of some sort," Lou said, looking at the bowl, "But I've never had a pet before. I have this fear of forgetting to feed it and it dying on us very quickly."

"I guess children have to learn about death," Diana said, "A pet is a good way of doing it."

"I don't really want to starve a hamster in front of Maddie just to get her to understand that's what's going to happen to all of us one day."

"You know what I mean," Diana said, having a sip of her wine.

Lou grinned. "Right, last one," she said, looking at the list, "Broaden Horizons. What does that mean, going back to college or something?"

"Oh, that one's a little bit special," Diana said, as she placed her glass back down onto the coaster, "I was thinking that if you help me with the other items, then I want to share number nine with you and take you on that cruise you want to go on. We can both broaden our horizons."

Lou's mouth fell open.

"You want to take me on a cruise? Why?"

"Well, it's like I just said; you're the one who's helping me. You got me to write this list. If you hadn't come over the other night I would still be sitting around moping, rather than feeling excited about the future. It's all thanks to you."

"But we hardly know each other. Wouldn't you prefer to take another member of the coven with you?"

The phrase was out of her mouth before Lou realised.

"The coven?" Diana questioned, "What do you mean?"

"Oh, well; I…er," she couldn't get out of this one, "It's what I've always called your little group of friends."

Shit, Lou thought; had she blown a new friendship before it had even got off the ground; **and** the chance to go on a cruise?

Diana laughed. Lou could only sit and watch while her face turned redder and redder.

"Oh I love that," Diana finally said, "The coven. Do you think we all wear long black robes and pointed hats when we meet up? Maybe I should get myself a black cat as a pet."

"Sorry," Lou apologised, "I don't think you're a witch. The fact that I'm sitting here proves that."

"Do you think that Joyce and Muriel are too? Not Muriel, surely?"

"No, I've always liked Muriel. I was talking about that Celia from the tearoom and the woman who used to own the amusement arcade before she died; and obviously Joyce. She's the worst; manipulative, nasty, selfish…"

"Oh now, I can't agree with that," Diana said, "Joyce is very forthright, I grant you, but her heart's in the right place. She's always getting up new committees to help the community. She's starting a new one now to help the local youth."

79

Lou had just picked up her wine glass but quickly placed it back down on the table again.

"Oh please," she said, "Joyce will be setting up curfews and doing all she can to get them out of her line of vision. All she does is help herself and Ryan Harbour is all the poorer for it."

"I don't know how you can say that," Diana said, astonished.

"Really? Go and take a look outside your window. How many people do you see?"

Diana got up to look.

"About fifty," she called back.

"What?"

"The boats will be leaving soon."

"Okay, bad day to use as an example," Lou said, "I mean usually. How many do you see?"

"Well it's very quiet around here. Most people like that, don't they?"

"It's deserted out there, Diana," Lou continued, "It's a beautiful harbour in an old town. The place should be buzzing. Why is no one coming down here? It's because of your friend Joyce and her committees; closing things down."

"I have to admit I agreed with her about stopping the stripping in The Smugglers. That's not the sort of thing one wants on the doorstep."

"I'm not talking about that," Lou said, coming over to the window, "I mean the shutting down of the smugglers tunnels. It was your friend Joyce who alerted the council about them; got her little underlings to write letters and then picket the offices until the tunnels were closed off. Now we have no tourists and the shops below are empty. It's just like a ghost town."

"But health and safety is an important issue," Diana reasoned, "I mean if the tunnels were no longer safe to use..."

"This has nothing to do with health and safety. Joyce wanted the tourists to stop coming so that the road her house lies on wouldn't get coaches down it any longer; that's all."

"I can't believe that's the reason," Diana said.

Lou turned round and returned to the dining table.

"There are a lot of things that get overheard in a supermarket you know," she said, "You find out all sorts."

Diana remained pensive while looking out at the people below. Was there an element of truth in what Lou said? Lou obviously believed so and if she did, how many others felt the same way? She saw the crowds start to wave.

"I think the boats are about to leave."

Lou drained her glass.

"Great. Are you ready to complete number one?"

Diana turned and looked questioningly at her.

"What do you mean?"

Lou smiled. She'd remembered what she'd said the other night.

"Number one, 'Do Something Liberating.' Let's flash the regatta."

"What?" Diana's eyes widened with horror.

"Come on," Lou said, fumbling under her t-shirt, "We're going to go out onto the balcony and flash our tits as the regatta leaves the harbour."

"We can't do that, someone might see."

"Diana, all eyes will be on the boats. Come on, what's more liberating than getting your baps out? They're what make you a woman."

Diana still looked petrified.

"Well, just a quick flash then," Lou suggested, "I've done it before, it's easy."

"I'm well aware you've done it before," Diana told her, "I remember your streak down the high street on your twenty-first."

Lou stopped grinning.

"How did you know that was me?"

"Because you stopped halfway down the road to give me the finger and I got a rather good look at a tattoo of your name."

Lou smiled again.

"Oh right," she said, "Yeah, I'm sorry about that. If it's any consolation, it really hurt to get it done down there."

She pulled her bra out from underneath her top.

"Come on then," she said, "Let's do this. You'll be doing something liberating and I'll be revisiting my youth."

Diana was silent but Lou sensed a slight change to her thoughts. Diana was considering it.

"No one will notice," Lou added, encouragingly.

"I'm not sure that's a compliment."

Lou laughed. "You know what I mean."

Diana took a deep breath and walked back over to the dining table. Lou thought she'd changed her mind but Diana had reached for her wine glass.

"'Do Something Liberating,'" she whispered, under her breath and downed the contents.

There were a lot of people in the harbour now, all cheering and waving at the boats. As Lou had said, all eyes were facing out to sea. The two ladies had both now removed their bras and were giggling, standing on the balcony, Lou in her t-shirt, Diana in her blouse that was undone but held tightly across her front.

"Ready?" Lou said, "After three, give the world a treat."

"I'm not sure mine were much of a treat forty years ago, let alone now," Diana told her.

82

Lou grinned. "Think of the list," she said, "Okay, one, two, three; go."

Diana gasped as she pulled open her blouse. Her first thought was that she hadn't put any sun cream on and it was very bright up on the balcony today. She certainly didn't want itchy sunburn, especially there. Her second thought was of joy and excitement. She'd done it. She was standing on the balcony showing her tits to the world. She heard laughter and realised it was her own. She looked across at Lou. She was also laughing while waving her t-shirt around her head and jumping up and down.

My God, Diana thought, she'll knock herself out in a minute with those two things bouncing about like that. How would I explain that to the paramedics?

Lou's whole face lit up when she laughed, Diana noted. Her long, brown hair was blowing around her face in the wind and it really brought out the green of her eyes. She was very pretty. Why hadn't Diana noticed that before? Lou looked over at her.

"How do you feel?" she asked.

"Elated," Diana grinned.

Lou laughed and began whooping while she spun her top around her head.

"Ssh," Diana said, "People will hear you."

"Relax. They're all still cheering the boats. Look, there's your mate with a load of other old people."

For the first time since coming out onto the balcony Diana felt embarrassed. There were Joyce and Muriel, standing by the slipway with the group of old folks they were going to take off to the church hall later on. What if Joyce looked up? Lou must have sensed Diana's fear. She began whooping loudly again.

"Look up Joyce," she called out.

"Stop it," Diana hissed, but Lou just laughed louder.

She swung her top around faster but a freak breeze caught it and it went sailing out of Lou's hand. She wasn't laughing now. The two ladies froze and watched as it floated gently down to the harbour below. It fell onto the head of an old lady in a wheelchair who was a member of Joyce's group. Even from two floors up the two women could hear the loud scream. As the rest of the crowd stopped cheering so a muffled voice shouted out,

"Sweet Jesus I've died. I'm coming to you Stanley. You'd better not be with that slut, Moira!"

All eyes were on the commotion as Joyce quickly grabbed the t-shirt from off the old lady's head. She looked at it and then up at the balconies. Other eyes followed hers.

Lou and Diana had already crouched down and were both frantically trying to get the door into the lounge open.

"It's stuck, I don't know why."

"Hurry up," said Lou.

"I'm trying," Diana snapped back, "But your breasts keep getting in the way of the handle. Can't you stand up a bit?"

Just at this crucial moment the two ladies heard another door opening nearby.

"Oh my God," Diana whispered, "Robert and Grace's balcony."

Thinking about all eyes being on the boats, both ladies had forgotten that every other apartment also had a balcony. Fortunately the one that was right beside Diana's, in the next block of apartments along, was separated by a thick, frosted glass panel; but the other side of the balcony was open to the elements to allow plenty of light into the lounge. As the two ladies slowly turned their heads to the right, looking across the

84

space where the windows to the bedrooms of the two apartments were, so they saw Grace sidle out onto her own balcony, a dressing gown pulled round her. Lou and Diana both froze. Grace looked out to sea and then turned her head to look at the people down near the slipway. She jumped when she saw Diana and Lou.

"Oh, hello," she called out, "How's the regatta going? Have I missed much?"

She took a better look at the two ladies.

"What on earth are you doing?"

Lou and Diana slowly stood upright. Lou moved behind Diana, who had now pulled her blouse across her front again.

"Erm, we were trying each other's tops on," Diana said.

"On the balcony? In full view of the world?"

"Yes, it does seem silly now," Diana agreed, reddening.

"Today of all days," Grace continued, "What a stupid thing to do. The harbour is full of people. What if someone saw you?"

Another gust of wind blew up and caught Grace's dressing gown, flinging it open to reveal a pink, see-through negligee underneath. A cheer went up from the crowd and Grace did a spectacular dive through the door back into her lounge. A second later a bewildered Diana and Lou heard her balcony door being gently closed from the inside. The cheer had been for the last boats leaving the harbour but Grace never did find that out.

*

"I can't believe you've never been in there before," Lou said, as she and Diana walked through the residents' car park on their way to The Smugglers.

"I suppose because it was always Richard's place to go,"

Diana replied, "He liked his Friday night in the pub and I didn't begrudge him that. Whenever the two of us went out together it was always to a restaurant or the theatre. I guess I've never been a pub person."

"Well I hope you're going to like it. I'm not sure how busy it's going to be. Still, it's a warm evening so we can always sit out on the harbour steps if there are no tables free inside."

"Perhaps you'll find your t-shirt," Diana said, and winked.

Lou grinned. As they arrived at the entrance so the door flew open and Old Joe wobbled out. He stood to attention when he saw the two ladies and gave them an over-exaggerated salute before tottering off.

"I'm guessing he's had more than his usual two pints," Lou said, laughing.

She stopped as they walked inside. The place was practically empty. Jamie and Gloria were stood long-faced behind the bar, he in a white, frilly shirt with black waistcoat; a headscarf tied around his head and an eye patch which he'd flicked up so he could see out of both eyes; and Gloria in a very low-cut, red top with short, ruched sleeves. Their customers just about outnumbered them. There was a couple sitting at one of the window tables that Lou didn't recognise and an old, white-haired man, who called himself the Colonel, was stood at the far end of the bar, his chin in his hands.

"What's happened?" Lou asked, as they made their way to two stools.

"It's been a disaster," Gloria said, "We've hardly had anyone come in at all."

"Really?" Lou asked, "No one?"

"A few came in for their free drink," Jamie added, miserably, "But then they left. No one even grabbed a handful of my salty nuts."

"Maybe it will pick up later," Lou said, trying not to laugh at Jamie's comment, "Perhaps people who are working today will come in once they've finished."

"What about your supermarket friends?" Jamie asked, hopefully.

"Oh, sorry; no they won't be coming down. Precious told me yesterday that she's off to the nightclub with some friends. They've been open all day today apparently, offering a complimentary barbecue and three free drinks if you're wearing a costume. Oh."

Lou realised she should have mentioned this to Jamie earlier. He sighed.

"No wonder we're empty," he said, "I can't compete with that."

There was a sudden squawking noise which made Diana and Lou jump.

"That's not helped either," he told them.

Lou and Diana both looked to where Jamie indicated. Just beyond the Colonel was a stand with a wooden perch on the top. Sitting on it was a parrot. As they looked so it squawked again.

"Hey babes!"

"Oh no," Lou said, "You didn't borrow Chris's mum's parrot did you?"

"It was free," Jamie blurted out, "I didn't know it had a lot of choice phrases."

"Bend over and smile."

Lou rolled her eyes. "Who do you think taught it all those expressions?" she asked.

"I don't think it's so bad," Gloria chipped in, trying to lighten the mood, "There are much worse things it could say."

"Back on to me, Gladys."

She shrugged her shoulders.

"What about your friend who was coming in?" Lou asked, looking round, "Has he gone?"

Jamie made a groaning sound.

"He's still here," he said, pointing to the table beside the main door.

Lou looked. She saw something slumped over in the bench seat.

"What is that?" she asked, "It looks like fur."

"Yep," Jamie sighed, "That was Nigel's take on my requesting an old, sea dog. He came dressed in a dog costume with a rubber ring around his middle."

"He looks a little the worse for wear," Diana suggested.

"I promised him free drinks and he's made sure he's had his fill. I'm just going to leave him there. At least it's another person in the room."

Diana ordered a bottle of one of Jamie's more expensive wines and asked him and Gloria to join them for a drink. That helped to lighten the mood. The Colonel, seeing free drinks decided to come over. He very quickly turned the conversation around to himself and one of his army stories.

"So anyway, the gambling in the camp among the privates was getting out of hand. It was poker, mostly. I asked one of my sergeants to keep an eye out. Anyway he…"

Lou leaned over and whispered to Diana,

"I don't think any of his stories are true. Makes you wonder if he is an actual colonel."

"But then I couldn't find him anywhere; my sergeant was AWOL," the colonel continued.

"Why would he lie?" Diana asked.

"Attention seeking. All his stories end with the same sentence. It's like his catchphrase. Wait and see."

"Anyway, I got a whiff of gossip about my sergeant from a fellow officer and followed his hunch. I marched down to the supplies room, threw open the door and there was my sergeant; playing with his privates."

"God, I bet he was surprised to see you," Gloria said.

"They all were."

"All?" Gloria questioned, frowning, "You mean he wasn't doing it alone?"

"My dear, how can you play poker on your own? He had three of his privates with him."

"Oh I see."

"The blasted man had tried to double-cross me. Anyway, I had to put each of them on a charge. They should have had a lookout or something; then I would never have found out. It's like I always say; don't get caught with your pants down."

"And there's the line," Lou said, to Diana, "Every story ends the same way."

"Surely not."

"Stick around, you'll hear another one."

The parrot began squawking.

"Quite a bird," the colonel said, "Had a run-in with one of those blighters in Borneo once."

"That one?" Diana questioned, frowning.

Lou rolled her eyes. The colonel really didn't need encouragement.

"Surely that's an African Grey."

The Colonel looked startled.

"Is it?" he said, "Oh yes, I'm aware of that. It belonged to the wife of one of the local dignitary's. They had a lovely house near Kanpur if I remember."

"Surely that's in India," Diana told him.

"What?"

"Kanpur is a place in India," Diana repeated, "My sister spent some time there. You said you were in Borneo."

The Colonel became very flustered, much to the amusement of the rest of the group. He nervously stroked his small, regimental moustache.

"Did I say Borneo? How silly of me. I've never been there. Don't know what made me say it. Yes it was India I was in."

"Lying bastard," squawked the parrot.

"Dear me, is that the time," the Colonel looked at his watch, "I didn't realise it was so late, I must go."

"I'm so sorry," Diana said, to Jamie, as the colonel rushed out of the door, "I seem to have lost you a customer."

"Who'd have thought it," Lou said, "Diana caught the colonel with his pants down."

Diana blushed. Jamie grinned.

"Don't worry about it," he told her, "Once he's checked his atlas he'll be regaling us with stories again. Besides, you've already doubled my profits today. I hope we see you in here more often."

Diana laughed. "I must say, I do like it in here. All those photographs of the past on the wall; it makes me feel quite nostalgic."

"Have you been here long?" Jamie asked.

"In Ryan Harbour? Over thirty years now. I moved here with my husband when his firm relocated. Your costumes are very good, by the way. Did you hire them?"

"I did," Jamie said. He turned to Gloria, "The rest of my team already owned theirs."

"What's wrong with it?" Gloria questioned, looking down at her low-cut blouse, "This is one of my best tops. Maybe it's a bit low but I think I can still pull it off."

"You offered to do that earlier to stop those guys leaving."

Lou was just about to take a sip of her wine but froze.

"Oh God mum, please tell me you didn't."

"Of course I didn't," Gloria replied, laughing a little too long.

She shot Jamie a look before picking up the Colonel's empty pint glass, leaning forwards over the bar.

"You don't get many of them to the pound," squawked the parrot.

Gloria smiled to herself. The couple at the table got up to leave, waving at Jamie as they left.

"Who are they?" Lou asked.

"Hopefully a useful profit," Jamie told her, "They're going to sing here next Saturday night. The price was pretty reasonable and they already have their advertising; look."

Jamie pulled an elastic band off of a rolled-up poster and unfurled it. A small photograph of the couple was in the top left hand corner. Lou read the words beside it aloud.

"Martin and Sarah performing at The King's Head. Come and enjoy the M & S experience."

"There's an online version I can download and just change the pub name on it," Jamie informed her, "Then all I have to do is add it to the community website and get some printed copies done to display around town."

"What sort of music do they play?"

"Well it's a bit folksy," he admitted, "But I thought that might help bring a range of people in. It's got to be better than today, hasn't it?"

91

Tricky Vince walked in.

"Have I missed the main event?" he asked, looking round. His eyes found Gloria's cleavage, "Ah, I see there's still a couple of delights on show."

Gloria giggled.

"Tosser!"

Vince looked all around him, unable to see where the voice had come from. Eventually he gave up and ordered a pint. Being the newest member of the group, talk inevitably fell on Diana. She didn't feel she had much to tell about herself and so mentioned the list.

"I'm thinking of learning to drive as my new skill," she told them, "It's something I always meant to get around to but never did. Mind you the roads are so busy these days I am a little nervous about it."

"I can give you a couple of lessons first, if you like," Lou said, "Before you start paying out for lessons from an instructor."

"They are expensive," Vince agreed, "But if you ever want to get yourself a run-around, let me know. I can always lay my hands on a decent car."

"Lying bastard!"

"Who the hell is that?" Vince asked, looking round the room again.

"It's only the parrot," Gloria told him, indicating the far end of the bar.

Vince walked over to it.

"What did it call me then?"

"Lying bastard," the bird repeated.

"How dare you!"

"It doesn't know what it's saying," Gloria said, coming

92

around the bar to stand bedside him, "It's not talking about you."

Vince was still eyeing the parrot, warily.

"Where did you get this in the end?" he asked.

"You know where I got it," Jamie told him, "Chris's mum."

"Oh God, I told her to say no."

"What was that?" Gloria asked, "Are you knocking off Chris's mum?"

"We're seeing each other, if that's what you mean."

"Well you kept that quiet."

"Of course I did," Vince told her, "I don't want the wife finding out now, do I."

Gloria's eyes opened wide.

"You're married! You didn't tell me that on our date, Vince."

At the sound of the name the parrot squawked again and then said, in a different sounding voice,

"Oh Vince; do it the way I like it."

Everybody fell silent.

"Give me that purple pecker."

"I knew it!" Vince shouted, "I knew the bloody thing was listening in."

Gloria gasped.

"You bastard," she spat, "I hope your purple pecker drops off."

Vince turned to Jamie.

"Well that's nice customer service from your staff, I must say."

"Hey, don't take your anger out on Gloria," Jamie told him, "And she's every right to be upset, seeing as you lied to her Vince."

"Don't worry, Vince;" the parrot said, "It happens to every man once in a while."

Vince's mouth dropped open.

"That does it," he said, and made a grab for the bird. The parrot squawked and attached itself to his finger.

"Ow! Get the bugger off," he shouted, trying to pull his hand away from the parrot's firm grip.

"It's your own fault for the way you treat birds," Gloria told him, "We all have feelings you know."

She turned and stomped back behind the bar. The parrot eventually let go

"That's done it," Vince said, while sucking on his finger, "You don't get any of this shit up at The Red Lion."

He turned and stormed out of the pub.

"Good riddance," Gloria called after him.

Although he agreed with her, Jamie couldn't help thinking that his idea for more customers had just cost him one of his regulars.

Chapter 5

Dr's Case Notes – Tuesday 1 September

It was a really busy surgery this morning. It always is the day after a public holiday. I was confused when Vince Jenson walked in as I was expecting old Mrs McAlpine for her test results. I heard the surgery door open and before I looked up said,

"You've got Acute Gastritis."

"Thanks Doc," Vince replied, "Is that Latin for bum?"

Mrs McAlpine's appointment had been cancelled first thing but Mrs Andrews neglected to tell me that. Apparently she'd been taken into hospital on Saturday and treated for shock. She'd been watching the boats leave the harbour for the regatta when somebody's t-shirt fell onto her head. Bless her, she didn't know what it was and thought she'd died when everything went black.

Vince came in with a tiny cut on his finger that he said he'd got from breaking up a knife fight. It looked more like something had just pecked at it to me. I told him his tetanus was up to date and not to worry. He seemed a little disappointed by that.

The rest of the morning surgery went without a hitch but I was far too busy to find any time to think about Dr Moore and that spectacular body. I thought I would be able to have a few minutes to myself once surgery had finished but Mrs Andrews' niece came in to visit with that appalling young son of hers. The child is so spoilt. He always gets everything he wants. Looking at the size of him now I think he's been demanding sides of beef. Mrs Andrews doesn't see it and I daren't tell her.

His visits are the only time she ever cracks a smile.

"Here he is," she said, as soon as they came through the door (he had to come in sideways to fit through), "Here's my little Nicky Nick."

Little?

The boy obviously wasn't that interested in seeing his Great Aunt. He had a half-eaten chocolate bar in his hand which took up most of his attention. Mrs Andrews came out from behind the reception desk, her arms spread open wide.

"Come to Auntie Tess, then," she said, "Come and have a tickle with your Auntie Tess."

She walked forwards and enveloped the boy in a hug, laughing all the time. Not that her hands could reach all the way around him mind you.

"That's it," she said, "Let me give you a tickle, a great big Tess tickle. And here's another one. A pair of Tess tickles; you love them."

That boy is going to grow up with so many issues. I'm glad I'm not his doctor. Anyway, Mrs Andrews let him go and play in the children's area but he very quickly got his head wedged inside the kiddies' basketball hoop. Well that caused pandemonium. The mum was shouting for the fire brigade and I got blamed for having a dangerous toy. In the end I had to drive everyone up to the hospital in Tenham to get the hoop removed and the boy checked over.

I was told off on the journey there when I said it was probably better to take that second chocolate bar off of him, as he might choke with a hoop stuck around his neck. Apparently "Little Nicky" suffers from nerves and only chocolate keeps him calm. I'm the one that needed to be calmed down. That basketball hoop cost a lot of money!

I've only just got back from the hospital. I'm exhausted but it's almost time for evening surgery. No rest for the wicked. Dr Moore just walked past my open door and gave me a lovely smile and wave. Do you think that means something? Could my feelings be reciprocated? I wonder if it would be wrong to suggest a drink together.

*

Lou slowly got out of the car. She was visibly shaking. Diana bounced out of the driver's seat.

"Are you sure you wouldn't like me to try and park it as well?" she asked, brightly.

Lou pressed her hand against her churning stomach.

"Er no, I don't think so; not on your first go," she said.

"I'm very grateful to you for taking the afternoon off to give me a driving lesson," Diana was totally oblivious to Lou's trembling and deep breathing, "How about I buy us a drink in the pub as a thank you; seeing as we're parking the car in their car park?"

"Without my screaming, 'stop' we'd have passed the pub and been in the harbour," Lou told her.

"Oh you're exaggerating," Diana replied, cheerily, "It is a rather old car. I think your brakes need adjusting. You should get them checked."

Lou was more interested in checking and adjusting her underwear right now. She'd been clenching so tightly the past twenty five minutes she worried surgery would be required to remove them. She walked past a grinning Diana, got into the driver's seat and reversed into the parking space.

"I don't think you're quite straight," Diana pointed out, helpfully.

"It's fine," Lou snapped, as she got back out again.

Diana shrugged her shoulders.

"If you say so," she said.

They made their way round to the pub entrance. Diana was still on a high.

"You know, I really think I'm starting to get the hang of it."

"You were on the wrong side of the road for ten minutes," Lou reminded her.

Diana laughed. "Yes I did keep doing that at first didn't I. Still, I'll be fine next time."

Lou stopped dead in her tracks.

"You want another lesson?"

"Oh yes, definitely, as soon as possible. But don't worry, I won't take up anymore of your time; I'll go to a driving school. I'll probably get more out of a professional instructor."

Lou was so relieved she ignored the slight at her teaching skills.

"Good," she said.

"I think I'll be driving around Tenhamshire before the year is out."

"God help us all."

"Sorry?"

"Nothing."

Lou and Diana walked into The Smugglers.

"Right, I'll be back in a few minutes," Lou said, making a beeline for the Ladies.

By the time she came back out Diana was in full flow, telling Jamie and Gloria all about her lesson. Two large glasses of white wine were sat on the bar. Lou felt the urge to down both of them.

"But I do think some of the bends around here are too tight," Diana continued.

"It helps if you don't take them at sixty," Lou told her, climbing up onto a stool, "And you really shouldn't shout out, 'wheeeeee' as you do."

"If they don't want people to drive fast around them then they should put signs up."

"They do. Didn't you see them?"

"Not without my glasses on, no," Diana admitted.

Lou's eyes opened wide with horror. She grabbed the glass of wine in front of her and took a huge gulp.

"Maybe that's where they should put the speed bumps," Diana mused, "They seem to be in entirely the wrong place in my opinion. Why on earth was there one on that side road up the hill?"

"That wasn't a speed bump," Lou told her, "It was Mrs Brady, well her foot anyway. That's kind of why we stopped and I got out and helped. It was just fortunate it was her false leg you ran over."

Diana waved her hand dismissively.

"She was obviously standing too close to the edge of the road," she said.

Lou looked at Jamie and Gloria and jumped on her stool to indicate that Diana had mounted the kerb. They both winced.

The pub door opened and the colonel walked in.

"Oh great," said Lou, "We'll get stories now of how he drove tanks during the Second World War. Never mind the fact he was probably a foetus at the time."

"Aah he's probably just lonely," Gloria said, smiling over at him, "He's very much the gentleman. Always calls me madam."

"He probably thinks you run a brothel."

Jamie's comment was met with a smack on the arm.

The colonel clocked Diana. He gave the two ladies a quick smile but then made his way up to the other end of the bar. Gloria went over to serve him.

"I guess he's not worked on his facts yet," Lou said to Diana, "Doesn't want to tell us any new stories in case you correct him again."

"At least I didn't scare him away from the pub altogether."

"That's true," Lou reasoned, "Blimey Jamie you're almost bursting at the seams today, what with the colonel and Old Joe sitting over there with Bill the Shadow."

Jamie laughed. "Those two have been gassing away as usual," he said.

Diana looked across at the two old men sat at the table on the far side of the room, beside the entrance to the kitchen.

"They're both just sitting there," she said.

"Exactly. That's all they ever do," Jamie told her, "They're like a couple of bookends. I don't actually think Joe likes Bill. As soon as he leaves, Bill always hobbles round and sits in the vacated seat. I've no idea why. One time Joe came back in for his hat and you should have seen the look on his face when he saw where Bill was sitting. He stood there watching until Bill moved back again."

"So are these your only regulars?" Diana asked.

Jamie's smile fell from his face.

"There are a couple of others who come in," he said, "every so often," he added, quietly.

"Mike the Wipe and Doug the Bug," Lou told her, "One hates germs and one loves insects. I'll let you work out which one is which."

"It's such a shame," Diana said, looking around her, "I find this place charming."

Jamie's smile returned.

"You're becoming pretty regular yourself," he told her.

Diana was concentrating on the fishing nets on the wall.

"I put that down to bran flakes every morning," she replied, absently.

Gloria walked back down the bar towards them, obviously miffed.

"What's wrong?" Lou asked.

"The colonel," she said.

"Another drawn out story was it?"

Gloria shook her head. "No, I was telling him about the singers coming here on Saturday night and how I was working a longer shift and he said he'll come along to make sure I'm not overdoing it."

"Well that's kind of sweet, isn't it?" Lou told her.

"Not really. He said we need to watch things at our age. Bloody cheek, I'm a darn sight younger than him. He told me exhaustion can come on very quickly and will lay me low for weeks. Preparation is the key, watch out for the little signs and get plenty of rest. That way I won't get caught with my pants down."

"I think he's a bit late telling you that," Jamie said, "How many times in your life have you been caught with your pants down?"

"Oi."

"Maybe the colonel just wants to get in them," Lou added, "That's if she's wearing..."

"Alright you two, that's enough," Gloria sighed, "Honestly, you're like a couple of school children when you start egging each other on."

Jamie and Lou grinned at each other.

101

"I'm glad you're here, Diana. You and I at least can add a bit of maturity to the conversation."

Diana smiled and nodded, not really knowing how best to respond. She turned to Lou.

"By the way, I know which skill I want to improve on; baking."

"Are you good then?" Lou asked.

"Well I've always thought myself a decent cook," she replied, "I never did that much with cakes or bread; more main meals and dinner parties for my husband's business contacts, but it's all following recipes and putting things in the oven isn't it. The college in Tenhman is running a short eight week course in basic baking. I'd probably be better with an intermediate but I thought I'd give it a try anyway. I'm sure I'll still learn something."

Lou nodded. "That's a good idea," she said, "I've always wanted to improve my cooking."

Gloria made a sound that was part laugh, part raspberry.

"You need to cook first before you improve on it," she said, to her daughter.

"I cook," Lou replied, indignantly, "I have to; I have a child to care for."

"Stabbing the film lid before popping it into the microwave isn't cooking."

"I don't cook ready meals all of the time."

"No, sometimes you get a takeaway."

"Why don't you come with me," Diana interrupted, before an argument broke out, "It's a basic course, I'm sure you'll find it interesting. It starts next Tuesday and when I put my name down, they said there were still a couple of places left."

"Hmm, I'm not sure," Lou told her, "Tony is bringing

Maddie back this weekend. School starts for her again next week."

"I'll look after her," Gloria said, "I'm sure His Nibs here won't mind my finishing a little early on a Tuesday."

"It's not like we're busy," Jamie sighed, "You know I'd like to do more food here. When the tourists used to come, the previous owner always did three-course meals for coach parties. Mind you, he could afford to employ a chef. Maybe I ought to go on a cookery course of some kind."

"I think you ought to tempt a few more people in here first," Gloria told him, "At the moment we can't even give our sandwiches away."

She looked out of the window.

"Oh, isn't that your friend, Diana? Are you meeting her here?"

All eyes turned in the direction of the harbour. Joyce had stopped by the window. She had a lead in her hand and was obviously berating her dog, who was hidden by the wall. Eventually she stooped down and picked it up.

"My God that's ugly," Lou said, "What's it supposed to be?"

"I think it's a cross," Diana said.

"Well its eyes certainly are," Gloria chipped in.

Joyce's gaze turned towards the bar. She did a double take and the poor, cross-eyed dog dropped to the floor with a yelp. Diana smiled and waved but Joyce turned on her heels and dragged the dog away.

"I take it she's not coming in then," said Jamie.

Lou shook her head and sighed.

"That's the only people who come down to the harbour now," she said, "The dog walkers. And even then you can't walk right along the front and out the other end like you used to.

It's all fenced off while the new apartments are being built."

"You're right," Jamie said, looking pensive, "There are a lot of dog walkers."

"Oh God," Gloria sighed, rolling her eyes, "He's got another idea brewing."

*

When Diana got home from The Smugglers there were three answerphone messages waiting for her; all from Joyce.

"I guess you're still out boozing," the first one said, "I'll call back later."

"My God, you must be comatose under the table by now," the second one said; ten minutes later.

"Call me back as soon as you're home; and sober."

Diana sighed as she rang Joyce's number.

"Have you only just got in?"

"It's six thirty Joyce. You saw me two hours ago."

"I couldn't believe my eyes when I looked through the window."

"It's not a crime to have a glass or two of wine during the afternoon, Joyce. Don't you and Norman share a bottle of red on a Sunday?"

"Only because it sends him off to sleep so I can get a bit of peace," Joyce informed her, "Besides, it wasn't the drink that made me so shocked."

Diana doubted that.

"It was who you were with. Louise Turner of all people; and being served by the mother!"

"Lou had just given me a driving lesson and I was saying thank you."

"But you don't drive."

"Hence the lesson."

104

"Don't get smart with me, Diana," Joyce said, "Have you thought of seeing Dr Bryant?"

"I think he's too busy to give me driving lessons."

"Honestly! How much have you drunk; or is the smart mouth Lou's influence?"

Diana bit her lip.

"Why do you want me to see Dr Bryant?" she asked.

"Because I think your sister's death has affected you more than you're letting on," Joyce said, "I'm concerned about you, Diana."

"I'm grateful. And yes, you're right; Frances' death has affected me; just not in the way you think. I'm making a few changes in my life, that's all. There's no reason to call the medics with a straightjacket."

"And you think Louise Turner is the best person to help you, do you? Diana, I'm your friend; talk to me. What is it you want to do; perhaps I can help."

"You can," Diana told her, "I want to join your new committee regarding the youth of the area."

"Of course you can help," Joyce replied, "I'm happy for you to volunteer; I've said so in the past. We could use some fresh blood in the group. Moo is becoming next to useless with the tea rota. We should be having our first meeting next Wednesday."

"That's great," Diana said, "Let me know a time later on. I have to go now but we'll speak soon." She put the phone down.

Joyce is wrong about Lou, Diana thought, she's the perfect influence. Perhaps I could get the two talking and then Joyce would see what I do. If she wants fresh blood on the committee; Lou would be ideal.

*

Robert hadn't been able to concentrate at work all day. In the afternoon departmental meeting he'd somehow managed to vote himself chief organiser of the firm's Yule Ball. Oh well, he could think about that tomorrow. Tonight he and Grace were going to try out a new position in bed. The sexy nightwear had been a disaster but this was a much simpler idea; just the two of them together in bed but with a bit of a twist; perhaps quite literally.

The usual Tuesday night dinner of chicken casserole proved a quiet affair. Robert was still excited and full of anticipation. Grace just felt fearful. She took a sip of her glass of Chablis.

"I'm still not sure about this," she said.

"Relax love," Robert replied, "There's no pressure. It'll be fun."

Grace very much doubted that.

"Don't you think we're too old to try something new?"

Robert sighed. They'd already had this conversation.

"I'm not expecting you to put your feet behind your ears or swing from the light fitting."

"Robert!"

"I've brought this book home with me," he told her, reaching across to his briefcase, "It demonstrates lots of different positions. We can have a look through it first and pick something we're both happy with."

"You didn't borrow that off of someone at work did you?" Grace asked, "I don't want everyone knowing about what we're doing. It's bad enough I flashed the regatta last weekend."

"I bought it, love."

"How much was it?"

Robert sighed again.

"I had to buy it didn't I," he snapped at her, "I don't think

106

the local library is going to stock this sort of thing now are they?"

"There's no need to raise your voice."

"Look," Robert said, "Let's both calm down. This is meant to be a fun and loving evening. It's not going to be if we keep arguing."

Grace remained silent.

"Fine," she said, eventually, and drained her glass of wine.

Robert's excitement was even more intense as he lay in bed, the book of positions on his bedside table. He hadn't really looked through it himself yet. He'd been embarrassed in the shop and had had to wait fifteen minutes before being able to take it off of the shelf as an old lady with a tartan shopping trolley on wheels was standing right by the display, reading a book entitled, 'Still Nobbing at Ninety.' Only after she'd dropped it into her trolley and legged it out of the shop without paying was Robert able to creep forwards and grab his book; adding an instruction manual on building model aeroplanes to it at the checkout; just to show the young girl on the till that he enjoyed a range of hobbies.

He thumbed through the book now while waiting on Grace, who was taking a suspiciously long time in the bathroom. The photographs looked a little graphic, even on the quick scan that Robert did. Grace wouldn't be pleased. Finally she opened the door of the en suite and came into the room.

"Right," she said, getting into bed, "Let's get this over with."

"How romantic."

She smiled. "Sorry love, I didn't mean being with you," she reached for her glasses, "Right, is this the book?"

"It's a bit graphic…"

Grace grabbed it from Robert before he could finish his

warning and began flicking through the pages; her mouth dropping lower at each turn.

"Dear God," she said, "Are these people making love or wrestling?"

"There may be some simpler ones towards the back," Robert replied, leaning over and frantically trying to turn the pages on to something a little less explicit, just in case Grace changed her mind. Unfortunately it appeared the further into the book, the more complicated the positions became.

"How can someone stay like that long enough for the photograph to be taken?" Grace asked.

"I don't know," Robert admitted, "I guess they don't have to say, 'Cheese' first so maybe it's not that long."

Grace began flicking back the pages, shaking her head.

"I'm sorry Robert, but I don't think I could have done any of these forty years ago, let alone now. I mean, look at this; how on earth can she move that up there? She could bite her own toe nails."

"Hang on," Robert said, turning a page back, "That looks familiar."

"What?!"

"It's like a wheelbarrow. You must have done that as a child. Your hands are on the floor and the person standing behind you holds your legs, like the arms of a wheel barrow. I was always doing that as a child. Didn't you?"

"Yes I did," Grace told him, "But always with my clothes on. I don't want to revisit my youth by having you push me around the park like that."

"No, you don't go outside...not unless you want to."

"Let's keep looking."

Grace turned a few more pages, tutting at each of them."

"How about that?" Robert said.

Grace examined the photo. She turned the book upside down and then righted it again.

"Do you really think you could straddle a wardrobe like that?" she asked.

"Forget the wardrobe, love," Robert told her, "I just meant the position; we could recreate that in bed."

"But they're using a wardrobe and a stuffed rhino head."

"Well we don't have to recreate the exact same scene," he snapped, "That woman's got long blonde hair and a shaved muff, are you going to do that bit as well?"

"You're getting coarse again, Robert!"

"I'm sorry, love; but this should be something easy."

Grace sighed. "Fine," she said, handing him the book, "You pick one and we'll give it a try."

"Really?"

"Yes, but nothing that might tear my nightie. You pick while I write a shopping list out for tomorrow."

That wasn't the most romantic of propositions but Robert wasn't about to argue. He began to silently leaf through the book, the only noise being Grace talking under her breath every so often.

"Do we need eggs? I'll get half a dozen anyway. What was I going to do with a parsnip? Oh yes, brush with honey before roasting. I'll have to buy a jar."

Eventually Robert settled on page eleven.

"There," he said, turning the book round to face Grace, "We'll do that one."

Grace perused the page.

"Are you sure you can manage that?" she asked.

Robert turned the book back and frowned.

"Of course I can," he said, "That's nothing. I could hold that position for hours. All arms and legs are touching the floor."

"If you say so."

"Watch me," Robert said.

Grace watched while Robert lay back and positioned his hands either side of his head. He raised himself up into a sort of crab position, his back arched so that his navel faced the ceiling.

"Pork belly!" Grace shouted out, and grabbed her list again. When she looked up Robert was still in the same position.

"Yes that's very impressive," she said, "You can get down now."

"I can't move," Robert whispered.

"Very funny."

"I mean it, Grace. I think my back has gone."

"Oh God, no." Grace sprang out of her side of the bed.

"I think you should call the doctor."

"Like hell I am," she said, "He's not coming in here and finding you like that, I don't care how much pain you're in."

"Grace!"

"Nope, I'm adamant about this. Now come on," she walked round to her husband's side of the bed and gently rubbed the base of his back, "This always helped before when you used to put your back out."

Eventually Robert was able to collapse down onto the bed, still wincing in pain.

"I'm such an idiot," he said.

"No you're not," Grace told him, soothingly, as she gently stroked his cheek, "You're just old."

That didn't make him feel any better.

*

Lou found herself whistling as she walked across the road to

110

work the following morning. When Chris let her in she even gave him a big smile. He grinned back.

"Did someone get some last night?" he said, lasciviously.

Lou sighed.

"Nah," he continued, "You couldn't replace me that quickly. Once a woman's ridden my love salami, she finds it difficult to get quality meat anywhere else."

"I had two chipolatas last night that were three days past their sell by date," Lou told him, "And they were a lot more satisfying."

"Oi oi; and where did you stick those then?"

"Oh God, I had them in a sandwich you disgusting creep!"

Lou walked towards the staffroom to get her overall on.

"You'll be running back to me soon," Chris called over to her. He pointed at himself, "How can you resist all of this?"

She turned round to face him, just as Simon walked out of his office.

"Why would I go back to a man who can't ejaculate without farting?" she shouted back across the floor.

Simon turned and retreated to his office. When Lou emerged wearing her overall she saw Precious had just walked in through the main door. She was looking at Chris with a puzzled expression on her face.

"I don't even like salami," she told him, before walking over to Lou.

"He gets worse," she said, "Really darling; what on earth did you ever see in that man?"

Lou sighed. "He caught me at a low ebb," she said, "I was struggling with a three year old child at the time and he was there and available."

Precious took a look back at Chris, who was now showing

Terry some sort of karate kick. He caught his foot in the basket of reduced produce.

"If I were you I'd have stuck with the low ebb," she said.

Simon, deeming it safe, came out of his office again.

"Could you gather round," he called out, "I just have two pieces of information to pass on to you before we open."

Everyone walked over to where Simon was standing; Chris limping a little.

"Right; now I'm sure some of you will be pleased to hear that the star of the Jesters Supermarket ads, Mr Pete Crick, will be visiting this store on his tour."

Lou felt her heart fluttering.

"I don't have an exact date yet but we must start preparing our advertising campaign for his arrival. This is a good opportunity to promote the smaller stores in the Jesters chain."

Chris nudged Lou.

"You told me once that I reminded you of Pete Crick," he said.

"When was that?" she asked.

"That weekend at my mum's caravan. I'd just bought my biker jacket and those white jeans with the 'go faster' stripe down each leg. You said I looked like Pete Crick."

Lou tutted. "I said you looked a complete prick."

"Anyway," Simon interrupted, "The second piece of news is more for Lou's benefit. The new clothing range has arrived. It's out the back. Don't worry, I'm not expecting you to put it all out on your own, I'm not that heartless."

Lou smiled.

"Terry is going to help you."

The smile disappeared, but reappeared on a very eager looking Terry.

There were a large number of boxes in the storeroom; all filled with, in Lou's opinion; tat. The company had relied heavily on the Jesters' logo with the head of a jester, in his three pointed hat with a bell at each tip, on many of the items. They'd also used the red and yellow striped costume as the main colours in their range.

"My God, who would wear this?" Lou said out loud, holding up a pair of red jeans with a jester head across the back.

"Every time you sat down, you'd be sitting on the Jester's face," Terry replied.

An image of Pete Crick appeared in Lou's mind.

"I wonder if they've got a size twelve?" she said, rummaging through the box.

A second later Terry called out to her.

"Lou, could you give me a hand?"

She looked up and was met with the sight of Terry in a yellow bra with jester faces on the cups.

"I just wanted to practice unhooking one," he told her, "But now I'm stuck."

Trying to supress a smile Lou walked over to him. She had trouble undoing it herself.

"I think this is a dodgy hook," she said.

Simon walked into the stockroom to see how things were going and was greeted by the sight of Lou standing behind Terry, trying to undo his bra.

"I really shouldn't leave my office," he said, before turning and walking back out again.

The whole morning was spent going through the clothes and planning where they would go in the display area. Although she wouldn't admit it to Simon, Lou actually enjoyed the experience; especially once she'd got rid of Terry and his

113

endless questions. 'What's the difference between a shirt and a blouse; how does cotton get mixed with polyester; why don't panties have a hole at the front so ladies can tiddle without having to take them off?'

It was about three thirty in the afternoon when Lou finally felt happy with the finishing touches she was putting to the display. She was just trying to stretch up to arrange a blouse over a metal rail when Grace and Robert approached her.

"Oh Robert, you're taller than me," Lou said, "You couldn't just drape this over the end of that rail could you; save me getting the ladder out."

"Afraid I can't," he told her.

"We're just off to the doctor's," Grace explained, "Robert's put his back out. We would have gone straight there but I remembered I'd forgotten the chops for dinner."

"I'm sorry to hear that," Lou said, "About your back I mean. I hope it's not too sore."

"Should be okay once I've got a few painkillers off the doctor," Robert said, "Sorry I can't help you though."

"Think nothing of it;" Lou told him, "I know you'd always help if you could. You're the first to bend over backwards for anybody."

Robert winced.

"I shan't be trying that again in a hurry," he said.

"Sorry?"

Grace tugged at her husband's sleeve.

"I must get you to your appointment," she said, "Come on Robert, we'll grab the lamb chops and go."

She fairly dragged her husband over to the meat aisle, the poor man flinching in pain at each quickened step.

Ten minutes later, after putting the ladder away again, Lou

114

stood back and admired the finished display. It was definitely eye-catching but she wasn't confident the red and yellow clothes would actually sell. Precious came and stood beside her. They were silent for a minute, just looking at the clothing.

"It kind of reminds me of a candy store," Precious finally said.

Lou laughed. A voice behind them said,

"Does that mean those panties are edible?"

Lou picked up a large pair of striped, old lady knickers and turned to Chris.

"Here you go," she said, "Try these. With luck, you'll choke."

"I've got something else you can choke on anytime you like, darling."

Lou had just formed the 'eff' sound of her response when Simon walked over.

"This looks great," he said, beaming, "Spectacular even."

"It's not exactly designer clothing though is it?" Precious told him.

"I don't think that matters," Chris interjected, "When a bird's got me down to my boxers she's too busy trying to get at the delight inside to start reading the name on the waistband."

He elbowed Simon in the ribs in a, 'lads together' sort of way. Simon just smiled back politely; not quite following Chris's train of thought.

"It's certainly colourful," Precious admitted, still looking at the display.

"Excellent," Simon said, admiringly, "Eye-catching will get the customers attention alright. Back in my last store we stocked a range of diarrhoea remedies that just weren't selling. As soon as we added some colour to the display they flew off the shelves."

"Really?"

Simon nodded. "Oh yes," he said, "Though of course it did coincide with Curry Week in the staff canteen."

He shrugged his shoulders.

"Do you think we'll sell any of it though," Lou asked, "I mean it's not really…well; tasteful is it."

"Isn't it?" Simon said, a frown appearing, "I'm not really up on women's fashion I must admit. Let's just see, shall we? Actually Lou, now that you've finished, could you come to my office; I'd like a quiet word."

As the two walked off Precious whispered to Chris,

"I guess his lack of interest in women's clothes dispels the theory from Jennifer over at the Pinstown branch about why he left his last store. She'd heard he'd been forced to leave after he was found down the pickles aisle wearing hot pants and a see-through boob tube."

Chris grinned. "I knew a girl like that once," his grin turned to a look of horror, "Which store are you talking about?"

In the office Simon indicated for Lou to sit down.

"I've had news that the company is going to be doing another round of management trainee programmes," he told her, "When it becomes official, I'd like to put your name forward for a place."

"Me?" Lou said, "That's silly."

Simon sighed, wearily. "It's not silly at all," he told her, "I've said before, you could manage your own store. This opportunity doesn't come up internally that often. Most of the time the programme is set up for newly qualified graduates. This is a great chance for you."

"But I couldn't manage a whole store," Lou said, "There's so much I don't know."

"And there's a lot you do. The rest comes with training. Honestly Lou, I wouldn't suggest this if I didn't think you could do it."

Lou looked at Simon's straight-faced expression across the desk and realised he was serious.

"But what about Maddie?" she said, "I can't just go off on some training programme or..."

Simon held up his hands and stopped her talking.

"I'm just asking you to consider it. There'll be plenty of time to organise things at home. Really Lou, consider it."

Lou nodded and got up.

How can that possibly happen, she thought as she left the room, the idea seemed fantastical. She'd spent twelve years stacking shelves. How on earth was that a qualification to become a manager?

Back outside she was surprised to see Jamie standing on the shop floor talking to Chris. When he saw her he waved and came over.

"Why is he talking about edible panties and salami?" he asked.

"Because Chris is an under-sexed tosser," Lou told him, "It's not often we see you in here."

"I've got a couple of posters left for the singers this Saturday," Jamie said, indicating the roll under his arm, "I should have thought of it before but do you think I could put one up in your window here?"

"I'm sure it will be fine," Lou replied, unrolling one, "I'll double-check with Simon but I can't see it being a problem."

"Thanks," Jamie said, giving her a peck on the cheek, "Must run."

Lou looked at the poster. It was like the one Jamie had shown her last week but there was something about it that wasn't quite right. She couldn't put her finger on it.

Chapter 6

Jamie was feeling nervous. On the one hand he was worried that no one would turn up to see the two singers. How popular were Martin and Sarah after all? He'd only booked them last Saturday for this Saturday. That wasn't really a positive sign of popularity was it? They said they toured the local pubs and festivals but Jamie had never heard of them. Did they have a following? On the other hand, what if they were very well-known and a huge crowd of people showed up, all trying to cram into this small bar? Would he and Gloria be able to cope? Lou, bless her, had offered to help out if needs be.

Jamie looked at his watch again; six thirty. Martin and Sarah were due to go on at half past seven. Old Joe had just left with a free cigar and at the moment, only the colonel and Mike the Wipe were there, sitting at a table together. Mike hadn't been in for a few weeks and Jamie assumed that he hadn't seen the posters. He usually avoided crowds to prevent anyone touching and contaminating him. He'd walked in tonight with his wet cloth in a plastic bag and had wiped down his table and chair as usual before sitting down. He was drinking bitter from his 'special glass;' happily cleaning his spectacles every five minutes while the colonel rattled off one of his stories.

At quarter to seven Lou walked in with Diana and a short lady that Jamie had seen Diana with before. He was surprised to see the woman wearing a rather lurid, red and yellow striped blouse. They walked up to the bar.

"Shall we share a bottle of wine?" Diana suggested, to her two friends.

They both nodded.

119

"Do you know Muriel?" she asked Jamie.

"I've seen you around," he said, nodding at her.

"She used to be my landlady when I first moved here," Lou told him, "That was a long time ago."

"Don't say that, you'll make me feel ancient," Muriel replied, smiling.

"Isn't there usually another lady that you're both with?" Jamie asked, as he brought over a bottle of chilled white wine and three glasses, "The one with the ugly dog?"

Lou's expression darkened.

"Oh, she won't be coming," Diana whispered, handing him the money.

Diana poured the wine and the three chinked glasses.

"Did I tell you I've got my first driving lesson booked for Monday morning?"

"No you didn't," Lou replied, feeling grateful she would be at work and therefore not on the roads that day.

"I'm so looking forward to it," Diana continued, "I wasn't sure whether to do one a week or go fast track."

"You mean a crash course? I wouldn't advise that for you," Lou told her.

"Yes, I thought that in the end. Perhaps if the lesson goes well I could drive us in your car to our baking lesson on Tuesday."

Lou missed her mouth with her wine.

"Erm; let's wait and see shall we," she said, wiping her chin. She quickly changed the subject, "I see you found my display at the supermarket, Muriel."

Muriel smiled again as she looked down at her new blouse.

"Yes, it is rather colourful isn't it," she replied, "This seemed to call out to me."

"I think it shouted," Lou grinned, "I'm glad someone has bought something though. I doubt we'll have many sales."

As she said this, Gloria walked through to the bar from the back. All three ladies mouths fell open. Gloria stopped when she saw them.

"What?" she asked, looking puzzled.

Silence remained as the three of them took in Gloria's new yellow top. It was very low-cut, even for her standards and had a red jester's face on the front. The two outside prongs of his hat followed the edge of the top up the sides towards the shoulders, creating the illusion of Gloria's ample breasts being pushed together. The third shot straight up the middle, the bell on the end pointing directly at her cleavage.

"I don't even remember seeing that one," Lou said.

"Oh," Gloria realised why they were staring, "Do you like it? I nipped into the supermarket before work and saw it. I've just popped it on."

"You're just about to pop out," Lou told her.

"It's not that low."

Jamie turned round from serving a customer.

"Jesus Christ!" he called out, getting an eyeful, "Stand back everybody, they're gonna blow."

"Oh stop it," Gloria said, running her hands down the sides of the top, which just pushed her breasts higher and made everyone gasp, "It's fun. Look, Muriel has the same idea. We're like twins."

Muriel took another look at her own short-sleeved, blouse that was buttoned up to the neck and felt she couldn't quite agree with that statement.

"It makes them look enormous, mum."

"I can't help the way I'm built," Gloria said, looking hurt,

121

"Besides; the girls would look a darn sight bigger if I tried to hide them in a high-necked top."

Lou shook her head.

"You're going to get a lot of comments," she said.

"Oh please, I'm sure no one will even notice," Gloria replied, before stepping over to serve the colonel as he came up to the bar with his and Mike's empty glasses.

The colonel's eyes couldn't help but drop to the cleavage but ever the gentleman; he quickly looked back up into Gloria's face and smiled.

"Hello my dear," he said, "I'll have two pints of your breast bitter please."

Gloria took the glasses and as she passed Lou, whispered, "Don't say one word."

Martin and Sarah walked in through the front entrance followed by a small group of people who were obviously fans. Jamie helped them set up their microphone and speakers before showing the two singers out to the room at the back beside the kitchen where they could, "meditate and channel their talent." By this time Lou, Diana and Muriel had retired to the table in the far corner where Old Joe sat during the day and which was away from the speakers. The group of fans were sat at the table right next to where Martin and Sarah would be singing. Two of the women, with flowers in their hair, had parked themselves on the floor in front of the microphones. A man walked in from the harbour front and came up to the bar.

"This is the right place for Martin and Sarah's performance isn't it?" he asked.

"Yes it is," Jamie said, "They'll be starting soon."

The man smiled.

"Excellent," he said, "The rest of the group are just parking up round the back and changing."

Changing? Perhaps they were groupies, Jamie reasoned, and were going to don outfits even more folksy than the group who had entered with Martin and Sarah fifteen minutes ago. Mind you, the guy standing in front of him didn't look folksy. He was wearing a black leather jacket, which looked pretty normal, but there was a tight vest top underneath that appeared to be made of some strange, space-like, shiny silver material.

"This is different from our usual venues," the man continued, looking around the bar, "But when I saw the posters I told the gang we should give it a go. It's nice to try out somewhere new."

"Well, I'm glad you did," Jamie said, "Do you know Martin and Sarah well?"

"I don't know them at all. As I say, I just saw the posters," the man replied, still looking at the walls, "What do you use those nets for?"

Jamie looked across at the boating memorabilia.

"Erm, it's decorative really," he told him, "More for effect. I do sometimes hang things off of it."

The man's eyes lit up.

"Cool," he said, "I wondered if you used it to tie people to those large oars."

"Sorry?"

"Or are those just for spanking?"

Before Jamie could reply, the rest of the group came in.

"What the hell?" Gloria said, coming over to stand beside Jamie, "I thought you said they played folksy music."

Jamie couldn't respond. The people that had just walked in were all dressed in a mixture of leather and rubber. One man had a black mask on in the same sort of shiny material of the original man's vest top. The other customers were all looking puzzled as well. The original man was quite relaxed.

"Tell me," he said, "Do you have your own dungeon? I assume with the rocks and caves around here it would be a great place for hooks and chains."

"I'm sorry," Jamie said, "I think there may have been some mistake."

Lou rushed up to the end of the bar and waved Jamie and her mother over.

"Oh God," she said, "I've just realised what was wrong with that poster the other day. I couldn't put my finger on it at the time."

"What do you mean?" Jamie asked.

Lou held out the one she had just torn down from the wall.

"It's meant to say, 'Martin and Sarah performing at The Smugglers Inn. Come and enjoy the M & S experience.'"

"Oh Jesus," said Jamie, "I deleted some of the text online by mistake when changing the pub name. I thought I'd typed it back in correctly. I've gone and put posters up all around town inviting people to, 'Come and enjoy the S & M experience.'"

"You mean all these people here…?" Gloria left the sentence hanging.

The man in the mask took off his coat. Underneath he was dressed in a black, rubber outfit. All that was visible was his bare bottom through two holes in the back.

"Roger!" Gloria shouted.

The man turned round to face her. He undid the zip across his mouth.

"My God; Gloria," he called back, "Is that you?"

"I'd have recognised you anywhere," she told him, walking over and reaching her hands across the bar where he gently took hold of them.

Lou watched, aghast, as her mother leaned forwards to let Roger kiss her on the cheek.

"I'm going to try and forget that just happened," she said.

Mike came up to the bar. He was a tall, bean-pole of a man, which was useful when squeezing through groups of people that you didn't want to brush against. His glasses looked like they were steaming up. He took them off and gave them another clean.

"I think there's been a bit of a blunder," he said.

"You're telling me," Jamie replied.

"Mind you, I must give them their due," Mike continued, "Their outfits are very clean aren't they. That girl over there with the whip, talking to the colonel; she just told me about the hygiene qualities she always insists on before she gets a piercing done. It's very commendable."

"I must be dreaming," Jamie said, to Lou, "What the hell do I do?"

"Well I think you'd better tell Martin and Sarah before they come out and..."

It was too late. Lou didn't have time to finish the sentence.

Even though she was in a long, shapeless, floral dress and he a very colourful waistcoat and sandals, there was a smattering of applause as the couple walked over to the microphone. Things were fine until Martin picked up his guitar and Sarah her tambourine. They sang three words before the S & M group began shouting.

*

"Actually they were very good about it in the end," Jamie said, once the pub had closed.

Lou nodded. "It's a shame Martin and Sarah and the rest of

their little group didn't see the funny side as well. I don't think they'll be coming back."

"I think they're against people wearing leather. It was nice of the S & M guys to stay for a couple of rounds of drinks though," Jamie said.

"I know. Sorry Diana and Muriel left, but it really was a bit of a shock for them."

Jamie shook his head. "No, it's fine," he told her, "It was a shock for all of us when the group walked in."

"Not that, I mean when the colonel expressed an interest in the group and pulled his trousers off to try on those leather chaps."

"Oh right, yes," Jamie said, "After all those stories about not getting caught with your pants down, who'd have thought he didn't wear any."

"I can't believe he decided to join the group," Lou continued, "He walked out of here wearing a studded dog collar and a smile."

"Someone had even pierced his nose for him!" Jamie winced, "I doubt we'll be seeing him in here again anytime soon. There was talk of a Rubber Weekend in Weston-super-Mare next week."

Gloria came out from the kitchen.

"Right, the back's locked up," she said, "I'm going to go now."

"Me too," Lou said, "I'll walk you to your car."

"And you can ask her how she recognised Roger," Jamie called after them.

"Oh, well you see…"

Lou held her hand up.

"Really don't want to know, mum. You weren't into that

stuff, were you?"

"It was nothing dirty; you see Roger liked it when…"

"No; I really don't want to know."

Jamie laughed as he locked up the door behind them but stopped when he turned round and looked at his empty bar. Now that the colonel had found a new interest he was another regular down. He had to think of a really good idea to attract people in. The image of the colonel in the collar made him recall the dog walkers.

*

The pub was in a beautiful village setting, overlooking the green. Diana had never been here before and was amazed that Joyce had heard about it.

"I can't remember who told me now," she said, "It's a bit off the beaten track so doesn't get too busy."

"I wonder that they make enough money to keep going," Diana said, looking round her at the near empty room. It was rustic and reminded her of The Smugglers. She couldn't help wondering how much longer Jamie could remain open with his lack of clientele.

"I like it," chipped in Muriel, she was wearing her new blouse from yesterday evening again, "It's been ages since I've been out for Sunday lunch. It was so nice of you to drive us, Joyce."

Diana smiled.

"I don't think it will be too long until I can do that too," she said, "I'm so looking forward to my lesson tomorrow."

"What's Norman doing today?" Muriel asked Joyce, "Did he not want to come with us?"

"Norman's having his dinner at home," Joyce told them, "We don't want him here butting into our conversation all of the time. I prepared his meal earlier; he's quite happy. You should have seen his little face when I stewed his plums this morning."

A strong, manufactured, floral smell wafted across the table, making all three ladies pull faces. A man, the wrong side of fifty, sidled up beside them.

"Hello my beautiful ladies," he said, in a strange, Italian accent, "I am Chico and will be your waiter for your lunchtime meal."

He was wearing the uniform of the rest of the staff, white shirt and black trousers, but his trousers were made of leather and the shirt had a ruffle down the front and was opened to the navel. He was bald on top but had a pony tail, which was obviously dyed as it was too black to be natural. Joyce looked him up and down with a disgusted look on her face. When she met his eyes he winked and a made a kissing noise at her. Diana supressed a smile.

"Drinks for your gorgeous group?" Chico asked, throwing in a little hip thrust.

"Soda water," Joyce said, abruptly.

"An orange juice for me please," Muriel added.

"A large glass of dry, white wine." Diana ignored Joyce's raised eyebrows.

Chico left with another hip thrust.

"Where on earth do they get their staff from?" Joyce said, "I'm not confident that man will get our order correct."

"Oh I thought he was rather sweet," Muriel said, watching Chico samba over to the bar area.

"You would, Moo. You see the good in everyone," Joyce said, as if this was a failing in her friend's character.

The three ladies perused the menu. Muriel let out a sigh.

"I don't like it when they give too much detail about the

meat," she said, "It says here the roast pork is made from Gloucester Old Spot pigs that were raised at Tyler's Green Farm. I've been there and can picture the little piglets running around. It's put me off ordering that."

"And the beef," Diana told her, not looking up, "They're serving Daisy. She had a happy life on the farm until an unfortunate accident with the combine harvester led to her being something delicious on your plate today."

"Oh God," Muriel replied, "I think I'll have the spinach quiche."

Diana laughed but her friends didn't join in and she soon stopped.

If Lou was here now we'd be crying with laughter at my little joke, she thought.

Chico came back with the correct drinks and took the food order. He grinned at Muriel when she asked for the quiche.

"Maybe you want some meat later?" he said, hip thrusting on the word meat. Muriel giggled and he winked before walking away.

Joyce dipped the end of her napkin into her soda water and wiped the rim of her glass before taking a sip.

"So," she said, "I hear your night out at the local, 'boozer;' is that the word, was a complete disaster."

"It was just a mix up, that's all," Diana replied.

A pained expression crossed Muriel's face.

"I saw things I never want to see again," she said.

Joyce patted her hand gently.

"I told you not to go, Moo."

"And I suppose that's my fault," Diana said, taking a large swig of her wine.

"Not at all," Joyce replied, "I think we all know whose fault it is Diana. And her influence isn't changing you for the better."

She indicated the glass of wine. Diana sighed.

"I wish you'd change the record Joyce," she told her, "I'm feeling happy and as my friend; that should make you happy too. You should take the chance to get to know Lou; she's not the woman you think she is. I was going to suggest she join your next committee."

Joyce choked on her soda water. Even Muriel looked shocked at the suggestion.

"Am I hearing you right?" Joyce said, once she'd recovered, "You want Louise Turner to join one of **my** committees?"

Diana remained defiant.

"Yes, I think she would be a great asset."

"How?"

"You're forming a committee relating to the youth of the area. I would have thought it made sense to have someone on the committee under sixty. Not only that but someone who has a child herself."

Joyce was shaking her head.

"Did she put you up to this?"

"Well no; I haven't actually mentioned it to her yet."

"Well thank goodness for that," Joyce said, "Because there's no way she would ever be welcome."

Muriel made a shushing sound before the two ladies voices rose any further. A couple at a nearby table were surreptitiously looking over to see what was going on.

Joyce sighed. "Look, I don't have a problem with your notion about having younger members at the meeting. I think that's a very good idea; someone to carry on our good work when we're no longer around or able to. I just can't believe that

Louise Turner is that person."

Diana remained silent; too worried her anger would boil over if she spoke.

"She's shown nothing but contempt for those of us up on the hill, ever since she arrived here," Joyce continued, "I actually feel sorry for her. What hope did she have with a mother like that?"

Diana opened her mouth to respond but Joyce cut in again.

"It's a question of breeding. Would someone of her class and background really be able to work for the good of our community? I'm sure she has her own…well; ideas shall we say, but I don't think she's the sort of woman who would stick at it; see things through to the end. It's not just the meetings, Diana. There's a lot of work that goes into getting things done; lots of people at the council to speak to; letter writing; phone calls…"

"And she has her kiddie to look after," chimed in Muriel, "Plus she works full time. I'm not sure she would want to give up any of her precious free time."

Diana was still silent. What Muriel had said made her think. Was she taking up too much of Lou's time? The last couple of weeks had been fun but Maddie was coming home today. Gloria had kindly agreed to look after her on Tuesday's for the next eight weeks so she and Lou could go to the baking class, but Diana couldn't keep infringing on Lou's free time. She needed to spend that with her daughter. What would happen to the list though? She knew it was a selfish thought but Diana really didn't think she could do all the things on it without Lou's help.

Joyce sighed again. "You know, our little area on the hill has changed so much," she said, "There are so many new,

131

young families; some of them frightfully noisy. Once upon a time our area was much more middle class."

"I still like it there," Muriel said.

"I wasn't really speaking about you, Moo. I meant more Diana and myself. We bought our houses there; you just inherited yours from your parents."

Muriel gave Diana a wink.

"We know how people should behave, you and me," Joyce continued, "We're a different breed. Our husbands both had very good jobs."

"Norman worked at the local post office."

"It was a Civil Service career, Moo!"

Muriel shrugged her shoulders at Diana, making her smile. Joyce was looking dreamily into space.

"We used to have some very high-up officials living there," she continued, "The mayor, several councillors; members of the armed forces. Do you remember the admiral?"

"Was that the one who killed his second wife?" Muriel asked.

Joyce waved her hand dismissively.

"The woman was always flighty," she said, "And far too young for him. I was talking about his character and his bearing."

"Oh yes, his bearing," Diana cut in, "He was bearing down on his wife with a pickaxe when a Jehovah's Witness knocked at the door, if I remember rightly."

"It did stop them knocking at that house ever again though," Muriel reasoned.

Chico showed up with the dinners. He placed Diana's and Joyce's down and then Muriel's. He gave her a little nudge.

"This is for you, cuteness," he said, "You look like a stripy sweet in that blouse and I want to give you a lick."

Muriel giggled. "Merci," she said.

Chico walked off, beaming. Silence returned to the table while the three ladies tucked into their meals. After a few minutes Joyce said,

"Well, this is disgusting."

Diana couldn't help laughing in agreement and the slight atmosphere that had developed between the two of them cleared.

"Shall I call the waiter over?" she asked.

All three women looked over to where Chico was standing, talking to a young waitress. He grabbed hold of his crotch with both hands.

"I think he looks a little busy," Muriel said.

"Yes, I don't think we'll order dessert," Joyce added.

They returned to their plates, although not much was eaten.

"Has William heard about his promotion?" Diana asked Joyce, as she gave up on her roast beef and put her knife and fork down.

Joyce beamed. "Oh yes, he did," she said, "The Chemical and Recycling Research Company are very pleased with him."

"That's good."

"He's solely responsible for all human waste in the entire North East now," she told them, proudly.

"Let's hope he doesn't take his work home with him," Muriel chipped in.

Joyce's eyes narrowed. "Is that an attempt at a joke?"

"No I mean it," Muriel told her, innocently, "You wouldn't want the stress rubbing off on the kiddies."

Joyce sat back in her seat.

"That's right," she said, "You wouldn't. Still, William

133

doesn't get stressed, he's very capable. Anyway, he and Wendy are taking the boys to Loch Lomond for a week to celebrate. That will be relaxing."

"That sounds nice," Diana said, "But I thought they would have come down here after cancelling their last visit."

Joyce's smile disappeared.

"Oh well," she replied, "Their friend has a cottage and it was only available next week."

"That's a shame. Couldn't you and Norman go up there and stay for a few days?"

"You suggested that, didn't you," Muriel said.

Joyce shot daggers at her friend before saying,

"Well the cottage isn't that big. It only has the three bedrooms and the boys aren't used to sharing."

The whole table fell into an embarrassed silence.

"Maybe we **should** look at the dessert menu," Diana said, "Or perhaps order some coffee."

She raised her hand and Chico came rushing over.

"Something sweet for all you sweeties?" he asked, as he cleared the plates.

"Just a regular coffee for me please," Diana said.

Joyce nodded to show she wanted the same thing.

"Me too," Muriel smiled.

"I'll bring you ladies over something hot and strong," Chico said, "And I've got something special right here to stir it with."

He began gyrating his pelvis at Muriel, right beside Joyce's head. She tutted loudly but he didn't hear her. Joyce was just about to tap him on his side to get his attention when Chico turned round so that Muriel could watch him sideways on and she accidently copped a feel. As Joyce screamed, Chico jumped and three plates of half-eaten food went crashing to the

134

ground. They didn't stay for coffee.

*

Lou finished stuffing magazines, toys and empty microwave meal cartons into bins, drawers and behind cushions to make the lounge look tidy before Tony arrived with Maddie. He'd said he was bringing her over late Sunday afternoon after stopping in at his mum's on the way but Lou knew he was always early.

At three o'clock the bell rang and Lou buzzed them in. She hadn't realised quite how much she had missed Maddie until she was cuddling her in her arms. Aside from the small suitcase Lou had sent her away with, she now had a bag stuffed with new toys.

"Sorry," Tony told her, when he saw Lou eyeing the bag, "More clutter for you I'm afraid."

"What do you mean; more?" she said, indignantly, "Look at the space in this lounge."

"It's impressive," he replied, his bright blue eyes twinkling, "But I guess there's not much room behind the cushions now is there?"

Lou couldn't help smiling.

"Coffee?" she asked.

Tony looked at his watch, an expensive make Lou couldn't help noticing.

"Hmm, Cheryl is expecting me back about seven; ah sod it; she can wait. I'd love one."

While Lou made the coffee, Maddie brought each of her new toys over in turn to show her mum.

"And this colouring book Cheryl bought to keep me quiet in her office when she had to go into work," she said, "We were meant to be going to the adventure park."

"And were you quiet while Cheryl worked?" Lou asked.

135

Maddie looked up at her mother resentfully.

"Yes," she said.

"Good girl."

Tony tutted. "She was so looking forward to that day," he said, as he watched Maddie rush off to her room to show her mother the next item, "I can't believe Cheryl went to work."

"And where were you then?" Lou asked, knowing full well the answer.

"Oh, well; I was at work too," Tony said, sheepishly, "It was really busy for me that week."

"So it's okay for the man to work but not the woman," Lou teased, "My, my; I never had you down as sexist Tony."

"I'm not," he replied, "I only meant…"

He saw Lou's grin and smiled.

"I forgot how annoying you are," he said.

Lou laughed.

"I know I'm in a different league to Cheryl jobwise," she said, bringing over the coffee, "But I understand what it's like to work full time and look after a child."

"I know you do," Tony said, "I'd like to help out more…"

"This isn't a rant," Lou interrupted, sitting beside him on the sofa, "It's just a statement of fact. You do all that you can. I mean, you even pay for Maddie 's after school care while I'm at work."

"That's nothing," he said, "It's only fair; but that's not what I meant. I really mean that I'd like to help out more."

Lou's face fell.

"You don't want more weeks at a time with her do you?" she asked.

"No, I mean I should make more of an effort at weekends; to get down to Tenhamshire."

Lou relaxed and sat back further against the cushion. She heard a snapping sound and realised she'd just reduced Maddie's princess doll collection by one. Hopefully it was that cheap one with the lazy eye.

"You don't want to keep driving down all this way," she said, "You'll be knackered."

"I'll soon adjust," Tony replied, "Besides it would be good to see mum more as well. I really see her getting older each time I do come."

"She's only sixty."

"Even so, I don't think she's as well as she makes out."

Lou thought back to the last time she'd bumped into Tony's mum, a couple of weeks ago when she'd come into Ryan Harbour to shop. They were having a chat together until she saw her bus coming. Lou had watched Tony's mum leg it up the high street to the bus stop at full pelt with three bags of shopping.

"Will Cheryl come with you," Lou asked.

"Haven't asked her," was the response, which Lou found puzzling.

Maddie came running in again from her bedroom, wearing the princess dress Lou had already heard about.

"You look beautiful darling," she said.

"Can I wear this to school?"

"No sweetheart. It will get ruined. Tell you what. You can wear it Tuesday evening when you go to Nanny Turner's house."

Maddie beamed. "I'm going to Nanny's?"

"Every Tuesday for the next few weeks. Mummy's going to a college to learn how to bake."

Tony spat his coffee back into his cup and laughed.

137

"What's so funny?"

"You're going baking," he said, incredulously, "You; baking?"

He laughed again.

"Why not? I think it will be useful. Besides I'm doing it more for a friend."

"Oh yes," Tony said, about to take another sip of his coffee, "Who's that?"

"Diana Carlton."

He froze, the coffee mug an inch away from his lips.

"Diana Carlton? You're not serious. That old witch?"

"She's not an old witch," Lou said, indicating for him to be quiet in front of Maddie, "We've kind of; well, bonded recently."

"My God, I don't come up for a few months and the impossible happens," Tony shook his head, "Don't tell me, next week you're going Line Dancing with Joyce Pendleton."

Lou laughed. It was nice to talk to someone who had been around during her early years living in Ryan Harbour. So many of her old friends had left. Well, so had Tony. Lou realised she was the only one of the original group still here. No one kept in touch these days either. There were always promises to catch up but it had all fizzled out pretty quickly. With a start, Lou realised that she didn't have that many friends. There was Precious but that was more a work thing. Precious was doing all the things Lou had done at twenty-two; pub crawls, clubbing until all hours and it wasn't something Lou really wanted to do again now, even if she could. There was Jamie of course and her mum…could she really include her mum; and now, Diana. That was all. How had that happened? She realised Tony and Maddie were both staring at her.

"Sorry," she said, "I was miles away. Do you want another coffee?"

"No thanks," Tony said, getting up, "I'd best be on my way." Lou watched while he said goodbye to Maddie. She smiled. It was nice for Maddie to have both her parents in the same room. It felt nice to Lou too. It's what she'd always envisioned when growing up with the various uncles; having a family of her own, which included a husband. Unfortunately, Tony was now somebody else's husband. Watching Maddie laughing while she rubbed her hands through Tony's fair hair while he pretended he was going to drop her, she couldn't help wondering if things would have been better if they'd stayed together.

Chapter 7

Dr's Case Notes – Tuesday 8 September

I've not been able to concentrate on anything today except Dr Moore's thighs. I got a quick glimpse of them this morning after a run. I wasn't the one running, obviously. The last time I broke into a sprint was the dash for cover I had to make that morning after Mrs Bryant's one day attempt at the cabbage soup diet. She'd added onions, mustard seeds and lentils to make the soup a little tastier. Honestly, it sounded like the Battle of Trafalgar in our bathroom. I wouldn't have minded but the surgery was still located in our house at the time. I had to pretend we had a problem with the drains.

I believe Dr Moore usually uses the gym over in Tenham but occasionally jogs down here to the surgery which is when I enjoy a quick glimpse of firm thigh. I don't get that at home. Mrs Bryant's thighs do have the appearance of someone who's tried to stuff way too much blancmange into two sausage casings. She's not been able to cross her legs since 1985. The last time she tried she managed to kick three teeth out of my mouth and suffocated the cat.

I got a real telling-off from Mr Bradley today. Apparently, while he was in reception waiting to see me about his test results, there was a young, pregnant mum who was having trouble controlling her other two children. Mrs Andrews leant over the desk and said, 'Will you two keep it down.' She then indicated Mr Bradley and added, 'Some people in here aren't long for this world; show some respect.' Well, he was obviously mortified; especially as his blood test had only been for cholesterol. I've put him on statins. I had to have a quiet word with Mrs Andrews afterwards. She told me she didn't like the look of him and thought statins were a waste of National Health Service money. She said he'd be dead before Christmas and I ended up having a ten pound bet with her on that.

I've been sitting here since evening surgery finished, enjoying a fantasy about Dr Moore giving me a full medical while wearing those jogging shorts. It's not the only fantasy I've had. My favourite is where Dr Moore is tied to a railway track, like in a silent, black and white movie and I've only got minutes to come to the rescue. The train is approaching fast, driven by Mrs Bryant, who's playing the evil role very convincingly. She's laughing and twiddling her long moustache (that's the only part that isn't fantasy). Of course I save the day, sweeping Dr Moore up into my arms before Mrs Bryant has her evil way. Oh God, that reminds me; Mrs Bryant wants her evil way with me tonight. Brace yourself, Cedric, and have a nip of brandy before you go home. I hope she doesn't leave scratch marks this time. That tongue piercing was a really bad idea.

*

"You've got to let it go," Lou said.

Diana had been complaining the entire journey.

"Driving isn't for everyone," Lou continued, "I'm sure you tried your best yesterday."

"The instructor said he was going to put me on some sort of list," Diana moaned, "He said that way, no other driving school will have to go through what he went through."

Lou supressed a smile.

"I'm sure there's no such thing."

"I don't think he was very professional anyway," Diana said, with an air of distaste, "I mean, should a qualified driving

141

instructor really shout out, 'Don't take me Lord, just the mad woman at the wheel' as his pupil goes round a roundabout?"

It depends which way you were going, Lou thought.

Diana shook her head.

"I can't believe I've failed so early on in the list."

"What do you mean?"

"Well, all I've managed to do is flash my breasts at a neighbour and get told by an instructor that I'm the worst driver to ever get behind the wheel of a car; and that's including an apparent mix-up where he only discovered his student was legally blind during an emergency stop."

Lou tried to turn her giggle into a cough.

"But that wasn't the objective, Diana," she said, "The whole point was to make changes to your drab life and you're doing that. Think back to that day when you heard the news about your sister. Would you have thought then that only a couple of weeks later you'd have got behind the wheel of a car and shown your baps to the world?"

"Well, no."

"Exactly. Your life is already changing. So what if you don't learn to drive. You had a go. It's not like you can't try something else."

Diana was silent for a moment as she took in what Lou had said.

"I suppose you're right," she admitted.

"And look at us now," Lou continued, as she pulled up into a parking space outside the college, "Going baking together. Now this is definitely my new skill."

Diana smiled. "You'll be fine," she said, "I'll help you if you get stuck."

"I'm feeling so nervous. I hardly ate any dinner with

142

Maddie earlier."

Muriel's words from Sunday about taking up Lou's precious time came back to Diana now.

"You don't have to come in, if you don't want to," she said, "I can always get a taxi home."

Lou turned round in her seat to face her, a puzzled expression on her face.

"Why did you say that?" she asked, "Do you not want me to come in with you?"

The thought of Diana being ashamed flashed into Lou's mind. Was she worried the group would be full of people she knew; like other members of the coven? Did she not want to be seen with Lou? Was she reverting back to type?

"I just don't want to take up your free time," Diana told her, "I realise now that your leisure time is precious. Why come out with me when you could be at home with little Maddie or out doing something else?"

"But I wanted to come," Lou replied.

"Really?"

"Truly."

Diana smiled again.

"Great," she said, "Shall we go in?"

The classroom was made up of four rows of two work benches complete with sink, oven and stove. There was an aisle down the middle for the teacher to walk through so that, in Lou's opinion, he or she could see every single mistake made. Around the edge of the room were shelves displaying a plethora of cooking utensils. Upon entering Lou made a beeline for the last row of benches but Diana called her back up to the front.

"I won't be able to see or hear anything properly from back there," she said.

Several other people walked in and everyone smiled and nodded at each other while they awaited the teacher.

Mrs Bailey entered the room like a huge cruise ship entering a tiny port. She stomped across to her desk at the front of the room and then clapped her hands a few times for the room to quieten down; even though it was already silent. Lou was transported back to junior school.

"Good evening everybody," she called out, turning to the whiteboard behind her. She picked up a marker and began to write her name as she spoke, "I'm Mrs Bailey."

Lou was reminded of her old history teacher, a very 'no nonsense' sort of a woman. Mrs Bailey even resembled her with her dark-grey, short, back and sides haircut and her sensible, masculine shoes. Once she'd finished writing her name she turned and walked round to the front of the desk.

"Now then," she said, her tweed skirt straining at her ample waist, "We're here to learn some basic baking skills. I believe these skills are fundamental to the running of a good home."

She began to walk down the central aisle, past Lou and Diana's benches, as she continued with her speech.

"Now I'm happy to see that each of you ladies has…" she stopped. Lou and Diana both turned round to see why.

"Oh," she continued, "I see we have a man in the class."

She sounded like she'd just spotted a little puddle on the carpet and was looking at the culprit. The poor, quivering man wasn't very tall but shrank further under Mrs Bailey's gaze. Lou decided then and there to make him her friend in the class.

"I firmly believe," Mrs Bailey continued, "That a man's uses are better placed outside of the kitchen but I suppose one must move with the times. You can try your best while you're here."

She walked back up to the front of the class again.

"Now, today we are going to make that simplest of cakes, the Victoria Sandwich. There's really no excuse to get this wrong so I shall be expecting six perfect cakes at the end of the lesson."

Lou's heart sank.

"You may have heard told of the 'all-in-one' method for preparing a sponge where butter, sugar, flour and eggs are all mixed together at the same time. Well, we're not going to be using the cheats' way today. Please get out your ingredients that you were told to bring while I hand you all a sheet showing the method for baking this cake. Try and keep them clean as I will want them back at the end of the lesson."

There were murmurings and bustle while everyone began emptying ingredients onto their benches.

"Perhaps we could all be a little quieter," Mrs Bailey called out.

Lou tipped her carrier bag upside down and let the ingredients fall out. She looked over at Diana who was carefully taking out small Tupperware boxes from her bag; filled with all the ingredients already weighed out.

Shit, thought Lou, should I have done that too? She looked around her and saw that Diana appeared to be the only one who had thought of this. Lou made a note to do the same thing next week. That was if Mrs Bailey let her back into the class after she saw this week's results.

When Mrs Bailey told them they could begin Lou felt the same sense of panic she'd had when beginning one of her school exams. She looked down at the recipe and read it through twice before starting; keeping her head down the entire time; especially whenever the teacher walked past the bench. She got an idea of what was going on at the other tables just

145

from what Mrs Bailey was saying.

"Half fat butter; this isn't Weight Watchers!"

"Gluten-free flour? What use is that?"

It seemed to be the poor man who was getting most of the flack.

"No, Mr Brown; that is a spatula, not a wooden spoon. Go over to the utensils and try again; hurry! Do you call that creaming? You must be more vigorous than that."

Lou wondered if Mrs Bailey treated her husband to similar sounding instructions at home. She tried to concentrate on her own work but as she was pouring the cake batter into the tins she did almost drop the bowl when she heard,

"No Mr Brown, I'll be showing you my soft, white baps on week four and not a moment sooner."

There's a treat to look forward to, Lou thought; and grinned as she placed the two tins into the oven. She let out a sigh and looked over at Diana's bench. Diana was vigorously mixing something in her bowl. She had flour in her hair and looked to be on the verge of tears. She caught Lou's eye.

"My mixture keeps curdling," she hissed, "I'm adding flour but it's not helping."

Lou was about to reply but Mrs Bailey showed up at that second.

"You should be further on than that Mrs Carlton," she bellowed.

"I know," Diana whimpered, "I don't know what's gone wrong."

"It's quite simple. You obviously didn't follow my recipe correctly. This isn't a cooking class where you can be free and liberal with instructions. This is baking and it must be followed to the letter…to the letter!"

146

She turned her gaze onto Lou, who felt her knees start to buckle.

"Very good Miss Turner, right on time. My only criticism is the mess of your bench. Try and clean up as you go along. A tidy workspace shows a tidy mind."

Although shocked by the praise Lou turned and frantically began to tidy her work station. By the time she had done this and washed and dried all of the utensils it was time to take the sponges out of the oven.

"I hope everyone has brought raspberry jam with them," Mrs Bailey called out, from behind the desk; leaning forward on her knuckles and surveying them all like a silverback gorilla, "That's the traditional filling for a Victoria sandwich."

A hand went up at the back of the room.

"I'm, erm; allergic to raspberries," Mr Brown confessed.

Mrs Bailey exhaled a long, drawn-out sigh and shook her head.

"I suppose I'll have to allow that," she said, "We wouldn't want you to have an anaphylactic shock or anything. That would be most tiresome. I will have to mark you down though."

Once the cakes had cooled and the jam had been applied, Mrs Bailey began her inspection; choosing to start at the back of the room. The strength of the verbal bashing poor Mr Brown received; Lou felt it would have been less painful for him if Mrs Bailey had just smacked his face into his sponge and ground it further in using the heel of her foot. There was a mixture of tuts and sighs for the other benches and then she came to Lou.

"I must say that's a very acceptable-looking Victoria Sandwich, Miss Turner."

Lou could have burst with pride. Diana was next.

"Well, what can I say about that?" Mrs Bailey admonished. Diana still had flour in her hair and also some jam on her face. Lou noticed a glob of butter behind her ear as well. She was still looking tearful.

"It's less of a sandwich and more of a pancake, my dear. I wouldn't eat that if I were you. Class dismissed."

Diana was very quiet on the drive home.

"Come on," Lou said, eventually, "It was only week one."

"Exactly," Diana replied, "This must have been the easiest night. What on earth will I be like next week?"

"You might be better," Lou told her, "Maybe it's just sponges that aren't your thing. Mrs Bailey isn't really a help either, the way she treats everyone like schoolchildren."

"You seemed to cope with her okay. I guess that's a skill you have to learn in your job, dealing with people."

"I never really thought of it like that," Lou said, contemplating the notion, "Mind you I'm not sure I used any skills with Mrs Bailey. I just kept my head down and hoped she wouldn't notice me."

"I should try that next time," Diana sighed, "I think I went in there trying to impress."

Lou smiled. "I'm glad you're going back again."

"Oh yes. I don't want this to be another fiasco, like the driving. My sponge might have been a disaster but next week my buns are going to be the talk of the room."

"That reminds me," Lou said, "Did you say you were going to look up keep fit classes?"

Diana couldn't quite see what had jogged Lou's memory but told her,

"Yes, there's a keep fit class at the village hall three lunchtimes a week. I believe they're beginner, average and advanced."

"Oh, lunchtime," Lou winced, "I'm not sure I could get active after a morning in the shop."

"I thought lunchtime would suit you better," Diana said, sounding a little miffed, "I didn't think you had any other time to spare."

"You're right, I'm sorry," Lou said, "Well, they do say, 'no pain, no gain' don't they."

"Who do?"

"Exercise people in general."

"Do they? At my age I prefer, 'No pain; that's great.'"

They both laughed and the atmosphere inside the car lightened.

"So, shall we start next week?" Diana said, "Mondays are the beginners' group."

"Definitely," Lou replied, "What's the worst that could happen?"

*

"What time is it?" Grace whispered.

Robert looked at his watch.

"It's a little after twelve," he whispered back.

Grace yawned. "Let's get this over with then."

Robert shook his head, resignedly. Why couldn't his wife show a little more enthusiasm? She'd enjoy it much more then.

"Are you sure there isn't a security camera in the lift?"

"Quite sure, Grace. There's only one in the ground floor lobby. We're not going to be seen."

Grace sighed and began mumbling under her breath,

"There's a perfectly good bed inside. What the hell are we doing it in an uncomfortable lift for; they usually smell of wee."

"Grace!"

"Ssh!"

"Will you stop complaining?" Robert hissed, "You agreed to give this a try and you're going to enjoy it. We've left it until everyone is in bed. No one's going to see us."

Robert pressed the button to call the lift up from the ground floor. A thrill of excitement ran through him. He'd only ever made love in bed before. It had taken lots of persuasion on his part to make Grace say yes to this. She'd agreed to making love in an unusual place but had made a long list of terms and conditions, which included nowhere out of doors, in case they caught a chill; nowhere too public and nowhere too far from home as she didn't want to be seen looking dishevelled in the car on the journey back. Robert had suggested they just do it in the car in the car park but Grace had pointed to item four on her list; nowhere too uncomfortable.

"I'm only thinking of you," she'd told him, "You don't want to put your back out again do you? Besides, the car is in the pub car park; we'd end up with an audience."

"From what I hear about customer numbers I doubt that," Robert had replied.

They'd decided on the lift in their apartment building. Robert would have liked to be outdoors somewhere but Grace was petrified of being seen. They'd waited until very late this Tuesday night when it was highly unlikely that anyone would be about. Lou and Diana had come in together about half past nine, both carrying cake tins and Old Joe had been home for hours so there shouldn't be any more movement on their floor now.

The lift doors opened and Robert rushed inside. He turned and saw Grace hadn't moved.

"Get in then, love."

150

Grace reluctantly moved forwards.

"Are you sure the doors won't fly open during?" she asked.

"They won't," Robert replied, "The lift will only move if someone outside calls it. If it moves we'll have plenty of time to straighten ourselves out; but it won't move as it's very late and everyone will be asleep."

The doors closed and Robert, not wanting to waste any time; pounced at his wife. Grace let out a yell.

"Jesus! You jumped right onto my foot then, you bloody idiot."

She smacked him across the arm.

"Ow. I'm sorry, alright. It was an accident."

So far the evening wasn't panning out as Robert had planned. He had to get things back on track. He swallowed his anger, smiled at his wife and gently placed his arms around her. They began kissing. It wasn't long before passions began to stir. Robert brought his hand up and was just about to have a gentle squeeze of Grace's right breast when the lift began to descend.

"Oh God!" Grace said.

The two of them pulled apart. On the ground floor the doors opened and old Edna Haney stepped inside.

"You're up late," she said, seeing Grace and Robert, "Where are you off to?"

"Erm, nowhere," Robert ad-libbed, "We've just come back. We pressed the wrong button on the lift panel."

"Good job I was here then," Edna replied, pressing the buttons for the first and second floors, "I usually take the stairs the one floor but my knee is giving me gyp."

At the first floor Edna got out. As soon as the doors closed Robert grabbed hold of his wife again and they began kissing as the lift returned to the second floor. They'd forgotten that Edna had pressed the button for their floor too. As the lift stopped so the doors opened. Grace screamed.

"Jesus Christ," Robert hissed, rubbing the side of his head, "That was right in my bloody ear."

"I'm sorry. I wasn't expecting the doors to open."

"No one's there. Let them close again."

They continued on. Robert began to kiss his wife's neck and his excitement returned when he heard her giggle. The next second he was shouting out in pain.

"Ssh," Grace hissed," Someone will hear you."

"What the bloody hell have you got on," he said, frantically rubbing his lips with his finger.

"What do you mean? Oh," realisation dawned on Grace's face, "Sorry, I rubbed a bit of that pain relief cream into my neck earlier."

"What? Christ, you could have told me," Robert moaned, his words muffled, "My sodding lips are burning."

"Well I'm sorry but I felt my rheumatism coming on. I only did it for you. If I hadn't rubbed any cream in, there was no way I'd be out here tonight."

A part of Robert thought it might be best to just call it quits now and return to the apartment; perhaps run an ice cube over his smarting lips, but he knew that if he did that; he'd never get Grace out here again.

Work through the pain, he told himself. Robert looked down at his wife and smiled.

"I'm sorry," he told her, "Thank you for thinking of me. Let's keep going."

Rather than kissing, Robert concentrated on exploring Grace's body with his hands. Soon the pain in his lips was forgotten as passions were aroused again. He unbuttoned Grace's blouse and put his hands around her. Just as he'd unhooked her bra so the lift moved down again.

"Shit!" Robert said.

He quickly pulled his hands away from his wife but her bra came too.

"Robert!"

There wasn't any time to give it back. Grace began frantically doing up the buttons on her blouse. Robert put his hands behind his back just as the lift doors opened on the ground floor. Edna Haney stood there. All three looked surprised and said,

"What are you doing there?"

"I forgot to check my post," Edna told them, eyeing the couple warily.

"But you didn't go down in the lift," Grace said.

"I don't need it to get down," Edna told them, "Only up. I have trouble getting up."

"You're not the only one tonight," Robert told her.

Grace would have smacked him but she couldn't while both hands were stretched across her front, trying to hold her breasts up.

"Why are you two still in the lift?"

"Hmm? Oh, well we…" Robert's brain wouldn't function.

"We forgot something in the car," Grace threw in.

"That's it," Robert added, relieved, "We've been out and we came back and we got caught in the lift and then we went upstairs and then we remembered we'd left something in the car."

Why couldn't he stop himself rambling?

"Why did you both come down?" Edna asked.

153

What's it got to do with you, you nosey bitch, is what Robert wanted to say.

"We forgot out front door key," Grace told her.

"But one of you could have waited in the hallway on your floor, surely," Edna continued.

"My God, you're like a dog with a bone, aren't you," Robert said.

"Sorry?"

"Nothing Edna," Grace said, pushing her husband out of the lift with her elbow, her arms still folded across her chest. She let Edna go in, "You get yourself off to bed. It's late."

"Oh I'm always up at this time," Edna said, cheerily.

"We've noticed that," Robert replied.

"Yes, I can't get off until about two. I usually have a walk along the harbour about now. It's quite safe. There's never anyone around," she pressed the button, "Anyway, don't let me keep you."

She waved as the doors closed. Robert waved back. The change of expression on Edna's face before the doors shut completely told him she'd spotted the bra hanging from his wrist. He hid it again before Grace noticed.

"What do we do now?" Grace asked, "I'd just started enjoying myself."

"Why don't we wait for the lift to come down again?"

"Because there's a high chance Edna will be in it."

Robert sighed and turned to look out of the glassed, front door.

"Grace," he said, an idea taking shape, "What about the harbour front?"

"What about it?"

Robert turned back to face his wife and smiled.

154

"Oh no," Grace said, shaking her head, "I told you, no outdoorsies. We might catch cold."

"It's late summer."

"Well we might be seen."

"But it's deserted. Edna said no one's ever there when she goes out for her walk."

"I don't know Robert."

He could tell his wife was wavering.

"Come on," he said, encouragingly, "There's that little garden area up the end. We can go in there."

"Garden area? Do you mean that flower bed with two trees and a small hedge? I'd hardly call that a garden."

"It's hidden."

Grace fell silent.

"Come on," Robert urged, "Let's at least go and take a look."

Grace made to walk forward but hesitated. Robert gently held out his hand to her.

"My bra!"

"Oh, yeah," Robert said, looking down at his wrist, "I keep forgetting that's there."

He rolled it up as best he could and stuffed it into his pocket.

"It's not worth you putting it on now. It'll be off again in a few minutes. Let's go."

He held the door open. Grace sighed and walked out.

"I hope we don't see anyone we know," she said, as they crept through the residents' car park, "Or someone we haven't seen in a long time."

Robert frowned.

"Why someone we haven't seen in a long time?"

Grace looked at him like he was an idiot.

155

"Well how the hell can I shake hands with them?" she questioned, "That will be a nice greeting won't it; my breasts dropping to my waist as I reach out. What if they want to hug me?"

"It'll be fine," Robert told her, "Look, we're opposite The Smugglers already and we haven't seen anyone. Look around you; it's deserted."

The main door to the pub opened and Jamie stepped out. He nodded and smiled at the couple standing across the road. As they'd never been in the pub before Jamie didn't recognise them as Lou's neighbours or even as residents of the apartments on the harbour front.

"Finally," he called over to them, pleasantly; "A cool, fresh evening."

"Erm, yes, isn't it," Robert replied, "A nice time of night for a walk along the harbour."

"Yes. I always think this is the perfect time to get some."

"What?"

"Fresh air," Jamie said.

"Oh yes, right," Robert was relieved, "Yes, that's why I'm taking my wife for a walk now. That's the reason. That's the only reason."

"Let's go," Grace whispered, "If we stay here any longer he might end up coming with us."

Robert nodded a goodbye to Jamie and led his wife off towards the garden area. Jamie, watching them go, suddenly remembered that the walkway at the far end was currently blocked off due to the building of the new apartments. Did this couple know about that? He called out helpfully to Robert,

"You can't go all the way if you're taking her up the other end."

Robert and Grace both froze. They stared at each other.

"Let's keep walking," Robert whispered, and the two headed off in silence without looking back.

They walked along until they reached the fenced off area where the new apartments were being built.

"Look," Robert said, "Here's the garden."

"It's not as hidden as I thought," Grace replied, wrinkling her nose up in disgust.

"It will be once we get round to the other side of the hedge; come on."

Robert pulled at Grace's arm and led her to the back of the garden.

"Here will do," he said.

They began kissing again, the pain in Robert's lips having lessened now to a dull ache. He could tell Grace wasn't really concentrating though and when he opened his eyes and looked at her, he noticed her focus was over his shoulder.

"Will you concentrate?" he hissed.

"I can't," Grace whispered, "I feel exposed."

"I haven't even got your blouse undone again yet."

"Not that sort of exposed. And excuse me, but you've already got my knickers off. I think that counts as exposed."

"I've not touched them."

"Don't lie; Robert. I think I can tell when my knickers are off. It's a cold wind that blows off the harbour you know."

"I haven't touched them love; honestly. I never move down there before having a play up top now, do I?"

They both frowned at each other and then looked down at the floor. Grace's knickers were round her ankles.

"Oh God, the elastic must have gone," she said, "Great! Now I'll have to walk back to the apartment without them. And you've got my bra in your pocket. No underwear; I feel like a right whore!"

"Ooh," Robert told her, "Would you like to explore that fantasy?"

"No I bloody wouldn't! For God's sake, let's just get on with this."

Grace grabbed Robert around the neck and pulled him down onto the floor. He cracked his knee as he landed but he wasn't about to start complaining at Grace's newfound forcefulness.

Five minutes later and the two of them were definitely engrossed in what they were doing. Robert's trousers and boxer shorts were round his knees.

Grace is right, he thought, that is a sharp wind off the harbour.

As they continued Robert became aware of something out of the corner of his eye. As he turned his head so the rest of his body stopped moving.

"What's wrong?" Grace asked.

She followed her husband's gaze. An ugly, cross-eyed dog was staring back at them; a ball in his mouth and his head cocked to one side.

"Oh God, that's Joyce Pendleton's," Grace whispered, "What's she doing out at this time of night?"

"Jock," she hissed, "Jock, get away."

The dog dropped the tennis ball it was carrying in its mouth.

"What should we do?" Grace whispered.

"Carry on?" Robert suggested, "I don't know how long he was there before I noticed. We could just quickly finish things off."

"With a dog watching?"

"I admit; it's not a turn on."

Jock barked, making Grace and Robert both jump.

"Oh Robert," Grace was so terrified of being discovered, "What shall we do?"

"Quick," he said, "Grab the ball."

He let out a yell and fell off his wife.

"I didn't mean one of mine, Grace!" he winced, "The dog's. I think he wants us to throw it."

Grace seized the tennis ball and threw it over the hedge. Jock went running off after it.

"He's gone," she said, relieved, "Are you alright, dear? You've gone very red."

Robert was still holding his crotch.

"Where the hell did you develop that grip," he asked her, "My God, I've got white flashing lights going off in my eyes."

"Sorry, but you said you wanted to finish off quickly; so I thought you meant…"

"Bloody hell! Did you really think that would help?"

"I'm sorry," Grace repeated, "I panicked and got confused."

They heard the patter of tiny feet and Jock reappeared, wagging his tail.

"Oh bollocks!"

"Robert!"

"Why is he here?" Robert asked, "Where the hell is his owner?"

In answer to that question, Joyce's voice rang out only a short distance away.

"Jock! Where on earth has he got to? I blame you for this Norman! Why weren't you watching him while I read that sign outside the pub? Can you believe they're going to let pets be taken in there? Of all the stupid…Jock!"

"They're coming this way," Grace hissed, "What do we do?"

"Jock, where are you?"

Jock gave a sharp bark.

"Ssh, you dumb dog!"

"Robert! He's not a dumb dog."

Robert threw himself forwards.

"Give me that ball," he said.

He took it and hurled it as hard as he could. After a second they heard a gentle splash. Jock remained where he was.

"See," Grace said, "I told you he wasn't a dumb dog. He's not going into the sea after that."

Robert sighed. "Okay I give in. Let's go, Grace," he said.

"Oh, are we not finishing off?"

"With an audience close by and my left testicle squished into the shape of a number eight; I don't think so."

"Jock, where are you boy," they heard Norman call out.

"He's not going to hear that puny voice of yours," Joyce remonstrated, before shouting, "Jock! Perhaps he's in that garden."

Robert and Grace looked at each other in horror before frantically pulling on their clothes. Jock barked again.

"Shut up," Robert hissed, "We don't have your ball. Go away."

"Jock, come here. Don't make daddy come in there to get you."

"Go Jock," Robert whispered, "We don't want daddy coming in here to get you either."

The dog put his head questioningly on one side again. He'd come in here with a ball and didn't want to leave empty-mouthed. He saw something on the ground. That would have to do as a replacement. He grabbed it and ran off.

"Hey," Grace whispered, loudly, "He's taken my knickers."

"Well you couldn't put them on anyway," Robert reasoned, "The elastic's gone."

"Yes, but I was going to replace that. They were a decent pair of undies. "

"There you are, Jock."

Joyce's voice sounded even closer than before and Robert and Grace were instantly silenced.

"Oh Jesus, Jock! Where the hell did you get those from?"

"What's he picked up now," Norman asked, "Not another muddy stick?"

"Well it's certainly something filthy. My God can this town get any worse? There was an old t-shirt that flew out of nowhere at the regatta the other week; now this. I bet it's kids in there, doing naughties."

"I doubt it," Norman replied, "They're hardly the sort of underwear a young woman is going to wear."

"And how would you know that? Do you have something you need to tell me, Norman?"

"Of course not, I just mean they look like old lady knickers, don't they."

"Bloody cheek," Grace whispered, to her husband.

"They're more like something you would wear, dear," Norman continued.

"How dare you," Joyce told him, "I wouldn't wear cheap, market crap like this."

"That does it," Grace said, and made to stand up. Robert pulled her down again.

"I guess if you wear cheap, you'll act cheap," Joyce said, "Will you stop fingering them, Norman. My God, how long have you had this fetish with underwear? Do I need to make you an appointment with Dr Bryant?"

161

"I don't have a fetish with anything," Norman replied, "How could I? It's been so long since I've seen a lady's undergarments."

"Meaning?"

"Well, when I said earlier that I couldn't sleep because I felt frisky; I wasn't expecting you to suggest taking the dog for a walk."

"Oh my God, Norman; we gave up on all that nonsense years ago!"

"You did, yes," he mumbled.

Joyce sighed. "This is my own fault for letting you watch Channel Five on your own after nine o'clock."

"I don't know why you're so shocked," he told her, "There's nothing wrong with feeling a little frisky. There was a time when you used to put little shows on for me in your underwear; do you remember."

"Shush Norman! We're going home; right now!" Joyce said, forcefully, "Leave those there on the floor. No Jock; if daddy isn't allowed to bring them home, neither are you."

She took once last look back at the hedge.

"You should be damned ashamed of yourselves," she called out, "I'd phone for the police if I thought they'd do anything. Come on Norman, I think you've had enough fresh air for one night. I wonder if Dr Bryant does Bromide on prescription."

Grace and Robert waited five minutes before they dared to get up. When they walked round onto the path they could see Grace's knickers lying on the floor. She picked them up and sighed, showing Robert the teeth marks. He really hoped they were Jock's and not Norman's.

Chapter 8

Lou spent a lot of her Wednesday morning at work reading. As she stocked the fresh food chillers she found herself looking at the cooking instructions on the packs of chops and chicken pieces; while she filled the grocery shelves she read the recipes on the backs of sauce jars; wine labels in the alcohol section told her what meals went best with that particular bottle.

Her Victoria Sandwich had been greatly enjoyed at coffee time by the rest of the team and she managed to sneak a couple of slices across to the pub in her lunch hour for her mum and Jamie to try. Gloria asked if she'd bought it, which was praise enough.

She knew it was only week one at college and perhaps she shouldn't run before she could walk, but Lou couldn't stop herself thinking about food and wondering what else she could cook. All she'd done last night was follow a recipe so why not try that again at home; maybe for a nice dinner for her and Maddie. All she needed was a cookbook.

Lou nipped up to the high street after leaving the pub and searched through, what felt like, hundreds of them in the shop before finally settling on a basic, all-round recipe book. She hurried back to the supermarket afterwards, only five minutes late. She almost collided with Simon who was pulling his rather tatty, moleskin, black jacket on as he rushed out of the store in the opposite direction.

"Ah, there you are," he said, running his hands through his hair, which just made it look even more untidy than usual, "I've got to get off to a meeting I'd forgotten about, must dash. I'm leaving you in charge. The others know about it. See you tomorrow."

He was gone before Lou could respond.

"Hey there boss, darling," Precious called out, as Lou walked in and across to the tills, "Can I have the afternoon off?"

Lou smiled. It obviously wasn't the first time Simon had been out of the shop since he'd arrived here but it was the first time he'd actually told Lou she was in charge. Chris came up behind her.

"Can I have a raise?"

She turned and lifted up two fingers.

"How about that?" she said.

He gave her his gummy smile.

"Alright, how about I raise something for you, eh; eh?"

Chris pulled a key ring with two keys on it out of his pocket and jangled them at her.

"I'll be locking up tonight," he said, importantly, "Or I could lock us both in. How about it; a night in the store, just the two of us? We could watch a DVD and open up some popcorn."

"Why would we need to be locked up in the store; I can do exactly the same thing at my house?"

Chris's grin widened.

"Thought you'd never ask," he said.

Lou shook her head but couldn't help smiling.

"Nice try," she told him.

"What do you think Simon's meeting is about?" Precious asked, "It was very sudden. Do you think it's got something to do with why he left his last store?"

"I doubt it."

Chris sniffed. "I heard he left because he was caught dipping his old man into jars of peanut butter."

"Really? Was it smooth or crunchy, darling?"

164

"Does that matter?" Lou said, "Who the hell told you that?"

"Security over at Tenham. They heard it from someone; can't remember the name."

"Honestly," Lou sighed, "These rumours are getting ridiculous."

"I always say there's no smoke without fire," Precious said.

"So you think the rumour you told me yesterday has some truth in it?" Lou replied, "That he had a nervous breakdown and ran naked through the bakery section, waving his baguette?"

"Waving it, dipping it in peanut butter, it all comes back to his todger," Chris reasoned, "The guy just needs to get laid; that'll solve all his problems down there."

"Oh for God's sake," Lou sighed, "You all need to stop listening to these rumours. There's nothing wrong with his todger…I mean…"

Terry walked over to them, saving Lou from digging herself in any deeper. He was looking about him, obviously searching.

"I've lost my thingy," he told them.

Chris sniggered.

"I had it in my hand not long ago."

The snigger turned into a giggle.

"Simon wants me to play with it more."

Chris laughed out loud. He smacked Terry on the back.

"Oh mate," he said, wiping the tears from his eyes, "You kill me, you really do."

I wish someone would, Lou thought.

"Anyway," Chris continued, "I need to go for an excavation, watch the store for me ladies," and he headed off for the staff toilets.

"Right then, Terry; tell me what Simon wanted you to do," Lou said.

"Announcements," he replied, "I've got a list of ads that I need to read out word for word, but I've lost the whatsit; the talkie thing."

Lou realised what he meant.

"You've lost the microphone," she said.

"That's it," he replied, obviously relieved, "I was practicing holding it earlier."

"You were pretending it was a lightsabre," Precious cut in.

Terry blushed. "I put it down somewhere and I can't remember where."

Lou sighed. Knowing the microphone was somewhere in the store didn't really narrow down the search area. This could take ages.

"Right," she said, resignedly, "Let's start looking."

She left Precious manning the till and she and Terry headed off in opposite directions to start looking. As Lou walked down the fresh fruit aisle she heard a plopping sound. She turned around on the spot, trying to find out where it was coming from. She heard the noise again. That was strange, it appeared to be overhead somewhere. Lou looked up at the ceiling, worried that there was a leak. That was all she needed on the first afternoon that she was officially in charge.

She heard the noise again, deeper this time, but then it was followed by a loud sigh.

"Oh God I'm glad that's out."

Terry rushed over to Lou.

"I've remembered where I left it," he said, excitedly.

"The staff toilet?"

Terry's mouth opened in shock.

"How did you know that?" he asked, "Are you physical?"

"The word's psychic, Terry," Lou sighed.

166

She closed her eyes but opened them again very quickly when she heard Chris's voice again through the speakers.

"Oh yeah, baby," he said, "Make it bigger for daddy."

"Oh God! Terry, go and get the microphone; quickly."

Terry rushed off. Chris was still giggling through the speakers. Lou looked around her. The customers she could see from where she stood had all stopped shopping and were listening in.

"Oh yeah, that's it, Precious," Chris said, "Show daddy a little sugar now."

Over at the till Precious dropped the packet of biscuits she was just about to scan.

"Yeah, get those long legs around my waist. Oh baby, we're almost there now."

Terry's frantic knocking at the toilet door could be heard but what he said was too muffled.

"What?" Chris said, "Give you my thingy? Fuck off, Terry."

Lou put her head in her hands.

"Okay Precious, Daddy's back."

As Lou looked up again she saw Precious staring back at her.

"Go and stop him," she called over, "It's too embarrassing."

Lou rushed over to the staffroom. How the hell had he managed to press the 'speak' button on the microphone anyway? Was he standing on it or had the weight of his trousers pressed the button down? Before she reached the door she heard a familiar groan.

Oh God, she thought; it's too late. It's about to get worse.

Chris's groaning became more forceful and then there was a final yell of, "yeah baby;" followed very quickly by a loud fart. About a minute later both Chris and Terry walked out onto the shop floor, grinning. Terry waved the microphone at Lou.

"I've given it a wipe over," he said, brightly.

There wasn't anything Lou could say to that so she just smiled encouragingly at him. The customers were all staring at Chris who grinned nonchalantly back at them.

"I just hope he's washed his hands," one old lady said, to her friend, as they walked past Lou and out of the shop.

The rest of the afternoon was rather quiet and no one really made eye contact with Chris; especially Precious. She looked embarrassed every time she saw him. He tapped Lou on the shoulder as she was rearranging the clothing display and said,

"Think she's finally fallen for me. She can't even look me in the eye, poor girl."

Lou let him have his little fantasy. She sighed as she looked back at the display. A lot of the stuff had actually sold, which Lou found hard to believe. There were so many women walking around town in red and yellow stripes it looked like Ryan Harbour was holding a rhubarb and custard festival. For some reason though, the underwear wasn't selling. If she'd been forced to buy something Lou would have gone straight for the underwear as no one else would see it. She picked up a pair of panties now and sighed again at the face of the jester that was staring back at her.

It would be alright if the face looked like Pete Crick's, she thought.

"How are you dear?" said a voice, beside her.

"Hi Grace," Lou replied, "Don't suppose you're in the market for a fresh pair of knickers are you?"

Grace dropped the carrier bag containing the chops for dinner.

"What do you mean?" she said, grabbing at the handles, "Who blabbed? Was it Joyce? I didn't think she saw."

"Erm, I don't really know what you're talking about."

"It was the dog; and his ball; not Robert's ball; although that has swelled up; I…I have to be going."

Lou hadn't seen Grace move that fast since…well, last week when Robert had his bad back. What the hell was going on with those two?

*

Although the nine women were sat around a dining table Diana felt like she was in a boardroom rather than in Joyce's house. It was a very formal meeting where all questions had to go through the chair (temporarily Joyce) and everything was voted on. The first item was to officially elect a committee chairman. Joyce was chosen pretty swiftly.

Just as they turned to the next item on the agenda, the door opened and Norman walked in, stooping forwards as always; displaying his bald pate to the world rather than having to make eye contact with anyone.

"Sweetheart, do you know where the…"

"Get out, get out; get out."

Norman very quickly backed out of the room, his question unfinished and unanswered.

"Now," said Joyce, to the group around the table, "I think we can all agree that something must be done about the youth in our community."

There was a general murmuring of agreement.

"They're spoiling the area for the rest of us."

Diana's head shot up. That wasn't what she thought Joyce had meant the other week. She was just about to say something when the door opened again and Muriel staggered in with a large tray loaded with cups of tea.

"You're a little early, Moo," Joyce called, staring at her

notepad, "Still, you're here now."

She remained seated where she was while Muriel struggled to manoeuvre past her chair.

"Here," Diana said, getting up and walking round the table, "Let me help you."

She took one side of the tray and helped set it down onto a couple of placemats. Muriel smiled gratefully at her.

"There's no milk jug," Joyce said.

"It's already in the cups."

Joyce tutted. "Fine, sit down then."

Muriel did as she was told.

"Now then," Joyce continued, after each woman had taken a cup of tea, "As I was saying; I think we need to come up with some ideas to rid our neighbourhood of all this anti-social behaviour by the younger members of the community."

"Excuse me, Joyce I…"

Diana's interruption was itself interrupted by Joyce.

"If you wish to speak you should raise your hand."

Diana raised her hand.

"The chair recognises Mrs Carlton."

"Thank you. Look, I thought you said this was going to be a committee to help the youngsters of the town."

"No, it's a committee to sort them out," Joyce said, "You can call it help if you like. After all, if we make an example of them, maybe they'll get the message that we're not going to be pushed around or shouted at or mooned in broad daylight anymore. Then we'll all be much happier. Now, as I was saying…"

"Who's been mooned at?"

"Raise your hand if you have a question."

Diana sighed and raised her hand.

170

"The chair recognises Mrs Carlton, again."

"Who has this anti-social behaviour been happening to? Is it any of us here?"

The room was silent.

"It's been well documented in the local paper."

Before Diana could interrupt again, Joyce continued on.

"There have also been several incidences that I've heard about through valuable sources. Plus, my own, dear husband, Norman, was viciously accosted by a gang of young girls at the junior school."

"When?" Diana asked.

"Only yesterday. The gang, unsupervised I might add, were sitting outside the school and were supposedly meant to be drawing that old elm tree. One of them, bold as brass; shouted out as Norman walked past, 'This old felt tip is all dried up.' Honestly, the poor man was so embarrassed. I know we're getting old but Norman isn't dried up."

Diana was confused. Joyce seemed to have forgotten the group was there with her.

"I mean I don't even know how the girl knew 'felt tip' was Norman's nickname in the army. I've never told anyone. Okay so the end of it is a little distorted but we still managed to have William..."

"Joyce!" Diana cut in. Joyce, startled, jumped in her seat, "A felt tip is a pen children use for colouring-in."

"Is it?" Joyce's face had reddened but she tried to maintain her composure, "Well, there are plenty of other incidences anyway. Now then ladies, I propose..."

Diana sat there and listened to what was said. Mostly the talking was done entirely by Joyce but the other women all nodded and made agreeing noises. Diana couldn't believe it.

Joyce was talking about curfews for the under eighteens and closing down the nightclub. What was it Lou had called them; the Coven? The name fitted. Diana felt angrier and angrier.

"And if they're banned from the high street between four and seven then that gives the rest of us a peaceful afternoon."

"Look," said Diana, "You've got it all wrong."

Joyce opened her mouth to speak.

"And if you tell me to raise my hand once more I'll be doing it with only two fingers!"

"Diana!"

"Look, I came here because I thought we were going to help the kids in this community. They've got nowhere to go and nothing to do. Things are different to our generation. We always had our mothers at home when we came in from school. The streets were a lot safer. Nowadays both parents have to work and the nine to five doesn't exist anymore."

"Huh," said Joyce, "They're working to buy more and more material possessions. Children would much prefer their parents' time than their gifts."

"I'm sure that's true in some instances," Diana told her, "But there are also plenty of cases where parents have to work to provide the basics, or would you rather they stay home and live off of benefits?"

Joyce remained silent. Diana continued.

"Whatever the situation kids are spending more time on their own and yes, I agree, some of them do get up to no good; but what they need is help. We should be organising after school clubs and trying to get the council to put an adventure playground in the park rather than having that single tired, old swing. We should be organising meetings with parents, with the kids themselves, asking them what they would like to see in

172

the community. Joyce, ladies; it's great that you're giving up your free time like this but really, we're not exactly a cross-section of the community here are we. We should get some fresh blood into these committees."

"I knew it," Joyce said, "This is all about your new friend, Louise Turner."

"Actually it isn't," Diana said, "I don't think she'd even want to be involved in one of your groups, although I still think it would be a great idea."

"Absolutely not," Joyce said, "I'm not having the likes of her in my house."

"You don't need to hold meetings in your house. If we're involving the community then we should use the hall. Let's face it, apart from your dreary little parties for the old folk and the lunchtime exercise classes, when else is it used?"

"Dreary little parties?" queried Joyce.

"It's a valuable commodity and we're wasting it," Diana said, warming to her theme, "There's so much we could do."

"I think we've heard enough," Joyce cut in, rather sharply, "Mrs Carlton, I'm not sure you're the right person for…"

Joyce was interrupted by the lady sat beside Muriel.

"We could set up a timetable for the hall," she said, "The vicar acts as caretaker and he's said to me before that the hall is underused."

Another lady at the other end of the table chipped in.

"The primary school already has a breakfast club for parents that work," she said, "I wonder if they could do a supper club?"

"The teachers probably wouldn't want to extend their already stretched working hours," added another.

"We could always ask for volunteers to watch the children."

"They'd probably need some sort of training to look after a

173

group of children."

"Well we could investigate that."

The conversation continued and lots of notes and plans were made. Joyce sat back in her carver chair, watching silently and seething. At one point Diana caught her eye and smiled warmly at her but she didn't smile back. Somehow she'd lost control of the room.

*

Diana couldn't wait to tell Lou all about her time at Joyce's meeting. She really felt she'd managed to get the ladies on side to help the youth of the area. Lou didn't have time that evening to talk when Diana popped over as she was cooking a dinner for her and Maddie from a recipe book that already had smudges and food stuck to the pages. Diana suggested a sandwich lunch at The Smugglers the next day as, for some reason; Joyce wasn't going to be working her usual shift at the charity shop and had cancelled their lunch date too. Diana and Lou were walking to the pub now.

"And I really felt they wanted to help," Diana said, talking nineteen to the dozen.

"What did Joyce have to say about that?" Lou asked.

"She didn't say much at all, really."

"I'll bet." Lou smiled, knowingly.

"But anyway," Diana continued, as she opened the door to the pub, "I think that..."

She stopped talking at the sight that greeted her. For once the pub was busy, but mostly with animals. Dogs were barking, cats were hissing and several species of bird were chirping and squawking. As they walked towards the bar they almost collided with a woman running in the opposite direction, holding a birdcage above her head while shouting out, "Come back here Captain Abraham."

"What the hell is going on?" Lou said, as she approached the bar.

Gloria looked accusingly at Jamie.

"It's my advert," he admitted, "I thought I'd attract a few more people in if I allowed the dog walkers that pass by here every day to bring their pets into the pub. Unfortunately in my haste to get the sign up I wrote, 'Pets Welcome' rather than just saying dogs."

"So you've managed to open Tenhamshire's first pet-friendly pub," Lou said, taking a quick look around her, "And judging by the way that cat is scratching itself over there I think it's brought its own pets in with it too."

"Oh God."

"At least the place is full," Diana added, kindly.

"Yes," Gloria told her, "Full of things that aren't trained to use the toilet. And most of the owners have spent so much time fussing over their animals they've neglected to buy a drink."

She eyeballed daggers at Jamie again. He looked so forlorn Lou couldn't help feeling sorry for him. She took another look around the room. Old Joe was sitting in his usual seat with Bill across from him. He had a hand over the top of his pint and took a quick sip when he was sure a bird wasn't about to fly over. Mike the Wipe was having a worse time in the opposite corner. He was pinned to the wall by a Great Dane who was sniffing all around his face.

"See," the owner was saying, brightly, "He likes you. He's just a big, old softie; aren't you, Caligula?"

Lou turned back to the bar.

"This is a nightmare," she said.

"That's what I've been saying all lunchtime," Gloria told

175

her.

"Oh come on," Jamie tried to reason; "It's not so bad. Lots of people obviously like the idea. Okay I hadn't bargained for quite so many to come in and that dog licking Mike's cheek right now is a bit too large for the bar but still; you've got to expect a few teething problems. No, I reckon I'm onto something here. What do you think, Diana? Are you on my side?"

Diana had also been looking around the room.

"Well, I must admit I do quite like the idea and there are plenty of happy faces in here," she said.

"Especially on that guy over there," Lou added, "His dog just stuck his nose in his crotch, leapt up onto his lap and started licking his face."

Gloria sighed, wistfully. "If I could find a man to do that, I'd be happy too."

She walked over to the tables by the window to clear a few glasses.

"Mind you," Diana continued, "I think if any of these animals gets eaten by another you might find you have a lawsuit on your hands."

"Oh, I hadn't thought of that."

Jamie made his way dejectedly, to the other end of the bar to serve a man with a gerbil poking out of his shirt pocket.

"I could have brought my goldfish down," Diana said, "Charlie seems to be doing a lot more floating than swimming these days. An outing might have cheered him up. He could have sat up here quite happily on the bar in his travel bowl."

"People would probably throw peanuts in it," Lou said.

Diana looked aghast.

"Oh no," she replied, firmly, as Jamie walked back up to the

176

soft drinks pump in front of them, "I won't allow any nuts near my Charlie."

The glass slipped in his hand, spilling half the contents onto the floor.

"Oops, clumsy," Diana said.

Jamie was still too shocked to respond. Mike the Wipe staggered over to them now that the lady with Caligula had left. He looked on the verge of tears with his glasses askew and face covered in slobber.

"Are you okay?" Jamie asked.

It took Mike a while to find his voice.

"What the bloody hell are you doing here?" he finally managed to blurt out, "I popped in for a swift pint and found myself in a safari park."

"Sorry Mike; just a few teething troubles."

"Teething troubles?" he replied, pulling a damp flannel out of his bag and frantically wiping his face with it, "You should have seen the set on that horse that had me pinned against the wall just now."

"Oh it was a Great Dane I think," Diana threw in, brightly.

"I'm aware of that!" Mike spat, "Oh God, and the size of its tongue. It's covered me with dribble and germs. Reminded me of the wife. I don't let her get that close these days either."

"Why don't I get you a nice, clean, fresh pint," Jamie suggested, "On the house."

Mike shook his head. "I need to go home and stand under the shower for two hours, scrubbing each little bit of me until I feel clean again."

"You'll go very wrinkly," Diana told him.

"That madam; is the least of my worries."

"Well I'll get you a free one the next time you come in,"

Jamie said.

Mike opened his mouth to reply but no sound came out. A look of horror appeared on his face. He stared down at the floor. As everyone else followed his gaze so a lady stood up beside him, holding a Yorkshire Terrier.

"Oops," she giggled, "That was very naughty of you Cookie."

"Cookie!" Mike exploded, "More like Leaky; the dirty, little bugger!"

"Don't you talk about my dog like that," the woman said, indignantly, "He's lovely; aren't you, Cookie?"

She held the dog up to her face and let him lick her all over the mouth.

"Cookie loves his kisses, don't you sweetheart."

"Oh God I feel sick," Mike said, "I'm going home now and I'm never leaving the house again."

He turned and walked towards the door; shaking the bottom of his trouser leg as he passed Gloria. She stormed up to the bar.

"Now look what's happened," she moaned, "I suppose I'll have to clear up the puddle this little rat with ears has left."

Cookie's owner gasped.

"I'm not staying here to be insulted," she said, and while she stomped out the front entrance, Gloria stomped through to the back to get a mop.

"Maybe we should get a bite somewhere on the high street," Diana said, to Lou, "I must admit I'm starting to feel a bit panicky. I really hate things flying and flapping around my head. That woman we saw on the way in is still chasing her parakeet around the room."

"Is that right?" Lou looked thoughtful, "You're scared of

things flying around your head?"

"Yes. I think it stems from my childhood and my sister's budgie. She'd let it out and it would always make a beeline for me. I spent most weekends with a magazine on my head."

"Interesting," Lou said.

Diana wasn't sure she liked the look on Lou's face but before she could say anything Gloria came back out with a mop and bucket, still muttering away.

"Honestly, we'll have to start putting sawdust on the floor."

"It's not that bad," Jamie told her, "I'll admit I'm having a few second thoughts but it could still work."

"Huh," Gloria said, as she walked round to the front of the bar, "I think this is aarrgghh."

Gloria shot across the floor at great speed. Naughty Cookie had obviously left more than just a puddle behind. As she slid towards the far side of the room, she managed to grab onto one of the fishing nets but that came away from the wall, which sent Gloria into a pirouette. She lost her balance and fell smack down into the bucket of disinfectant. If Jamie hadn't got the message then that this was all a fiasco, Captain Abraham's message into Gloria's cleavage certainly rammed the point home.

"Yeah okay," he called over to her, "I'll go take the sign down."

*

Lou was surprised to receive a phone call from Tony on Sunday morning. She had decided to cook a roast dinner for her, Maddie and Gloria and had just begun to put stuffing into a chicken when the phone rang.

"Am I disturbing you?" Tony said.

Lou looked at the chicken still sitting on her other hand.

179

"No it's fine," she replied, "I'm just preparing dinner."

"Oh right, do you want me to wait while you open the tin of baked beans. How's the toast coming along?"

"Cheeky bugger. I'm actually cooking roast chicken; with all the trimmings."

"Jesus Christ, you have one lesson and suddenly you're a gourmet."

"It turns out I'm actually very good at it," Lou informed him, "I made a spaghetti bolognaise from scratch in the week."

"Impressive. What are you going to give me next weekend?"

"I'm sorry?" Lou asked, a little taken aback.

"I'm coming up to Tenhamshire next weekend. I was hoping to see a bit of Maddie if that's okay. I was going to take her out somewhere but maybe I should just invite myself round for dinner."

Lou laughed. "Maybe I'll surprise you."

"I still remember the last time you told me that…and you did."

Lou felt herself blush as that particular memory came back to her too. Surly it was wrong of Tony to bring up that night after so long, especially now that he was married to someone else.

"Anyway," Tony continued, "I'll give you a call when I'm here. It might be Friday evening or it might be Saturday morning, I'm not sure yet."

"That's fine," Lou said, "Oh, I just remembered; Maddie has a party Saturday afternoon. She's being taken to Billy Burgers in Tenhman and is really looking forward to it."

"No problem, I'll work around you guys. See you next weekend."

180

After he rang off Lou returned to the kitchen. She managed to prise the chicken off of her wrist. Her thoughts returned to that memory Tony had just awakened. Lou smiled and began to hum.

Chapter 9

Lou didn't really feel like going to the exercise class with Diana today. Her Sunday lunch had been a success and after Maddie had gone to bed that evening, she'd finished off an opened bottle of red wine as a treat to herself. It had been so enjoyable she'd opened up another and drunk half of that as well. She'd felt pretty crappy this morning and dealing with Maddie's tantrum hadn't made her feel any better either. Maddie wanted her mum to cook breakfast for her, just like she had Sunday dinner. Lou had to drag her to breakfast club at school, kicking and screaming, which made her late for work. It had been a busy morning too and Simon had remained in his office for most of it, leaving Lou to deal with all of the issues that arose.

"He's been very quiet lately, hasn't he, darling? Do you think he's on the move again," Precious whispered; during a quiet moment, "Maybe that rumour about him and the area manager is true after all."

"Another rumour?"

Precious nodded, knowingly.

"There was no CCTV footage to prove what happened between the two of them but apparently the conveyor belt on till twelve at his last store showed a bit too much wear and tear, if you know what I mean."

Lou sighed, shook her head and walked away. These rumours were getting out of control.

She kept looking at the clock, as the morning progressed; hoping to slow time down but a quarter past twelve came around very quickly. She went off to the staffroom and changed into a pair of shorts and a T shirt. When she emerged

Diana was waiting for her by the main door, grinning excitedly and wearing a tight pair of red and yellow striped, cotton trousers and matching top.

"Is that what you're wearing?" Lou asked.

Diana's smile dropped as she looked down at herself.

"What's wrong with it?" she said, "I bought it here. It's comfortable. The trousers are a little snug but I thought that would be a good guide for improvement. You know; when they fit better then I'm toning up. Anyway, what about you?"

"What about me?" It was Lou's turn to take a look down at her outfit.

"That t-shirt is very loose. I haven't forgotten our balcony incident when you were jumping up and down. You could have given yourself a black eye."

"Well I wasn't planning on taking it off and exercising with my tits out."

Diana winced. "I just meant, wouldn't something a little more fitted be better? Why don't you get something from the clothing range here; like I did?"

Because I'd rather not look like Bozo the Clown's mother, is the thought Lou didn't voice out loud. Instead she said, as she led the way out of the store,

"It's fine. I don't think we'll be doing that much jumping about and I've got my sturdy bra on anyway."

The two ladies began walking up the hill to the church hall. The grand, bay-fronted Victorian houses on the main road faced out to the sea. It was very tranquil walking along and Lou saw Diana smiling.

"Do you miss living up here?" she asked.

Diana thought for a moment before admitting,

"In a way. I did love the house Richard and I owned but the

apartment is plenty big enough for me and I now have a lovely view from my own window, rather than just from the end of the road I lived on.

Lou looked around her.

"It is lovely," she agreed, "I do like the proportions and features of these houses but I always felt the area was very snobby when I rented a room off of Muriel. Being on the hill, even the houses look down on the harbour and people below."

Diana laughed.

"I suppose I felt jealous really," Lou admitted, "I'd love to own one of these places. Not that that is ever likely to happen."

"Would you want to live next door to Joyce?"

Diana watched Lou's expression change to a look of horror and laughed. Lou joined in.

"By the way," she said, "Are you doing anything Wednesday morning?"

"Not that I can think of," Diana replied, "Why?"

"I'm going to take the morning off of work. I think it's time to tick, 'Face a fear' off your list."

"Where are we going?" Diana asked, an ominous feeling beginning to churn in the pit of her stomach.

"No questions," Lou replied, smiling, "Don't worry; you'll be fine."

Diana doubted that very much.

At the top of the hill, just beside Joyce's house; the ladies turned right, down a small, no-through road where the church stood at the far end. Just before it, on the left; was the village hall. They walked in to find several other people already waiting. Lou felt embarrassed and completely out of place as the other women all seemed pretty old.

"Hmm," Diana said.

184

"Is something wrong?" Lou asked, hoping Diana was going to say, 'Let's leave.'

"That committee I've joined," Diana said, "I suggested we use the village hall as a place to run clubs for children."

"Sounds like a good idea."

"Joyce told me there's an ancient covenant on the place that limits the amount of people that can use it at any one time."

"She's making it up."

"There's no reason why she should," Diana said, "And she is a warden of the hall so she would know about these things. I was just wondering what the limit is as there's still quite a few people here today."

Lou took a look around the room. It wasn't vast but there was certainly enough space for children to run around or to sit and do some kind of arts and crafts. The tables and chairs were piled up around the edge of the room under the windows. There was also a useful car park outside for parents to drop their children off. Joyce had to be pulling the wool over Diana's eyes, Lou felt; but why would she do that? Diana was her friend.

"I'm sure you can find somewhere else for a kids club," Lou said, "Would you like me to ask at the school?"

Diana smiled. "That would be great," she said.

The two ladies walked over to where the other women were waiting. In the middle of the space various pieces of equipment were set out in a large circle. There was an assortment of light dumbbells beside a step-up box and a skipping rope next to that and so on. A young, blonde lady dressed in a blue vest top and jogging bottoms with a matching headband came over to them.

"Are you new?" she asked, while jumping around on the spot, shaking her arms and moving her head from side to side.

Lou and Diana both nodded.

"Lovely. Right, I'm Donna," said the lady.

It might just have been the height of the ceiling that caused her voice to echo, but Lou felt Donna probably spoke at the same level whether she was taking a class or talking to a friend on the phone.

"What we do here is a basic circuit training session," she continued, "Over the next thirty minutes you move from one piece of equipment to another. I'll be here to assist you with any problems. Now then, do you have any illnesses or injuries that I should know about my darlings?"

Both ladies shook their heads.

"And can I ask how flexible you are."

"Oh, well," said Diana, "If you change the day then I can't do Thursday afternoons; I volunteer at the Charity Shop in the high street."

Lou sniggered.

"No my lovely," Donna replied, calmly, "I mean flexible in a 'touch your toes' kind of way. Never mind. Come over and we'll begin the warm up."

Donna arranged the group into a semicircle in front of her and began rotating her shoulders and arms and lifting her legs up and down, giving instructions the entire time. At the end of the warm up she instructed them to slowly bend forwards and reach their hands towards their toes as far as they could go. As they did, a loud ripping sound filled the air. Lou saw Diana shoot straight back up again. Lou stood upright as well. Diana's face had gone the same colour as the red stripe on her outfit and her hands were placed around the back of her trousers.

"My trousers have split," she whispered, "Stupid, cheap

186

rubbish."

Lou couldn't help laughing.

"It's not funny," Diana said, "How am I going to get home?"

"Let me see," Lou replied, "It might not be that bad. You might get away with a safety pin."

Diana turned round.

"Okay you're not going to get away with a safety pin," Lou told her, "Black underwear, eh? You devil, you."

Diana threw her hands over her bottom again.

"Is there a problem?" Donna asked, coming forward.

She looked at Diana and tutted.

"Never mind," she said, her voice still echoing around the room for everyone to hear, "I can drop you off home at the end of the lesson in the van if you need a lift. Now then, I can lend you a pair of something now if you'd like or you could just exercise in your panties."

Diana looked shocked at such a suggestion.

"I shall sit this out," she said, regally, and backed her way to the side of the room.

Lou rather enjoyed the lesson. The comments she heard Donna make to the other ladies helped her mood too.

"No Mrs Richards; the pile of chairs by the wall isn't part of the circuit training. Please don't climb them again. Don't you remember last week when you got trapped behind them? We had to call the fire brigade out to you. I wouldn't attempt a squat again Mrs Henderson; not if your bowel trouble still hasn't cleared up yet. I don't know where the mop is. Really Mrs Edwards, in your case; when I say relax your body I don't mean the buttocks. You're still eating the cauliflower, aren't you?"

Lou really threw herself into the exercises and appeared to

be the only one sweating at the end. She helped Donna load the equipment back into her van before cadging a lift with Diana.

"You know, you're very good," Donna told Lou, speaking across Diana who was sat in the middle seat in the front of the van, "You're definitely too good for that broken hip class." Lou made a conscious effort to keep looking at the road and not at Diana.

"I think you'd do much better at one of my other classes."

"Thanks," Lou said, "But I work all week so don't get much time."

"Not a problem," Donna replied, "Come to my Saturday morning class at the sports centre over in Tenham. It's a fabulous workout that you can also adapt for doing in your own home the rest of the week."

"I have my daughter to look after."

"Again, not a problem," Donna said, "There's a crèche at the sports centre. Your daughter will have a fab time and it's only for an hour while you exercise. Why don't you come up this Saturday and give it a try at least."

Donna seemed to remember that Diana was sitting beside her. She patted her on the arm.

"Come back next Monday my darling with a decent pair of jogging bottoms," she said.

Diana didn't reply.

Donna stopped the car at the corner by The Smugglers. Lou rushed off to the supermarket to use the shower before her lunch break finished. It meant she didn't have to watch Diana walk across to their apartment building, spilling out of a pair of bright, red cycling shorts; which was all Donna could find to loan her.

*

188

Dr's Case Notes – Monday 14 September

Dr Moore seemed a little preoccupied today. I'd have liked to have helped but what can you say to someone when they're bent over the photocopier clearing a paper jam? The only phrase that came to mind was, 'God, you've got a great arse,' and I didn't think that would be too helpful. I'll just have to keep a careful eye out I think; see if any situation or problem develops. I haven't suggested a drink together yet. Maybe I should. I could ask then if anything is wrong; be a shoulder to cry on.

I'd hate for Dr Moore to leave. I know it's difficult when you move to a new area, especially somewhere like Ryan Harbour, which is still relatively small. The locals don't always take kindly to change and I've noticed that a lot of them won't see anyone else except me. I don't know why, I'd love to spend more time in Dr Moore's surgery. I could strip off and get a full medical check. Just imagine feeling those delicate, soft hands roaming all over my body. I've not had that in years. Mrs Bryant isn't the most gentle of women in the bedroom. The last time she attempted an intimate massage on me she treated my manhood in the same way that she attacks the roll of cling-film when she can't find the end. All that was missing was the whack against the kitchen countertop when she finally gives up.

Diana Carlton came in for a late appointment this evening. I was surprised really as Mrs Andrews never usually lets anyone have one of the empty emergency appointments. Mr Bennett was so desperate to see me that time, with his suspected angina attack, that he had to faint first. Even then she made him wait outside in case his pallor upset the other patients. Mind you Diana is one of her friends so I guess that's why.

She told me she had just joined a keep fit class and said she

189

felt she should probably get the all clear from me first before she goes again due to her advancing years. I got the feeling she wanted me to tell her not to go because when I said it's a good idea but take things gently to begin with, she seemed disappointed.

It's no fun getting old. People ask me if I'm looking forward to retirement but the thought of all day everyday with Mrs Bryant sends shivers down my spine. We all have our little habits to get used to. Mine is sniffing the milk at the breakfast table. Mrs Bryant's is flossing at the breakfast table. How she manages without a mirror in front of her I don't know. You'd think that was the time of day when one's teeth were at their cleanest but you'd be surprised what gets stuck up there. Half a sardine flew towards me across the table the other morning. Of course Mrs Bryant does have rather large gaps between her teeth. She doesn't use actual dental floss, preferring a thick type of garden twine instead. The action doesn't resemble flossing so much as a tug-of-war.

If I was with Dr Moore I'd retire tomorrow. Imagine all day everyday with that beautiful individual. I'm sure my pension would be sufficient for both of us to live on. What the hell, with Dr Moore I could live on air and be happy.

Would an affair be so bad? If we kept it quiet then no one would get hurt would they? I suppose if Mrs Bryant found out I'd get hurt. I remember early on in our marriage when I was working at a practice over in Spratling Kershaw and she thought I was having an affair with the church organist. I didn't think Mrs Bryant was the type to eavesdrop outside of doors but if you're going to do that, at least make sure you hear the whole conversation before jumping to conclusions.

The poor lady organist needed an injection but was terrified of needles; hated looking at them. I'd just got her into position and said, 'Brace yourself, I'm about to give it to you anally' when Mrs Bryant came rushing in. The organist was pushed off the medical table and the blood pressure sleeve was around my testicles with Mrs Bryant squeezing that pump for dear life before I realised what was going on. It was only as the sleeve tightened that I found my voice. We moved to Ryan Harbour not long after that.

Still, an affair with Dr Moore is worth the risk. God knows I need some excitement in my life. I guess Mrs Bryant and I are very much set in our ways; especially since the kids left home. I like to read the paper and have a potter in the garden when I'm not working and she likes to build dry-stone walls and play with her ferrets.

I'd like to try something new with Dr Moore. Perhaps running barefoot through bluebells while holding hands or enjoying a midnight picnic together while holding hands. How about something daring like being strapped together on a tandem parachute jump while holding hands? I'd try anything, just so long as we were holding hands.

Do you know what, I'm going to do it. To hell with Mrs Bryant. I'm going to march right into Dr Moore's surgery now and suggest a drink together; tonight.

*

Seven o'clock Monday evening saw The Smugglers completely empty. Jamie sighed. Old Joe had left a couple of hours before. Bill had then moved into his vacated seat, as usual and had one more pint before leaving too. It was often on a Monday that Tricky Vince or Mike the Wipe would turn up for a quiet drink but Jamie wasn't expecting either of them to come back again. This morning he'd received a postcard from the Colonel, who was off on some kind of hedonistic holiday in the Caribbean. Everything seemed to have gone wrong lately. Gloria came through from the kitchen.

"I've put that food in the bins out back," she said, "It's past its sell by date."

Jamie sighed again. "Look at this place," he said.

"I know," Gloria replied, "It's bad isn't it."

Jamie didn't answer.

"Look," Gloria continued, "I can see how things are, if you need to cut my hours you only have to say."

Jamie smiled. "It's not come to that yet," he told her, "Besides, I need you here. Without you I might just as well shut this place down."

Gloria smiled back at him and busied herself by wiping down the already spotless bar.

"I just wish I could do something right," Jamie said, "I really thought my ideas would work, but since the regatta…" He left the sentence hanging.

"I don't think there was anything wrong with your themed day idea," Gloria said, wiping around the Bitter pump handles, "It was just bad luck that it ran parallel with the Nightclub event. Of course it might have been the type of theme that was the problem."

"What do you mean?" Jamie asked.

Gloria stopped wiping and looked across at him.

"Well it was pirate-based wasn't it?"

Jamie shrugged his shoulders in a, "yes, so what" kind of way. Gloria continued.

"I mean I know this area was known for pirates back in the day, but after all; this place is called The Smugglers Inn. Maybe we should have concentrated on that rather than the pirates."

Thoughts began racing through Jamie's head. Gloria was still talking and had returned to her cleaning.

"Of course it is difficult to dress up as a smuggler. What would I wear? I always imagine they would have on a pair of jeans and one of those thick, white, woolly fishermen jumpers. I don't have shoes and a handbag to match that. And how would you theme a smugglers evening anyway? They have loot. I suppose that's a kind of treasure, like the pirates. Maybe they're not so different after all."

Gloria stopped talking as she realised she was getting no response.

"Are you okay?" she asked.

"Booty."

"I'm sorry?"

"That might work."

"What are you talking about? Are you going to get the strippers back?"

Jamie came out of his reverie.

"What? No. Can you give Lou a call," he asked, "See if she is free Saturday afternoon? And see if her friend, Diana can come; and that other friend of hers that came in; the munchkin."

Gloria looked puzzled but still picked up the phone and dialled. The pub door opened and Chris walked in.

"Here I am, let's get the party star…" he stopped talking as he surveyed the empty bar, "Are you open?"

"Of course," Jamie said, "What can I get you?"

"Hello, Lou; it's mum," Gloria said, into the phone, "Am I disturbing you? Sorry? You're doing what with an aubergine?"

Jamie and Chris both looked across at her.

"Stuff it; that's a nice way to talk to your mother…oh I see!

193

No it's nothing important; Jamie's got another whacky idea for the pub."

"Oi!"

"Are you free Saturday afternoon?" she asked, ignoring Jamie, "What? Is he definitely coming up? Well if Maddie's at a party he won't come over will he? What? No I don't have details yet but he wants you to ask Diana too; and that little friend of hers; Muriel. Yeah I know; what disaster is going to happen this time. Speak to you soon."

She was still laughing when she turned round but stopped when she saw Jamie's face.

"She'll try and come but Tony is coming up at the weekend to see Maddie."

"I hope she can make it," Jamie said.

"What's all this about then?" Chris asked, blowing a kiss over at Gloria, who tutted.

"A Treasure Hunt," Jamie said, "I've only just thought about it but I don't see why it couldn't work."

"A Treasure Hunt?" Gloria questioned.

"Yes. You get a group of people and split them into teams. Then you give them the first clue which will lead them around the town to the next one, and so on. The last clue will lead them to a prize. I thought we could have a trial run on Saturday. If it goes well there's no reason why we can't have one each week," Jamie's blue eyes were shining, "We could involve other businesses as well. At the end everyone comes back here for the prize giving and a few drinks."

"Count me in," Chris said.

Gloria tutted again. "Oh please," she chided, "How can your two brain cells hope to solve clues?"

Chris leaned back on his stool.

"It's true; I rely on my looks for my success."

"Actually, you should come along," Jamie said, ignoring Gloria's angry gaze, "It would be good to have a few teams to test out if this will work."

"Great," Chris grinned, "Saturday's my day off this week."

"How fortunate," Gloria spat.

He winked at her again, missing the sarcasm in her voice completely. Jamie was smiling to himself. Here was an idea he could try out with no need to spend any money. All he had to do was create a few clues. He bent down behind the bar to find a pen.

Chapter 10

Diana was feeling nervous. She looked across at Lou in the driving seat, who was still wearing that same, 'knowing' smile on her face that she'd had since knocking at Diana's door half an hour ago.

"I don't know why you won't tell me where we're going. I'd feel a lot better if you did."

"This is your, 'Face a fear,'" Lou told her, "I can't tell you and risk you chickening out."

"I still might do that when we arrive."

Lou laughed. "Trust me," she said.

Diana sighed inwardly

"I think my, 'Face a fear' has become Mrs Bailey at the baking class," she admitted.

"I thought she was a bit too hard on you last night," Lou replied, "But then she does hate it if her instructions aren't followed to the letter."

"It said put the dough in the fridge and chill for twenty minutes. I did that."

"I know, you sat yourself down with a cup of tea and a magazine," Lou said, "Didn't it occur to you that it was just the pastry that had to chill?"

"Not until Mrs Bailey came over and started shouting at me to tidy up my work station."

Diana shook her head.

"I won't be going back next week," she confessed, "I'm obviously no baker; unlike you. Mrs Bailey said your buns were delicious."

Lou grinned. "I remember Tony telling me that once," she

said.

"Sorry?"

"Nothing. I think we're here."

Diana's stomach was doing somersaults. As the car turned off the road into a driveway she caught a quick glimpse of a sign but only had time to pick out the word, 'Butter.' What could that mean? Was it a dairy farm of some kind? Diana wasn't scared of farms. In fact she rather liked them; the produce, the animals; especially the animals. She remembered a lovely day out with Richard, years ago, at a fair at Tyler's Green Farm. It was like a smaller version of the county show and Diana recalled watching all the animals in the Show Ring, being judged. She and Richard were stood right beside the exit gate. Thinking back now, Diana remembered congratulating one man on his smashing pair of bullocks. She still didn't know why he had looked shocked and Richard had started laughing.

"Right, here we are then," Lou said, bringing Diana back to the present.

Diana looked out of the windscreen as they parked up in front of a large, brick and glass building and read the sign above the main entrance; Hillview Butterfly House.

"I don't get it."

"You told me the other day how much you disliked having birds and things flying around your head," Lou said, "Here's your chance to deal with that."

Diana looked shocked. "You mean we have to walk through a room where there are lots of butterflies flying around."

"Yep," Lou said, opening her car door, "They'll be all around us. Come on; the sooner we're in the sooner you can face your fear."

"I wouldn't really call it a fear," Diana told her, slowly

getting out of the car, "It's more a dislike, that's all."

"Well, it shouldn't be a problem for you then," Lou winked, "Come on; we're going in."

Two minutes later they were standing in the queue. Lou was shaking her head.

"They won't let you in like that," she said.

Diana sighed and pulled the magazine off the top of her head.

"A part of me wishes we were already in there," she whispered, "Standing in this queue I'm getting more and more nervous and apprehensive. Why won't they hurry up in front?"

The two ladies Diana indicated were paying their entrance fee by debit card and were happily chatting to the receptionist while the payment went through. They were probably younger than her, Diana felt; but their rather old-fashioned-looking outfits of tweed skirts, sensible blouses and wide-brimmed straw hats made them appear older.

"We were here in Tenhamshire last year, weren't we Josie," the shorter of the two said.

Her friend nodded.

"Yes, we came on a coach tour. Unfortunately that company is no longer in business so Suze and I decided to rent a little run-around for a few days and came back this year under our own steam."

The receptionist nodded, not really paying much attention to what the two women were saying.

"I must say, the car is performing splendidly, isn't it Suze. What it's called again, a Toyota Clitoris?"

"Something like that," Suze replied, cheerfully.

The startled receptionist heard that bit and almost dropped the card reader. The receipt began to print and she quickly ripped it off and handed it over to them. The two ladies nodded at Diana and Lou as they passed by and headed off towards the entrance to the butterfly house.

As soon as they stepped forward, the receptionist confiscated Diana's magazine.

"We have strict rules as to what people can and can't take into the main area," she explained. "I'm sure you wouldn't start swatting at the butterflies or birds but someone might and we have to treat everybody the same way."

"You've got birds in there too?" Diana said, her eyes widening with horror.

"Just a few lovebirds and finches. They're very beautiful to look at."

Diana would have been quite happy to turn round and leave but Lou had just paid the entrance fee so she reluctantly followed her through the double doors and down a small, dark corridor. At the end of it was an opening that was covered in long, thick strips of see-through plastic that ran from floor to ceiling and overlapped one another. For Lou it was very reminiscent of the entrance into the storage freezer at work but the effect on reaching the other side was the complete opposite.

"My God it's hot in here," Diana said. She sniffed the air, "And there's a distinct pong too."

"You're determined to enjoy yourself aren't you," Lou replied.

The room they had just entered was vast. The glass panelled ceiling rose high above their heads; letting in the dappled sunlight of the day outside. The space was filled with lush, green shrubs and trees, many in flower and Lou could see the butterflies flitting between them. In the centre was a large pond, spanned by a wooden bridge and behind this was a small waterfall that gently cascaded down a craggy, black rock face.

"It's lovely, isn't it," Lou said, turning to Diana, "Like a rainforest."

Diana was looking all around her and every few seconds flinched, even though there were no butterflies where they were standing. Lou couldn't help grinning.

"It's not funny," Diana told her, "This is really difficult for me."

The two old-fashioned ladies were standing beside Lou, looking at the leaflet they'd been given at reception. The shorter of the two gently tapped her on the arm.

"Is your mother okay," Suze whispered, as Diana flinched for the eighth time, "I was a fulltime carer for my late husband. I know each day can be stressful so I just wanted to check if you needed any assistance."

"Erm no thank you, I'm actually…"

"This must be a very stimulating place to bring her to," Josie interrupted, "All the different colours and movement."

"No really, you see…"

"Butterflies are wonderful creatures," Suze agreed, "I try to attract as many as I can to my garden each summer. I love it when I see the first Brimstones and Red Admirals of the season."

"I have a penchant for Naked Ladies," Josie admitted.

"Do you?"

This seemed an odd time to come out of the closet, Lou thought.

"They're Painted Ladies, dear," Suze corrected.

"Didn't I say that?"

Lou managed to cut into the conversation.

"Diana is a friend of mine," she said, "She just has a bit of a fear of things flying around her, that's all. That's why we're here today."

"Oh I see."

Suze turned to Josie and they both laughed. Diana, having decided the immediate area was safe turned her attention to the group, just as Josie said,

"Why don't you both walk round with us? We can chat along the way and help your friend settle down and relax, can't we Suze?"

"Ooh yes, that's a great idea."

Lou couldn't think of a reason not to and so, after proper introductions were made, the four of them headed off down the main path.

"The flowers on these shrubs are absolutely beautiful," Suze said, as they approached an area dense with foliage, "Look at this pink colour, Josie. It's so vibrant."

Josie nodded.

"I agree, dear," she said. She turned to Diana and Lou, "I must say; I'm glad now I decided not to get rid of my Chlamydia."

"What?" Lou asked. Why did this woman keep confessing things to her?

"It's such a lovely shrub," Josie continued, "It flowers by the conservatory door in December and carries on right through January too."

"Do you mean a Camellia," Diana said.

Josie beamed.

"That's it," she told them, "What did I say?"

"It doesn't matter now," Lou replied, relieved.

Suze and Josie continued to chatter amongst themselves while Diana continued to flinch, grabbing Lou's arm every so often when a butterfly flew past right in front of them. It wasn't until they walked onto the bridge and Diana noticed the goldfish in the pond that she smiled for the first time that day.

"I do love fish," she said, "I find them so relaxing to watch."

"I agree with you," Josie replied, "I've got an aquarium of tropical fish at home. My son is looking after them while I'm away. I can sit for hours watching them."

"I just have the one goldfish," Diana admitted.

"Oh my dear you should always have more than one," Josie said, "Unless it's a Siamese Farter of course. They prefer to be alone."

"So they should with a name like that," Lou interjected.

Josie looked a little puzzled until Diana told them all she thought the fish was called a Siamese Fighter. Lou turned and looked over the opposite side of the bridge. She felt like she was in some kind of farce. It didn't help when Diana's voice floated over to her.

"I think you're right. My Charlie could do with a bit of company."

Lou rubbed her forehead, sensing a headache coming on.

"Shall we move on," she said.

The four ladies stepped off of the bridge. Diana sniffed the air again.

"That pong from earlier is definitely getting worse. Can't you smell it?"

"Actually I can," Lou replied. They were by a bird table covered in fruit, "It can't be this, surely."

Diana leaned forward to give it a sniff. At that moment a well-camouflaged butterfly flew up into her face.

"Aargghh."

"Diana, ssh," Lou said, as Suze and Josie both jumped in

202

fright, "You'll have Security in here in a minute; thinking you've been attacked."

"I have been! It's alright for you," Diana told her, rubbing her face, "This is a genuine fear."

"Who was it we knew who had a similar phobia," Josie asked Suze.

Suze screwed up her eyes as she tried to remember.

"Oh, wasn't it Ellen Aldridge," she said, "Used to live up the top end of the village. Had that one acre of land she kept pigs on."

"That's it," Josie replied, smiling. She turned to Diana and Lou, "Yes, lovely woman but what with all the pigs, you wouldn't want to spend too long talking to her, if you understand what I mean."

She waved her hand under her nose.

"The local kids used to call her Smelly Nelly," Suze added.

"Now **she** had a fear similar to yours," Josie continued, "Loved animals but was scared stiff of birds. Now I'm sure she found a way to get over it."

"Really," Diana said, feeling hopeful, "How?"

"Erm," Josie rubbed her chin, "What did she do, Suze?"

"She died."

"Oh of course she did. Yes, she had a heart attack when that Crow flew in through her kitchen window. Sorry, that's not much help really is it?"

Diana stood looking at Josie with her mouth open, unable to find any words to respond. Lou tried to supress a grin.

"Perhaps we should move on again," she suggested.

Josie and Suze walked on ahead. Diana grabbed Lou's arm.

"Those two aren't really helping me settle down," she whispered, "Can't we go?"

"Let's just walk around this last bit," Lou replied, "I'd like to see what's on the other side of the pond's rock face."

Further along the path was a small seating area where another bird table was set up with fruit. Diana muttered disgust when a bright, orange butterfly flew up and landed on Lou's cheek. Suze told everyone it was a lucky sign.

"It's very gentle," Lou said, as the butterfly flew off ahead of them, "It felt just like when Maddie was a baby and used to stroke my face."

"I'll take your word for it," Diana wrinkled her nose, "That smell is getting really bad here isn't it?"

Lou winced as she took a sniff.

"It can't be, but it smells just like…"

They rounded the final corner and found the source of the smell. In front of them was a large flowerbed filled with shrubs displaying flowers in vibrant shades of yellow and orange. It was breath taking, but what was really taking their breath away was the stuff stuck to the sole of a red and white striped trainer that was hanging off the end of one of the branches. Josie and Suze moved towards it and leant over for a closer inspection.

"Is that dog poo on there?" Diana asked, stepping forwards as well, "That's disgusting."

"Not at all," Suze said, brightly, straightening up, "There's a lot of nutrients and goodness in there that many butterflies love. Well, you can see, can't you?"

"Oh God," Lou said, "That orange butterfly that was on my face just now is lapping it up."

Diana smiled.

"Not feeling so lucky now, are you?"

"Whose shoe is it?" Lou asked, ignoring her friend.

In response to that question a member of staff came limping

round the corner, wearing the other trainer. Her pink sock on her shoeless foot had a hole in the top where her big toe was poking through.

"Ah, you've found my little secret," she told them, brightly, limping over.

"It's not that secret," Diana replied, "You could smell it as soon as you walked in."

The woman smiled and nodded at her.

"Yes you can, can't you?"

She took a healthy breath in.

"I trod in it on the pavement outside my house this morning," she continued, "I was going to grab a stick but then thought, 'Why waste it? The butterflies will love this.'"

"Oh I agree wholeheartedly," Suze told her.

Josie nodded her approval too.

"Yes," she said, "It is a very good idea. I think more people should be aware of what nature needs. In fact I might start doing something similar myself, at home. My Sphincter provides so much of the stuff."

Lou gagged.

"It's a Pinscher isn't it, dear," Suze queried, "Your dog's a German Pinscher."

"That's what I said, didn't I?"

Diana looked at Lou and shook her head.

"We need to leave, now," she whispered.

"Have you conquered your fear?"

"My list said face a fear; not conquer it."

"Okay, that's good enough for me. Let's go."

They left Josie and Suze in deep conversation with the member of staff, about all the merits and wastefulness of poo. Back out in the main area another staff member asked Diana if

205

she wanted to become a 'Friend of Hillview Butterfly House' for an eighty-five pounds a year membership fee. Diana's ten minute rant not only made him wish he'd never asked but also that he'd never been born. Once she'd managed to drag her outside, Lou drove them to a nearby coffee shop.

"I think we're getting through your list pretty quickly," Lou said, once the two of them were sat at a window table with their drinks.

"I'm not sure I've been that successful though," Diana replied, "I'm rubbish at baking, I can't drive a car to save my life and I managed to split my trousers during the first exercise warm-up."

"Well, put like that…" Lou winked, "Remember, the point is that you're trying. You wanted to change your life and you have; you are."

Diana smiled and took a sip of her tea.

"There are still a few items left," she said, "Working with animals for one."

Lou was just about to have a drink of her latte but placed the tall, glass mug back onto the saucer.

"I had a thought about that one," she told her, "I was planning on taking Maddie to Bunbury Zoo over the summer but we didn't get around to it. They offer one of those, 'Be a keeper for the day' type things. You could do that and Maddie and I can come and watch one Saturday. I know she'd love it."

"Hmm," Diana said, thinking, "I quite like the sound of that one myself. If I really enjoy it perhaps they'll let me be a volunteer or something. They haven't got a butterfly house have they?"

"No, just dangerous wild animals like lions and bears."

"What a relief."

They both laughed.

"And what else is left on the list after that," Lou asked.

"There's the makeover of course," Diana replied, and then blushed, "Oh and the, 'Find companionship' one too."

"Ooh yes," Lou said, grinning, "The dating scene. I should get my mother to help you with that."

Diana laughed again.

"Do you think she and I should go clubbing together?" she asked.

"You laugh; if I suggested that to mum she'd jump at the chance."

They both fell silent as they drank their drinks.

"Truth be told," Diana finally said, "I'm still a bit nervous about dating. I'm not sure I'm ready."

"How long have you been widowed for?"

"Twelve years."

"And you're still not ready."

Diana smiled. "Maybe I'm just scared," she said.

"I can understand that," Lou told her, "I've only just dumped Chris but the thought of entering the dating scene again is daunting."

"Maybe you're just not ready to move on."

"From Chris; I was ready to move on three weeks after meeting him."

"You say that now but you were together for two years."

Lou conceded the point.

"Yeah, you're right," she said, "I can't have thought him that bad back then. I suppose I stuck with him because he was the kind of guy everyone expected me to go out with."

"What do you mean?"

"Well Tony was always driven. He'd done well at school

and when we got together he was already planning out his career. I overheard several conversations at the time where people were asking what he was doing with the likes of me. They thought I was holding him back."

"That's terrible," Diana said.

"It wasn't anything I hadn't already wondered myself," Lou confessed, "We had so many differences but it did kind of work; for a while. When I met Chris he made me laugh at the start and I suppose I stayed with him because he never made me feel insecure."

"Richard and I were very different if I think about it," Diana said.

"He must have been a pretty special man if you're still mourning him twelve years after his death."

Diana looked pensive.

"I wouldn't say I was still in mourning," she replied, "Don't get me wrong, I miss him every day; but I have moved on. I think it's probably the nature of his death that still haunts me."

"Why, how did he die?"

"He was killed by a hit and run driver."

Lou's mouth dropped open in shock.

"I had no idea," she said.

"I don't often talk about it," Diana told her, "I guess it must have happened just before you moved to Ryan Harbour. Richard had gone into Tenham; I'm not sure why; probably something to do with a client at work. Anyway, a car was driving too fast along a rather busy stretch of the high road so I was informed. Richard was crossing the street when he was hit."

"That's awful. And the bastard never stopped?"

Diana shook her head.

208

"He wasn't killed instantly but had died by the time the ambulance arrived."

Lou didn't know what to say.

"The one piece of comfort I've always had is that a woman came over and sat with him after the accident. Obviously people crowded round but she sat down on the ground beside him, so I was told; and held his hand. He was unconscious apparently but she just sat there until he died and then disappeared amongst the crowd," Diana was looking into the distance, remembering; "Maybe he knew someone was there, maybe he could feel his hand being held; perhaps he didn't. I'm just glad he didn't die alone. I wish I'd met her, so that I could have said thank you."

Lou was still at a loss as to what to say. She looked at her watch. She had to work this afternoon.

"Shall we grab a quick sandwich here?"

"Okay," Diana said, "Will we have time afterwards to go back to the Butterfly House?"

Lou was shocked.

"Do you want to face your fear again?" she asked.

Diana shook her head.

"No," she told her, "That bloody receptionist has still got my magazine."

Chapter 11

Jamie was pleased with the turnout. He hadn't had this many people in the pub on a Saturday afternoon since...well, he couldn't remember. Diana had managed to bring along her friend, although he'd overheard her tell Lou that Muriel had been reluctant about coming. Mind you the last time she'd been here was when the S&M group had arrived and she'd been distressed by the sight of a naked colonel. That probably had something to do with her reluctance.

Jamie had never met Lou's ex, Tony, before but he looked a decent enough sort of guy, although Jamie didn't like the way Lou kept laughing at all his little jokes. They weren't that funny. But at least the atmosphere was good seeing as there were two of Lou's exes in the same room. Aside from their height the two men were totally different. Tony was dressed casually but in an expensive-looking shirt and designer jeans. He obviously spent time at the gym as well. Chris was wearing a crumpled, old t-shirt that was too tight for him and showed off his paunch. There was a faded picture of a trumpet on the front with the caption, 'Come blow my horn' written underneath it. He was currently winding up Gloria. Actually he was just sitting at the bar but that seemed to be enough.

Lou had also spotted a reaction to Chris but it wasn't her mother's. When he had called over, 'Hello darling,' and winked at Muriel, Lou saw the look that Diana gave him. It was the same haughty, condescending expression that she had often been on the receiving end of in the past. Lou thought Diana had changed in the last few weeks; less of a snob and more accepting of others and it shocked her to think that she could be wrong about that. Was it only herself that had been accepted into Diana's world? Surely not. After all, she was getting on well with Jamie and her mother too. Maybe it was just Chris. Lou felt a bit sorry for him. Not that he seemed too bothered. She smiled and nodded at him as she walked up to the bar to talk to Jamie.

"Are you expecting anyone else?"

"No this is it," Jamie told her, "It's just a test to see if I can pull off a Treasure Hunt."

"What about Old Joe and Bill," Lou teased, nodding her head over to their table, "Are you sending them around town looking for clues too?"

"If I thought they were capable of walking that far, definitely."

Lou laughed. "I'm not sure how far I can walk to tell you the truth," she told him, "I went to an exercise class over in Tenham this morning and now my legs are killing me."

"Exercise classes too now? Is this to burn off the calories from all the cakes you're baking?"

"I hadn't thought of it like that, but now you come to mention it," Lou said, "I can't believe how much I'm enjoying baking and cooking. Tony came over for lunch today and I jerked a chicken."

Chris spluttered into his lager.

"You dirty bitch," he laughed, "You jerked his what?"

Lou rolled her eyes. "It's chicken in a marinade, you arse."

"Yeah, right," he replied, getting off of his stool, "Of course it is. And I jerked a jumbo sausage before I came here today."

Perhaps she could understand Diana's expression after all. Chris walked over to talk to Tony.

"So what's the deal with Maddie's dad?" Jamie asked,

211

seeing where Chris had gone.

"There's no deal," Lou replied, "He came up for the weekend to see Maddie. He wants to spend more time with her, which I can understand. She's at a party this afternoon and is then straight off afterwards for a sleepover at a friend's house, which I'd forgotten about; so Tony was at a loose end and I invited him along here."

Lou leaned further across the bar.

"I don't think all's well at home though," she whispered.

Jamie wasn't sure what he was meant to take from that statement.

It was time to get the treasure hunt started but before Jamie could call for everyone's attention the pub door opened and a big, bearded, silver bear of a man walked in.

"Surprise."

"Hey, Doug the Bug," Jamie said, as the man stomped over to the bar, "Haven't seen you in ages."

"I've been on a camping safari for eight weeks in the Congo," he bellowed, his rich, booming, baritone voice making everyone turn and listen to him, "Fascinating it was. We were studying moths and had to travel through some of the densest forests you've ever seen to get to them."

Gloria rushed over, beaming.

"Hello stranger," she said, shoving Jamie aside and leaning forward over the bar.

"Ah, the delectable Gloria," Doug said, taking her hand gently in his huge hairy paw and kissing it, "It was only the thought of seeing those big green eyes of yours again that got me through the dysentery."

Gloria giggled. "Oh you," she said, slapping him playfully on the arm with her other hand before surreptitiously giving his bicep a gentle squeeze.

"Can I get you a drink?" Jamie asked, "The usual?"

"Actually no, I can't stop," Doug said, extracting himself from Gloria's grip, "I've just popped in to ask a favour. You know about the, 'Save the Tenhamshire Lesser-Spotted Beetle' campaign?"

"Well, vaguely," Jamie said.

"I'm part of the team and we're desperately trying to get some new members to help with the project. Do you know we believe there aren't any breeding pairs in the wild now? We've got two females in captivity to try and swell the numbers."

"And you want me to join?" Jamie asked.

"No."

"What about me?" Gloria breathed, "Would I do?"

"Good God, no," Doug replied.

Gloria's face fell.

"We're looking for people to get hands-on with the project," he gently took Gloria's hands again, "These delectable fingers should never be made dirty," he said.

Gloria giggled. "You are a naughty boy," she said, "I ought to put you across my knee."

Doug laughed as he let go of her hand.

"Alas I haven't the time."

"I'm free tomorrow."

Jamie cut in. "So what is this favour you want?"

"I need a venue," Doug told him, sounding more business-like, "Where we can hold a talk about the campaign. I've come back from my trip and nothing has been organised. Would you mind if I held it here? We'll organise all of the advertising, naturally; but perhaps you could lay on some sandwiches and people can buy their own drinks; how does that sound?"

213

"Sounds good to me," Jamie said, trying not to grin too widely.

"Only problem is, it's for this coming Thursday night. I know it's short notice but is that an issue?"

"I'm sure I can rearrange a few things to fit you in," Jamie lied; "No problem."

Doug visibly relaxed. "Thank you," he said, shaking Jamie's hand.

He blew a kiss to Gloria, who almost fainted on the spot; and then left.

"Oh, what I'd like to do for that man," she said, wistfully, "He's so rugged and brave and yet so charming and such a gentleman."

"He spends most of his time with bugs," Jamie pointed out.

Gloria shrugged her shoulders.

"I could cope with that," she said.

"Don't think you're his type, babes; if you get my meaning," Chris had obviously been listening in, "I heard last year he was in Thailand; looking for lady boys."

"That was ladybirds, you idiot," Gloria corrected.

"Right then everybody," Jamie called out, "If I can have your attention for a few minutes. Firstly I'd like to thank all of you for coming here to help with this event. If today proves successful I hope to roll it out for the whole town to enjoy."

Chris sniggered. "Roll it out."

Gloria shot him a dirty look.

"Now then; I've arranged several clues in a Treasure Hunt. Clue one you get here. I'd like you to pair up and try and solve the location of the next clue together from what's written on the card. When you know where that is, go to that part of Ryan Harbour where the next clue will be waiting for you. There are

214

four clues in all. There'll be a prize for the first one to solve all four. Any questions?"

There was silence.

"Great. Okay, pair up and I'll hand you the first clue."

*

Robert was trying not to get too excited about this afternoon. With the complications that had occurred after their recent attempts to spice things up, he didn't know whether Grace would make it through to the end of a porn film; but at least she was willing to give it a try. She was a lot happier with something they could do inside their apartment together; just so long as the sound on the TV wasn't turned up too loud.

Robert had promised her he would get hold of an erotic film that was about love and respect. He picked up the DVD from the armrest of the sofa now. 'The Theft of my Virginity' probably wasn't quite the film Grace had in mind. Still, it was the only one Robert was able to get in the end and hopefully it would put them in the mood for a little afternoon action.

Grace stood up from putting the lunch things in the dishwasher and came and sat down beside her husband. She picked up the DVD case while Robert loaded it into the player.

"What's it about?" Grace asked.

"I've not seen it," he replied, sitting back down.

"Who's in the cast? Is there anyone I would know?"

"I doubt it."

"What about the director?"

Robert gently took the DVD case from Grace's hand.

"Look love," he explained, "This isn't your normal sort of film. It's an adult movie. It's meant to…well, get you in the mood. Let's just sit back and watch it."

Grace nodded and Robert pressed play on the remote control.

There was a lot of flickering before the opening credits appeared.

"It's not a very good copy is it," Grace said.

Robert couldn't deny that.

The opening scene showed a shower cubicle, all misted up as hot water poured out of the shower head. A woman could be heard humming. The scene cut to outside where a big, muscular man in a striped, tight t-shirt and carrying a sack over his shoulder was making his way around the house, looking for an open window or unlocked door. He stopped by the patio doors.

"We used to have curtains like that in our old house, didn't we," Grace said, "Do you remember; it was in the back bedroom. I think the colour was called Dusky Apricot."

The scene flicked back to the shower where the woman was still singing and then returned back outside to where the man was entering the house through the patio doors.

"Well that's asking for trouble," Grace said, "Why on earth didn't she lock that if she was going upstairs? I always lock the balcony door when I go off to have a shower."

"But we're on the second floor," Robert replied.

"It pays to be careful," she told him.

By now the man was walking up the stairs. He could hear the shower and the humming.

"Oh God, what's he going to do?"

Robert tutted. "It's an adult film," he told her, "I doubt he's going to try and sell her a pack of dusters."

"Well there's no need to be sarcastic."

"Let's just watch and see."

The man was standing outside the bathroom door. The shower had stopped but the woman was still humming. He opened it a crack and watched the reflection of the woman in the mirror, towelling herself dry.

"Well that's wrong for a start," Grace said, "That mirror would be all steamed up wouldn't it."

"It doesn't matter, Grace."

"Of course it matters. We could both see how hot the water was. The cubicle was misted up, why wasn't the mirror?"

"Let's just watch the movie."

The man was now grinning and the camera panned down to where he was rubbing the front of his jeans.

"Oh my, do we really need to see that?"

"It's a porn film, Grace. Of course we need to see that. It's meant to be turning you on."

"Well if that rubbing is turning you on Robert then we really need to have a serious talk."

"Let's just watch the movie," Robert repeated, a little louder than before.

Grace sighed.

As they watched, the man on the screen flung the door open. It banged loudly against the wall. The woman screamed and dropped her towel, standing there completely naked. She looked down towards the guy's crotch and her eyes lit up.

"Well that's not very realistic is it," Grace interrupted, "She'd be screaming the place down if a man broke into her house. I know I would."

Robert closed his eyes and counted to five. When he opened them the scene had moved on to the bedroom.

"Oh God, I don't believe it," Grace said.

"What?"

"That bedspread; I saw the exact same one in town last week. I was thinking of buying it for the spare bedroom. I shan't now of course. This film has cheapened it."

The man's jeans were around his ankles and the woman was performing oral sex on him. Robert felt a little embarrassed and turned to see if his wife was feeling the same. Grace was looking puzzled. Surely she knew what the woman was doing.

"Are you alright, Love?"

"I'm trying to look at that bedside lamp on the table but the woman's head keeps getting in the way," she told him, "Honestly, can't she hold still for one minute? I think it's one mother used to have."

"Grace, you're not meant to be looking at the furniture," Robert fumed, "You're meant to be watching what the couple are doing."

"I've seen what the couple are doing," she replied, "But she's taking an awfully long time on it and I've got bored."

There was no response to that.

"And the film title is all wrong, by the way," Grace added, "'The Theft of my Virginity?' You can't tell me she's still a virgin."

Robert shook his head and didn't bother replying. Pretty soon the roles on the screen had reversed and the woman was lying back on the bed while the man pleasured her orally.

'Oh yeah,' she kept saying, 'That's it baby; oh yeah.'

"There's not a lot of dialogue is there," Grace said.

"Well what do you want them to say?" Robert replied, exasperated, "I don't think either of them are interested right now if she forgot to buy lamb chops at the supermarket."

Grace's head whipped round.

"What's that supposed to mean?"

"I just mean she's not going to say much while a man has his tongue up her chuff!"

"Robert!"

218

"Look, Grace; please. It's an erotic film. It's not a classic; it's not going to be up for an Academy award. It's meant to be watched and enjoyed for what it is. Now please; let's just watch the bloody movie."

Grace pursed her lips tightly together and folded her arms. She sat back on the sofa, obviously in a huff but at least she remained silent. They continued to watch the film. The couple had sex on the bed and then moved across to a chair by the window.

"My grandmother used to have a set of dining chairs like that," Grace said.

Robert bit his lip.

"Of course **we** only ever sat in them for a meal," she added, as the woman on the screen straddled it, face forwards while the man took her from behind, "It'll take more than furniture polish to get that clean."

'Fuck my ass!' The woman on the screen shouted out.

"Oh my goodness," Grace said, "I'm sorry but there's no need for language like that."

Robert sighed. "It's all part of the experience," he told her, "Dirty talk is meant to be a turn on."

Grace stared at him.

"This stuff really turns you on?" she asked.

"Not right now it's not; no."

Grace stood up.

"I'm sorry," she said again, "But this is worrying. Do you want me to behave like that? Do you want me to be all effy effy? Is that what this is all about?"

"No," Robert whined, "It was just meant to get us in the mood."

Grace took a final look at the screen where the woman was

getting taken roughly while bent backwards over the linen basket. She turned back to her husband.

"I thought I knew you," she told him. She shook her head and left the room.

Robert threw himself back on the sofa. On screen the couple were joined by the woman's sister. An image of Grace's seventy-five year old, warty sibling with one leg shorter than the other entered Robert's head. That was the final straw. There was no way this film was going to turn him on now no matter what happened. He pressed the stop button on the remote control and picked up the local newspaper.

*

"Hurry up, Diana!"

"Muriel, please. I can't walk any faster."

"Lou and Tony are already ahead of us. I can't believe we didn't solve this earlier."

She read out the clue and solved each line as they walked.

"*Off you go to the indoor fair.* Well we now know that's the supermarket. *Something treasured you'll find there.* What was that bit again?"

"Lou's colleague is called Precious."

"That's right. *To solve the clue and complete the task; All you have to do is ask.* I suppose she'll give us the next clue."

"I think so."

The two ladies were just passing the entrance to the pub car park.

"You know I think this smacks of cheating really," Muriel said.

"What; why?" Diana asked.

"Having a clue where Lou works and having it about her friend. No wonder she's ahead. I think Jamie did that because

220

he fancies her."

"What, Lou? Do you think so?" Diana hadn't considered that before. It made a lot of sense now that she came to think about it.

"Look, there's Lou and Tony now; leaving the supermarket," Muriel said, "They must have the next clue. They're the ones to beat. I don't think we've got a problem with that gummy clown or the old trollop behind the bar."

"Muriel! What's come over you?"

"I don't like to lose," she replied, "I'm too competitive, I know that; but you would insist on my coming today. You'll have to deal with the consequences. Now come on, Diana; let's go!"

She grabbed at her friend's arm and dragged her into the road.

"Muriel, careful," Diana shouted, as a car's brakes squealed and the driver tooted. Muriel threw the guy two fingers and carried on across the road and into the supermarket.

Back outside the pub, Gloria had just emerged, looking thoroughly fed up.

"Will you come along," she called back, through the door.

Chris followed her out, slipping on his leather, biker jacket.

"I should have known what this meant," he said, indicating the clue in his hand, "I heard Precious talking about it to Terry yesterday."

Gloria rolled her eyes. "You tell me that now? Oh God, how did I end up partnered with you?"

"Luck of the draw, babes," Chris told her, "I was hoping for that little cutie with the old girl."

"Well you're stuck with me…or rather I'm stuck with you.

Let's just get this over with and will you please try to not say anything stupid."

Chris grinned. "Can't promise anything babes," he told her.

Lou and Tony had walked away from the supermarket and round the corner onto the main high street to read the next clue.

"Right," said Tony, "*To find the way to your next clue, Try and think of something new, Bricks, cement a big erection, But what about the artist's section?* What the hell does that mean?"

"I don't know," Lou replied, taking the clue from Tony and reading it herself, "There's a builder's yard off the high street; maybe it's that. Mum said Jamie talked about involving other businesses in the treasure hunt."

"Well let's walk towards it while we think," Tony suggested.

They began walking in silence. Eventually Tony said,

"I'm still impressed by that dinner you made us today."

Lou felt herself blushing.

"Oh it was easy really," she said, "I cheated on the marinade as it was already prepared in a jar."

"Are you learning how to make that from scratch in next week's lesson then?"

Lou laughed.

"It's baking classes I go to, not cooking; although I'm enjoying experimenting with both at home. I've become a lot tidier too. It was the one thing Mrs Bailey, the teacher, commented on, my first week at college. I was too scared of her not to begin tidying my work area. I channel her now when I cook at home and that makes me keep a tidy kitchen."

"Not just the kitchen," Tony said, "I didn't feel anything when I leant back again the cushion on the settee."

Lou smiled.

"Once I started I couldn't stop. Poor Maddie has to go searching through three different cupboards now, looking for her toys."

Tony made a huffing sound.

"It's worse than that at mine," he said, "Everything has its rightful place. I came home from work one day when I had Maddie and found her and Cheryl making labels for everything."

"I'm sure they were having fun."

"Cheryl definitely was."

Silence returned. Lou broke it.

"Is everything alright between you and Cheryl," she tentatively asked, "I don't want to pry and you can tell me to mind my own business if you like, but you seem; agitated."

Tony sighed.

It's nothing," he said, after a pause, "We're...I don't know. She just seems to take everything so seriously. I can't remember the last time we laughed at something silly or did something stupid together...like go on a treasure hunt."

He grinned. Lou smiled back but then she stopped walking.

"I've been an idiot," she said.

"No you haven't," Tony replied, "It was my fault really, but I..."

"The clue," Lou interrupted, "It's not the builder's yard. *Something new* the clue said and we've ignored the *big erection.*"

"Well I try not to draw attention to it."

"It's the apartments on the harbour," Lou said, ignoring Tony, "We're going the wrong way."

"Right," he said, grabbing her hand, "Let's go."

"It's the apartments near you," Muriel said, as she and Diana crossed the road from the supermarket.

"Are you sure," Diana replied, "What about the *artist's section* part? What does that mean?"

Muriel sighed.

"We'll find out when we get there," she snapped.

"I don't like the competitive you," Diana said, "You're nasty."

"I'm not nasty; I'm just impatient. It's no good coming second and I don't want to be surrounded by idiots."

"You made that poor girl in the supermarket cry. She came in especially today, just to hand out the clues."

"She was taking too long with the envelope," Muriel replied, "If she spent less time calling me darling and asking how I was, I wouldn't have had to snatch it off of her. It wasn't my fault one of her fingernails caught on the envelope. Anyway, here we are."

The two ladies had reached the temporary fence that surrounded the building site by the harbour where the new apartments were being built.

"Right," said Diana, "What are we looking for?"

"The clue, Diana," Muriel said to her, sounding like she was addressing an idiot, "We need the next clue; start searching."

"Hang on," Diana replied, staring at the piece of paper in her hand, "Let's try and work out each line first. It will save time."

Muriel sighed again. "It's you that's wasting time. Just start looking."

"Ssh," Diana said, "Now then, *bricks and cement* refer to this sight. What about the *big erection*? Muriel, what experience have you had of big erections?"

Muriel stopped her search and turned to face Diana.

224

"What the hell do you think that is?" she said, pointing at the almost completed apartment block."

"Oh right," Diana replied, following her gaze, "Why did I think it referred to something else? Okay, *But what about the artist's section?* What does that mean?"

"I don't know, start looking. Lou and Tony could be here any minute."

"I know what it means," Diana said, staring up at the boarding and grinning.

Muriel, who had continued her search of the floor, looked back at Diana. Diana pointed up at the advertising on the boarding.

"This is new," she said, "Photographs of the apartments' interiors. Only they're not photographs; they're artist's impressions."

She walked to the end of the advertising board and reached up. She pulled down an envelope and walked over and gave it to Muriel. Muriel looked at it and then up at her friend.

"Well you took your time about it!" she said, and stormed off.

Gloria was walking a few steps ahead of Chris along the harbour front. She stopped and turned round to face him.

"Will you please stop laughing," she said.

"I can't help it; *A big erection.*" Chris went off into hysterics again.

Gloria sighed and started walking off.

"Honestly, you're only a small step up from pond weed," she said, "We've just passed Lou and Tony who have obviously found the third clue. I'm not sure why he was limping. I reckon Diana and Muriel have already been up here too."

They reached the apartment block and Gloria looked along the advertising board until she found the envelope.

"Yep, they've all been here," she said, "This is the last envelope."

"If I'd been them I'd have nicked the other envelopes," Chris told her.

"That doesn't surprise me in the least," Gloria replied, "Now then. *There are many along the street, But how to choose the one to greet, This one's full of old world charms, And it likes to spread its alms.*"

She looked up at Chris.

"What do you think?" she asked.

Chris started laughing again.

"I'm more into spreading legs, if you catch my drift," he said.

Not for the first time in the past twenty minutes, Gloria rolled her eyes.

"This one was obvious," Muriel said, out of breath as she walked as quickly as she could up the high street.

"Yes, it was the *alms* part that gave away it was the charity shop," Diana agreed, "But don't you think this smacks of cheating?"

Muriel stopped walking. "How can it be cheating?"

"Well, you said that it was cheating for Lou when it was the supermarket. We both volunteer at the charity shop."

Muriel started walking again.

"That's completely different," she said, "Now come on. We don't want the others catching us up."

"That's hardly likely since you tripped poor Tony on our way back along the harbour."

226

"I didn't trip him," Muriel said, "He just got in the way of my foot. He shouldn't walk that close to someone."

"You swerved into him."

"Let's not split hairs," Muriel snapped, "At least we should now have a bit more time to get the…"

She stopped talking as a car tooted as it passed by them. Tony was driving and Lou was leaning out of the passenger window. She grinned at the two ladies and then gave Muriel the finger. The two ladies stood and watched as Tony pulled up on the double yellow line outside the charity shop and Lou rushed in. Two seconds later she was back out with an envelope in her hand.

"Come on!" Muriel shouted, and Diana watched as her seventy year old friend sprinted up the road.

"How far up this bastard high street do I have to go before I can turn the car round," Tony said, clearly agitated.

"Just a bit further," Lou replied.

"Are you sure you've worked out that clue correctly this time," he snapped, "You were too slow with the third one."

"Hey! Don't blame me because your foot hurts," Lou told him, "I didn't trip you."

"I can't believe that woman. She carries a lot of weight for someone so small. If she wants to start treading on people; well, two can play at that game. I'll squash the bitch so far into the ground moles will feed on her carcass. Now, are you sure you've worked out the answer."

"Yes! It's really obvious. *The prize is close so don't lose heart, Return your team back to the start, In Old J's spot is where it is, The prize will pop and bubble and fizz.* It can only be a bottle of champagne that's in the seat where Old Joe sits."

"I'd like to crack the bottle of champagne over that midget's head."

"Let it go, Tony. Now, turn this car round will you. It won't take the others long to work this out."

Diana and Muriel were practically running back down the street towards the harbour and The Smugglers.

"Muriel," Diana puffed, "You can't outrun their car you know."

"They can't turn it round until they're up by The Green Man," Muriel called over her shoulder, "Now, keep up wimp or go to hell."

"Where's all this traffic come from?"

"Tony, it's a zebra crossing; that's why we've stopped. Be a little patient, will you."

Tony leaned out of his window.

"Get that crate moving will you!" he shouted.

Lou pulled him back inside the car.

"That's Mr Pinkerton," she hissed, "He's ninety and his wife in the wheelchair is eighty-eight. They can't move any faster."

Tony banged the steering wheel.

"This place is full of old fossils," he moaned, "And that midget wrinkly isn't getting her paws on the prize."

He pressed his hand down on the horn.

"Keep up Chris!"

"We don't know where we're going, babes."

"**We** don't, but **I** do. It's the charity shop."

They were walking back along the harbour front from the new apartments.

228

"How did you work that out?"

"*Spreading alms.*"

Chris began laughing again.

"Spreading," he said, "Big erection. That Jamie's a legend."

Gloria sighed for the hundredth time.

"My God, can no one say anything that you can't turn into something rude?"

"It's a gift, babes."

"Honestly she said, I…what the hell?"

The two of them had just reached the slipway beside The Smugglers. Gloria was looking up the road towards the high street. Muriel was hurtling across the road towards them. Cars brakes squealed as they tried to stop. At one point Gloria was sure the old lady leapt across a bonnet. Diana was behind, waving apologies at all the drivers. Suddenly a blue car careered through the gaps at an alarming speed and screeched to a stop five foot from where Gloria and Chris stood, blocking the route down to the slipway into the harbour. Lou and Tony leapt out. Muriel was yelling at them.

"They know where the prize is," Chris whispered into Gloria's ear. She was almost sure he sniffed her hair afterwards, "Let's follow them."

"But we haven't got all the envelopes," she told him, following Chris as he chased the others.

"Screw that," he called, "I want the prize, whatever it is."

Jamie was smiling to himself. He wondered how everyone was getting on and hoped they were enjoying his hunt. He felt rather proud about the clues he'd set; getting them to rhyme like that. Maybe he should start working on some more for the next hunt. It was pretty quiet in the pub at the moment. Old Joe had just left and Bill, as usual, had moved round into the vacated seat. Jamie looked over there now and smiled. The prize was all set up ready. He felt sure everyone would laugh at his joke.

The door to the pub flew open and the entire room was filled with the noise of shouting and yelling as six people tried to get in at once. Lou squeezed through first on all fours. Tony was behind with Muriel on his back. She had two fingers up his nose and was frantically trying to pull him backwards out of the pub. Jamie looked on, open mouthed. They'd only been gone half an hour. What had happened?

Having thrown Muriel off, Tony slipped inside the door and then the space was free for the other four to follow. Lou had just stood up but the five people behind her moved as one and all six flew at Old Joe's table. Bill let out a whimper as he disappeared under the throng.

"Where is it?" Lou shouted.

"It must be under the cushion," Diana said.

"Just rip it open;" Chris called out.

Jamie ran round the bar. No one was ripping up his seats.

"Stop that," he shouted out, "What are you doing? You're going to…"

"It's mine!" he heard Muriel yell, "Do you hear?"

"That's my bollocks you're squeezing, you undersized Harpy!" Tony called out.

"Guys, guys," Jamie tried to get everyone's attention, "Hey!" They all stopped struggling and looked up at him.

"What the hell is wrong with you?" he asked them, "This was meant to be a fun afternoon for you all."

"Where's the champagne?" Lou said, "The clues led us here to Joe's seat. Where's the bubbly?"

"It's in *Old Joe's spot*," Jamie told her, smiling, "Look, it's

230

right in front of you on the table."

Six pairs of eyes looked down and saw a bottle of lemonade.

"Is this some kind of joke?" Lou whispered, in a very hostile sounding voice.

The smile fell from Jamie's face.

"It was only a test run," he reasoned, "I thought the lemonade would be funny."

The six of them began to struggle to their feet.

"Funny? You made me trounce round the harbour with the missing link and you think that's funny?" Gloria said.

The group stood together against the landlord.

"Four clues led to this?" Diana said; who had picked up the lemonade bottle, "I've spent the afternoon with devil woman, for a bottle of lemonade?"

"Give me that!" Muriel snatched the bottle; the prize. "Yes," she shouted, punching the air.

"I can't believe I've come down all the way from London," Tony fumed, "Got my foot kicked and my testicles crushed, for pop?"

"I thought you'd come down to see your daughter," Lou accused.

"I wish I'd gone with her to Bobby Burgers."

"I think it's Billy," Diana told him.

"I don't give a shit!"

"Well there's no need to be like that."

"Guys," Jamie cut in, "Will you all just calm down. You're behaving like animals."

"Don't talk to me about animal behaviour," Gloria told him, "I had to clear up what they left behind in here after your other so called 'great idea.'"

"Oh for God's sake," Jamie said, totally fed up, "Will you all stop moaning."

A groaning sound came from behind them.

"I said stop moaning!"

The group parted as another moan came from under the table.

"Oh God, Bill." Jamie ran forward and helped the old man back onto his seat.

"Am I dead?" he asked, "Is this heaven?"

"Jesus, I hope not," Gloria told him.

Jamie threw her a look.

"I think I ought to take him up the hospital to get looked over," he said, "Bill, do you think you can walk to my car out the back?"

The old man nodded and Jamie helped him up.

When he got back to the pub several hours later, after Bill had been admitted with concussion and a fractured elbow, a party was in full swing. Lou and Tony were slow dancing together while Chris and Muriel were attempting the cancan. All appeared to have been forgiven. Gloria and Diana were sat on stools at the bar. Gloria waved over at Jamie when she saw him. He walked down behind the bar to talk to her.

"Everything okay?" he asked.

"Wonderful," she replied, "I got a round of drinks in, on the house, after you left. I hope you don't mind."

Jamie shook his head.

"Good," she told him, "Because I got another four in after that. But it seems to have done the trick."

Jamie could see that. Muriel and Chris had joined Lou and Tony now for a slow dance; the four of them leaning on each other, Muriel with her hand on Tony's bum. She'd got hold of quite a lot of him today, Jamie thought; well, rather her than

Lou anyway.

"How's Bill?" Diana asked.

Jamie sighed. "He's going to be okay," he told her, "But his daughter wasn't too happy with me when she showed up at the hospital. I felt guilty telling her he'd just fallen off his chair but what else could I say? She thinks he's drinking too much and has found him a place in a retirement home near to where she lives in Cunden Lingus. I guess we won't be seeing him in here again."

"That's a shame," Diana said, "Another regular down."

Jamie really didn't need reminding of that fact.

Chapter 12

Lou didn't particularly like going on the till but as Precious had
had to go home sick there was only her or Terry to choose from;
none of the part-timers being able to come in at such short
notice. The last time Terry had been let loose on the tills he'd
used the handheld scanner as a gun and kept 'shooting' the
customers. It wasn't a tough decision who to pick.

It was a slow afternoon, unusual for a Wednesday. Lou
couldn't really stray too far from the till and so had to content
herself with straightening out the greetings cards stand
whenever she didn't have any customers. She managed to
rearrange the entire display three times.

Still, at least she'd had the good news from Simon that Pete
Crick was going to be visiting the store Saturday week. She'd
also been charged with the task of planning something for the
event. Simon's other news was that the management training
courses had been officially announced and Lou had until
tomorrow to put her name forward. She still wasn't sure what
to do about it. So lost in thought was she, she didn't see the
customer standing beside her and jumped when Grace gave a
little cough.

"I'm so sorry," Lou said, scanning the lamb chops Grace had
forgotten to buy earlier.

"You looked miles away," Grace told her, smiling,
"Something on your mind?"

"Oh, this and that," Lou replied, "Work stuff mainly. How
are you and Robert?"

"We're fine, thanks," she picked up a copy of the local paper
from the stand behind the till and tutted as she put it down on

the conveyor belt, "Honestly; this is terrible, isn't it?"

Grace nodded at the front page. Lou read the headline as she scanned it through the till; 'Local Couple Held at Gunpoint.'

"I know what you mean," she said, "People say it's just the world we live in now but that makes me scared for Maddie's future."

Grace shook her head. "I heard a story recently about a woman being burgled while she was at home."

"Did you?"

"Now who told me about that? She was in the shower and a man came in through the French windows…"

Grace stopped as she realised she was telling Lou the plot of that awful porn film. All Lou saw was a look of horror appear on her neighbour's face.

"Are you okay Grace? I shouldn't worry too much about it. These stories in the paper are always blown up out of all proportion to sell a few more copies. The public is just a pawn in the journalists' sensationalism."

Grace's gaze flicked onto Lou.

"What did you say, did you say porn?"

"Pardon?"

"Who told you? How?"

Grace grabbed the carrier bag with the chops and the newspaper in it.

"I'm going," she said, "I must go home and get the meat in; oh I mean the chops on, I…"

She left the sentence hanging and ran out of the shop. She almost collided with Joyce and Muriel who were on their way in.

Oh God, that's all I need, Lou thought.

Muriel looked over and waved brightly. Lou smiled back.

Joyce's gaze followed Muriel's but showed no recognition of Lou; preferring to stare right through her instead. It was about ten minutes before the two ladies came up to the till. Muriel was holding the basket and Joyce took out the bits that were hers; which was most of the contents, Lou noted.

"Would you like help with your packing?"

"No."

Lou began pushing the items through the scanner as quickly as possible so that they would pile up at the end of the conveyor belt and make Joyce's packing harder.

"Diana told me this morning that she's given up the baking class," Muriel said.

"I know," Lou replied, "She's not really had a successful time there so I can't blame her. I think yesterday was the last straw. I'd persuaded her to have one more try, but the results weren't good."

"She says you're doing well."

Lou heard a huffing sound behind her but chose to ignore it.

"I do seem to have taken to it," she said, loud enough for Joyce to hear, "I'm cooking all the time now. I do think it's right for a child to be brought up with a healthy diet."

"Oh I agree," Muriel told her, "I'm glad you're enjoying it."

Joyce walked back up to the till to settle her bill. Lou told her the amount and twisted the card reader towards her for her to pay.

"I'm having Diana and my mum over to mine tonight for dinner," she told Muriel, "I'm grilling some lamb steaks with oregano and doing a wild rice risotto with it."

"Sounds lovely."

"I thought it would be nice for her to relax with friends after such a trying morning."

"Oh, she was only at a committee meeting at Joyce's this morning," Muriel said.

"I know."

Lou passed over Joyce's receipt. Joyce folded it and placed it inside her purse. Then she turned her gaze onto Lou.

"Enjoy your time with Diana," she said, "It won't last long. She'll soon come to her senses."

"I think you'll find she's already done that," Lou replied, "She's finally enjoying herself with a friend who allows her to be herself."

Joyce smiled. "Oh I think her real friends are those who've always been there for her. Not the sort of person who used to bad-mouth and disrespect her."

"I'll just pay for the bread and milk," Muriel chipped in, sensing trouble.

"Some friends hang around too long," Lou replied to Joyce, "Like a very bad smell."

Joyce's smile wavered ever so slightly. She picked up her bags of shopping.

"Diana's still in mourning for her sister," she said, "And is going through a phase, that's all. She'll soon come to her senses and see you for what you truly are."

"And what do you mean by that?"

"Just the milk, forget the bread."

Joyce leaned in closer to Lou and whispered,

"You're nothing but a common, little tart. Like mother, like daughter."

Lou wasn't sure how she managed not to head butt the woman in front of her. Maybe it was the chance of becoming a store manager that was still at the forefront of her mind and Diana having commented recently on her customer care skills.

Instead she smiled back at Joyce.

"Thank you for your custom. Have a nice day and do come back again soon."

The smile fell from Joyce's face and Lou realised in that second that she had wanted her to retaliate. Joyce would have happily received an ear bashing or actual physical harm, just so she could go and complain to management and get Lou sacked. Lou was shocked at the woman's loathing for her but also felt empowered that she hadn't risen to the bait.

"Let's go, Moo," Joyce said, and she walked away from the till.

Muriel took Joyce's place in front of Lou and gave her a big smile.

"She doesn't mean it," she said.

"Oh I think she does," Lou replied, putting the milk and bread through the scanner and placing it into Muriel's bag for her.

"She does really care for Diana," Muriel said, "She truly wants what is best for her."

"That's not strictly true," Lou replied, "She wants what **she** thinks is best for Diana."

Muriel opened her mouth to reply but closed it again. She smiled again and left. Once they were out of sight Lou took a few deep breaths to calm down her thumping heart. Joyce was the nastiest woman she had ever met but she'd voiced a thought Lou had had herself. What if Diana was going through a phase? She was trying all these new things but so far had failed at driving, baking, and Lou knew for a fact that she hadn't gone back to the keep fit class on Monday. What if Diana did decide not to continue with the other items on her list and returned to her old life? Lou realised that she didn't want to lose her as a friend, but how could their friendship develop when Joyce Pendleton was resting on Diana's shoulder?

*

Dr's Case Notes – Wednesday 23rd September

I've started following Dr Moore around. I don't mean in the surgery I mean once we've closed for the evening. To home, to the park, to the supermarket; I'm following Dr Moore's every movement. That's not healthy is it? As a doctor myself I should know that. I'm worried Mrs Bryant is getting suspicious at my getting in late each night. I've told her I'm catching up on admin but, as she reminded me, I used to bring that sort of thing home. I've said I'm doing it at work so that I don't disturb her new hobby but I'm not sure she's convinced. She's told me that once she's in that wrestling ring and covered in mud; nothing is going to distract her from ripping Mrs Jefferson's face off.

I like that she's found something new to keep her busy. The ring is more of an inflatable swimming pool really but I still wish she hadn't set it up in the front room as the mud gets splashed everywhere. Mind you I'm hoping it will help clear up her outbreak of blackheads.

I really need to get a grip on this infatuation though. I should have been getting home early today as there's no evening surgery but as I was about to leave I heard the shower being turned on in the little bathroom that's beside my office. I could hear Dr Moore singing. As much as the voice was beautiful and rhapsodic, I was concentrating more on the fact that there was a gorgeous, naked doctor only a wall away from me.

My imagination went into overdrive. I fantasised that I was a washing machine repairman and Dr Moore had a pumping

239

problem only I could fix. (I saw an adult film about that once while Mrs Bryant was away on a deer hunting weekend). I offer Dr Moore a good servicing. Oh God! As that beautiful form bends over to show me exactly where the problem is I get a glimpse of bare flesh. I gently reach forward, my fingers about to stroke the delicate, smooth skin and... The bloody phone rang. I was leaning right back in my chair with my eyes closed. The noise seemed so loud I jumped and both the chair and I went flying into the wall. Still, at least Dr Moore came running to my aid; dripping wet in just a towel. I feigned a blow to the head so that those delicate hands would gently caress my cranium. I wish now I'd said I'd hurt my groin.

Oh God; I so wanted to tug the towel off that luscious body. My hand did reach up, just like it had in the fantasy but then the blasted phone rang again and Dr Moore returned to the bathroom to dry off. Mrs Bryant was on the other end of the line, wanting me to pick up some raw braising steak on the way home. She likes to rip it with her teeth before a bout; it helps her get in the mood, so she says.

I started wondering why Dr Moore was having a shower at work. I supposed there could have been a problem at home with hot water but more likely, Dr Moore was going out somewhere. Oh my God, was there someone else? I had to know.

I didn't have far to follow. Dr Moore left the surgery and went straight across the road to The Smugglers. I gave it a few minutes and then wandered over myself. I stood outside and peaked in through the window. The place was practically deserted. I spied Dr Moore at the bar; alone, thank the Lord. I wondered if I should go in. I keep saying I'm going to suggest a drink together; wouldn't this have been the best time? I could pretend I'd decided to stop by for a drink too. Perhaps admitting my feelings would help control the infatuation.

But what would happen if Dr Moore was actually meeting someone? I don't think I'd be able to stand there and watch the two of them smiling at each other or leaving together. My disappointment would surely show on my face. Even if Dr Moore wasn't meeting anyone the place was too empty for me to talk about how I felt. The landlord and barmaid would be able to hear my every word.

I decided to wait around outside for a while to see if anyone showed up. I thought I was well concealed but Mr Jacobs from one of the apartments above my surgery saw me and came over to ask about his wife's foul-smelling discharge. I wasn't in the mood to give a diagnosis and told him she should contact her gynaecologist directly. He thought this odd as apparently the discharge is from her ear.

Several other people came over with different medical questions. Usually the harbour front is deserted but suddenly the world and his wife were here and all wanting medical advice. Honestly, it's no wonder Mrs Bryant and I never venture out of an evening for a meal or anything. Mind you she's not the daintiest of eaters. I saw her eat a quail whole once and then spit out the bones one by one. She was a bit over zealous and one landed on my plate, another on the neighbouring table and the last one she got the waiter in the eye with as he passed by holding a tray of cocktails. That turned into a very expensive evening for me. The dry-cleaning bill alone still makes me shiver when I think about it.

I decided to leave my vantage point outside the pub and head off home. I only needed to pop back to the surgery to write up these notes and grab my wallet to buy the raw braising steak, but before I'd even crossed the slipway I was accosted by old Miss Daniels. She hoisted up her skirt and asked if what I saw looked normal. Call me old-fashioned but I don't think crotchless panties and a tattoo saying, 'This way up' on an eighty-eight year old woman could ever look normal.

*

Everything was prepared for dinner when Lou heard a knock at her front door. She'd expected to be delayed and panicky as it had taken so long to get Maddie to bed. As soon as she knew nanny was coming over with Auntie Diana she wanted to stay up. It was a very sulky little girl who told her mother she hated her before hiding under the bed covers.

Diana walked in with a nice bottle of dry, white wine but she wasn't smiling and, to Lou, looked almost nervous.

"Are you okay?"

"Is your mum here yet," Diana whispered, looking down the hallway towards the lounge.

"No, why."

"I just wanted to apologise before she got here. I believe I caused an altercation at the supermarket today."

"A what?"

"An argument."

"Oh right. No it wasn't you at all, it was Joyce," Lou said, the anger rising again as she remembered.

"But it was about me, wasn't it?"

Lou walked down to the lounge and Diana followed.

"No it was Joyce spoiling for an argument and trying to get me sacked from my job."

"Oh she wouldn't do that."

"Yes she would, Diana. Your friend is a nasty bitch when it comes to me. Ask Muriel, she was there. She saw what happened."

"I'm sure Joyce is just looking out for me."

Lou stopped her search for a corkscrew in the kitchen drawer and looked at Diana.

"And what do you think I'm doing?" she asked, "Who's the person helping you with your list? Who's the person taking you to keep fit classes and baking lessons? Who's the person who wants to see you happy and enjoying life?"

"I know that and I'm grateful," Diana said, "I just don't want to hear that people have argued over me."

"You were an excuse to Joyce, Diana. She hates me and I hate her. You're not going to change that. I could tell you what she called me but I won't. I'm sure she's told you everything I said and more."

Diana remained silent and Lou knew she was right.

"All I ask," she continued, "Is that you don't assume I am to blame. I don't want you to end your friendship with Joyce; you've known her for years; but she obviously feels differently about your relationship with me and is trying to end it."

"Oh I'm sure she isn't…"

"She thinks you've gone crackers by the way. Thinks all this is a phase because of your sister's death."

"Still? I thought she'd got over that theory."

"Well anyway, let's not dwell on this shall we otherwise I shan't enjoy the evening."

"No, okay," Diana said, sitting down.

Lou found her corkscrew and uncorked Diana's wine.

"I really do appreciate all you've done," Diana said, "And I'm glad of our new friendship."

Lou smiled. "So am I," she said.

It was difficult to get rid of the atmosphere completely while just the two of them were in the room but as soon as Gloria showed up, apologising for being late, the mood lightened.

"I had trouble getting the car started," she said, "A rather nice young man gave me a jump."

"Is that why you're puffing?"

"No it isn't! I walked up the stairs."

"Why on earth did you do that," Lou asked, handing her mother a small glass of wine, "Is the lift out of order?"

"I thought I'd take a leaf out of your book," she replied, "I need a bit of exercise. I'm always in the car. I thought I'd start out slowly by climbing the four flights up here, but it was knackering. I had to stop half way."

"How was your class on Saturday, by the way," Diana asked Lou, "In all the confusion of the treasure hunt, I forgot to ask."

"Oh it was great," she told her, "I mean it was difficult but I really enjoyed it and Maddie liked the crèche area. I've done some of the exercises here in the evenings so that, hopefully, I'll feel less like a newcomer next week. I heard you didn't go back to yours on Monday."

Diana took a guilty sip of her wine.

"No," she said, "I haven't had a chance to buy a new exercise outfit yet; but I will go again; honestly."

"You should take mum with you," Lou called out, as she dished up the plates.

"I can't go Monday lunchtimes," Gloria said, "I'm working. Not that we're exactly busy then. Besides, I'm not really built for jumping about."

Lou put the plates on the table and the three ladies sat down to eat.

"I'm not sure the village hall is the best place for the exercise classes," Diana said, halfway through the meal, "This is

244

delicious by the way. Maybe if they were able to convert the current toilets in some way to incorporate a shower; you know; improve the facilities. That would benefit everyone. Perhaps Joyce would reconsider using the place for a kids' club then."

"Did you manage to speak to the headmistress at the school," Lou asked, "About using that for an afterschool club? I told her to contact you."

"Yes," Diana said, "And it's a no go, I'm afraid. I believe the caretaker said he wouldn't be able to keep it open; I'm not sure why."

"Didn't the headmistress tell you?"

"No. I think she was surprised herself."

"That's a shame," Lou said, "I thought it would be fine. The school's always open early for the breakfast club. Oh well, I'm sure you can come up with somewhere else."

"That's just it, there doesn't seem to be anywhere."

"What, nowhere?" Lou queried.

Diana sighed. "All of the suggestions have come up against problems; the hall, the school; even the vicarage."

"What about the pub?" chipped in Gloria, "Jamie would jump at the chance of some new faces?"

Lou shook her head.

"Probably not a good idea for a kids group," she told her.

"No," Gloria agreed," I suppose not."

"Here's a thought, Diana," Lou said, "What about one of the empty shops below here?"

"What about them?"

"Maybe one of those could be used as a place for a kids clubs. They already have kitchens and toilets. I'm sure the council would be glad of one of them being used in some way. Aside from Dr Bryant's surgery, they're empty. I don't know

245

who actually owns them but I'm sure your group could find out."

Diana grinned. "That's a great idea," she said, "I'll start investigating that tomorrow and bring it up at the next meeting."

"Probably shouldn't mention to Joyce that it was my idea," Lou said, and winked.

"You can tell her I suggested the pub," Gloria said, "I don't care. Do you know; we've got a talk going on in there tomorrow, about beetles? I hate creepy crawlies. I hope they don't bring along any live ones."

"They probably won't," Lou told her, "It's for the rare, local beetle isn't it? They must be too precious to transport around. I'm sure it will just be photographs."

"I hope so," Gloria said, "At least it should attract a few more people which will be good for Jamie."

"He seems a very nice man," Diana said, remembering Muriel's comment at the weekend, "Does he not have anyone special in his life?"

"Aside from me you mean?" Gloria joked.

"He's never mentioned anyone," Lou said, topping up Diana's glass, "A shame really as he is such a lovely guy."

"Yes," Diana replied, and smiled.

"It's not easy trying to meet someone these days anyway," Gloria said, "Believe me; I've tried."

"Believe me, we know," Lou told her.

"Well it isn't. I've tried it all; speed dating, online dating…"

"Hanging around outside pub doorways dating."

"Oi you," Gloria said, "You make me sound like a prostitute. You may have cooked a lovely meal but that doesn't mean you can be cheeky."

"I've not had to date since before I was married," Diana

admitted, "The thought of doing that now is terrifying."

"But you're going to try," Lou told her, and turning to her mother added, "It's one of the things on Diana's list."

"It is a scary world out there, Diana," Gloria said, "Do you know, when I first tried online dating I had a man send me a photograph of himself wearing some kind of see-through rubber dress."

"And what did he wear on your date?" Lou asked, grinning.

"I sent a polite reply to his e mail," Gloria said, firmly, "Telling him there are probably better sites for him to be a member of rather than a dating one."

"I don't know what I would have done if that had been me," Diana said, "Of course, I haven't got a computer."

"Oh that wasn't the worst of it," Gloria continued.

"Mum, stop it. We're trying to get Diana to go dating not make her join a convent for the remainder of her life."

Gloria shook her head.

"She needs to be prepared if she's entering the dating scene. A lot of men that advertise on the websites are only looking for sex, not a relationship. I've been sent so many photographs of nobs I've had to save them onto a separate memory stick."

Diana's mouth opened in shock.

"Shall I clear the plates if everyone's finished?" Lou asked, trying not to laugh.

"Why can't dating be like the old days," Gloria sighed, sitting back in her chair, "You meet a man and you 'walk out' together? You take his arm as you stroll down the street and he opens doors for you."

"And how far back are we going?" Lou asked, taking a tray out of the oven, "Before women had the right to vote?"

"Diana knows what I mean," Gloria said, "Even thirty, forty

years ago it was a more innocent time. Sex wasn't all in your face like it is now on TV programmes and posters. The internet has ruined dating as far as I'm concerned. People want to meet up just for sex. Why doesn't anyone want to just date? I'd love to go out for an evening with a man who only expects a kiss at the end of the evening and not someone who is spending all night wondering how he can get into my knickers."

"It's not all like that," Lou said, bringing dessert over.

"Well it seems like it to me."

"I'm not sure my going dating sounds like a good idea now," Diana said.

Lou sighed.

"Great mum. Now look what you've done."

"I didn't mean it was impossible; just harder than it used to be," Gloria sighed, "I'd like to meet a man during an evening out; you know; somewhere where there's a crowd of people all enjoying a few drinks. He'd offer to buy me one and we'd start chatting in a natural environment. Is that so much to ask?"

"Perhaps there's somewhere nearby that holds a singles night you could go to for that sort of evening," Lou told her.

Gloria sat up in her chair.

"I should get Jamie to hold one at the pub," she said, "I'll suggest that to him tomorrow."

"Great," Lou said, "And I can bring Diana along."

Diana looked petrified. She downed the wine in her glass.

Gloria happily picked up her spoon.

"These smell good," she said, looking at the dessert.

"It's what I made at baking class last night," Lou told her, "I've just warmed them through."

"I think going on that course is the best thing you've ever done, Lou," her mother told her, "How are you enjoying it,

Diana?"

Diana sighed. "Not very much," she said, "Mrs Bailey got very cross with me yesterday when my flapjack began leaking at the end of the lesson."

"Yes it's horrible getting old, isn't it," Gloria said, absently. Diana looked confused.

"Er, mum; could you get the custard for me?" Lou asked, trying not to laugh.

Gloria got up from the table and Lou decided to change the subject.

"I've got a bit of a decision to make, workwise," she said.

"They don't want you to increase your hours again, do they?" Gloria asked, coming back to the table with the custard.

Lou took a deep breath. "No, Simon wants me to apply for a place on the management training programme."

"That's wonderful," Diana said, "Congratulations."

Gloria sat down, a confused look on her face.

"So it does mean more hours then."

"Sorry?"

"If they want you to be a manager, it will mean longer hours," Gloria said, "Weekends, late evenings, that type of thing."

"Well it will probably mean a change of hours, yes;" Lou conceded, "But I'll be the person in charge once I'm trained up. It will be my store so I'll be the one to sort out work times."

"Exactly," Diana said, "Well done you. You really deserve it. You practically run that store as it is. I rarely ever see the actual manager."

Diana was obviously excited for Lou but her mother was still looking questioningly at her.

"What about Maddie? Have you thought of her?"

"No mum," Lou replied, "She slipped my mind while I was thinking about me."

"There's no need to be sarcastic. It's a perfectly reasonable question. What about Maddie? She barely gets to see you now."

"That's unfair, mum," Lou said, "I have to work. Besides, she's full time at school now. I have to think of the future; our future. I'm on my own. It would be nice to have a bit of a career and earn a bit more money. Who knows, maybe I could afford a mortgage at some stage or just be able to save up a bit of cash to start replacing some of this crap furniture I've had for years; a new sofa or a dining table that isn't stained and has four matching chairs."

"But Tony provides for Maddie."

"So? And what if he and Cheryl have children together? He'll have less money to splash about. He's very generous at the moment but he won't be if he has more mouths to feed. This is a great opportunity mum. Don't you think I can do it?"

"Of course you can do it," Gloria said, reaching over and placing her hand on top of Lou's, "You can you do it blindfolded with one hand tied behind your back. I just want you to think of the problems before rushing off into this."

"Believe me I've thought about all the problems. Anyway, it's just putting in an application. There's no guarantee yet that I'll be accepted."

"Well then," Gloria smiled, raising her glass, "Here's to you."

Diana grinned and raised her glass as well; which was still empty.

At the end of the evening Lou and Diana waved Gloria off as she made her way downstairs; using the lift. Before returning to her own place Diana turned back to Lou.

"Thanks again for a delicious meal," she said.

"You're welcome."

Diana smiled. "Do you know, I think my list of things to do is probably working out better for you than for me?"

"Sorry?"

"Well, look at you; Little Miss Organised with your cooking and cleaning and getting fit. Now you have the confidence to embark on a new career too. It's all going well for you."

"I'm sorry," Lou said, looking shocked, "I never meant for…"

Diana chuckled. "I'm not complaining," she told her, "It's just an observation. Maybe it wasn't just me whose life needed a good kick. Have you noticed how much you've been smiling recently? I'm very happy for you."

"Thanks Diana," Lou replied, grinning, "I guess you're right. I have been enjoying myself these last few weeks. Fresh starts for both of us, eh?"

"Why not?"

"Next stop; boyfriends," Lou winked.

Diana winced. "Your mother really scared me tonight."

"Yes she has that effect on people."

"I meant about dating."

"I'm sure she's exaggerating. Besides, if Jamie does hold a singles night in the pub, that could end up being fun to go to. We don't have to look around for dates we can just watch everyone else doing it."

"I don't know."

"Come on," Lou said, "We'll be able to watch my mum try and get a date. For you it will be like watching the master at work."

Diana laughed. "Okay, maybe," she said.

"We can get a makeover beforehand and that will be two ticks on your list."

"Now that's an idea I do like. Well, I'll say goodnight. You know, maybe you will meet someone in The Smugglers. Someone you've not thought of before."

"I think Joe's a little old for me," Lou joked.

Diana smiled as she thought about Jamie. She really hoped she'd planted a seed.

*

Jamie had left Gloria in charge of the bar while he prepared the food for the group coming to hear the talk about the Tenhamshire Lesser-Spotted Beetle. Doug had called yesterday with an idea of numbers and Jamie was making an effort with the sandwiches, doing chicken, ham and cheese in both white and brown bread.

Gloria poked her head round the corner.

"More people are beginning to arrive," she said.

Jamie covered the last plate in foil, put it in the fridge with the others and returned to the bar. He was surprised to see six people waiting to be served. Gloria was currently getting an order of drinks from a group of five.

"No just an orange juice for me," he heard, "I'll have a lime cordial. A soda water over here, thanks."

They weren't exactly going to make Jamie's fortune. Still, people in the pub, was people in the pub. Aside from Old Joe, who had come in later today for his regular two pints, they were his only customers. As he finished serving the six Doug came in with the main party. The group were carrying posters and pamphlets; badges and collecting tins.

They really want to save this beetle, Jamie thought.

"Hello Doug," Gloria called over to him, waving her hands and breasts in his general direction.

Doug raised his hand and then quickly turned his attention back to a young, blonde next to him whose buxomness gave Gloria's a run for her money. She was just placing an aquarium-like structure down on one of the tables. It was full of greenery.

"Are they okay in there?" Doug said to her.

"I think so," she replied, "I was very careful carrying them in."

"Bless you." Doug patted her gently on the shoulder and she grinned.

Jamie walked across to Gloria.

"Blimey," he said, "Doug's brought a live one in."

"Yes I can see that," she snapped.

"He said the other day he had a couple of breeding females."

"Alright, don't rub it in," Gloria told him, adding ice to a glass in a rather aggressive manner.

Jamie looked at her, a puzzled expression on his face.

"I was talking about what's in the tank," he said.

"It's what's holding it that's getting more attention. My God, look at the way she's behaving in front of him."

Jamie looked over to where the girl was crouched down looking into the tank.

"It's disgusting," Gloria continued, "Why doesn't she just shove those huge tits into his face and be done with it?"

Jamie couldn't help smiling to himself. Doug came over.

"I think we're all set," he said, brightly, looking around him.

A projector and screen had already been moved into position while the pamphlets and badges were distributed to each table. The young, buxom girl walked up to the bar.

253

"We're probably ready to go, Doug," she said, looking up at him, admiringly.

Doug looked down and smiled warmly at her, the lines on his weather-beaten face creasing up like lots of little grins. He placed an arm around her shoulder.

"Isn't it wonderful that the young want to get involved in projects like this?" he said to Jamie and Gloria, "Not just us old fogeys."

"Speak for yourself!" Gloria told him, firmly.

"Martha here is in charge of the breeding programme."

"That's obvious."

"She's brought in the only two breeding females that we've got in captivity. They're in that aquarium over there."

"Perhaps I should stay with them," Martha said, and returned to the tank. Doug watched her go.

"She's an amazing young woman," he continued, "So dedicated. I'm thinking of asking her onto my South America trip. I'd love to take Martha up the Amazon."

"She looks the sort to let you, too," Gloria spat, and walked off to the kitchen; leaving behind a very bewildered-looking Doug.

"She's just gone to get the sandwiches," Jamie said, trying not to laugh, "I'll go help her; won't be a sec."

Gloria must have gone right out the back of the building as she was nowhere to be seen in the kitchen. Jamie collected all the plates of sandwiches together from the fridge and took them out front. The talk had already begun so he had to keep ducking and apologising as he placed a plate on each table.

After twenty minutes the speaker took a break and everyone came up to the bar to order drinks. Gloria hadn't yet returned so Jamie found himself dealing with the first rush he'd had in a long time. When the next speaker started up he busied himself with clearing away the empty glasses.

It was just as he was picking up Old Joe's empty glass after waving the old man off that the speaker said, "And now we'll take a look at the actual beetles themselves," and there was a sharp cry from Martha.

"The slats come open in the lid," she called out, frantically moving bits of the greenery around the tank, "I think they've escaped."

"Oh my God," Doug said, "Nobody move. We've got to find them. They're the last two breeding females."

Jamie had stopped dead with the pint glass in his hand as soon as Martha called out. It was now that Gloria decided to walk back into the bar, carrying an empty tray.

"Sorry I was so long," she said, "Let me help clear up."

As she walked behind the bar she saw something move on the countertop. It was one of those moments seen in slow motion. Jamie knew what Gloria was going to do but wasn't able to stop her. She screamed and brought the metal tray crashing down onto the bar. As she did this Jamie took a step forward to stop her and heard a sickening crunch. When he lifted his foot, all he saw was a lesser-spotted mess.

All hell broke loose after that. People ran round looking at the squashed beetles. Some were shouting, others were crying. One man suggested mouth to mouth resuscitation. Doug marched over to Jamie who was now standing behind the bar with Gloria, watching one of the speakers scraping bits of beetle off of the tray, while sobbing.

"What the hell is wrong with you two?" he shouted, "You've managed to wipe out an entire species."

"I'm sorry," Jamie replied, "It was an accident."

255

"An accident? A whole species gone forever and you call it an accident?"

"Now just wait a minute," Gloria shouted back, "If this was such an endangered species what were you doing bringing them in here in that tank with you in the first place? It sounds like a bloody stupid thing to do; like putting all your eggs in one basket."

"We haven't got any eggs," Doug whined. Gloria ignored him.

"If anyone is to blame then it's her over there; the one with torpedoes for tits. She let them out. If they were so precious she should have kept a closer eye on them instead of giving you the big doe-eyes all of the time."

Doug opened his mouth to respond but stopped briefly as what Gloria had said sunk in. He smiled.

"Does she; does she really?" he asked.

He remembered the reason for his anger and the smile dropped from his face.

"Anyway," he said, "Whoever is to blame this is still a catastrophe. I think it's best if I start drinking in The Red Lion from now on."

"You do that!" Gloria told him.

He turned and made his way over to Martha. He scooped her into his big arms and she cried on his shoulder.

Gloria made a huffing sound as she looked over at him.

"That's another bug that needs squishing," she said; and walked back out to the kitchen.

Chapter 13

Lou was still feeling self-conscious even though it was the second time she'd been out for a run this week. She felt everyone around her was watching as she jogged by. Perhaps she was doing too much too soon but after her second Saturday in Donna's class at the sports centre she felt she wanted something else to challenge her during the week. Doing the same exercises from Saturday at home wasn't ideal; especially living in an apartment. There was a lot of stomping across the floor and jumping up and down and poor, old Edna Haney from the floor below had come rushing up last Thursday, not sure if Lou was being attacked or having aggressive sex (her words). Donna had suggested jogging and sold Lou a very expensive pair of trainers.

Weaving her way through the Wednesday shoppers on the high street, Lou made a mental note to get out the street map and plan a better route for future running sessions, somewhere she could be a bit less conspicuous. She was puffing heavily when she returned to the supermarket ten minutes later.

"I always get the girls panting," Chris leered, as she walked through the front door, "It's going commando in tight jeans that does it."

Lou was too tired to respond and headed off towards the staffroom. She'd only got halfway across the floor when Chris called out,

"Just one zip in my trousers stands between you and all the pleasures of a meat feast."

An old lady beside Lou stopped dead in her tracks and picked a box out of her basket.

"I've gone right off this pizza now," she said, and threw it onto the nearest shelf.

The shower was welcoming and as she let the warm water pour over her, Lou's mind drifted to the coming weekend. It was going to be busy. Jamie had listened to her mother's suggestion and Friday evening was going to be Singles Night at The Smugglers. Lou hoped, for his sake, that it was a success. She liked Jamie and admired him for his efforts to improve the pub's takings but felt all his little schemes so far for attracting new customers to the bar were a little amateurish. When was he going to stop playing at being a publican and start looking at things seriously? He surely couldn't continue on for much longer the way things were. What if he sold up and moved away? Lou realised she'd miss him; a lot.

The only problem with Singles Night was that Lou had to work the following day. Saturday was Pete Crick Day at the supermarket. She'd already worked hard on getting everything prepared. Jester's advertising department had taken care of the publicity but what the individual stores did was up to them. The posters and cardboard cut outs of Pete to display in the store were ordered, the local newspaper had confirmed a reporter would be there and a separate audio system had been hired so that Pete could give a speech using a proper microphone and not rely on the shop's crappy public address system. Lou had also managed to borrow a DVD projector to show Pete's best film, 'The Theft of Purity' on a loop throughout the day. Simon had offered to get the film, which; seeing as it only had to be ordered online, wasn't exactly too taxing. Perhaps, Lou thought; if Jamie were more organised like this he'd have a successful pub by now.

She switched off the shower and dried herself. As she wiped

258

the towel through her hair Lou wondered if she should have it cut shorter for Friday night. As she was working Saturday this week Lou had taken Friday off and she and Diana were going to Tenham for the day to have a makeover before going onto Jamie's singles evening. If Diana managed to meet a man then there were only two things left on her list to do; work with animals and broaden horizons.

Working with animals was sorted, Lou thought, as she dressed. Maddie was looking forward to going to the zoo. As for the last one, Lou wasn't sure if she would have the time to go on a cruise, especially if she was about to embark on training to become a store manager. She'd put her application in last week and was now just waiting to hear if she'd been accepted. Besides, there was also Maddie to think about. Diana hadn't mentioned taking her with them.

Anyway, Lou thought to herself as she dressed, if Diana did manage to find herself a man on Friday she'd probably end up going away with him instead; and that was fine.

Back out on the shop floor Lou was in charge again, Simon having taken the day off. Precious was on the till and one of the part-timers was stacking shelves. For the first time Lou felt she really could run this place herself. Of course it certainly wasn't set in stone that she would get the chance to run this particular store, even if she passed the course. That was one of the concerns she had. If she was assigned a store, how far away would it be? Would she and Maddie have to move? If so, Lou realised how many people she would miss around here; Diana, her mother; Jamie. Yes, Jamie. It felt to Lou like the two of them were destined to be parted; either by his failure or her success. She really didn't want that to happen. Lou shook the thoughts from her head. All this was a long way off. Right now she had a supermarket to run. She walked over to the storeroom.

"Terry," she called through the door, "How are you getting on with tidying those back shelves in there?"

The sound of boxes toppling over and tin cans rolling across the floor met her ears. After a brief silence a voice called back, "Getting there."

"That's great." Lou made a mental note that she may need to discount the next batch of tinned sweetcorn before they went on the shelves.

Jamie walked into the shop as Lou was straightening the bouquets of cut flowers. Perhaps it was just because he was so recently in her thoughts but she jumped at the sound of his voice.

"That's sweet of you," he said, as she turned to face him, holding a small mixed bouquet, "No one's ever bought me flowers before."

"And they still haven't," she replied, moving the bunch out of his reach, "What do you want?"

"Do you know; it's the polite, customer service that keeps me coming back here."

Lou grinned. "Sorry," she said, "I meant to say, what can I do for you, sir?"

"That's better. I want to pick your brains."

"I'm afraid Jesters doesn't offer that facility. Have you considered the charity shop in the high street? They're a funny lot up there."

Jamie laughed. "I'm looking for ideas," he said, "And you're the girl who usually has the good ones."

"Flattery won't get you anywhere; you've still got to buy something."

Jamie took a step forwards and leaned towards her. Lou almost gasped but in a second he'd stood back again, the bunch of flowers Lou had been holding now in his hand.

"Right," he said, "I'll take these. Now then, Friday night's singles evening; I was thinking of a red rose in a vase on each table."

Lou regained her composure, not really understanding what had just happened to her.

"Erm, well; that idea's okay, although it could prove to be expensive," Lou indicated the bunch of flowers in Jamie's hand, "The Carnations in there are a lot cheaper than roses. A flower's a flower after all."

"You old romantic, you. What about food? Do you think I should do some kind of free buffet?"

"Maybe you should just stick to snacks; crisps and nuts, or maybe some popcorn in bowls on the tables. If the evening goes well you could always look into doing food another time. Perhaps you could hold a proper date night for all those people you bring together on Friday."

Jamie smiled and stared into Lou's eyes.

"Brains and beauty," he said.

She suddenly felt embarrassed and looked down at the flowers in Jamie's hand. She hadn't noticed before but he had rather nice fingers; not too long or too fat and his nails, although short were trimmed neatly and not bitten.

"That sounds like a great plan to me," he continued, "I guess I'd better pay for these and get back. I've left your mum alone with Old Joe."

Lou looked up again and smiled.

"She'll probably be sitting on his lap by now, getting his credit card information."

261

Jamie laughed. "I should tell her you said that. Mind you, she'll be barking up the wrong tree with poor Joe."

"What, is he gay?"

"No I meant about the credit card. I doubt he's even got a bank account let alone a credit card."

"Oh right. You don't have to buy those, by the way," Lou said, indicating the flowers, "I was only joking."

"Nope, I'm willing to pay for your time Ms Turner."

Jamie walked over to the till. Lou continued with her tidying. When he came back he handed Lou the bunch.

"Keep them in water until you get home tonight," he said.

He winked at her and left the shop.

Lou looked down at the bunch of flowers in her hand and smiled.

*

"So," said Joyce, to the committee members around her dining table, "I think we can safely say that this idea of Mrs Carlton's of trying to start up a group to help the local delinquents is now dead in the water. Perhaps we should move on to my original…"

Diana raised her hand.

"Yes?" Joyce said, in a very tiresome voice.

"One thing, no two things now actually," Diana said, "Firstly I'd like to say that my; or rather our," she indicated around the table, "Idea was to help the youth of the area. There was no mention of delinquents by any of us; bar one."

She shot a look at Joyce. Joyce opened her mouth to reply but Diana continued.

"Furthermore, the idea is not dead just because we have been turned down by the village hall, school and the vicarage."

"Some people would take that as a sign," Joyce said. Diana

ignored her.

"As most of you are aware, I live along the harbour front. Now, up until the smuggler caves were closed off to tourists, the area was vibrant. Since then it has become an area that not many of us ever visit, which is a shame as it's beautiful down there."

"Is this just an advert for your home or is there a point to all this?"

"There are a number of premises along the harbour front that are currently empty. I've discovered that the one right beside the doctor's surgery is owned by the council who are keen to either sell or lease it out at a very reasonable rate. I propose we speak to them about using it to house a youth club. The property is relatively new and has all facilities catered for; i.e. toilet and kitchen facilities. Now does anyone have a contact at the council whom we could ask?"

"I hardly think…" Joyce began but was interrupted by another member of the group.

"My friend works in Housing. She might not be the right person herself, but I'm sure she would know who to ask."

"Excellent," Diana said, "If you could ask her before the next meeting it would give us something to discuss next time."

Diana turned back to Joyce. Joyce smiled.

"Perhaps this would be a good time to break for tea?" she turned towards the serving hatch and shouted, "Muriel!"

Once the meeting was over and the other ladies had left, Joyce, Diana and Muriel sat down in the lounge with a fresh pot of tea. Although south facing; with the net curtains and highly patterned wallpaper, Joyce's lounge was never bathed in sunlight. The glass-fronted display units that were jammed full of knickknacks were made of dark mahogany and these too, like

263

the wallpaper; ate up any light that dared to enter. Not that there was much sunlight today anyway. The black clouds outside were threatening a heavy rain shower.

"You went very quiet in the meeting today," Diana said. Joyce held up her hand to stop her.

"I never discuss meetings once they've finished, Diana. In them, we are merely colleagues; now, we are friends enjoying a cup of tea together on a Wednesday afternoon," she picked up a biscuit and put it back down on the plate again, "And as a friend, Moo; I can say these biscuits aren't your best batch."

Muriel just smiled kindly and ate hers.

"I hear there's a singles night at the pub near you," she said, to Diana.

"Yes, that's right, this Friday. Would you like to come, Muriel?"

Joyce's cup banged down into the saucer.

"Don't tell me you're going?" she said.

Diana nodded. Joyce placed her teacup and saucer back onto the tray on the coffee table.

"I've heard it all now," she said, "I suppose this was another of Louise Turner's hare-brained ideas."

"No; it was her mum's."

Joyce opened her mouth in astonishment.

"Actually it wasn't," Diana said, "I mean the evening in the pub was her idea but meeting someone new was mine. I put it on my list."

"Why on earth would you want another man at your age?"

"I'm sixty-seven Joyce not a hundred and four. I'm lonely. If I'm lucky enough to live to be eighty, that's another thirteen years of loneliness."

"You're not lonely," Joyce told her, "You've got us."

264

Diana couldn't help smiling.

"That's not the same thing," she replied.

"What can you get from a man that you can't get from us?"

"I would have thought that was obvious," Muriel chipped in.

"Thank you, Moo! We don't need the conversation reduced to that sort of level."

"It's not about sex," Diana said.

Joyce baulked.

"It's the companionship I think. Having someone special in your life is different from friendship. Take us three for example. Remember when I said we should go to the theatre a few months back? Did we ever do it; no. We couldn't get a date we all had free, then we couldn't agree on which play to see. With a partner those things don't matter. I could say, 'let's go to the theatre,' and he'll reply, 'okay, I'll book the tickets.' It's things like that I miss."

"I don't remember you and Richard swanning out every night," Joyce said.

"I don't want to be out every night. Richard and I had lots of Socials with his work but when we weren't out we were at home together," Diana smiled as she thought about a past memory, "I think it's Sunday mornings when I miss Richard the most. When we lived up here on the hill we'd sit in the conservatory on a Sunday morning with the newspapers. We had the radio on quietly in the background and, even though we weren't talking, we were both there together, sharing the experience; does that make sense to you? Now I hate the radio of a Sunday morning."

"I know what you mean," Muriel said.

"How could you, Moo?" Joyce threw at her, "You've never been married."

"I'm talking about being alone," Muriel replied, "After dad had passed on and mum was sick, I spent most of my time running up and down the stairs for her, but Sunday mornings was our relaxing day together. It was similar to Diana. I'd take the newspapers up to her room and we'd sit together reading them. Ever since she died, I no longer read the Sunday newspaper."

"Well I don't get it," Joyce said, "I have to throw Norman out into the garden to get a bit of peace on a Sunday. Besides, you can't feel sorry for yourselves. It's sad when someone passes on but you've got to deal with it and move on."

"And that's what I'm doing," Diana told her.

"No, you're just trying to replace Richard."

"Of course I'm not," Diana snapped, "Nobody can replace him. But he's dead and I'm not."

"Diana!"

"What? It's true. My life didn't end because my husband's did. I'm my own person. Not that I always felt that way when we were together. At his work parties Richard would introduce me as, 'The wife, Diana' rather than, "This is Diana, my wife."

"What's the difference?" Joyce asked.

Diana sighed. "That's what Richard used to say. There's a big difference. The first way I was a wife first before being an actual person; a commodity Richard possessed; but the second way I was a living, breathing individual who just happened to be married to Richard."

"Humph," Joyce said, under her breath, "Silly."

"You can think that," Diana told her, "But I know I'm right. At Richard's funeral none of his work colleagues came up and spoke to me. They didn't see a person in mourning, all they saw was that woman Richard lived with; that woman who used to

266

hand out canapés at his parties and who was still doing the same thing at the funeral. They felt I was there for them that day, whereas they should have been there for me. I never heard from any of them again afterwards."

Diana sipped her tea. Neither Joyce nor Muriel could think of anything to say.

"I mean it when I say my life hasn't ended," Diana said, once she had placed her empty cup and saucer on the tray, "I spent years after the accident wondering what we would be doing together if only Richard hadn't gone to Tenham that day. After I gave him a good send-off I stayed at home and missed him every day, but I'm not going to live in the past anymore. He wouldn't want me to either."

"That was a lovely service," Muriel said, remembering, "And that funeral director did you proud. It's a shame he was so expensive. I couldn't afford him for mum and dad."

"I thought him very expensive too," Diana agreed, "Mind you, I paid for the funeral on my Jester's credit card. I got so many points I bought a new fridge freezer."

Diana and Muriel caught each other's eye and started laughing. Joyce remained tight lipped.

"Is that the one that broke down just out of its guarantee," Muriel asked.

"That's the one," Diana replied, "I think Richard was getting his own back.

"When you two have quite finished," Joyce said, firmly, "Honestly, you're howling like a couple of banshees. It's death we're talking about here."

"No it's not," Diana told her, "We're talking about life; my life. I still have one and I'm going to a singles night in the local pub. I probably won't meet anyone. I may get cold feet and not

want to meet anyone but regardless, I'll be having an evening out with friends and that's fun."

"Friends? You mean Louise and her mother?"

"That's right."

Joyce shook her head and sighed.

"With those two influencing you I suppose we should just be glad that there's no chance of you having a baby."

The atmosphere of the room changed immediately.

"Yes," Diana said, quietly, "I'm always aware of that."

"I'm sorry," Joyce said, "I didn't mean…"

"I know."

The room fell silent. It was two very long minutes before Muriel looked at her watch.

"I guess I should be going."

"Me too," Diana said, standing up, "My plant I keep by my front door is looking peaky. I must go and buy some plant food."

As they moved towards the door to the hallway so it opened and Norman poked his head in.

"Where are the plasters, dear heart?" he asked, "I've snipped myself on the scissors while cutting out those articles from the local paper you wanted."

Joyce tutted.

"Oh Norman, you're so annoying at times," she turned to her friends, "Could you see yourselves out?"

They both nodded. Joyce pushed her husband out of the room.

"Come on," she said to him, "I'd better get the first aid box out."

The two of them disappeared down towards the kitchen.

"You'd better not have bled all over my kitchen table!"

The kitchen door closed behind them. Muriel and Diana smiled at each other.

"I like your idea of using the shop on the harbour for the youngsters," Muriel said, as they made their way to the front door, "I hope they let you use it."

"Me too."

"It was a shame about the school," Muriel continued, "Joyce knows the caretaker as well. I'm surprised he said no."

"Joyce knows the caretaker?"

"Yes, he's the son of someone she knows, I can't remember who. I believe he owed her a favour. Oh well, let's hope we have better luck with the shop. We'll find out at the next meeting."

Muriel opened the door and put up her umbrella before walking out into the rain. Diana did the same but her mind wasn't on the next meeting. She was thinking back over the previous ones and some of the things said. Surely Joyce hadn't…Diana shook her head. No, she was being silly.

*

Robert put his key in the lock and opened the door.

"Hello love, had a good day?" Grace called, from the lounge.

"Ye-es."

As usual for a Wednesday evening, a lamb chop dinner was waiting on the dining table. Grace rattled on for ages about the puddles in the car park after the heavy rain earlier, but Robert wasn't really listening. Their attempt at watching the porn film, 'The Theft of My Virginity' hadn't ended well. They'd not discussed the issue of sex since and Robert was worried that Grace thought he'd given up on the idea of spicing things up. He hadn't, but he wanted to make sure the next thing they tried didn't end up with another part of him suffering pain. The new position had caused a bad back, outdoor sex had left him in agony with a swollen testicle and the porn film initiated an earache with Grace's lengthy discussion afterwards about lack of screenplay, direction and cinematography. Robert was ready now to try something new, but what?

After dinner he stacked the dishwasher and settled down in the armchair with the latest edition of the local paper. Grace sat across from him on the settee, knitting some blue monstrosity that was apparently going to be a cardigan for their recently born great nephew.

Robert didn't really know why he read the local paper at all but Grace always picked one up so he usually ended up having a browse through. It seemed to always be full of bad news such as various local crimes and the latest cutbacks by the council. There were never any happy or heart-warming stories these days and it left him with a feeling of depression about the state of the local community. It probably wasn't the right impression to have. At the end of the day, he supposed, crime sold more newspapers than an article about who had won the church raffle.

He glanced at the obituaries, which didn't take long. People did seem to go on living around here. Robert wasn't a morbid kind of guy but he did enjoy reading an obituary; learning about someone else's life; what they did, who they were. The last decent one in the local rag was for Selina Johnson, the old lady who had owned the parade of arcades next door where the new block of apartments was nearing completion. She was a formidable woman; managing to prevent her little empire getting swept away with the earlier redevelopment of the harbour.

All change now though, Robert sighed as he thought about the new building next door. He'd never used the old arcades and they had been a bit of an eyesore, but even so; Robert worried that this new development was just the start of a lot more to come. With The Smugglers hardly seeing a customer and the teashop next to it now up for sale, how long would it be before those beautiful old buildings were knocked down to make way for something new?

"There's not a lot of cheerfulness in there this week, is there," Grace said, having heard Robert's sigh.

"Not really, no," he replied.

He turned the page to the advertisements. One instantly caught his eye. The Smugglers was having a date night for single people. Robert's mind went into overdrive.

"Grace, we haven't got anything planned for Friday night have we?"

She thought for a second before replying,

"No, there's nothing special on. I was going to get steaks for dinner as usual."

"Great," Robert said.

Grace beamed. "I'm so glad you like them," she replied, I always think it's due to the coating I put on before grilling."

"I didn't mean the meat, I meant good about Friday night. We're going to go out."

"Oh lovely; we've not been out in ages."

"We're going to The Smugglers," Robert said.

"Oh," Grace's face fell, "That's not very far away really is it."

Robert showed her the advertisements page in the newspaper.

"We're going for this."

Grace squinted at the page.

"Two-for-one on contact lens solution? Do they sell that

there?"

"Next to that advert."

"Erotic, Oriental massages; couples only. Call Bendy Brenda on…"

"Oh for God's sake; I mean the singles night at the pub!"

Grace looked puzzled.

"We're not single," she said.

"I know, but we could pretend to be."

This did nothing to enlighten his wife.

"We could return to our first date all over again," Robert suggested, "I could see you in the pub and chat you up, just like I did all those years ago."

"If memory serves me correctly you were too nervous to ask me out and built up a bit too much Dutch courage; resulting in you throwing up into my handbag."

Robert squirmed in his chair.

"We don't have to recreate the actual event," he said, "I think it would be nice for me to see the most beautiful woman in the room and walk over and start talking to her."

Grace smiled. "I guess it would be nice to have a night out," she said.

Robert grinned. "We don't have to be ourselves either if we don't want," he told her, "We could create new pasts for ourselves. I could be a pilot; you could be a well-known actress, doing a show at the local theatre."

Grace looked confused again.

"Why would a well-known actress come to our tiny, little theatre?"

"Okay, forget that bit. We can just be ourselves but act like we've only just met. I'll come over to you and buy us both a drink. We can relax, have a bit of a laugh and then…well; see where the evening takes us."

Grace smiled again but it very quickly disappeared.

"Hang on, what if we see someone we know?" she said.

"It's unlikely," Robert replied, "Who do we know who would go out to a singles night?"

"There's bound to be someone."

"Well, we'll pretend we didn't know it was a singles night. If anyone asks, you can say we decided to come out for a drink together."

Grace still looked worried.

"I'm not sure," she said, "It's starting to sound complicated. I'm not good with lies."

"Don't worry. I'll come over and chat to you in the pub straightaway," Robert told her, "You won't be on your own. No one will come over to you before I get there."

Grace threw down her knitting.

"Oh thanks very much for that," she said, miffed, "A second ago I was going to be the most beautiful woman in the room, now no one is going to want me. Why not? What's wrong with me?"

"Grace, I didn't mean it like that," Robert told her, exasperated, "Look, we're going to go out to the pub on Friday evening and we're going to have a good time; okay?"

"When you put it like that, how can I refuse?" Grace replied, sarcastically.

That was as close to an affirmative response as Robert was going to get.

Chapter 14

"I'm worried about my Charlie."

Lou almost swerved the car into a ditch.

"Sorry?"

"My goldfish, Charlie," Diana said, "He doesn't seem to swim around his bowl like he used to. He either sits at the bottom or floats near the top."

"Oh, well perhaps he's just old," Lou suggested, still reeling from Diana's initial sentence.

"I think that lady from the butterfly house, Josie, was right. I shouldn't just have one fish. He's lonely. I'm in the apartment a lot less than I used to be. I think he knows it."

"Come on Diana, fish are known for having hardly any brain. He doesn't even know who you are."

"Well he knows when feeding time is. He's always waiting for his food in the exact corner where I put it. I actually think he's very intelligent; just lonely."

"Well you can buy him a playmate at the pet shop today after we've had our makeovers," Lou told her, "And if you find yourself a partner tonight at The Smugglers then you'll both be happy."

Lou wasn't as excited about today as she had been earlier on in the week. The thought of her hair and make-up being done was great, but it was Diana who was paying for the two of them. There was no way she could have afforded to pay for this herself and, if Lou was honest, even if she had put some money aside, there were other more important things to spend it on than a frivolous makeover. With that in mind she was feeling guilty about the day ahead rather than animated.

Diana had booked their appointments at a hair salon in Tenham that also did make-up and nails. Lou was worried. Diana herself had confessed to going to the same hairdresser in Ryan Harbour for years and she couldn't help wondering if she was going to end up in a place where they excelled in shampoo and sets. Fortunately, upon arrival at the salon in the shopping mall, the place looked modern and trendy; but also very expensive.

The two ladies sat down on a comfy, brown leather sofa in the salon with coffee and croissants while they had discussions with the beauticians and hairdressers about what they wanted to have done. Lou thought Diana would be the nervous one but she was happily looking through magazines and picking out, what seemed to Lou, extortionately priced make-up and nail varnishes. Lou kept pointing at the cheapest products she could see. When Diana had finished with her choices she leaned over to see what Lou was picking.

"No, go for that other eye shadow the beautician is suggesting," she told her, "It will really bring out your eyes. I agree with her about that blusher as well. It will be perfect for your complexion."

"It's so expensive," Lou managed to whisper to her friend.

"Don't worry about the cost," Diana replied, kindly, "This is my treat. Just enjoy it."

But Lou continued to feel guilty.

Eventually choices were made and the makeovers began. The girl that did Lou's nails was a sister of one of her old school friends and she was able to relax more while they chatted together over old times. It was also funny to overhear Diana admit she was thinking about a colour for her hair and the stylist telling her all about her grandmother's blue rinse.

By the end of the morning both women were feeling incredibly happy with the results in the mirror. They headed off to find somewhere for lunch in a very buoyant mood.

"I really like what they've done with your hair," Lou told Diana, "Thinning out the sides has made such a difference. You look ten years younger."

Diana smiled. "Thanks," she said, "I like it too. I'm worried I'm wearing too much make-up though. I'm not seventeen anymore."

Lou laughed. "It looks great, honestly."

"I doubt I'll be able to recreate this look at home," Diana confessed, looking at her reflection in a shop window, "But I must admit, I'd like to try."

She turned back and smiled at Lou.

"I love that short bob on you," she told her, "It looks very sophisticated; just the look for a Manager of a store to have."

Lou grinned. "I should hear next week if I've been accepted."

Diana crossed her fingers.

They found a rather plush-looking, bistro-type café to have lunch in, which was situated in a corner of the mall; enabling the two ladies to watch the world go by.

"Don't look over there," Diana whispered across the table, after their lunch order had been brought over, "There's a woman breast-feeding."

Lou automatically turned her head.

"I said don't look!"

"Oh Diana," Lou sighed, "It's a perfectly natural thing to do. A baby's got to be fed and I think the woman is being very discreet about it. I wouldn't have noticed if you hadn't pointed it out."

Diana shook her head.

"I'm sorry but I can't help feeling a little embarrassed. I certainly wouldn't feel comfortable getting my breasts out in public."

"But on your balcony is fine," Lou winked.

Diana's face reddened.

"That was different," she said, "I suppose you were more than happy to whip your booby out to feed Maddie."

"I didn't have to make that decision," Lou told her, "With Maddie being so premature she wasn't able to breastfeed. I had to express instead. Honestly, having a suction pump clamped to my nipple each day, I felt like I should have just hung a bell around my neck and changed my name to Daisy."

"I didn't know Maddie was premature."

Lou wiped her mouth with a napkin.

"Yes, about eight weeks. That was a shock when I went into labour so early. Tony and I were pretty much separated by then. It wasn't official but he was already away a lot in London with his job. He'd planned to be there for the birth but that went out of the window."

"Were you alone then?" Diana asked, concerned.

Lou nodded. "Yes," she said, "I thought I'd be okay with it just being me and the hospital staff in the delivery room, but with the birth so premature it was all too much for me. That's when mum came properly back into my life again. We'd hardly spoken in seven years but I called her, desperate for help; and she was there for me. We became close after that."

"That's nice."

"I suppose my being a single mother, to all intents and purposes, made me realise what she had been through when I was a child. She could have given me up but she didn't. I always resented all of the 'uncles' I had but really, I think that was mum's way of trying to get me a father figure. She didn't know how else to act."

"Did you not know your real father?" Diana asked, tentatively.

"Apparently I did meet him a few times when I was very young, but I can't remember what he looked like or anything," Lou told her, "All I can remember is a smell of cigar smoke."

"That doesn't really narrow it down, does it," Diana said, "So many people smoked back then. I've always hated that smell. My Richard used to enjoy a cigar but he had to smoke it in the garden."

"Anyway," Lou continued, "He stopped coming after a while. I was too young to ask why. Mum and I never heard from him again. I guess that's why I never had the urge to go looking for him; even when mum and I weren't getting along I didn't have any desire to seek him out. He obviously didn't want either of us so I didn't want him."

"That's understandable," Diana said.

"Actually though, it turns out he used to send my mum money every month; right up until I was eighteen. I never knew until after I had Maddie. Although Tony would see Maddie as often as possible and provide for her, I didn't really want him to give me an allowance each week. I know that sounds strange. I guess I just wanted to make sure that he only spent money on his daughter, not on me. I'd show him the receipts for clothes and food and he would then give me money that way. I always paid our rent and utility bills."

"That must have been a struggle," Diana said.

"It was tough to begin with," Lou admitted, "But then mum came over one day and gave me a wad of cash. She explained about the payments my father had made. She'd spent the money on me as a child but when I left school at sixteen and started working in a shop here in Tenham, earning a wage; she set the monthly payments aside to give me as a present when I turned eighteen. We had our major bust up just before then and I left home to go and live in Ryan Harbour but she never spent it herself; kept it in a savings account until we spoke again. It was a godsend. Maybe that was the only time I thought about seeking out my dad but mum also told me that he'd died. Come to think of it; I don't know how she knew that."

"Do you have any idea of who he was?" Diana asked.

Lou shook her head. "No," she said, "His name isn't on my birth certificate. I presume he was married. Mum obviously knows who he was but she's never told me and I've never really asked. There's no point in my knowing now anyway."

The two ladies fell silent. It was a lot of information for Diana to ingest but she was glad that Lou had felt able to confide in her.

"What time do we need to leave for you to pick Maddie up?" she eventually asked.

"By three really," Lou replied, "I thought I ought to collect her from school today rather than let her go to the child minders. We can spend a few hours together before I drive her over to Tony's mum's house later."

"I'm not keeping you away from her am I?" Diana asked, "I mean we don't have to go to this singles night tonight."

Lou raised her eyebrows.

"Is this a genuine feeling or just cold feet?"

"A bit of both if I'm honest," Diana confessed.

Lou grinned. "You're not keeping Maddie and me apart. She likes to spend time with both her nans. They're so different. My mum will sit back and watch Maddie play whereas Tony's mum gets on the floor with her. Maddie likes that, although she does confide in me that she sometimes thinks Nanny Poole is enjoying herself more than she is."

Diana laughed and then looked at her watch.

"Hmm, that only gives us a couple of hours to go dress shopping. I've never selected an outfit that quickly before."

"Really?" Lou said, shocked, "I usually buy the first thing I see on the rail that I like."

Diana frowned. "But don't you need to try it on first to see if it will fit?" she asked, "Don't you think about what you already have in your wardrobe to go with it? What about accessories; shoes or a handbag?"

"I'm more your jeans type girl. Most things I pick up always go with those."

Diana opened her mouth to respond but something must have crossed her mind and she closed it again. Lou thought she knew what that something was. She was proved right after Diana's next sentence.

"You know, when I said the makeover was on me, I meant everything. I'm happy to pay for an outfit too."

Lou shook her head. "Honestly, it's fine," she said, "The makeover was wonderful, but I don't need clothes bought for me."

"It's all part of the thank you," Diana told her, "You've done so much for me. You've changed my life. I'm not thinking of it as charity or anything."

Lou smiled. "I realise that," she said, "But I'm fine. If I see a dress I like; I'll buy it."

With lunch over, Lou insisted on paying the bill. As she looked at the receipt, trying not to baulk at the total at the bottom, she couldn't help noticing Diana out of the corner of her eye; looking worriedly at her. It made her feel pitied which in turn, made her angry. When they headed off to look at outfits the two were almost cagey with each other, but once Diana had picked up a pink leather skirt in the first shop and called out loudly to the assistant to see if they had it in a size fourteen, they both laughed and normal relations were restored.

After an hour of searching Lou had seen six dresses she could happily have bought. Diana had tried on numerous but didn't like any of them. Lou sighed as she stood at the end of a row of dresses that Diana was perusing. It was an expensive shop and she hadn't even bothered to look for herself.

"It's so difficult to choose," Diana said, for the hundredth time.

Lou leant back against the wall and stared up at the ceiling.

"Ah, now that's beautiful," she heard Diana say.

Turning to look Lou was surprised to see Diana holding a rather lovely knee-length, red dress. It was sleeveless but had wide shoulder straps with a row of red sequins on the outside, which mirrored the same pattern across the bust line.

"I've never seen you in red before," Lou told her.

Diana smiled. "This is for you, not me. Why don't you go and try it on?"

"I've never worn anything like that before," Lou said.

"Just try it. Go on, for me."

Lou sighed again and took the dress. The changing room only had a half-length mirror so Lou had to come out of the cubicle to see the result. She didn't recognise the woman in the reflection. That woman had expensively cut hair and was wearing make-up that brought out the green in her eyes. The slender dress accentuated the trim, hourglass figure. Diana stepped into view behind her, grinning.

"See," she said, "I don't know about you but I see an elegant, sophisticated young woman; a woman who's going places with her life and her career. Does this say, 'Manager' to you?"

Lou couldn't respond. She was still staring at herself.

"Now," Diana said, "We must find shoes and a bag to go with it."

"Sorry, what?" Lou said, coming out of her reverie.

"Well you've got to have it, haven't you? I mean, look how beautiful you are."

"Thanks Diana but…"

Diana held up her hand. "If it's a question of money…"

"It's not!"

"I'm only offering a loan. Pay me back later if you don't have it right now; that's all I'm saying."

Lou used her credit card.

What the hell, she thought, trying not to wince at the price of the dress, shoes and handbag, I can always bring them back if I'm careful tonight.

After another half an hour, Lou and Diana returned to the first department store they'd been to after lunch.

"I think that plain, black dress I originally saw was definitely the best," Diana said, as they stepped onto the up escalator to the Ladies department.

"Then please get it," Lou replied, sounding completely tired and fed up.

"I'll have to try it on again to be sure though."

"Really?"

Diana nodded.

"I'd like to see it on with this jacket I'm wearing. I hope it will work as an ensemble."

Lou sighed inwardly.

"I do so like this jacket," Diana continued, as they stepped off onto the second floor, "I know it's more white than black but I think it could work with the dress. I hope so; it's my favourite."

Diana grabbed the dress from the back of the rail where she'd hidden it earlier and the two of them headed off to the changing room. While Diana went into one of the cubicles Lou plonked herself gratefully down onto the circular sofa in the middle of the room.

A middle-aged, well-built woman walked in with a tiny, much older lady on her arm.

"Here we are, mum," the woman shouted, into the old lady's ear, "You can try your dress on in here."

"Oh right."

The old lady bent forwards and began to pull up her skirt.

"Not right here, mum! God, what are you like? Go through this curtain."

The woman smiled and rolled her eyes at Lou as she helped her mother into the cubicle beside Diana's.

"Are you sure you don't want me to help?"

"No I'll be fine," the old lady replied, in a quiet, croaky voice, "There's a nice stool I can sit on."

"Well, don't fall asleep on it," the daughter told her. She pulled the curtain across but then flung it back again, "And don't get confused and think it's a toilet either! We're still banned from Debenhams."

After closing it again the woman came over and sat beside Lou.

"Mother's eh," she sighed, "You love 'em but they can be a right pain in the arse can't they."

283

Lou smiled back as a response.

"Are you waiting on yours?" the woman asked, indicating the cubicle Diana was in.

"No, I'm here with a friend."

"That's nice," the daughter turned her attention back to the other cubicle and shouted out, "You alright in there mum? Keep your bra and panties on. Remember you're trying on a dress not putting on a hospital gown."

"I'm doing okay," the old lady replied, quietly.

"Bless her; she does get confused at times," the daughter told Lou, "We're looking for a new dress for my niece's wedding."

"Oh, right."

"Don't know why she's bothering with a big do really. She's already got four kids. The money it must be costing. Anyway it's mum's only granddaughter so she said she wanted to splash out on a new outfit and here we are."

Lou nodded and hoped Diana wasn't going to be much longer.

"Is it on yet mum," the woman shouted out, "Have you managed to pull it over your hernia?"

"Almost there," came the reply.

"Good."

Diana pulled back her curtain and stepped out wearing the dress and her jacket, smiling broadly.

"What do you think," she asked, turning around, "Does it go together?"

Lou opened her mouth but the lady beside her responded first.

"It's a lovely dress my darling, if I might butt in; but that jacket is hideous."

"Sorry?" Diana stopped spinning.

284

"I'm surprised an expensive department store like this would sell something so old-fashioned. Who wears black and white squares these days? No my lovely; you stick with the dress and give them back that old tat of a jacket."

Diana stared haughtily down her nose at the woman.

"This is my own jacket," she told her, regally.

"Is it? Whoopsie," the woman replied, brightly, "I'm always putting my foot in it. Don't mind me. If that jacket is an old favourite then you keep wearing it sweetheart."

Diana, exasperated, turned to Lou but she was leant over, rummaging about in one of her carrier bags on the floor. The way she was visibly shaking as she did told Diana she found this all highly amusing. Diana turned on her heels and headed back to the cubicle, theatrically pulling the curtain across.

"I think I've upset your friend," the woman said.

Lou sat back up.

"Mmm," was all she could say; fearing she'd laugh out loud if she opened her mouth.

"Oh well, I'd best go see how mum's doing," the woman said.

She got up and disappeared behind the curtain.

Diana emerged from her cubicle, carrying the dress in one hand and her jacket in the other.

"That was a quick change," Lou said.

"I want to escape while that fashion critic is in the other cubicle."

Lou grinned as she picked up her bags and followed Diana to the exit out to the main floor. As they passed the occupied cubicle they heard the daughter say,

"Oh mum, it's Debenhams all over again."

*

285

Dr's Case Notes – Friday 2 October

Dr Moore and I were having a coffee and discussing patient notes, as we always do every Friday after our home visits. I say discuss, usually I let Dr Moore do all of the talking while I sit there and fantasise. At the end we both walked out into the reception area where Mrs Andrews was tidying the newspapers and magazines. Well I say tidying; she was sat with her feet up reading this week's local paper. She was looking at the ads and informed us about a singles night The Smugglers is having this evening. Dr Moore already knew about it…and is going!

I experienced so many emotions at the same time. Firstly, elation that Dr Moore is definitely single; secondly, fear that that might not be the case after tonight, and thirdly, determination that I needed to thwart any attempt on Dr Moore's affections this evening. That would involve pursuit and surveillance. Mind you I've been doing that for weeks already. I know Dr Moore's entire routine; the journey home from work, the exercise classes, the bowel movements.

Perhaps I should just go along myself this evening and chat up Dr Moore. But how could I explain my presence there? I could go in a disguise of some kind I suppose. Would that work? I used to do amateur dramatics in my youth; Shakespeare mostly. I was always comfortable up on stage although I remember being terribly nervous at my debut performance in A Midsummer Night's Dream. I needn't have worried though. That night I gave the audience my Bottom and they gave me a standing ovation.

But let's face it, if I entered the pub in disguise, Dr Moore would soon recognise me when I started talking. I don't want my locum thinking I'm a total idiot. I guess the only way I could legitimately go in was as a single person. How could I manage that in about four hours? I'd have to kill Mrs Bryant, make it look like an accident and then tell everyone I needed to move on straight away. Could I get away with that?

Let's face it, could I even murder Mrs Bryant anyway? It wouldn't be the easiest thing in the world to do. I don't mean because I love her too much, I mean because the actual process would be difficult. A few years ago she was hit by a Range Rover on the high street. The only injuries sustained were a cracked windscreen and two smashed headlights. Then there was that time she accidently drank poison in my surgery up at the house. She was on her third glass of it, mixed with some tonic and crushed ice before we realised. **She** suffered no ill effects although I almost passed out on the fumes every time she burped.

Mrs Bryant isn't someone who scares easily either. I remember that attempted mugging when we were out with friends in London. She has the skin of a hippopotamus and that knife bounced right off of her. I'd thought the screams of a woman having a difficult labour were bad, but when Mrs Bryant swung that guy around her head by his testicles...well, that shrieking still haunts my dreams to this day.

No, I know what I'll do. I'll hide outside The Smugglers and watch what goes on with Dr Moore's evening. I've got a bit of time to come up with some kind of disguise that will help camouflage me into the background. I doubt I'll be spotted. Mrs Bryant is out tonight anyway; in a weightlifting tournament. She doesn't like me being in the audience as it puts her off for some reason. That's fine with me. Mrs Bryant in a tight, purple leotard, grunting aggressively while lifting weights isn't a particularly attractive sight. Although I must say, her snatch is very impressive.

287

Chapter 15

Grace felt very uncomfortable. She'd never gone into a pub on her own before but Robert said it needed to be done this way for their fantasy first date to work. They could hardly walk in together if they were meant to be strangers. The plan was for her to go in and sit up at the bar and wait. If she saw anyone she knew before Robert arrived she could say she was meeting him for a drink and hadn't realised it was a singles night. Otherwise Grace had been told to stick firmly to the fantasy.

Robert was meant to follow her in, fifteen minutes later, but she'd been here almost half an hour now. She'd practically downed her first glass of wine due to nerves and the second one was pretty close to empty. Grace was surprised at how many people were here. She'd been a little taken aback when Lou and Diana had walked in just now. They looked fantastic, she noted, as they reached the bar. When they said hello to her, she panicked and began explaining why she was here in a very quick and jerky way.

"I'm-meeting-Robert-here-for-a-drink-but-didn't-realise-it-was-a-singles-night-but-Robert-should-be-here-soon-so-I'm-fine-and-we're-just-having-a-quiet-drink-together-and-we're-not-on-a-date-or-anything-silly-like-that-you-know."

The two ladies shot each other a puzzled look before turning aside to speak to Jamie and Gloria. Grace downed the rest of her drink and pretended to root around in her handbag. When she looked up again Lou and Diana had moved off to sit at a table by the window. Grace sighed.

What must they think of me, she thought, looking across at them; and why on earth is Dr Bryant staring in through the

288

window? Is that a fake moustache he's wearing?

She looked away, not wanting to catch his eye.

"Hello," said a voice beside her, "Can I fill that glass up for you?"

Grace relaxed. Finally Robert was here. She looked round, relieved; but it wasn't Robert. She let out a little squeak. The man smiled. He looked to be around sixty, but a well-preserved sixty. He had grey hair that was quite long on top but some product was keeping it perfectly in place. He had large, kind, brown eyes and the little creases in the corner when he smiled made his whole face light up. Grace couldn't help being impressed.

"Erm, no; I'm fine actually," she said, smiling too, "I'm waiting for someone."

The man raised his eyebrows.

"I didn't know it was a singles night," Grace added, "I'm waiting for my husband. We're having a quiet drink together."

The man shrugged his shoulders in defeat.

"He's a lucky man," he said.

As he patted her arm and walked away, Grace spotted Robert in the doorway staring at her. She blushed. He looked like he was scowling but eventually he composed himself and walked up to the bar, standing a little way away from where she was sitting.

"What can I get you?" Gloria asked him.

Robert had forgotten Lou's mum worked here. He'd planned to ask the barmaid to, 'freshen up the drink for that lady at the end of the bar' but how could he point to Grace and ask Gloria that when she knew them both? It would sound silly. Gloria was still staring at him, waiting for his order. He needed to come up with another line but his mind had gone blank. Not that Gloria was making things easier, standing there in a very low-cut, red and yellow top. Was that a jester's face on the front? My God, his hat seemed to be moulded around her considerable bosom. Robert found it difficult not to stare.

"Erm, can I have two white wines please," he asked, "Chablis, if you have it."

Gloria nodded before turning to get the drinks. Robert tried to concentrate on the fantasy date. Getting two drinks was a good idea. He could then walk over and offer Grace one of them.

While Gloria poured the wine Robert looked over at the man Grace had been speaking to. He was now sat at a table beside Diana and Lou. Who was he and what was he doing talking with his wife?

Gloria came over with the drinks. Robert couldn't help gasping as she leaned forward while placing the glasses onto the bar.

"I've got two large ones," she said.

"Yes, I can see that."

"I hope they're not too dry for you."

"Not at all," Robert told her, "They look lovely."

Gloria giggled.

"I meant the wine," she said.

"Oh…yes; me too," Robert replied, his face reddening.

"Well don't spoil it." Gloria winked.

Robert handed over a twenty pound note and after receiving his change he quickly walked over to where Grace was sitting. He put the two glasses down and leaned nonchalantly against the bar and smiled at her.

"Hello," he said, "Can I give you one?"

Grace's eyes widened with shock.

290

"One of these, I mean," Robert added, hurriedly pushing one of the glasses forward. Grace smiled and took the drink.

"Thank you," she said, giggling, "Whoever you are."

"You're welcome," he replied, grinning, "I'm Robert, what's your name?"

"Mary-Lou, Jane, Ariadne."

"What? Play the game, Grace," Robert whispered, clearly ruffled.

The smile dropped from Grace's face.

"I am playing the game," she hissed, "You wanted this, remember?"

"I wanted to meet you again, not Mary…June…whatsername."

"Mary-Lou, Jane, Ariadne," Grace repeated, "And for your information she's a very lovely woman. That man over there who's talking to Diana thought so."

"Yes, what did he want?" Robert asked.

"He wanted to buy me a drink."

"What on earth for?"

Grace looked at her husband incredulously.

"Why wouldn't he want to buy me a drink?" she said, "I'm all dressed up. I've made a special effort with my make-up. Just maybe he thought I looked attractive."

Robert realised how his last sentence had sounded. He looked at Grace properly. She was right, she had made an effort. She was wearing her favourite 'going out' blue dress. Robert couldn't remember the last time he'd seen her wearing it.

"I'm sorry," he said, "You do look lovely tonight. I was so busy trying to focus on the fantasy I didn't pay enough attention to you."

291

Grace smiled again. "You're forgiven," she said, "Look, we may as well forget this now. Why don't we enjoy this drink and then go on to a restaurant, just the two of us?"

"But we haven't really tried to make this work yet," Robert told her.

"Do we need to?"

"Yes, I think so."

Grace sighed. "Fine," she said, "I'm Grace, it's nice to meet you Robert."

That was better. Robert's grin returned.

"Why's a great-looking woman like you drinking alone?"

Grace giggled. "I'm not drinking alone."

Her smile turned to horror.

"Oh God, I forgot the coleslaw for tea tomorrow."

"Grace!"

"Sorry, it just sprang into my mind," she said.

Robert tried to maintain his composure, and the fantasy.

"I like a girl who knows her wine," he told her, turning Grace's glass around on the bar, "You remind me of this particular one."

"This is our usual," she replied, "You always say it's cold and crisp. Thanks very much."

"I mean," Robert added, quickly; taking Grace's hand and kissing it between each word of description, "It's delicious, fragrant and aged to perfection."

"Your brother phoned today as well," Grace informed him, "Apparently it's still not gone down so he's going back to the hospital with it in the morning."

Robert let go of her hand.

"Bloody hell, Grace! I'm really trying here."

"Well I'm sorry but I think it's stupid," she replied, "Why

292

can't we just be ourselves now and enjoy a night out together?"

"Because it's meant to be exciting, that's why. It's something new, a change from the norm. It's meant to be a break from the usual dreary evenings we always have!"

Robert fell silent as he saw tears appear in his wife's eyes.

"You think I'm boring," she said, reaching for a tissue in her handbag, "I knew it."

"I didn't mean that," Robert started.

"Really? Well you certainly made it sound that way," she got off the stool, "I'm going home. I'm going to eat a boring meal in front of the boring television. Why don't you go off and have fun on your own somewhere!"

She stormed out of the pub, Robert ran after her, calling her name. He bumped into Lou as she emerged from the Ladies and muttered a quick apology. He didn't hear her sigh.

*

When Lou knocked at Diana's door that evening she found her in a state of panic and in her underwear. Dresses were spread all across the bed.

"I'm worried about the one I bought today," Diana said, pointing out the black dress on top of a pile of three others that all looked the same to Lou, "I'm not sure it goes with anything."

"Diana, it's black, it goes with everything. Calm down."

"Well it doesn't go with my favourite jacket. That was pointed out to me today in no uncertain terms. Maybe tonight is all a mistake. I looked at myself in the mirror this evening; I don't look like me anymore."

Lou placed her hands on the sides of Diana's arms and gently sat her down on the edge of the bed.

"You're just nervous," she said, "This is another big step for you, I understand that. Just think of it as an evening out. I'll be there. If you don't want to talk to any men, you don't have to. It's a drink in The Smugglers, that's all."

Lou could see Diana begin to relax so she picked up the black dress and handed it to her.

"Now, go put this on. You'll look great."

Diana smiled and stood up.

It wasn't a chilly evening for the time of year but both ladies shivered as they crossed the road from the apartment block to The Smugglers. Diana was still feeling anxious. Lou felt excited. She loved the outfit she had on and couldn't wait to see her mother's reaction to it.

"Well, here we are," she said, as the two ladies stood outside the pub.

There was a sign out the front advertising Singles Night and they could both hear soft music coming from inside. They squeezed each other's hand for strength. As Diana reached up to push the door open, something caught Lou's eye.

"There's someone over there," she whispered.

Diana looked over to where Lou was staring.

"That's Dr Bryant," she whispered back, "What's he doing there? And why on earth is he wearing a blonde wig?"

"Maybe he's off to a fancy dress party?" Lou offered.

The door to the pub opened as a giggling, young couple left, arm in arm; so the two ladies took the opportunity to walk inside. There was a larger crowd than Lou had anticipated. Some she knew, like Precious; who was holding court with three young men towards the back of the room, and Chris who obviously wouldn't miss out on a night like this. He was currently chatting to two women who looked disgusted with whatever joke he was telling them. His eyes scanned the room as he laughed. They passed over Lou with no signs of recognition. Did she really look that different; or had he finally realised she was out of his league?

"Do you think Dr Bryant is keeping an eye on Dr Moore?" Diana asked, also observing who else was in the room.

"I doubt it," Lou replied, "I don't think Dr Moore is in need of a chaperone."

"I was just wondering what the man was doing outside."

"Maybe he's planning to cheat on Mrs Bryant and is trying to build up courage to come in."

Diana snorted. "I don't think he's the type," she said, "Besides, do you think he'd dare?"

Lou laughed. "Mrs Bryant would kill him and eat him for breakfast if he did."

They walked up to the bar, saying hello to Grace who couldn't have seen the sign outside. She acted very strangely when they said hello, but perhaps that almost empty glass of wine in front of her wasn't her first.

When Gloria saw Lou she got all teary.

"Oh God," she said, dabbing her eyes, "My little girl is all grown up."

"Stop it mum," Lou said, but only half-heartedly.

She turned to Jamie and caught him looking her up and down. She found she didn't mind. When he looked into her eyes he smiled.

"My God," he said, "What's the name of the beauty parlour that turned you into a lady? They deserve a medal for achieving the impossible."

Gloria smacked him hard on the arm. Lou laughed.

"You're not looking so bad yourself," she said, "Is that suit new?"

"What this old thing?" he replied, tugging at the lapel of the jacket, "First thing that came to hand in my wardrobe."

"You look taller," Lou said, "Are you wearing lifts in your shoes?"

"No."

"But that's definitely padded shoulders isn't it?"

"It's all me, baby."

Although Lou had been making a joke she realised she was quite impressed that it was indeed 'all Jamie.' She caught his eye and realised she had been staring. Jamie winked.

"You look great," he said, "Both of you," he added, looking at Diana.

Lou took in her mother's Jester's top.

"I see you're planning on pulling this evening," she said, "Had any bites yet?"

"It's only a matter of time," her mother replied, arranging the top more snuggly around her breasts, "The girls are in position and ready for anything."

"They look ready for an escape attempt," Jamie told her, and received another smack.

"Well good luck anyway," Lou said.

"I don't need luck on a night like this," Gloria told them, "A load of desperate men looking for love; just give me and the girls ten minutes and I'll have half a dozen of them panting for me."

She sidled over to serve a customer; leaning forward over the bar and smiling as she did.

"I wish I had some of what your mother's got," Diana said.

Lou's mouth dropped open.

"I was talking about confidence," Diana added, quickly, her face reddening; "I didn't mean…those. I wouldn't know what to do with them."

Jamie got Diana and Lou's drinks and they moved over to an empty table by the window where they had a good view of the room. Diana was still feeling nervous. There didn't seem to be too many people here of her age, not men anyway; and she wasn't sure if she was glad or disappointed by that.

As she took another look around the room Diana did notice one man who seemed to be within her age group. He'd just stopped at the bar and was talking to Grace. He was very attractive, she noted; one of those smart-looking men who looked completely at home in a suit. A gentleman, Diana thought.

"I wonder what Robert will think?" Lou said, looking in the same direction.

"We're about to find out," Diana replied, noticing Robert in the doorway.

When she turned her attention back to the bar she saw the man had walked away from Grace and was now walking towards her. Diana realised she was staring. He came and sat down at the table beside them. Her heartbeat quickened.

*

Jamie felt all his planning for tonight was paying off. After placing adverts about the singles night in the various local papers and on the community website he'd been worried about the number of people that might turn up, be it too few or too many. Learning from previous mistakes and having listened to Lou the other day in the supermarket, he hadn't prepared food for the evening and had only ordered a little extra alcohol in his delivery that week.

The only real expense had been the candles in decorative glass jars that he'd decided to place on each table. Still, he could use them again another time and was rather pleased with the effect they gave; it wasn't over the top. Gloria had walked in to begin her evening shift and straight away asked where the balloons and party poppers were. She was still suggesting she go buy some when Lou walked in. She did look wonderful, Jamie had to admit that. It wasn't just her new, shorter hairstyle or the dress she was wearing; there was a new quality to her somehow. Sophisticated; that word sounded right. Some might say her outfit was conservative but it still showed off her lovely figure without the need to display as much flesh as possible. She looked so happy and confident in herself.

There was a nice amount of people in the bar, now Jamie noted; although there was still room for a few more. Perhaps Dr Bryant, standing outside and staring in through the window in a pair of large, round sunglasses would eventually come in and join the others. His locum was already here, chatting and laughing with a young man. Jamie didn't want to get his hopes up but perhaps this was the answer to his problems, a weekly singles evening. Perhaps one day there would be a Smugglers wedding.

*

"Right," said Lou, standing up, "I'm just popping to the Ladies. I'll be back in a minute."

"You're not going to leave me here on my own?"

"Well I can't stay here and pee in a glass," she told Diana, "Jamie doesn't allow it. Don't worry, you'll be fine."

"I'll look desperate, sitting here on my own. I'd go and talk to Robert and Grace except they look like they're having a bit of a row."

"Well just sit here and look available then."

Lou grinned and walked off to the Ladies. Diana picked up

her drink and stared at it, her nervousness returning.

"Excuse me," said a deep, well-spoken voice beside her.

Diana looked up. It was the man who had been talking to Grace. He was smiling at her, the creases at the outer corner of each eye just adding to his attractiveness.

"Would you mind if I take that spare beermat off your table," he asked, "The leg's wonky on mine and I'd hate to spill my drink."

Diana picked up the beermat.

"Here you are," she said. She couldn't help smiling.

As the stranger took hold of the coaster the tips of his fingers just barely touched hers. She felt a thrill pass through her.

"I don't think I've ever been somewhere where a table is perfectly level with the floor," he continued.

"I've noticed that too," Diana said, "It can't be a wonky floor every time."

The man laughed; a tender but strong enough sound that made Diana think he had actually found her comment funny and wasn't just being polite.

"Apart from the table this is rather a charming little bar," the man said, looking around the room, "I've never been here before."

"Oh it's my local," Diana replied.

She realised that might make her sound like a bit of a lush.

"Erm, I mean it's the nearest one to where I live. I don't come in here that often myself."

That wasn't smart either, she thought, telling a complete stranger practically where she lived.

"I have a house on the outskirts of Tenham," the man told her, "It's handy for my work in the town centre. I saw the advert for tonight in the Tenham Herald and thought I'd bite the bullet and come over."

He looked into Diana's eyes.

"I'm glad I did."

Diana felt herself blushing. The man held out his hand.

"I'm Keith," he said.

Diana reached out her hand and he gently took it.

"Diana."

"A lovely name; for a lovely lady. Is that too corny?"

Diana laughed. "It's borderline," she replied.

Keith smiled.

Lou emerged from the ladies, zipping up her handbag. Someone ran passed in front of her, making her start. Robert Keane followed close behind. He muttered an apology to Lou as he brushed against her in pursuit of his wife. Lou sighed as she looked down at her dress and the small tear in the front where Robert's watch strap had just snagged three of the sequins. It wasn't so noticeable that she would have to rush home and change but it was looking unlikely that she could get away with taking it back to the shop now.

She was about to walk back to the table but saw Diana deep in conversation with a man.

You little devil, Lou thought to herself, and smiled. She turned and walked over to the bar instead.

"How's it going, mum?" she asked.

Gloria was looking pretty miserable, sat on a stool behind the bar with her arms crossed.

"Not great," she sighed, "I don't get it. I'm not even getting eyed up, let alone have comments made about the girls. What's happening?"

"Maybe it's because you're working here. Perhaps the men don't realise you're available."

A man came up to the bar with what looked like a scotch in his glass. Gloria jumped up.

"Ooh, is that a large, stiff one," she asked, giving him a wink.

Lou rolled her eyes. A man would have to be in a coma not to realise that her mother was available.

The guy looked confused.

"It's just a single," he told her, "I wanted a splash of soda put in it. Gloria snatched the glass out of his hand and walked over to the mixers pump. Jamie came in from the kitchen with a large box filled with packets of crisps.

"Selling drinks **and** snacks," he said to Lou, as he placed the box under the counter, "It's going well so far."

"Yes, it's a good idea for one night a month," she told him.

"What do you mean?" he said, "I'm thinking of making this a regular weekly event; perhaps twice a week."

"Do you think that would work," Lou replied, "I mean it's something different for a couple of nights, but either people will match up and not need to come again; or those that don't get matched up won't keep coming if they're not going to meet anyone new."

Jamie's smile fell from his face.

"You know how to wind a guy don't you."

"Sorry, I didn't mean to rain on your parade. This is a successful evening," Lou said, "It was a great idea."

"It was your mum's idea, not mine; remember?"

Jamie walked off to serve a customer at the other end of the bar. Lou sighed. She hadn't meant to upset him but honestly, when was he going to stop playing at being a publican and sort out a proper plan to make the business a success? Did he really think a regular singles night was going to solve all of his problems? The guy was dreaming.

Lou saw the man talking to Diana get up from his seat. He gently took her hand in both of his and they spoke for a moment before he walked out of the pub. Diana watched him go, spotted Lou and came over.

"Can you believe it," she said, her eyes shining, "I've got a date."

"What happened to the nerves?"

"I know; I was being silly. Keith's a very charming man. He's taking me out to dinner tomorrow night," Diana couldn't hide her excitement.

"Where?" Lou asked.

"Oh, just at The Green Man up the other end of the high street. Keith suggested it, which I thought was a good idea. It means I can meet him there and I didn't have to give out my address to be picked up or anything. I'm sure he's lovely but I thought that wise."

"Very sensible," Lou told her, smiling at her friend's obvious enthusiasm.

"I'm going to go now," Diana said, "Is that alright?"

"Of course."

"What about you?"

"Oh I might stick around for a while," Lou mused. She really wanted to talk to Jamie again.

"Okay then. Not too late though; you have an important day tomorrow. Who knows; you may sweep that actor man off his feet."

Lou laughed. "Hardly," she said.

"He'd be lucky to have you."

"Thanks. You are still going to pop into the shop aren't you? I'll probably be a nervous wreck and could use the support."

"Of course."

"Good. In case I don't get the chance to say it tomorrow, I hope your date goes well."

Diana smiled. "Me too," she said.

*

Jamie noticed the crowd was beginning to thin out. He looked at his watch and was surprised to see it had only just gone nine. Perhaps Lou was right. Once people were paired up they didn't need The Smugglers anymore. She was still here, talking to her supermarket colleagues but her friend, Diana, had already left.

Gloria was collecting glasses. He could only see the back of her over at one of the window tables but he could see the face of the old man she was talking to. He looked petrified. Suddenly Gloria began to bounce up and down on the spot. The man's expression changed to horror. He grabbed his chest and stumbled past her out of the door. She watched him go and then stomped over to the bar.

"Well, you certainly cured his hiccups," Jamie told her.

Gloria huffed. "Honestly, what's wrong tonight?" she said, "I thought this place would be filled with desperate men looking for a piece of me, but I can't even get the oldies interested."

"Is jumping up and down part of your usual routine; because if it is I think I may have found the flaw in your chat-up technique."

"That's never failed me before," Gloria said, more to herself, "I mean it's always the last desperate shot, but I've never had the girls fail me."

She looked up at Jamie.

"It's finally happened," she said, "I've lost my sex appeal. The eyesight's not what it was, I get pains in my right shoulder

303

just before it begins to rain and now the allure is leaving me as well. I'm old."

"You're not," Jamie replied, "It's just an off night. Perhaps you're trying too hard. Guys can sense that."

"And who are you, the love doctor?"

"I only meant…look, I don't think it's time for you to hang up your dating boobs yet."

"You mean boots."

"I know what I mean."

Gloria smiled. "Actually I do have some dating boots," she confessed, "They're red leather and come right up to my…"

"What can I get you," Jamie said, turning quickly to Lou, who had just walked up to the bar.

"Just a small, white wine thanks."

Gloria returned to clearing tables. Jamie poured out a glass of wine and refused Lou's money.

"Thanks," she said, climbing up onto a barstool, "Sorry about earlier. I didn't mean to suggest that this couldn't be a regular event."

He sighed. "I think you were right what you said. It's thinned out already, and it's still pretty early."

Lou checked her watch.

"I see what you mean. Well, don't be disheartened. Looking on the bright side, once these new couples have all got to know each other, they'll start fighting; split up and then you can have another singles evening."

Jamie laughed. "That's a nice thought," he said, "But unfortunately I need a slightly more regular income."

"How bad are things?" Lou asked.

Jamie pulled a face.

"Let's just say it could be a lot better. I could really do with some back-up funds to take care of a few repairs. That sign outside desperately needs repainting and, between you and me, there are a few leaks in the roof that are starting to concern me."

"Well, you know what you could do," Lou said.

"I'm not bringing back the strippers; no matter how much your mother begs."

"No I meant you could buy a large screen TV and start running all the sports fixtures. This place would be packed."

Jamie screwed his nose up.

"I don't really want that sort of a pub. Besides I don't think this place lends itself to that."

Lou sighed. "No," she told him, "You want a place that will appeal to everyone; a place that's known for good conversation, good food and a pleasant atmosphere."

Jamie smiled. "Am I that easy to read?"

"I just know you," she said, "But you're certainly going to need a lot of spare cash to create your ultimate dream."

The smile dropped from Jamie's face.

"I know."

"Do you?" Lou asked, "This place isn't big enough for the gastro pub that you want. In an ideal world you could buy the tearoom next door that's up for sale and then knock through. Then you could open up the living quarters on the floor above and use that as part of the restaurant too. That would really utilise the harbour views. Outside space will always be a problem but there's room for a few tables. That would be great for the summer months. Mind you with patio heaters…"

Jamie placed his chin in his hands and lent on the bar while Lou rattled on. Eventually she noticed him.

"Well, it's just a few ideas off the top of my head," she said.

"Yep, thanks for that. If I ever need a business manager I'll give you a call."

Lou didn't smile.

"But what I've just said is all a pipe dream anyway, isn't it."

"Not necessarily."

"Of course it is!" Lou snapped, "I worry about you. You have big dreams for this place but you're never going to make them work if you carry on as you are."

"I'll get there," Jamie said, standing upright again, "It'll take some time but…"

"You don't have the luxury of time do you," Lou interrupted, "Be honest with me, Jamie."

Jamie found he couldn't respond. Lou felt a rush of feeling for this despondent man standing in front of her.

"Look," she said, "Why don't you just concentrate on the food side of things? That's what you really want to do most isn't it."

"I do," Jamie sighed, "I've done all the food and hygiene courses but I really need a chef to create the food I want and I can't afford one."

Lou huffed. "You see, that's your problem," she said, "I mention food you start talking about employing a chef. Why can't you rein things in a little and concentrate on what you can do with the resources you currently have."

"That's what I have been doing," Jamie retorted, feeling miffed, "All my recent ideas have been on a budget and where have they got me? I need something big. People don't want to come in here for a sandwich or a Jacket potato."

"Well, not the plain ones you're serving, no," Lou told him, a feeling of frustration building inside her, "But if you make them a speciality; maybe offer sweet potatoes as another option, that would be a start. You could serve them with a decent salad and then do something similar with the sandwiches; widen the fillings, put wholegrain mustard in with some thick-cut ham, offer a hot steak sandwich with mushrooms; serve them all with those posh-looking crisps. Then all you need is a little advertising and you're away."

Lou got off of the stall she was sitting on.

"Why don't you give that some thought and please, for your own sake; just stop messing about with these crazy one-off ideas that aren't working for you."

She stomped off to the Ladies. Lou didn't know why was she getting so angry with Jamie this evening but for some reason, he was infuriating her. She so wanted him to succeed and to stay in Ryan Harbour but that wasn't going to happen the way he was going. Then what? He'd have to sell up and leave.

Lou looked at herself in the mirror as she washed her hands. Her new look seemed different now. Earlier, back at her apartment, it had been soft but attractive. Now she seemed to be turning into a hard bitch. She thought she knew why. It was due to Joyce Pendleton and the rest of the narrow-minded members of the coven. Lou knew that if she'd bumped into any of them on the way here tonight they would still only have seen the drunken, loud, stupid tart they thought she was. She wanted to show them that they were wrong. Why did it matter to her so much? Lou couldn't answer that question but she was going to show them who she really was; starting tomorrow with her well thought out, well planned 'Pete Crick Day.' It was going to be a great success.

*

Jamie had been taken aback by Lou's sudden outburst. What had he said or done to cause it? They'd been getting on so well only a moment before. He saw her come out of the Ladies.

307

Hopefully she would come back over and talk but before she got a chance to, a man walked into the pub and stopped her. Jamie saw the huge smile appear on her face.

Oh God, he thought, why can't she look at me like that?

*

Lou came back out of the Ladies ready to go over and apologise to Jamie. Before she could, someone stepped in front of her.

"Tony! What are you doing here?"

"Oh I decided to come up last minute. I was tired of London."

"Maddie's over at your mum's house."

"I know. I just put her to bed and thought I'd take advantage of mum's babysitting and come over to Ryan Harbour to meet you for a drink. Well, that was only if you were on your own of course."

Tony indicated one of the Singles Night signs.

"Oh that," Lou replied, "No that was for Diana really. I just came along for moral support."

"Oh yes," Tony said, knowingly, "And do you usually dress up like that, just to provide moral support? You look amazing by the way."

Lou couldn't help grinning.

"Thanks," she said.

"Have you lost weight? Not that you needed to, but; have you?"

"Maybe," Lou said, looking down at herself, "Perhaps the healthier meals and exercise is starting to pay off."

"Can I get you a drink?"

As Lou glanced towards the bar she thought she caught Jamie's eye. He looked a bit annoyed.

308

"Erm, would you mind if we had a drink back at mine?" she said, "I was just about to leave."

"Sure, that sounds good," Tony replied, "Let's go via the off licence."

*

Lou hadn't planned on drinking much more but she and Tony kept laughing together about old times and soon the bottle of wine he'd bought was empty. Lou opened one of hers.

"And then you told the old girl in the arcade exactly what she could do with her bingo balls."

Lou was laughing and blushing.

"My God," she said, "I'd forgotten how bad I was."

"You weren't bad," Tony told her, grinning, "You were just standing up for yourself."

They continued laughing.

"I miss those times," Tony said, eventually, "I'm really starting to hate London."

"But that's always where you've wanted to be," Lou told him, topping up his glass from the new bottle, "Working on the trading floors in the City."

"I know and it was great to begin with. Those first couple of years I worked hard and played hard, it was exactly how I thought it was going to be. I began to excel in my career and then I met Cheryl who shared my passion for work. It was all going great but now," Tony shook his head, "I don't know. I guess I'm starting to feel a bit bored. I mean I'm at a level in my job where I thought I was happy to stay, but then I think, 'I've got thirty more years of this. Is this all it's going to be?'"

"What about Cheryl?" Lou asked, placing her drink onto a coaster on the coffee table, "What does she say? Have you told her how you feel?"

"We don't talk much about feelings and stuff."

Tony took a swig of his wine and put it down. He looked at Lou.

"Then there's you," he said.

"Me?"

"Yes. Look at you. You're still moving your life forward. You look after our daughter, you're about to improve your career and you've never looked better."

Lou smiled. "That's not all my doing," she said, "It's thanks to Diana really. It's her wanting to change her life that has actually helped me change mine. I've only lately realised that my life was stuck in a rut too."

"Really?"

"Yes. You say that I'm **still** moving my life forward, Tony, but that's not true. For the past five years it hasn't moved at all. Don't get me wrong, I love Maddie to bits and I wouldn't have things any other way; but all I've done these past five years is go to work to the same job I've had since I was eighteen and then come home each night and be a mother. I don't see any of the old crowd, well most of them have moved away. It wasn't until Diana came along that I realised how lonely I had become."

Lou couldn't stop tears forming in her eyes. It was probably the drink that was making her emotional but what she'd said was true enough. Tony placed his arm round her.

"While you left to find your own life," Lou continued, "Mine stopped. I lost confidence in myself. I'd become the woman those damn bitches up the hill always thought I was. A single mother; 'like mother; like daughter.' If I was in a mess then it served me right."

"I'm sorry," Tony said, cradling Lou's cheek in his hand, "I didn't realise what a state I'd left you in."

"It wasn't your fault," Lou told him, "It was all mine. I played into those gossips' hands. I wish I could just ignore them, but even now; they still hate me."

Lou thought of Joyce's cruel words in the supermarket that day she'd been on the till. She couldn't deny that it had hurt. She began to cry. Tony kissed her on the cheek. As she looked up so their eyes met. They both leaned in and kissed each other on the lips; one quick kiss to begin with but a second, longer one followed. Soon they were pawing at each other and pulling at their clothes. Lou heard another ripping sound and knew for sure that her new dress was not going back to the shop for a refund.

Chapter 16

Lou's alarm went off at seven-fifteen and she was instantly awake. The big day was here; 'Pete Crick Day' at the supermarket. After all her planning for the event, today she was finally going to meet the man she'd had a crush on for years. It was just a shame she wasn't feeling or looking her best right now. Her head was pounding after last night's wine and she actually jumped in bed when she caught a glimpse of her reflection in the dressing table mirror. It was certainly a different looking Lou from last night. Her hair was sticking out at all angles and yesterday's salon-applied make-up had smudged its way around her eyes and across her cheeks. To Lou, the image in the mirror reflected an aged clown who'd had all the air let out of his face.

Who needs Pete Crick's attention anyway, she thought, smiling to herself while remembering last night. Tony wasn't in bed beside her but Lou could hear movement in the apartment. After giving her face a quick rub with a make-up remover wipe and patting down her hair; she grabbed her dressing gown from the back of the door and made her way down to the lounge area.

As she entered the room she saw Tony standing over by the French doors leading out onto her balcony overlooking the car park. He was already dressed and his mobile phone was pressed up against his ear.

"Yes," he said, "If you want to get the details we can view the property when I get back. What did you say? Oh right, yes Tuesday evening will be fine."

There was a gap as the other person spoke.

"I love you too," Tony said, "See you tomorrow night, Cheryl."

He hung up and turned round. He didn't jump when he saw Lou; just smiled as if the phone conversation hadn't taken place.

"I was going to put some coffee on," he said, "Do you have a coffeemaker or is it instant?"

Lou couldn't respond.

"I'll stick the kettle on, it'll be quicker."

He made his way across to the kitchen.

"Are you and Cheryl buying a new house?" Lou managed to ask.

"Hmm? Oh, yes; yes we are. We thought we'd rent out our current one in London and make a move to the suburbs. We want to buy a rundown house to do up. If we make a bit of money on it we could maybe buy another and perhaps start a property let business."

Lou couldn't believe what she was hearing and Tony's nonchalant attitude was pissing her off.

"So what was all that talk last night about, then?" she asked.

"What talk," Tony said, checking the kettle for water before switching it on.

"I mean all your chat about being fed up with London and Cheryl."

Tony held up his hands.

"Hang on; I said I was fed up with my job; hence the possible property business. I never said I was fed up with Cheryl."

"Well you've dropped some bloody big hints about the state of your marriage." Lou was having trouble controlling her anger, "What was all that tripe about the two of you not talking?"

313

Tony looked puzzled.

"I don't get what all this is about," he said.

"What? Tony, we slept together last night. Does that not mean anything to you?"

"Last night was fun," he said, "It was nice to revisit the past."

"The past? What sort of person do you think I am?"

Tony frowned.

"I really don't understand why you're so upset," he told her, opening up the cupboard above the toaster and getting two mugs out, "Didn't you enjoy last night. You sounded like you did."

He winked at her and Lou lost it.

"Get out of my house right now."

"Lou."

"I mean it, Tony! Who the hell do you think you are? You start waltzing back to Ryan Harbour whenever you feel like it; telling me how tough things are for you in London. You tell me I'm looking good and admire how well I'm doing…"

"Well you are."

"Then why have you just treated me like some fucking whore?"

Tony's eyes opened wide in shock.

"I haven't. You were all up for last night too."

"Was I? All I remember was crying on your shoulder while I told you about loneliness and how the local coven still make me feel worthless. I don't recall asking you to come to bed."

"Well you didn't say no; did you?"

"You bastard!" Lou spat, "You don't even see it, do you."

"Obviously not," Tony replied, "I guess I should forget the coffee."

He made to leave but Lou was still standing in the doorway out to the hall, preventing his escape.

"You think of me the same way they do," Lou whispered, tears springing to her eyes, "You came here last night and thought I'd be an easy lay."

"That's not true. I didn't plan for last night to happen. I'm starting to wish it hadn't now."

"There's something we can both agree on," Lou told him, "My God what a mug I am."

"What did you think," Tony asked, "Did you think I wanted us to get back together? I never said that."

"So you do think I'll sleep with someone at the drop of a hat then?"

"Of course I don't! Look Lou, if I gave you the wrong impression, I'm sorry. I…"

"Just go will you. I'm feeling embarrassed enough as it is. Go and spend time with your daughter. I'll be picking her up from your mother's at six thirty; make sure you're not there."

Lou moved to one side. After a beat Tony walked past and left without saying anything more. When she heard the front door close Lou dropped to the floor and cried.

*

Her eyes were still a bit puffy when she rushed into the supermarket at nine o'clock.

"Are you okay, darling?" Precious asked, "You don't look well."

"I'm fine. I didn't get much sleep last night," Lou replied, "Worried about today I suppose."

"Me too. I'm so nervous. I've never met a celebrity before."

"What about me," Chris sidled up to the two women, "I'm a bit of a legend around here. Are you alright babes, you don't

315

look well?"

"I'm fine."

Simon came out of his office.

"Ah, Lou," he said, walking over, "Glad you've arrived. Are you okay, you don't look well?"

"I'm fine!" she snapped.

Simon baulked.

"Sorry," she said

"Bit of a snag," he told her, regaining his composure, "The audio equipment you hired hasn't arrived."

"Where is it?" Lou asked, instantly in work mode.

"Not even in the county I'm afraid," Simon told her, chuckling.

"Oh God, I'll have to see if I can borrow something else," she said, starting to panic, "He's getting here at ten."

"I doubt there's time," Simon looked at his watch; "We'll just have to use our public address system. I've got the DVD of Pete's film and that's all ready to go once he arrives. Oh and the posters and cardboard cut outs are here. They're in my office. Shall we get those unpacked and set up now?"

"I thought you were going to do that yesterday after the store closed."

"Yes I was," he told her, "But I thought I'd have a quick listen to that CD you got him first and then I forgot to."

"That CD that I took ages to find?" Lou said, an ominous feeling starting to grow in her stomach, "One of only a few copies of an aria by that famous opera singer that he loves and always talks about in interviews?"

Simon nodded.

"Hang on, I'd already wrapped it."

"I think I can manage a bit of rewrapping, Lou," Simon said,

"But anyway, I didn't have to in the end."

That awful feeling in her stomach was getting stronger.

"Why not?"

Simon laughed again.

"Well," he said, "You'll never guess what happened. I'd just removed it from the CD player (it was lovely by the way; absolutely beautiful) but I'd been eating some cheesy crisps beforehand and the thing slipped out of my hands onto the floor. In my haste to pick it up I'm afraid I trod on it; left a nasty scratch down the front."

"So it's ruined," Lou said, quietly; trying to control her temper, "That very personal gift can't now be presented to him."

"Well it doesn't matter," Simon replied, trying to jolly her along, "It's not like he was expecting it. What he doesn't know can't hurt him. He's getting paid by Jesters to do this tour anyway."

"But all the other stores have given him gifts," Lou told her boss, "I've seen the presentation photos on the company website. What the hell are we going to do?"

"Well we are a shop, darling," Precious interjected, "Perhaps we can give him something from here."

"Oh yes, great idea," Lou told her, "We'll get him up on the stage and present him with a bag of potatoes and a tin of spam. Oh God! Where's the stage?"

"Same place as the audio equipment," Simon replied.

Lou sighed. Could this day get any worse? When she unrolled the posters in Simon's office, she was able to answer that question with a big, fat yes.

"This isn't Pete Crick," she said.

Simon looked at the poster, questioningly.

"Isn't it?" he replied, "I can't really tell when he's not in the jester costume."

"This is terrible," Lou said, as she pulled out one of the cardboard cut outs and saw that was wrong too. She felt like bursting into tears again.

"It's not that bad," Simon consoled, "If I couldn't tell it wasn't him I'm sure most other people will be fooled too."

"Except maybe the man himself."

"Oh right, yes; I suppose that's true."

Simon didn't seem too bothered about these disasters. Lou was feeling worse by the minute. All of her planning had been for nothing. What would Pete Crick think when he turned up to find no images of himself around the store? She pictured all those photos online from his visits to other branches, standing on a proper stage giving a speech; posing beside his cardboard cut outs, waving at the crowds. Maybe he was the sort of guy who would just laugh it off. Perhaps the crowd of fans that had already gathered outside now would be enough for him.

When Lou walked back out to the shop and sensed the buzz of anticipation in the air it made her feel a little better. She couldn't see Diana anywhere. Lou hoped she'd be here soon for some moral support. Gloria was standing over by the entrance and waved at her daughter. Lou could see she was wearing her favourite leopard print dress (low-cut as always) under her mac. Other people just coming in were closing down umbrellas.

Great, Lou thought as she walked over, to top it all off it's raining now as well.

"All ready?" Gloria asked, brightly.

"Not really."

"It'll be fine, don't worry. Now," Gloria took hold of her

daughter's upper arm and pulled her across to the wall, out of earshot of other people, "What happened with Tony last night? I'm not prying, it's just that I saw the two of you leaving together and this morning I clocked him stomping over to his car in the pub car park. He looked pretty upset."

"Mum, now is not the time," Lou said, gently removing her mother's arm.

A big, black car pulled up outside.

"Shit he's early." Lou's stomach lurched, "And the reporter and photographer aren't even here yet."

She waved over at Simon and the two of them raced outside. As the car door opened so a cloud of smoke emerged before the person did. Pete Crick stood there looking up at the supermarket building, puffing away on a cigar. The smell reminded Lou of her one memory of her father and the association took away a little of the attraction for the actor. Mind you, so did the scowl on his face and the stench of alcohol.

"Jesus Christ," he said, his large, brown eyes narrowed against the daylight, "What shithole have I been brought to now?"

"Erm Mr Crick," Simon called out, rushing forward; hand outstretched, "It's a pleasure to welcome you to our Ryan Harbour branch. We're all very excited to have you here."

"I'm sure," Pete said, still looking at the building.

Finally he turned his gaze onto the two people staring up at him. Lou's first thought was that he looked more hung-over than she did; but there was still an aura of charm about him; especially when he winked and grinned at her.

"There are some bags inside," he said to Simon, indicating the car. He looked over to the entrance where Gloria was stood right at the front of the crowd, waving, "And I see there's one or two in the store as well."

While Simon rooted around in the car, Pete Crick stuck his arm tightly round Lou's waist.

"Okay darling," he said, "Let's get this over with. Show me where I can have ten minutes to myself."

"Er, certainly," Lou replied, feeling the hand move lower, "You can use my manager's office."

In the short time it took to walk from the car to the entrance, Pete Crick transformed. With the cigar discarded Lou was amazed to suddenly see a happy, fit, handsome man walk tall through the crowd of people.

"Great to see you all," he called out, in a very well-spoken voice as he made his way to the office; Lou by his side, "I'll be out in a few minutes to chat and sign whatever you want me to sign."

There was a ripple of laughter.

"Thank you," he said, as the crowd started clapping.

At the office door he turned, flicking his head in a way that made his brown hair bounce suggestively; like he was starring in a shampoo commercial. He gave his fans one last wave and disappeared inside. By the time he'd slumped into Simon's chair the Pete Crick that had emerged from the car was back.

"God I hate doing this stuff," he said, pulling a hipflask from his jacket pocket and draining the contents.

"I guess it must get tiresome," Lou replied.

"You've no idea, doll."

Pete looked around him.

"This is a mess," he said, pushing the rolled-up posters across the desk, "I usually get more of a welcome than this, "Where are all the photographs and gifts; or is this dump such a dive that you can't afford it."

"There was a problem with the posters and cardboard cut outs I'm afraid," Lou explained, "They only arrived today and erm; well, they're not quite right."

Pete made a huffing noise.

"Fucking supermarket," he said, shaking his head, "I should have stuck with the Royal Shakespeare Company."

He waved his hipflask at Lou.

"Any chance of getting a refill, babe?" he asked.

"Erm, I'm sure that's possible."

Lou didn't know what else to say. She was alone in a room with her dream man but it wasn't exactly a fantasy.

"Single malt," Pete told her, as she took the flask, "Ten years old. And none of the shit this place sells."

Lou turned to walk out the door.

"Hide it somewhere on you for fuck's sake," Pete called out, "I don't want the fans to see it do I? Use your nut."

"Right, sorry."

As Lou walked out the door so Simon walked in, carrying two holdalls. She left him to provide the small talk with Pete while she searched out her mother.

"What's he like?" Gloria asked, as Lou came up to her.

"A bit different to what you'd think," she replied, "Look mum, could you go to the pub and get this filled up for me?"

Gloria looked down at the silver-plated hipflask.

"Is this his?"

"Yes," Lou sighed, "And I reckon it was full up this morning."

Gloria wasn't listening. She took off the top and lifted it to her lips.

"Now it's like our lips have touched," she whispered.

Lou grimaced. "Oh God, mum."

"What?"

"Can you please get this filled up at the pub with a decent whisky. Tell Jamie to send over a receipt later and I'll reimburse him from petty cash."

Gloria rushed off to the pub and Lou returned to Simon's office, getting stopped every few seconds by people asking when Pete was coming out and what was he really like. Upon opening the door Lou could instantly tell that Simon's customer relations skills weren't going down too well.

"I wasn't in that one," she heard Pete say, tight-mouthed.

"Weren't you?" Simon replied, nonchalantly, "Oh, who am I mixing you up with? Anyway, that was a great series wasn't it; very popular for BBC2."

Lou coughed.

"Excuse me," she said, "Everyone outside is so thrilled and excited that you're here, could I let them know that you're ready to meet them?"

Pete sighed. "Fine," he said, resignedly, opening up one of the holdalls and getting a mirror out of it. He winced at the reflection, "Give me five minutes to freshen up and change. Where am I going to talk to my fans? I didn't see a stage area or a microphone on the way in."

"Oh that's quite a funny story…" Simon began. Lou cut across him.

"You remember I mentioned the posters and cut outs," she said, "I'm afraid the stage and microphone order went through the same people."

"The cut outs; that's who I'm confusing you with," Simon shouted out. To Lou's horror he unfolded one of them, "It's this guy. He's great isn't he?"

If looks could kill all that would have been left of Simon was two smoking shoes. Pete focussed his gaze on Lou.

"Have you got my hipflask?" he asked.

"It's on its way," she turned to Simon, "Why don't you go and put the film on and check the replacement microphone and speakers are ready to go?"

Simon nodded. "That's a good idea," he said, walking to the door, "I got Terry to take a look at the public address system last night. Apparently he's very good with electronics."

Lou closed her eyes. When she opened them, Pete was staring at her. He'd taken off his t-shirt, revealing an impressive physique for someone who enjoyed a good drink and smoke.

"Have I got this straight?" he asked, pulling a bright, white shirt out of his holdall that somehow still looked crisp and fresh, "He's **your** boss?"

Lou couldn't help smiling.

"He's very good with the customers," she lied, "I just don't think he's much of a film or TV buff."

Pete laughed as he pulled on the shirt and all of Lou's feelings for him came rushing back.

"I'm to blame for this total cock-up," she admitted, "I was tasked with making this day special, I guess I'm just not up to it. I should have got the posters in earlier and the audio equipment. But we're going to show that wonderful dark comedy film of yours, 'The Theft of Purity.' It's my particular favourite. I thought you were great in that."

She smiled shyly at Pete. He smiled back at her as he buttoned up his shirt, holding her gaze until Lou felt like she was going to faint. A knock on the door broke the spell. It was Gloria.

323

"Here it is," she said, loudly, as she stood in the doorway; waving the hipflask for all to see.

"Mum!" Lou hissed, "Don't show everyone."

Gloria's response to that was to enter the room.

"Hello," she said, brightly, walking over to the desk and leaning across it, "I'm Gloria. I work at the pub across the road. Here's your drink, Pete."

She grinned up at him, fluttering her eyelashes.

"I like a man who enjoys a good scotch. There are some things in life that need a bit of age on them to give the best pleasure, don't you agree?"

"Fucking hell," Pete took a step backwards.

"Yes thanks for that Mrs Turner," Lou said.

She pulled her mum up off the table by the collar of her mac which made the front of it fling open. Gloria let out an 'ooh' sound and winked at Pete Crick as 'the girls' were thrust forward. He took another step back and pressed himself right up against the filing cabinets.

"I'm sure Mr Crick will be happy to give you an autograph later," Lou continued, as she walked her mother to the door. Before she was able to get her through it, Gloria turned round.

"I'll be waiting," she called, and indicated exactly where she wanted him to sign his name.

Lou pushed her out and shut the door.

"Jesus Christ," Pete said, "I've never been scared of a woman before now. Are they all like that around here?"

Lou didn't answer, instead she said,

"I think we're ready for you. Simon has started playing the film."

Pete took a large swig from his hipflask. Whether that was to meet his public or to steady his nerves after Gloria, Lou

324

didn't know. She opened the door. After a final check in his mirror, Pete made his way out onto the shop floor. Lou followed. She was surprised to hear silence. There was supposed to be some entrance music; the song Pete had had a minor hit with about five years ago, and she thought the crowd would have started clapping him again. He'd stopped dead, right in front of her. Lou had to walk round him to see what was happening. All eyes were facing the screen, watching the film. A naked woman had just emerged from the shower and an obviously excited man was watching her.

"What the fuck is this?" Pete spat, "Is this some kind of joke?"

Simon was standing by the public address system just outside of his office.

"What are you doing?" Lou whispered, picking up the DVD cover, "This isn't, 'The Theft of Purity'. It says, 'The Theft of my Virginity.' It's a porno film. What the hell is wrong with you, Simon?"

"Well I didn't know. I assumed he was going to show up in this in a little while so I left it running."

Lou turned round to face the shop floor. Most people still seemed to be transfixed by the screen. She saw Grace rushing out the entrance, rather red faced. Pete Crick had retreated to the office.

"Turn it off!" Lou said, and ran into the office after him.

Inside Pete was throwing his old t-shirt and mirror into one of the bags.

"I don't know what the fuck is going on here," he called over to her, "I'm in some kind of backwater hellhole. Hopefully I'll wake up in a minute."

"Mr Crick, I'm so sorry," Lou said, "It's entirely my fault. I

325

should never have taken yesterday off of work. I should have been here to oversee all of this."

"Do you spend your life apologising?" Pete asked, zipping up the bag.

"Sometimes it feels like it," Lou whispered.

"Well, you're going to have to apologise to that crowd out there. I'm not staying here a second longer. This place is the pits."

"I'm sorry," Lou said, again, "Really, this isn't the norm, I promise you. Won't you stay a bit longer; just to give out a few autographs or pose for a couple of photographs? You're very highly thought of around here."

Pete tutted. "With my luck today I'll get stuck having a photo with the fat tart that came in here; Miss Huge Honkers, 1961. It'll turn into a scene not unlike the one you're showing on the screen out there. That'll do my reputation a lot of good."

"What will walking out of here in a strop do for your reputation?" Lou asked.

Pete stopped what he was doing and glared at her.

Oh God, she thought, he's going to shout at me. Instead his face relaxed into a smile.

"You're too clever for this place," he told her. "Do you know that?"

He sighed and sat down in Simon's chair; picking up his hipflask and taking another healthy swig.

"I hate all of this," he admitted, "As if dressing up as a jester on an advert isn't bad enough, I now tour supermarkets. This isn't the life I'd planned."

He took another draught from the flask.

"Most of us don't end up with the life we planned," Lou said, walking over to stand beside him, "But you just have to try and make the best of it."

"Shit, is that the best motivational speech you can come up with?"

Lou laughed. "After what you've seen so far today, are you surprised?"

Pete looked up into Lou's eyes.

"You're okay," he said.

A second later he grabbed her arm and pulled her down into his lap; kissing her fiercely on the mouth. Even in her shock Lou couldn't help thinking, 'Oh my God, I'm kissing Pete Crick.'

She felt a hand reach up and squeeze her right breast. She tried to move it but couldn't. He squeezed harder and it hurt. Lou wanted to tell him 'no' but he was locked onto her mouth and she couldn't break away. The hand finally moved but downwards. As Pete's hand slid underneath her skirt so his mouth broke away from hers.

"Come on darling," he whispered, the fumes of his whisky breath strong enough to make Lou feel light-headed, "Don't say you don't want this. I know you do, you all do."

"I don't," Lou squirmed in his lap, "Let me go."

Pete's hand pulled at her panties.

"Get off me!" she shouted out.

"Ssh," Pete kissed her again only now, Lou felt nothing but revulsion.

She tried pushing him off but he was too strong for her, not that she stopped trying. A few moments later she thought she'd succeeded when his mouth was ripped away from hers. Suddenly another pair of hands appeared and yanked Pete out of the seat. Lou fell to the floor. What was happening? She turned round and saw Chris had the actor pressed up against the filing cabinet.

"Come on pal," Pete was saying, "We were having a bit of fun. You look like a man of the world. Come on, she was begging for it. All these slappers want a piece of me."

Chris dragged him away from the filing cabinet.

"You don't even look at her," he said, ferocity in his voice Lou had never heard before.

He pulled back his arm and punched Pete hard in the face. He flew backwards through the open door, out onto the main floor. As Pete Crick hit the ground so Simon finally switched on the entrance music. It was the wrong song.

*

Diana was in a panic. She'd woken up feeling anxious and the emotion wouldn't go away. She couldn't believe she'd actually made a date with a man; a complete stranger. Her first instinct was to cancel, but as neither of them had exchanged phone numbers that couldn't happen. Not turning up wasn't an option either. It was an impolite thing to do but Diana also couldn't help picturing an angry Keith hunting her down to find out why she'd stood him up. What if he found her in the charity shop and started shouting in front of Joyce and Muriel? That would be embarrassing.

Diana wished Lou had found someone too so that they could have double-dated. That would have been so much easier. Mind you, she thought, Lou would probably be too exhausted to go out for the evening anyway. That celebrity was visiting today and Diana had promised to pop in to lend her support. Mind you, would Lou really miss her if she didn't manage to get there? There must be so much going on and Diana was sure there'd be a crowd. Not that she was a fan of the actor. He might be good looking but from what she'd read about him in the newspapers, he seemed to be a rather arrogant young man with an ego far greater than his talent.

After all, she thought, putting a slice of bread into the toaster for breakfast; besides the advertising campaign what else had he done lately?

No; as far as Diana was concerned, once the adverts stopped the public would only be seeing Pete Crick on one of those ridiculous reality television shows, alongside all the other talentless has-beens craving attention.

After breakfast Diana tried a relaxing bath but she still spent her soak worrying. She'd resigned herself now to going on the date but what to wear. It certainly wasn't a fancy place but she wanted to make an effort. Yesterday Keith had seen her at her best. How on earth was she going to recreate that look? She considered going back into Tenham again to get the make-up redone but that was rather expensive and she'd have to go on the bus.

Diana spent the rest of the morning choosing a dress; walking around the apartment in each one to see how they flowed; sitting down in them to see what gaped or if any part of her poked through. She asked Charlie's advice but he was very non-committal and remained at the bottom of his bowl.

Once I've decided on the dress, I'll pop over to the supermarket to see how it's all going, Diana promised herself; but then she caught a glimpse of her hair in the hallway mirror. I'll just try and tame this first.

By the time she'd got her hair right and had a late lunch, Diana felt she ought to make a start on her make-up. That took a lot longer than anticipated. When she was finally happy with the result, she realised it was too late to go to the supermarket now anyway. The event would be over but she was sure Lou had made it a great success.

At seven o'clock that evening Diana was sat at a table in the restaurant section of The Green Man, her nerves still in tatters. She didn't like being at the table in the centre, especially as everybody else around her were all sat in couples, chatting together and enjoying their meals. What if Keith was the one not to turn up? How long should she sit here and wait for him?

Diana poured herself a glass of water from the jug on the table to give her hands something to do. She drank it very quickly and poured herself another. Now she needed to use the toilet. What if Keith arrived while she was in there and assumed she hadn't turned up? She couldn't leave her bag behind at the table as it had her purse in it. She couldn't take off her sparkly cardigan and place that on the chair either as her dress was sleeveless and Diana was a bit self-conscious of the loose skin on her upper arms. Why hadn't she put on the black, long-sleeved?

The fear of wetting her knickers trumped all other worries and Diana quickly rushed off to the Ladies. When she returned Keith was sat at the table, looking quite relaxed. He stood up and grinned as she walked over; gently holding her arm while he leaned in to kiss her on the cheek.

"I'm sorry," Diana said, "I was just…well I…"

Fortunately Keith interrupted her.

"My apologies for being late," he said, "I got waylaid by a phone call."

They both sat down.

"You know," he continued, "I didn't think it was possible for you to look more beautiful than you did last night."

Diana smiled and looked down shyly at her menu. The waiter arrived to take the drinks order.

"Is white wine okay?" Keith asked.

She nodded.

"The Sancerre," Keith said, gruffly; to the waiter, not making eye contact; "And make sure it's properly chilled."

He thrust the wine menu at him. When he turned his attention back to Diana, Keith was all smiles.

"So," he said, "How has your day been?"

"Oh I've not done much really," Diana said, "How about you?"

"Very boringly I had to go into the office."

Keith began speaking about his work.

He can't find it that boring, Diana thought, when he was still going ten minutes later; but she was glad that he found it easy to talk. She still felt tongue-tied.

Diana discovered that Keith headed up a Finance team for an insurance company based in Tenham. He'd been widowed for several years and hadn't dated much since. Diana spoke a little about Richard. She mentioned how he too had been in insurance at a different company. She told him he had died but didn't say how.

By the time coffee was ordered Diana was hooked. Keith didn't resemble her Richard at all physically, but there was something about him; perhaps the way he spoke confidently about his career and how he seemed to give off a kind of aura that said he would always be in control of any situation. Diana found that comforting. He was kindness itself to her, but the way he spoke to the waiters; well, Lou wouldn't like him, and that was a bit of a worry.

They made plans to see each other again on Tuesday evening. As he opened the pub door for her at the end of the date, Diana smiled. She was happy. This was exactly what had been missing from her life. She was already looking forward to the next date with Keith. Maybe she should give it a little while though, before she introduced him to Lou.

*

Lou slowly opened her eyes. Something was different, she could feel it; but what? Not the pain in her head; that was exactly the same as yesterday morning; another day, another hangover. How come she had another hangover? Why had she been out drinking? Lou shot up in bed and let out a moan as everything went white behind her eyes.

Maddie? No, hang on, it's okay; she stayed the night with Tony's mum. Why was that? Oh yeah, the nightclub. After the disaster of 'Pete Crick Day' she'd decided to go clubbing with Precious. They'd gone to The Red Lion first for shots and then went to the club and that's where she bumped into...

An icy chill ran down Lou's back. Very slowly she lowered her hands and opened her eyes to look at the room. The shelf along the opposite wall beside the door still had the display of model cars on it while underneath was the familiar poster of a naked woman with a puppy between her breasts. Lou took a deep breath and turned her head to the left. A big, gummy grin was staring back up at her.

"Morning babes."

"Oh my God!"

"I always knew I'd get you back in my bed again."

Lou's hands returned to her face, covering her eyes. So that's why there was a smell of stale farts in the air. She should have realised sooner.

"What the hell am I doing here," she asked?

"You insisted," she heard Chris say, "Said I was your hero and that you felt safe with me."

Chris had come to her rescue yesterday; that was true. It had been an awful situation to be in but Lou felt it was all her fault. She should have seen it coming. She should have been in control of everything. So much for being able to run a store of her own, she couldn't even get a small event to go right. They'd piled Pete Crick back into his car; much to the amusement of the chauffeur, and sent him on his way.

Simon had been chilled about the whole thing. He told Lou there'd be no repercussions as a friend of his in head office had told him that Pete Crick was being dropped from the commercials anyway and this tour sparked the end of the contract. His drinking had apparently got out of hand and everyone in the store had seen his hipflask fly out of his pocket as he landed after Chris had punched him. Lou still blamed herself though. She'd wished Diana had been there. She always made her feel confident. Where the hell had she been?

It was the way Pete had come onto her that had affected Lou the most, especially after her night with Tony. Did all men see her as some kind of easy lay? Was that the persona she gave out? Is that what the coven saw? Well she'd just proved them right, waking up for the second day running in the bed of an ex-lover.

If only Diana hadn't had a date last night. Lou could have gone home and spoken with her about the day rather than going out and getting drunk; then this wouldn't have happened. Chris said she'd insisted on coming back here. Was that true? Probably, Lou thought. She couldn't really remember anything, which perhaps, was a blessing.

"I've got to go," she said to him, "I've got to pick up Maddie."

"Of course babes," he replied, throwing back the covers.

333

Chris got up and began stretching in front of the window. Lou quickly turned and faced the other way, gathering her clothes towards her while she held the duvet up to her chin.

"Is your mum about?"

She really didn't want anyone else knowing about this.

"No," Chris replied, "She's gone away on another one of her 'Spa weekends.' Honestly, she must realise by now that I know she's having a dirty weekend with her latest fella."

"Perhaps she really is at a spa."

Chris laughed. "Yeah right," he replied, "I know what 'treatment' she's getting right now."

He turned round to face her.

"Do you want me to drive you home?"

Lou averted her eyes.

"No; thank you. I'll call for a cab," she said, sitting up straighter in the bed, "Look Chris, I'm not looking for us to get back together, last night wasn't…"

"I know," he interrupted.

"You do?"

"'Course babes. I'm not that much of an idiot. You've moved on. You're going places."

Lou smiled. "Do you know I think that's the nicest thing you've ever said to me?"

Chris looked puzzled.

"Can't be," he told her, "I must have mentioned you've got cracking tits before."

Lou realised the duvet had dropped and became very self-conscious of her 'cracking tits.' She pulled the duvet up again. Chris laughed, watching her as he stood there naked by the window.

"I'll turn round if you want, while you get dressed."

Lou smiled. "Thanks," she said.

As Lou pulled on her clothes Chris stood looking out of the window, whistling. He seemed in no hurry to dress himself. When Lou glanced over she was sure he waved at someone outside in the street.

"Right," she said, as she picked up her handbag, "I'm off."

"It was good having you, babes."

Lou froze as she reached for the door handle.

"To stay, I mean."

"Right, thanks Chris."

She nodded and opened the door.

"You're a classy bird, doll. Don't forget that."

Lou looked back to say thanks. Chris had just picked last night's t-shirt up off the floor. He gave it a sniff, shrugged his shoulders and put it on, turning round to look for the rest of his outfit. She couldn't help wincing.

"I'll see you at work tomorrow then," she told him.

"Yep," he replied, and bent over to retrieve a sock, "I'll be there at the crack."

Lou turned and fled.

She went straight home and jumped in the shower. What the hell had happened to her in the past twenty-four hours? She'd woken up yesterday feeling positive and confident, albeit slightly hung-over. Today she was feeling depressed, low and still hung-over. She'd managed to sleep with two different men and got groped by a third. It was a wake-up call. She'd become too confident in herself; gone above her station, that had to be the reason this had happened. She dried off and sat down at her dressing table, looking at the reflection in the mirror.

"My God you've been a silly bitch," she said, "New hair and a dress you can't afford won't change who you really are. **You** can't change that either, no matter what you try and do. Just accept things as they are, Lou Turner. Stop reaching for the stars."

Chapter 17

If she was totally honest with herself, Lou didn't want to go back to how her life had been before becoming friends with Diana but it very quickly seemed to do just that. Three weeks had passed since that night with Chris. She hadn't realised until then just how much her world had changed, and for the better. She'd enjoyed spending time with her new friend; taken pleasure from exercising and loved her new-found interest in cookery. She'd gained so much confidence and self-worth that other things started happening, such as the chance for promotion at work, but after the events with Tony and Pete Crick, that confidence had taken a battering. She'd aimed too high, that was Lou's conclusion. It was time to rein things in.

She'd hardly seen or spoken to Diana since the singles night at The Smugglers, just an occasional word here and there. She knew Diana was still seeing the man she had met, not that Lou had been introduced to him. Was Diana embarrassed by her? Had Joyce Pendleton been right when she said Diana was only going through a phase? She'd said Diana would soon see Lou for what she truly was; a common, little tart. Isn't that what Lou had seen herself, in the mirror that morning after she'd come back from Chris's? She'd slept with two different men in the space of twenty-four hours. The reflection that had stared back at her was the woman Joyce Pendleton and probably the rest of Ryan Harbour, saw.

Without Diana and the list in her life, Lou's world had reverted to the supermarket and home. Would the list ever be completed? There were only two items left, work with animals and broaden horizons. Lou had long since given up hope of

going on a luxury cruise but Maddie hadn't forgotten she'd
been promised a trip to the zoo to see Auntie Diana be a zoo
keeper. She kept pestering her mother about it and Lou often
lost her temper with her.

Lou's irritability wasn't all Maddie's fault, however. She
had so many things on her mind; Jamie for one. She hadn't set
foot inside The Smugglers since Singles Night as she was trying
to avoid alcohol. Of course this meant that she'd never got
around to apologising to him for her outburst about the way he
was running his bar. Did he think she was still angry with him?

She was angry with herself. What right had she to tell him
he was doing it all wrong? He obviously knew a lot more about
the pub game than she did. The longer she left it though, the
harder she found it to go and see him. Why was that? Why did
she keep putting it off? It didn't help that every time her mother
saw her she kept trying to ask what had happened with Tony
that night and why Lou was so noticeably not herself at the
moment.

She'd stopped going to the exercise classes and hadn't been
to the baking class since baps week. Jogging was the one thing
she had kept up of a lunchtime, although with the weather
turning colder, Lou wasn't sure how long that was going to last
either. It was a break from the monotony of work though.
Simon had heard nothing about the management trainee course
and Lou had convinced herself that she didn't have a place.
Why would the supermarket bosses think she could run her own
store anyway after so many years of just stacking shelves? The
work had become boring and Lou felt dejected. When Jesters
decided to drop its clothing line, Simon wanted ideas of what to
do with the freed up space. Lou just shrugged her shoulders
when asked.

"Why not put it back to how it used to be," she'd said.

Simon had looked disappointed and made the decision to turn it into a bargain section for sales items and 'two for one' offers instead. He'd ordered signs for the display and that's what Lou was hanging up now from the ceiling, while Terry worked below, stocking the display shelves and baskets.

"I can see your scrunchie from down here," he called up to her.

"What?"

Lou almost fell off the ladder. She looked down and saw the band she used to tie her hair back with was hanging out of the pocket of her overall.

"Thank you, Terry," she said, stuffing it back in.

"I liked you with long hair," he added, blushing a little.

Lou smiled. "Thanks," she told him, "I'm going to grow it again."

She came down off the ladder.

"That's as straight as I can get it," she said, looking up.

"Should we really be telling customers to bog off?" Terry asked, also looking up at one of the signs.

"It's only the initial letters of each word that spell that, Terry. The phrase is, 'Buy one, get one free.' The words are written up there too."

Terry squinted. "They're written very small," he said, "All I can see from down here is B.O.G.O.F. down the left-hand side."

"It's a well-known phrase. No one will take offence."

Lou closed up the ladder. Terry was still staring at the signs.

"What about that other one for the clothing sale?" he asked, "Will that not cause offence?"

Lou sighed and looked up as well. She frowned.

"Oh, I do see what you mean."

The other sign read, 'Sale. One Day Only. Fabulous Fashions."

"I'd better take that one down," Lou said, resignedly, "We really can't tell customers to sod off."

She opened the ladder and climbed back up. Why hadn't she noticed that before hanging it up? A few weeks ago she would have. Lou looked at her watch as she came back down.

"You're due on tea break aren't you, Terry? Why don't you head off and I'll finish filling these shelves. Could you put the ladder back for me on the way, thanks?"

It was a quiet Monday morning and Precious soon wandered over when there were no customers to serve at the till.

"Bog Off?"

"It's fine," Lou told her.

Precious didn't say anything else and kept looking around, idly.

"Is something wrong?"

"Hmm? Oh, no; nothing's wrong."

She continued to loiter there. If Lou didn't know her better, she would have said Precious appeared nervous. She heard her sigh.

"Chris seems to like his new uniform," she said.

"Yes, he does," Lou replied, looking over to where Chris was sat by the public address system in his blue jumper and black trousers. He was miming into the microphone.

"Navy Blue is definitely his colour," Precious continued, staring at him, "It really compliments his eyes."

"Okay, now I know something is wrong," Lou said, standing up from the bottom shelf she'd been filling, "Come on, out with it."

Precious made a groaning sound.

340

"It's Chris," she admitted.

"He's not been sniffing your hair again has he?"

Precious shook her head.

"What about waving his crotch at the barcode scanner?"

"No."

"He's not still drawing faces on blown up condoms and putting on puppet shows over your till?"

Precious giggled. "That's quite funny really," she said, but then sighed, "I...well I just can't stop thinking about him," she confessed.

"He is a bit difficult to forget," Lou agreed, watching him scratch his armpit and then sniff his fingers.

"I don't mean like that," Precious told her, "Oh God, this is so difficult to say to you after your history together."

Lou turned back to face her friend.

"You're not telling me you fancy him?"

Precious nodded. There was a pause as Lou tried to find words to reply to this revelation. In the end she settled on, "How?"

"It was three weeks ago, on 'Pete Crick Day;' when he came to your rescue like a knight in shining armour."

"Oh, that."

"I just thought he was so brave and manly."

"It was really good of him, I'll admit that," Lou said, "But even so, this is Chris we're talking about. I'd be less shocked if you told me you fancied Terry."

Precious grinned. "He's just a boy, Chris is all man."

This conversation was starting to turn Lou's stomach.

"So erm, what are you going to do about it?" she asked.

Precious shrugged her shoulders.

"That's up to you."

341

"Why me?"

"Well, you and he were together for so long."

"Yes, but that's been over for a long time."

Lou hadn't told anyone about what had happened between them three weeks ago.

"I don't want to tread on your toes," Precious said.

Lou couldn't help smiling.

"That's very sweet of you," she replied, "If you really want to date Chris then be my guest. I don't have a problem with it, but honestly…this is Chris."

Precious sighed longingly again.

"I know," she said.

Fortunately Simon opened the door to his office just then and beckoned Lou over so she didn't have to continue on with this surreal conversation.

"I have some good news," he told her, once they were inside, "You've been accepted on the management trainee program."

*

Diana realised she was humming as she applied her make-up. The past three weeks with Keith had been great. She couldn't remember the last time she'd felt this way. They'd seen each other so often it seemed to Diana like they'd known one another for years. Every time he phoned her to see if she was free she felt a thrill. She'd been going out a lot less; preferring to wait indoors in case he rang. She really must get herself a mobile phone. They'd been to dinner, the theatre, had walks in the park. Everyone Diana had introduced him to found him charming. Granted that was only Joyce, Muriel and Celia but still. She so wanted him to meet Lou but was scared of what her reaction would be.

Diana wasn't stupid; she knew Keith fitted in very well with her old friends. She'd seen the way he spoke to waiters in restaurants and listened to him moaning on about how he was treated in stores by 'god-awful shop staff.' She knew Lou would hate him on sight and accuse Diana of reverting to type, but she liked Keith a lot. He had lots of other qualities and was fun to be with. He made Diana feel special and beautiful every time they went out. She hadn't met any of his friends yet but then they did tend to spend time together here in Ryan Harbour rather than over at his place in Tenham. As Keith had explained to her; when your home life and office life are in close proximity it's nice to get away from it all somewhere else and relax; especially when there was a beautiful lady to relax with.

They'd also enjoyed that trip to London the previous weekend where they'd stayed overnight and finally shared a bed. Since then they'd enjoyed several other love-making sessions together in Diana's apartment. They'd not even made it out to dinner. Not that Diana minded. It felt wonderful and so natural for her to be with Keith.

He'd called her earlier this morning to say he was free around lunchtime and could he come over and satisfy his appetite. Diana had giggled. She'd been due over at Joyce's for a special meeting regarding the new program for the youth of the town but they could do without her just this once. They were making great strides with the council regarding the use of the empty premises beside the doctor's surgery. Diana was sure the meeting would run smoothly and besides, she could catch up with Joyce tomorrow.

After finishing her make-up Diana rushed down to the lounge and quickly put some food into Charlie's bowl before making her way over to the kitchen to check the soup on the stove. She'd made it for a meal with Keith last week and he'd said he loved it. It took hours to make but Diana had spent yesterday preparing a fresh batch, ready for the next time he came over. The soup was bubbling away nicely and the salad was ready on the plate. She wouldn't put the steaks under the grill until after he arrived.

She'd nipped over to the supermarket earlier to buy them. Lou had looked like she wanted to tell her something but Diana had stopped her and explained she had to get back home again. She knew she was neglecting her friend but time with Keith had been so lovely and precious. Perhaps she'd pop across to Lou's one evening this week with a bottle of wine and have a proper catch up.

The buzzer sounded on the intercom. Diana's heart began thumping in her chest and she ran to answer it. She buzzed Keith in and while she waited for him to arrive did a final check of her appearance in the hall mirror; making a few corrections to her hair. Keith entered through the open front door.

"My God that's a rare treat for a man to see on a Monday lunchtime," he said.

He grabbed Diana's arm and pulled her towards him. She laughed. He kissed her hard on the lips. In a second his hands were raking through her carefully styled hair and he was pushing her backwards to the bedroom. Half an hour later he dressed, kissed Diana on the forehead and left. She'd have to put those steaks in the freezer for another time.

*

Robert pressed the button for the second floor and felt the lift begin to ascend. It had been a very long three weeks. After their argument at the singles evening Grace had refused to speak to him for the rest of the weekend; and for Grace; going two days without talking showed how angry she really was. By the Monday she had thawed and life returned to normal with Robert working and coming home to the same meals on set days as before. The first week had been bearable but by the second Robert's desire for change began to grow again. He was still tentative about talking to Grace but by week three he knew he had to broach the subject again about spicing things up.

"It's just a case of finding something that works for both of us," he had told her last Friday, "I mean; Rome wasn't built in a day. So we've had a few failures; doesn't mean we should stop altogether."

Grace wasn't convinced but resignedly told Robert to come up with an idea over the weekend, but one where they both had to sit down and discuss it first.

"Hello love, had a good day," Grace called out when she heard Robert's key in the door.

"Ye-es," he replied.

Robert had a quick wash and then entered the lounge with the sex toys catalogue. All through dinner Grace kept eyeing it suspiciously.

"It's not going to bite you," Robert eventually said to her, "It's only a catalogue."

"That's not a catalogue," Grace told him, as she cleared the plates, "A catalogue sells clothes or household goods."

"Well this one is full of sex toys."

Grace shuddered. "I don't know how it's acceptable to advertise things like that so freely, I really don't. The world's gone mad, in my opinion."

Robert decided it was best to remain silent and let Grace have her rant.

"A catalogue should just be one filled with pictures of men and women in seasonal clothing," she continued, firmly, "I used

345

to love receiving my catalogues through the post, especially the autumn/winter editions; all those lovely cardigans and pullovers. Mind you, I was a little embarrassed when they started advertising men's underwear. They didn't really need to have models wearing them; especially under the slogan, 'Get your hands on a package this Christmas.'"

Robert sighed. Was this going to turn into another disaster? He thought his wife was on board this time. Okay so she was shocked at first when he'd initially suggested looking at toys but that's just because she'd got hold of the wrong end of the stick.

"You're not involving Mr Snuggles in anything sordid," she'd told him, "I've had that bear since I was a little girl. It would be immoral. I wouldn't even let him watch."

It had taken Robert a while to explain what he'd actually meant.

With dinner finished and the dishwasher stacked they both sat down on the sofa together.

"Once we've chosen what we want this will be a lot simpler than the other ideas," Robert promised, "We'll already be in bed together and can just lie back and try a few new things; see what tickles our fancy."

"I don't want my fancy tickled, thank you very much," Grace told him. She looked warily at the catalogue in Robert's hands, "I don't know where you keep getting hold of all this stuff."

"It doesn't matter. Let's just have a browse through, shall we."

"Alright," Grace said, moving closer, "But just so you know, I want nothing to do with those long, buzzing things. You're not putting a dodo inside of me."

346

"A dildo."

"Or that."

"Okay love."

Robert opened up the catalogue.

"And you can forget all about those for a start," Grace said, pointing at a page full of whips and handcuffs, "The only whipping being done in this apartment is when I'm making meringues. Oh that reminds me, I need some eggs."

She grabbed a piece of paper and a pen while Robert turned to the next page. When Grace looked back she frowned and leaned nearer to the picture.

"That looks like a rosary," she said, "But it can't be."

Robert squinted at the tiny writing underneath.

"They're anal beads."

"They're what?"

"Anal beads. That's what it says here."

Grace sat back and thought to herself.

"What on earth do you do with those?" she asked.

Robert had continued to read the description.

"It says here that the beads are attached together in a series and you insert them into the anus."

"Really?"

"Yep; through the anus and into the rectum."

"Isn't that what you strum a guitar with?"

"No, that's a plectrum," Robert told her.

Grace was still looking puzzled.

"But what's the point of doing that," she asked.

"It says here that once they're in, you pull them out at varying speeds and it's meant to be pleasurable."

Grace grimaced. "I can't see how that's pleasurable," she said, "I expect it would feel like a loose bowel movement."

Robert was still reading.

"That's interesting," he said, "It says here that the ring at the end of the line, that you use to pull them out with; is also there to prevent the beads from getting lodged inside of you."

"Oh God."

"And that you should count the beads once you've pulled them out."

"Like on an abacus."

"Well it's to make sure they're all out rather than doing sums," Robert told her, "You don't want to leave one inside."

Grace shook her head, slowly.

"You live and learn don't you," she said, "And people really use these?"

"I guess so," Robert turned the page again, "Oh, this seems more our kind of thing; love eggs."

"Ah," Grace smiled, "That sounds lovely. What is it?"

Robert remained quiet as he read the description.

"Oh," he said, finally, "Maybe not."

"What is it?" Grace repeated.

"Erm, well; it's an egg-shaped...well it's a bit like a vibrator that you insert into your...lady parts."

"How big is it?" Grace asked, "It sounds like it would be tricky to get in."

"It goes in like a tampon apparently, according to this."

"Oh dear," she replied, "I never really got on with them."

"It says here it can vibrate at different speeds inside of you, which is meant to give pleasure. They can be on a wire or they can be remote controlled."

"Remote controlled?"

"Yep. It says here, 'for distance teasing.'"

Grace looked incredulously at her husband.

348

"So you could switch it on while I'm over at the supermarket and it would start whirring about inside of me? What if I was just reaching up for a pint of milk? I could flood the place."

"I doubt it would work at that distance," Robert said.

Grace shook her head.

"Well I'm not taking any chances," she told him, firmly, "Turn the page."

Robert did as he was told.

"Oh, they look nice," Grace said, "I didn't know they did jewellery. I'm looking for some hooped earrings."

"They're not earrings, love."

"What are they then?"

"Cock rings, it's got written here."

Grace raised her eyebrows.

"What, they put them on a cock?"

Robert nodded.

"Well I think that's cruel," she said, "Surely they don't need to be tethered like that."

"What?"

"Well, when I was young, the local farmer told me that after a few days with the chickens a new cock would stick around."

"It doesn't mean a cockerel," Robert said, exasperated, "It's a man's cock!"

Grace's hands flew up to her face.

"Oh my good God," she said, "What on earth is the point of that? You can't tell me that's sexual."

"Of course it is. It wouldn't be in here otherwise. It's placed around the base of the cock…"

Grace tutted. "Will you please not use that word?"

"There's nothing wrong with it. I think it's a scientific term."

"Oh really," she questioned, "Like the other term you used earlier; 'my lady parts?'"

Robert sighed. "Fine," he said, "It's placed around the base of the penis to slow the blood flow."

"And is that meant to be pleasurable for you; because it sounds damn painful to me."

"It makes the, you know, the tent pole last longer," Robert told her, blushing a little.

"And what's the point of that?"

"To give you pleasure for longer!"

"Well that's ridiculous," Grace said, "I think ten minutes is enough for any woman."

Robert was reading under his breath. Eventually he said, "Blimey you really have to read these things carefully. It says these shouldn't be worn by a man who's on blood thinning medication or who has heart disease, isn't that interesting. And you also shouldn't wear one for more than half an hour."

"Half an hour! My God, what sort of sexual deviant wants to do it for that length of time?"

Robert felt it wasn't the right moment to raise his hand.

"They can be made in rubber, metal or even leather," he continued.

"How common!"

"It could get entangled in your hair it says here. I guess I'd need to get a trim before wearing one."

"But you're not due at the barbers for another two weeks," Grace said, "It's written on the calendar."

"Not that hair," Robert sighed, "I mean down there. How is it going to get entangled in the hair on my head?"

"Well I don't know!"

Robert turned to the back page before they started arguing

again.

"Butt plugs," he read out loud.

"Oh charming, back in that area again," Grace said.

"Inserted into the rectum for sexual pleasure."

Grace tutted.

"Can have animal tails attached to them," Robert read.

"What was that?" Grace looked over at the page.

"Animal tails can be attached to the butt plugs to be used in," Robert squinted at the small printing, "Animal fantasy play, such as the human pony."

They both looked at each other.

"No," Robert said, "I'm not sure what that means either. I guess you pop one in and pretend to be a horse."

"It's a sick world out there," Grace said, getting up, "Sorry Robert but I feel the need to bathe. I'm going to have a shower."

"Hang on love, we haven't decided on anything."

"Well I'm not using any of those things in there."

Robert looked back down at the catalogue.

"I don't know; the animal fantasy has given me an idea."

Grace's eyes widened with horror.

"What do you mean? You don't want to be a horsey do you? Is this about whips and things?"

"No. I meant the fantasy part."

Grace sighed. "Haven't we been there already?"

"No, I was thinking of costumes," Robert said, "Isn't there someone you've always fantasised about?"

Grace shook her head.

"Of course not, Robert," she told him, "I've only ever wanted you."

"Well that's lovely but I mean, I don't know; do you like

351

firemen's uniforms for example or did you fancy Tarzan in his loincloth; that type of thing. I could dress up for you."

Grace thought for a few seconds and then a smile appeared on her face.

"I did quite like the man who came and read the gas meter at our last house," she said.

"Well I can hardly dress up as him for you now, can I."

"He had lovely shoes," Grace continued, dreamily, "Always took them off before he came into the house. Big feet but lovely manners."

Robert was starting to really hate this guy.

"I wonder what ever happened to him," Grace said, still miles away, "Probably retired long ago."

Robert grinned. Perhaps a little fantasy role play wouldn't go amiss right now. He stood up.

"Would the lady like me to follow her into the shower so I can take a look at her gas meter?"

Out loud that sentence sounded wrong to both of them.

Chapter 18

Diana was surprised when she walked into Joyce's front room on Tuesday morning.

"No Muriel?" she asked, "I thought we were meeting for tea."

"No," Joyce replied, "I wanted the two of us to have a little chat."

"That sounds ominous," Diana said, sitting down in one of the armchairs, "You're not about to lecture me on my love life or something, are you?"

Joyce smiled. "Of course not," she informed Diana, "I think you're managing that okay on your own. Keith seems to be a very charming man. Even Norman said so. He's been raving about him all week. I can't shut him up."

Diana doubted that but she said aloud,

"Thank you."

The smile left Joyce's face as she moved into efficiency mode.

"No, this is about the committee meeting that you missed yesterday."

"Oh yes."

"Mmm," Joyce put on her glasses and reached for a piece of paper, "It was quite an important one. I'm afraid we can't use the premises in the harbour."

"What? But it was practically all settled."

"Not settled enough my dear. It looks like Dr Bryant is going to expand his surgery into the premises we were hoping to use. He's done a deal with the council," Joyce removed her glasses and put down the sheet of paper. She smiled again, "So that's that."

"What about one of the other premises," Diana asked, "Maybe we could contact the owners…"

Joyce raised her hands in a calming gesture.

"It's over, Diana," she said, "We put it to a vote. I felt, as many of the others did, that we have spent long enough on this project. You must admit, it has turned into a bit of a wild goose chase, trying to find premises; what with the village hall, the school and now the shop beside Dr Bryant's."

"But we had so much planned for activities," Diana said, dismayed.

"These things happen," Joyce told her, getting up.

"So what's next?" Diana asked.

"What do you mean?"

"Well, is there going to be another project?"

Joyce sighed and moved across to sit on the arm of Diana's chair.

"I think it's probably for the best if you sit the next one out," she said, patting Diana's hand, "You see a few of the ladies felt a little put out with your presence."

"What?"

"I'm sorry Diana, these aren't my words; but you must try and see it from their point of view. You came into the committee as a new member and worked everyone up; trying to get your ideas off the ground. They've all helped you by giving their free time and what is there to show for it; nothing."

"But I never wanted them to…"

Joyce interrupted her again.

"I know, I know. But I've got to think of the committee as a whole, Diana. I'm afraid you're out of the group," Joyce stood up again, "Now then, I've managed to stop them having a vote to get rid of you, I thought that wouldn't be fair; instead I'm going to say that, due to other circumstances; you've decided you don't have enough time to commit yourself to worthy causes."

Joyce looked at her watch.

"Now, I've got a meeting with the vicar, so if you wouldn't mind?"

Diana looked up and realised Joyce wanted her to leave. She stood up, feeling a bit dazed and left.

As she walked down the road towards the harbour Diana tried to think over all of the previous meetings. The ladies had seemed excited about the project. What had happened? It wasn't her fault that the village hall had some covenant on it or that the school caretaker didn't want to keep the school open later; and how was she to know that Dr Bryant had plans to expand the surgery? My God, he'd not long moved into the harbour premises, wasn't it a little soon to be thinking of expanding again?

As she turned down the side road to the slipway so she heard her name called. Turning she saw Gloria waving at her from the backyard of the pub. Diana walked over.

"How are you?" Gloria asked, "I haven't seen you in a while."

"No, I'm sorry about that," Diana replied, "I've been a bit busy lately."

"So I've heard," Gloria winked, "So how's it going with the new man?"

Diana smiled. "It's going very well," she told her.

"I'm so jealous."

"I'm sure the right man is out there for you too," Diana said, "Maybe he'll be at the next singles event."

Gloria sighed. "I don't think there's going to be another one."

"Why not, it was a success wasn't it?"

"Oh, His Nibs has got some other idea he's been working on," Gloria told her, "Anyway, you should bring your new man into the pub for a drink some time. God knows we could do with the custom."

"I will," Diana said, "I've meant to, it's just…"

She couldn't say she was worried what Lou would think of him. Gloria formed her own opinion of Diana's silence.

"Is it too early?" she suggested, "Has it not got serious enough yet?"

"No, that's not the reason," Diana replied, "We've actually seen rather a lot of each other. It's just that we spend most of our time at my apartment, just the two of us. Well, the three of us if you include my Charlie."

Gloria giggled and slapped Diana playfully on the arm.

"I'm glad one of us is getting her oats," she said.

Diana looked confused.

"Anyway," Gloria continued, "That's not why I called over to you. Have you seen Lou lately?"

Diana's guilt returned. "Erm, no; not really."

"I'm a bit worried about her," Gloria said, "She seemed to be so happy, but since that singles night; I don't know, I think something is wrong. She won't say anything to me. I thought perhaps you could ask her. She might talk to a friend rather than her mother."

"I will, yes; definitely," Diana said, "I'll pop over this evening."

Gloria smiled. "That's great, thanks."

Diana had planned to go over with a bottle sometime this

week. It would be nice to have a chat with Lou. If she told her about getting thrown off of the committee she knew Lou would have a good laugh about it and that would make her laugh too. Diana smiled. Yes, she'd knock tonight. After all, she had something she needed to confess to her.

*

Dr's Case Notes – Tuesday 27 October

It's been quite a busy few weeks really. So busy in fact that this is the first entry I've been able to write for a while.

It all started about three weeks ago when Mrs Andrews, my receptionist, mentioned; completely out of the blue, that there was a possibility of my expanding the surgery further into the premises next door. I'd never even thought about it but, as she pointed out, with those new apartments nearing completion, Ryan Harbour was steadily growing. She said she'd heard the council were looking very favourably on any ideas to get the harbour front rejuvenated. I don't know how she knew this but it started me thinking.

By the next day I'd phoned the council up and Mrs Andrews was proved right. This sent my mind into overdrive and I've been busily making plans for expansion ever since. Only this week I entered into a contract with the council to purchase the premises next door. Of course the real reason for my excitement is that this would mean offering a permanent position to Dr Moore. God there's lots of positions I'd like to offer Dr Moore. I haven't brought up the subject yet as I wanted to get the plans in place first, but I will; very soon.

I've talked it over with Mrs Bryant. She seems to think I'm expanding and getting in new doctors so that I can semi-retire and spend more time with her. God forbid! Fortunately since giving up the wrestling she no longer needs a ringside assistant on competition nights. Honestly, rubbing her thighs between rounds is like stroking the back of a wild boar. And her aim isn't great when spitting into the bucket. I was yawning once and almost drowned.

She's still weightlifting but has also begun a new hobby; singing. I'm a tad worried about it really. When she first told me I thought she meant she was joining a choir. Turns out it's a new band, singing some sort of cross between heavy metal, hard rock and anarchic punk. She's considering getting a spider's web tattoo across her face. I told her, once the tattooist has weaved it around her pimples, scars and stubble; it will look more like a mangled hubcap.

I wonder if Dr Moore has any secret, intimate tattoos. There's only one way to find out. Well actually there are two. I could just ask but where's the fun in that? No, I want Dr Moore to show me. Oh God, do you know what? I can't wait any longer. I'm going to go and mention the premises expansion and permanent job offer; and then we can go and celebrate our new partnership with a drink at The Smugglers. Do they serve Champagne?

*

It had seemed a very long day to Lou. Tuesdays were always slow at the supermarket but the hours had dragged by. Even though she was feeling a lot more positive about things after being accepted on the management trainee course, she just felt exhausted right now and didn't know why. She kept yawning as she walked across to the pub car park to get in the car and go and collect Maddie from the child minder.

"God, I can see what you had for lunch from here."

Lou looked round and saw Jamie standing out the back of the pub, smiling at her. She felt her stomach lurch as she

358

remembered she still hadn't apologised. Well now was as good a time as any. She walked over to him.

"It's been a long day," she told him.

"Yes you look absolutely knackered," Jamie told her, "Utterly worn-out."

Lou couldn't help grinning. Suddenly everything felt okay again.

"Yes, thanks for that," she replied; "I guess I won't be making it into the Ryan Harbour Beauties calendar this year, like you."

Jamie laughed.

Lou stopped smiling. "Actually, I've been meaning to come and see you," she said, "I wanted to apologise for my little outburst at singles night. I really don't know what came over me."

Jamie waved his hands, dismissively.

"You've got nothing to apologise for," he said, "In fact I wanted to thank you."

"To thank me?"

"Yes. You made me stop and think about what I really wanted to do with the pub and you were right."

"I usually am."

Jamie grinned at her. "Have you got a second?" he asked.

"Only a second," Lou said, looking at her watch, "I'm off to pick Maddie up."

Jamie rushed back inside the pub and emerged less than a minute later holding, what looked like, a cream-coloured, laminated piece of card. He handed it to Lou.

"A new menu," he explained.

Lou read down the list.

"This is great," she said.

"It was all your idea," Jamie told her, "Deep-filled sandwiches on a range of artisan breads, lots of new fillings for jacket potatoes, homemade soups. I've been experimenting with flavours for weeks. Each plate will have a proper side garnish. I've worked really hard on all aspects."

"I can see that," Lou said, handing back the menu.

"And I've also got a great idea of how to advertise it."

Lou started to feel worried.

"I know what you're thinking," Jamie told her, "But to be honest, with the outlay for food and the price for getting these menus printed, it's going to cost me a pretty penny. There's nothing left for a good advertising campaign."

"What are you going to do?" Lou asked.

"I'm going to hold an eating competition," Jamie grinned, "One of those all you can eat type things with a prize for the winner. All the food will be items on the new menu. I've spoken with the local paper and they sounded keen and said they'd probably do an article on it, so there's my advertising."

"Actually that sounds like a really good idea," Lou replied, "When are you going to have it?"

"I've not set a date yet. I want to make sure I've got everything right first; but soon."

"Well you know I'll always help out, if I can," Lou said, "I must go now."

She smiled and walked back to her car. As she drove to the child minder, Lou found that she was still wearing that same smile. Jamie seemed so excited by his new project and had obviously worked so hard on it. Lou was happy for him. He deserved success. The smile fell from her face once she'd picked Maddie up.

"Why can't we go to the zoo?" she whined.

360

Lou sighed. Maddie just wouldn't let this go.

"We're waiting for Auntie Diana to organise her zoo keeping day," Lou told her, for what felt like the thousandth time."

"I want to go to the zoo now."

Maddie kept repeating that same sentence the entire journey home.

"Ok fine," Lou said, resignedly, as she parked the car, "We'll go on our own."

"When?"

"How about this Sunday? You won't want to go Saturday as you'll be out trick or treating for Hallowe'en with your school friends. God I hope that Amber with the allergies isn't coming this year. Her mum demands that no child picks a peanut snack and then she has an argument at each house when the owners don't offer a range of gluten free treats."

"Sunday," Maddie cheered, as Lou let her out of the car, "Put it in the diary."

"As soon as we're indoors."

What the hell, Lou thought; they could always visit the zoo again when Diana finally decided to sign up to be a keeper.

Maddie skipped along to the apartment quite happily. Inside she raced to the drawer in the kitchen where Lou kept her diary.

"Hey madam," Lou said, "You're not meant to touch that are you. It's mummy's diary."

"Put it in, put it in," Maddie said, jumping up and down.

Lou laughed. "There," she said, "See, I've written it in there for this Sunday."

Happy at last, Maddie rushed off to her room. Lou grinned and absently flicked through the last few pages of the book. The smile dropped from her face. She turned back a few more pages; a little more frantically. A whole week; how had she lost track?

Shit, she thought; I'm never late.

Chapter 19

Diana was enjoying the day out but she still felt guilty that she hadn't got around to telling Lou about it. She'd planned to confess Tuesday evening after speaking with Gloria earlier in the day but Keith had phoned and invited himself round for dinner, so there hadn't been time. Diana had asked him to stay the night after they'd had sex but he'd told her he had an early start at work the next day and left, which she'd found disappointing. Diana always liked a cuddle after making love.

The rest of the week had passed by very quickly. Now it was Sunday and too late to speak to Lou anyway; she and Keith were here at the zoo, being keepers for the day together. When she had told him about the list on one of their early dates, Keith had been impressed. She'd mentioned Lou's zoo keeper idea and, on their trip to London, he'd presented her with an envelope. Upon opening Diana saw two passes for being a keeper at Bunbury Zoo.

"It sounded such a good idea," Keith had said, "I thought I'd do it too."

He hadn't given Lou any consideration at all but Diana still thought it a lovely gesture on his part so didn't say anything. There was always the cruise that she planned to take Lou on anyway. She hadn't mentioned that to Keith yet.

During the morning there had been a lot of poo clearing, especially in the rhino house but Diana had loved feeding the farm animals in the children's zoo and the Giraffes in their enclosure. The day was turning out to be very informative and she and Keith were able to get a lot closer to the animals than Diana had thought they would.

To be honest, she told herself at lunchtime; as she enjoyed a private meal with Keith, looking out across the elephants' pasture; it wouldn't have been much fun for Lou and Maddie if they had come along anyway. They wouldn't have been able to have gotten as close to the animals as she and Keith had or seen much of what they were doing throughout the day.

Just as they were about to head out for the afternoon their keeper was called away to tend to an emergency with one of the Zebras. That left them with Bob as their guide. Bob was five foot four in his builders' boots but strutted about like he was six feet tall. Diana felt his driving skills were far worse than hers as he sped round tight bends in the small golf cart he was driving them in, the trailer they were pulling along behind veering dangerously close to walls, fences and visitors. She sighed with relief whenever they stopped.

"I survey the zoo while on my rounds," he told them, at one such stop, while he swept up two crisp packets with his long-handled dustpan and brush, "And see what jobs need tackling. It's a very important role and, I have to say, some days the zoo wouldn't open without me."

"You all seem to have busy jobs here," Diana told him, trying to sound polite.

"It's a vocation rather than a job," Bob corrected, swaggering across to the trailer to empty his third bin.

There was a lot less for Diana and Keith to do, with Bob taking control of everything; telling them how many years of practice and experience were needed before they would be qualified to do what he was doing. Diana felt that clearing rubbish and filling up vending machines didn't look too difficult to master. Not that she voiced that opinion. She didn't want to hurt Bob's feelings and she knew Keith wouldn't like her saying anything like that either. Still, she was glad when a message came through Bob's walkie-talkie, asking him to take the two of them over to help Laura in the Chimp House. It was just a shame it meant a long, hell-raising journey to the other side of the zoo in the golf cart.

Bob just about managed to avoid crashing into the group of people crowded round the chimp house, all staring in through the glass at the front and laughing at the antics of the chimps inside. He led Diana and Keith round to the side of the building where he knocked at a thick, wooden door. An attractive blonde woman of about thirty opened it and smiled warmly at the three of them.

"I'm Laura," she said, "Shaking both Diana and Keith's hands."

Diana wasn't sure but it looked like Laura almost had to tug her hand out of Keith's grip as he grinned at her. She shook her head.

How silly of me, she thought, I'm acting like a jealous teenager.

"I'm going to be feeding the chimps soon and could use some help chopping up some of the carrots and lettuces," Laura told them, "Bob, would you mind hanging around for a few minutes to take the remnants away for the compost heaps?"

Bob looked at his watched and sucked air in through his teeth.

"Hmm, I guess I can," he said, "If I rearrange my schedule."

Laura led them into a long narrow room behind the area where the chimps were playing. It had a table down one side with buckets of fruit and veg on top. The sounds of the chimps playing out front seemed almost deafening to Diana now that she was closer to them.

"I always prepare their food back here," Laura shouted out, over the noise, "We give the chimps some carrots and lettuce as well as some oranges and bananas at this time of day. They're noisy right now because they know it's feeding time. If you could grab a knife each and perhaps Keith, you could cut off the bases of the lettuces and Diana, you could cut the carrots in half for me."

The two of them got to work, glad of something to do. Bob wandered around in the background, looking at his watch every so often and tutting impatiently.

"Do you go inside the cage to feed them?" Diana asked Laura.

She shook her head. "No, we put the food into their outside enclosure, that's why they're currently inside. We don't always bring them in and at those times we'll throw the food to them instead, but today I'll take you round the outside enclosure and we'll hide the food so it takes them a while to find it. It helps to keep the chimps stimulated."

"What about this one?"

All eyes turned to Bob. He was standing over by a separate cage where a large chimp was sat staring back at him.

"Oh that's Agnes," Laura said, "She had a bit of a run in with one of the other females and we're keeping the two apart at the moment."

"They're so human-like, aren't they," Diana said, "Having arguments, making up. I'm sure she's been listening to every word we say."

"And understanding a lot of it too," Laura agreed, "They might not know all of the words but they're always aware of what is going on and can sense our emotions."

Bob made a huffing sound.

"What rot," he said, "You'll be telling me next they understand different languages."

Keith laughed.

"You'd be surprised, Bob," Laura told him, "Agnes there is very intelligent. I'd be careful what you say in front of her."

It was Bob's turn to laugh.

"Yeah, right," he said, "A dumb animal like that is going to understand me."

Something round and brown flew out of the cage and hit him up the side of the head.

"Eughh," he said, falling sideways, "What the hell was that?"

"I did warn you," Laura said, matter-of-factly; scraping the chopped veg back into a bucket, "That's her poo Agnes has just thrown."

Bob had been rubbing the side of his head but stopped abruptly. He slowly lowered his arm and stared at the brown mess all over his hand. A look of horror and disgust appeared on his face. He took one last look at the group, let out a cry and bolted for the door.

"Not a bad judge of character that chimp," Keith said, as Bob passed him.

Diana enjoyed the next half hour, putting the food out into the Chimp's enclosure and then watching them being let out afterwards to locate and eat it. Once that was done the zoo keeping day was over and the two of them were free to look round the zoo on their own. After a short meander Diana felt rather tired and had a sit down on a bench while Keith walked across to the gift shop.

The sun was shining and the bench she was sitting on was sheltered from the wind. Diana undid her jacket. She sat back on the seat, closed her eyes and lifted up her face to the sky. She could feel herself smiling. It had been such a lovely day. Well, maybe not for Bob who was still probably trying to get **real** poo out of his hair using **sham**poo.

That's quite clever, Diana thought, perhaps I'll tell Keith that.

"Auntie Diana," a voice close by called.

Diana opened her eyes and looked to where the sound had come from. Squinting to see through the sunlight her stomach lurched as she saw Lou and Maddie standing in front of her, staring back. Maddie had a soft toy elephant in her hand and was grinning widely. Lou's surprised look, Diana felt; probably resembled her own.

"Hello," she said, standing up; and then added, "Fancy seeing you here."

"I see you've completed another item on your list, then," Lou told her, indicting Diana's T-shirt which blatantly showed the words, 'Zoo Keeper' on it.

"Oh, erm yes," Diana said, pulling her jacket across her front, "It was a surprise treat from Keith. I was going to tell you but; well things have moved so fast."

"I've got an elephant," Maddie said.

"Isn't that lovely," Diana told her, and then to Lou, "I see you came here without me."

"My daughter couldn't wait any longer to come here," Lou replied, abruptly.

"Look I'm sorry," Diana said, trying not to raise her voice in front of Maddie, "I really am. I didn't plan this; Keith did."

"Oh yes, good, old Keith. What a great guy. Well, how the hell would I know since I've not even met him?"

"It's been tricky," Diana said, "I've wanted to but…"

"But what?"

Before she could reply, Keith returned from the Gift Shop.

"Honestly," he said, to Diana, "Bloody shop staff again. That incompetent girl in there couldn't find her own arse with both hands. Where do they get these people?"

"Erm Keith, this is my friend, Lou; and her daughter Maddie."

For the first time Keith realised that Diana hadn't been standing there alone. His whole manner changed.

"I'm very pleased to meet you," he said, smiling and taking Lou's hand, "You were at the singles night with Diana weren't you. Yes, red dress, sequinned, great fit."

Lou pulled her hand out of his grip. Keith laughed and turned his attention to Maddie. He bent down and shook her hand. She giggled. He spent some time talking to her about her elephant. Lou was just beginning to think that perhaps her first impression about him had been wrong when he stood up and said,

"Surprised you managed to purchase anything from that dippy girl in there," he shook his head, "I've had better service at a three star hotel. Honestly, don't they give any kind of training to these idiots before they let them loose on the shop floor? It's the same wherever I go; but honestly, that dippy girl in there…"

"That dippy girl, as **you** call her," Lou told him, firmly, "Only started working here yesterday. I took the trouble to ask if she was okay, seeing as she looked so upset. The computers are down and they're a staff member short due to sickness and she's doing her best to help out."

"Well that's hardly my problem is it, sweetheart," Keith replied, "I mean, she's only got to be able to fill a shelf and open a till. Everything is barcoded now, it's hardly rocket science is it, running an item through a scanner."

"Lou's in retail," Diana chipped in, sensing trouble brewing, "She works...she's about to move into management."

"Oh," Keith replied, "Well that's great. I'm sure you'd soon whip her into shape, or sack her."

Diana laughed, trying to lighten the atmosphere.

"There is rather a lot more to working in a store than 'filling a shelf' or 'running an item through a scanner,'" Lou continued. She looked Keith up and down, "Like learning how to deal with pig-headed customers for a start."

"We probably should be heading off," Diana said.

Keith smiled.

"You're a feisty, little thing aren't you," he told Lou, "I like that."

Lou opened her mouth to respond but Diana cut in.

"Let's go Keith, I'm really feeling quite tired."

He turned his attention to Diana.

"Can't wait to get me back to your place, eh?"

He smacked her on the bottom. Diana grinned as she jumped. Lou looked incredulously at her.

"We must catch up again soon," Keith said to Lou, "I enjoy a good spat."

He began to walk away.

Diana whispered to Lou,

"We'll catch up later; promise," and then she rushed off after Keith.

Lou watched them go. Keith was talking as he strode towards the exit gates. Diana was jogging beside him to keep up, hanging on his every word.

"Is that Auntie Diana's new husband?" Maddie asked.

"I hope not sweetheart," Lou told her, "I hope not."

*

Jamie was sat at the far corner table by the window which looked out onto the harbour but he wasn't concentrating on the view. He was looking at figures he'd written down on a piece of paper and then at a bank statement. Gloria could see his frown lines from her position behind the bar.

Jamie had gone ahead and ordered the new menus after Lou had given the sample her approval. They were more expensive to get produced than Jamie had first realised. The figures on the piece of paper were calculations for the food bill for the eating competition which weren't exactly small either. He was determined to get this right. He'd spoken with the newspaper again and told them the competition was going to be for next Saturday and they had promised to send a reporter and photographer to oversee the event.

The menus were due to be ready by Wednesday and posters were arriving tomorrow. He'd put a large add on the community website for contestants and already there was interest. Yep, next Saturday was going to be a success.

Decisions made he looked up from his notes. Gloria was serving Old Joe his second pint. She looked tired. It was the first time Jamie had ever seen her like that. True, she didn't normally work on a Sunday but it was only for a couple of hours while he worked on his plans; she could go home soon. Was something else wrong, perhaps? He really needed her on board for this last attempt to turn the pub's fortunes around. And it was going to have to be Jamie's last attempt. It had to work, there was nothing left. He gathered up his notes and walked over to the bar. He grabbed a cigar.

"Here you go, Joe," he said, "On the house."

371

Without looking up Joe shook his head and took his pint over to his usual table.

"That's a first," Jamie whispered, to Gloria.

"What is?" Gloria asked, not really paying attention.

On closer inspection she really did look fed-up.

"What's wrong?" he asked.

Gloria sighed. "Oh nothing really; it's silly."

"Come on, you can tell me. You know I'll tell you honestly if you're being silly."

Gloria managed a smile.

"I don't doubt that for a moment," she said, "Oh I don't know. I think I'm just feeling a little sorry for myself."

"Why's that?"

"I spoke with Diana Carlton in the week. I've never see her looking so happy and she was only walking along the street."

"She must have lost it," Jamie replied, matter-of-factly, "No one who's normal walks along grinning away to themselves. Do you think we should alert the police?"

"You know what I mean," Gloria said, "She wasn't grinning, she just; well she gave off an aura of happiness. She looked radiant."

"Oh I see," Jamie replied, realisation dawning on his face, "It's because she's found herself a man isn't it."

"No it isn't. Well, partly," Gloria looked thoughtful, "I think it just hit me how much Diana has changed since she and Lou embarked on this list of hers. Whenever I'd seen her before she'd always seemed shy and awkward. Lou called it snobbishness but I didn't agree. Now, she seems alive and so happy and I'm a little jealous. She was lonely and I've realised, so am I."

"Well you can always do what she has done," Jamie told her,

"Try out new things or start a hobby."

"I'm not sure that's enough for me."

Jamie was silent for a while and then asked,

"Are you seeking out a raise?"

Gloria laughed. "Well now you come to mention it," she said, "But no that's not what I was looking for. Maybe I'm just a little bored with everything and, for the first time in my life; a man isn't the answer."

She shrugged her shoulders and walked out to the kitchen.

It's certainly a day for surprises, Jamie thought as he turned round. Old Joe had just walked out the door, leaving behind his untouched pint of bitter.

*

Diana waited until nine o'clock before popping across to Lou's. She thought it would be better to wait until Maddie was in bed so that they could talk properly. Mind you, Keith had only just left her apartment anyway, after a bite to eat and a rather enjoyable half hour together in the bedroom; although his imitation of Tarzan beating his chest had been a little embarrassing. And calling her Laura during an intimate moment hadn't helped the mood either. That was the name of the woman in the chimp house. Keith apologised and Diana tried to laugh it off.

After all, she'd thought afterwards, at least he hadn't call me Agnes; after the chimp.

She smiled warmly at Lou when the door opened and held up a bottle of wine. Lou told her to come through but she didn't return the smile. She opened the wine silently and poured a glass out for Diana, screwing the lid back on without pouring herself one.

"Bit of a headache," she said, to Diana's questioning gaze.

Diana felt odd drinking alone. She thought that Lou might perk up now that they were sitting down together but she still seemed unsettled.

"How have you been?" she asked.

"Fine."

"Sorry I've not seen you as much as I would have liked but, well...as I said earlier, Keith and I have been seeing quite a lot of each other."

"I heard."

A one-sided conversation was always difficult. Was Lou's mood purely because Diana hadn't taken her to the zoo? That was silly, she thought, friends don't always see each other all of the time.

"How's Maddie doing?"

"She's fine."

"Yes she looked well when I saw her. Look, I'm sorry again that I didn't tell you that Keith had already planned the zookeeper day."

"It's fine," Lou repeated again.

This was getting ridiculous.

"It doesn't sound fine."

Lou sighed.

"I'm sorry," she said, "It's not you, I've just got a few things on my mind right now."

"Oh? Anything I can help with?"

"Not really."

Lou stood up and walked over to the kitchen counter to get a tissue.

"I don't like this tension between us," Diana said.

"I've just told you; it's not you," Lou replied, forcefully.

"It obviously is," Diana responded, "I mean I..."

Lou turned round and Diana was shocked to see tears in her eyes.

"Really, have I behaved that badly?"

"Oh God, Diana; not everything in my life revolves around you!"

Lou wiped her eyes and then grabbed another tissue to wipe her nose. She looked into her friend's face.

"I think I'm pregnant, okay."

Diana was shocked. She didn't know what to say.

"But how?" she finally blurted out, "No, that sounds ridiculous. I mean, who; when?"

"I'd rather not talk about it at the moment," Lou told her, looking down at the floor.

"You do know who, don't you?"

The sentence was out of Diana's mouth before she realised how it sounded. Lou's head snapped up.

"What do you mean by that?"

"Sorry, that didn't come out right."

"Well how else was it meant to sound?"

Diana couldn't find the words to reply. Lou began to pace up and down the kitchen floor.

"Honestly, three weeks away from me and you've reverted completely to type haven't you?"

"That's not true."

"You've picked a man exactly like your husband; someone who only has to bark an order and you come running."

"That's ridiculous. Yes, he is a little like Richard in that way but…"

"I bet he's had the seal of approval from all your old snobby friends but you didn't want me to meet him did you. No, because you knew we wouldn't hit it off. You knew I'd see the

375

type of person he is."

"Well it was a bit difficult, I'll admit," Diana was getting flustered, "But really, if you give him time…"

"He's just like all your other friends," Lou finished, "Wouldn't want to have anything to do with the likes of me. I'm only a shop assistant. I noticed you didn't tell him that; just mentioned I was going into management. That really hurt Diana."

"You're being very unreasonable," Diana said, "It's not like that, it's…well, it's just…"

Lou stopped pacing and stared at her.

"You see," she said, exasperated, "You can't even come up with a lie. I'm right aren't I? You thought him too good to meet me didn't you? And I bet you've been at his beck and call for the past three weeks; waiting around at home in case he phones you. I saw how you were today; hanging on his every word. My God, you were getting interesting for a while but you've so quickly gone back to what you were before; a snob with your snobby friends and a doormat to your boyfriend, just like you were to your husband."

Diana stood up.

"Now just wait a minute," she said, riled, "You know so very little about my husband and you know nothing about Keith."

"And whose fault is that?"

"Look, I'm not going to keep on apologising for the past three weeks," Diana said, "This hasn't all been a one way friendship you know. When I came into your life as a friend you started smiling and feeling good about yourself. You got the chance to improve your career and finally had the confidence to go for it. I don't see you for three weeks and suddenly you're knocked up and God knows who the father is!"

Lou's mouth dropped open. Diana was too angry to want to take that last sentence back. If Lou thought she'd reverted to type then she'd show her.

Standing in the kitchen all Lou saw was Diana give her that pitying look of loathing that she hadn't seen for ages. She felt like something stuck to the bottom of a shoe.

"I'm not the only one who's reverted to type, obviously," Diana whispered, vehemently, "Another accident is it, this pregnancy? Like mother, like daughter."

She turned and stormed out of the apartment.

Chapter 20

Dr Bryant's surgery always ran late on a Monday morning. Muriel only needed to get the results of a blood test. She'd be in and out in two minutes but unfortunately all those in the queue in front of her seemed to need much longer with the doctor. She'd leafed through two magazines already and was now sat watching the clock on the wall as it ticked twenty-five minutes past her allotted appointment time.

Muriel was pretty sure the fidgety woman on her left was before her. She kept scratching her bosom every couple of minutes; at one point, placing her hand up her jumper to have a go. What with that and the old man on her right continuously sniffing, Muriel wished now she'd had the courage to ask the scary Tess Andrews to change her appointment to Tuesday.

"Mr Wilson, doctor will see you now," Mrs Andrews called out, from behind the reception desk, "Hurry along there will you, doctor's busy and hasn't got all day."

Mr Wilson quickened his pace with his walking frame.

"Surgery number two," Mrs Andrews shouted after him, "Dr Moore's going to deal with your chronic diarrhoea problem."

Joyce strode in through the front door and up to the reception area. She and Tess conversed quietly together before Joyce turned round and saw Muriel. She started, but quickly regained her composure and came over.

"I didn't know you had an appointment today," she said, accusingly; standing over her friend.

"It's just the results of my B12 blood test," Muriel told her.

"Who are you here to see?"

"Dr Bryant."

"Good," Joyce said, nodding her approval, "Good. You'll get more out of him. Dr Moore is still wet behind the ears in my opinion."

The buzzer sounded behind the desk.

"Mrs Fenwick, Dr Bryant is ready for you now," Mrs Andrews called out.

The lady with the itchy bosom got up and walked down the corridor to the surgeries. Mrs Andrews watched her go over the top of her glasses.

"I'm sure he'll have to don two pairs of surgical gloves before he goes anywhere near that weeping rash of yours," she added, for the benefit of the waiting patients.

Joyce had been about to sit down in the vacated seat but quickly changed her mind. She took the one beside it and beckoned her friend to shift over into Mrs Fenwick's seat instead.

"I think I'm next," Muriel told her, "Are you here to see the doctor as well?"

"Hmm? Oh, no I'm fine," Joyce replied, "I just wanted a quick word with Tess about the last committee meeting."

Muriel sighed. "It's a shame Diana has decided to quit," she said, "She was doing so well and was very popular."

"Yes, well; she has her new man now," Joyce told her, sounding disgruntled.

"Still, I'd have thought she could have found time for the committee."

"Don't you go asking her about it," Joyce said, firmly, "She's made her decision."

The telephone rang. Mrs Andrews sighed and watched it for three rings before answering. She began talking to the caller in a loud voice.

"Sorry, it's a bad line. Yes of course **Miss** Turner. How far along do you think you are? Okay, well I'll make you an appointment for when you're six weeks, unless there are any problems beforehand. That's fine; I'll give you a call back. Goodbye **Miss** Turner."

Mrs Andrews put the phone down and saw that she'd achieved her desired affect; Joyce and Muriel were both looking up at her.

"I think it's time to start knitting booties," she said.

*

Lou stood beside the old entrance down to the now closed smuggler caves. The precipitous steps were still there but the way down had been blocked off by a new brick wall. The red bricks weren't in keeping with the rock of the cliff or the clapboard buildings along the harbour front but right now it did provide Lou with some shelter from the cool breeze. She still pulled her coat a little tighter around her as she looked out across the harbour.

She'd phoned in sick at the supermarket, unable to face anyone. Booking the appointment at the doctor's had somehow made the pregnancy seem more real. She'd planned to crawl under the duvet until it was time to pick Maddie up from school but the apartment had felt claustrophobic and Lou had escaped here to the harbour front where she stood, leaning on the railings; thinking.

She didn't want to have another child, not now. It was ruining all of her plans. Lou knew she wouldn't get another break like this to become a store manager. If she turned the chance down now, why on earth would they ever offer her the opportunity again? She wasn't trying to be selfish; it was Maddie's future she was thinking about too as well as her own.

And then there was the question of the father. There was no way of knowing which of the two men it was until DNA tests could be done. Lou felt ashamed. Diana's words had certainly hit home last night. She didn't know who the father was. How could she have slept with two different men on two consecutive nights? She and Tony had obviously taken precautions but accidents do happen; there may have been a problem with the condom. It was an old one Lou had found in the back of her bedside cabinet. How long had it actually been there? With Chris she had no idea what had happened but they'd always been careful in the past and assumed they would have that night as well, but she couldn't be sure. She sighed. What a terrible state to have gotten into.

What would Tony or Chris say once they found out? Tony had already made his feelings quite clear. There was no way they were getting back together. Still, she supposed he would be there for the child as he was for Maddie...or would he be? How would he react when she told him? Cheryl would have to know they'd slept together. What would that do to their relationship? How would he react knowing it was only a possibility that he was the father? Lou and he weren't on the best of terms right now. This news may make him sever all contact, which would be a travesty for Maddie.

Then there was Chris. Lou really didn't want any ties to him, but if the baby was his then he'd probably be in her life for ever. She shivered as last night's dream came back to her. She'd been in labour and when the baby emerged it gave a gummy grin and said, "Alright babes." Lou had woken up screaming.

She put aside thoughts of the father. At the moment this was her problem to deal with. She didn't want a baby. That was the problem in a nutshell. Could she get rid of it? Lou shivered again. She'd tried not to think about that but the thought had been there; slowly pushing its way to the front of her brain. She didn't have to have the baby. Why call it a baby anyway? What was she, three, almost four weeks gone? It was just a collection of cells inside her wasn't it?

No; Lou couldn't think that way. She had a human life inside of her, growing; how could she get rid of it. What if she'd done the same thing five years ago? She couldn't imagine life without Maddie. The poor girl had had to deal with her mother's mood swings this past week. Lou would shout at her for being noisy and then scoop her up in her arms and cry. That wasn't good for a five year old to witness.

Lou shook her head and turned round to begin the walk back towards the slipway and the entrance to her apartment block. The cool breeze was getting stronger and appeared to have changed direction. She wanted to get back home to the warm. She sighed. She didn't want to have a baby but was going to have one and that was entirely her own fault. How else could she look at it? A new baby should be a source of joy. At the moment, no matter how hard she tried; Lou couldn't see it that way.

As she neared The Smugglers Jamie walked out of the entrance and stood staring back at the window, a frown on his face. As she reached his side she saw a poster advertising the eating competition.

"I'm not sure that's noticeable enough," he said to her, "It's just black writing on a white background. I've got several of these to be displayed around town. Do you think I should have used some colour? It was more expensive but maybe…"

He left the sentence hanging.

"I think people will notice," Lou told him, grateful to be able to think of something else, "It's a big poster and after all, size is everything."

Jamie smiled. "Isn't that just a fallacy," he said.

"Believe that if you like," she replied.

He laughed but then stopped abruptly.

"Hang on," he said, "Why aren't you at work?"

"Oh, I'm not feeling that great," Lou replied.

Jamie took a step back.

"God, get away from me then," he said, "I don't want to catch anything you've got, not with the competition coming up."

"You'll catch a fat lip in a minute."

Jamie laughed.

"You're still going to be able to come along on Saturday aren't you?" he asked, "I could really use the moral support. Only if you're feeling better mind you."

"Of course," Lou replied, "I wouldn't miss it."

Jamie smiled warmly at her.

"Brilliant," he said, now go home and rest. You do look peaky."

He kissed her on the cheek, gave her a hug and walked back inside the pub. Lou had a sudden urge to cry.

If only the baby inside me was Jamie's, she thought; then everything would be okay.

*

Dr's Case Notes – Monday 2 November

I'm losing interest in this expansion business. Before I had a chance to suggest a drink and make the offer of a permanent position, Dr Moore visited me in my surgery and told me that a move back home to the Lake District was on the cards.

Apparently Dr Moore's father is also a doctor and is looking to retire from his small, village practice in about six months. My Dr Moore is going to take it over.

What am I going to do? I've sat here all day going through all sorts of scenarios. I don't think I've really given my patients the best care or attention they deserve. I mixed up some test results and told Muriel Green her prostate was showing signs of abnormality. We both needed a medicinal nip of brandy after that diagnosis. And before that there was poor Mrs Fenwick with the rash. I mistakenly advised her to rub live yoghurt into her breasts. I had to rush out of the surgery after her. I only caught up with the woman as she entered the supermarket. In front of a queue of people at the till I grabbed her, waved a prescription in her face and yelled out, "You haven't got thrush, it's a fungal infection." That didn't go down too well.

I've been wondering if I could sell this practice and move north too. I could work with Dr Moore in the Lake District. It's meant to be a beautiful area. I don't know how Mrs Bryant would take the news. I think she'd be shocked if I told her I was leaving. What am I saying; she'd beat me to a pulp. She's been in some very scary moods these past few days while training for the eating competition at The Smugglers. Last night she ate a dozen oysters in thirty seconds. Their aphrodisiac qualities soon emerged and a horny Mrs Bryant chased me round the house, cornering me in the kitchen. In a flash I was bent backwards over the butchers block and she had me, right there and then. I cried myself to sleep last night.

What should I do about Dr Moore? What would happen if I declared my love? Would that change any future plans? Oh why am I such a wimp? I should march straight into Dr Moore's surgery now and shout out, "I love you!" Do you know what; I'm going to do it. Nothing ventured, nothing gained.

Chapter 21

Jamie didn't usually listen to gossip. By the time it had been passed from person to person the story had always grown and there was very little truth left in it. He'd always fancied telling someone he had an ingrowing toenail on a Monday and then wait to see if he was dying by Friday. The gossip that reached his ears this Tuesday morning however, was different. He'd only popped up to the high street first thing as he had a poster for the eating competition left over and thought the butchers would be a good place to display it.

The owner, Rita (or Reet the Meat as she was known), told him what she'd heard from Gay Alan, who had popped into the shop late yesterday afternoon for a Cumberland ring. Alan had been speaking with Clepto Carol who'd bumped into Ginger Phil as she raced out of the chemists with some dental floss and a packet of feminine hygiene wipes up her jumper. Phil's cousin had been in the doctor's surgery yesterday morning and the news was that the young woman from the supermarket, Gloria's daughter, was pregnant. There was some other garbage about a woman having thrush on her breasts and a Mr Wilson shitting himself when he fell over his walking frame, but Jamie put the extra details to one side.

Lou was pregnant. Whether that was true or not it was being spoken about quite freely. Mind you, she had looked peaky yesterday. If it was true, who was the father? Jamie pondered that thought back at the pub while stacking glasses. Not that prat of an ex-boyfriend of hers, surely; but who else? Tony had been down a few times recently but that was just to see Maddie. Besides, he had a wife in London. Mind you hadn't Lou

mentioned something about a bad patch? Even so, Lou
certainly had more respect for herself than to jump into bed with
him, hadn't she? Jamie sighed. Whoever the father was he felt
a real rush of hate for him. He wondered what Lou was going
to do. He wanted to help in any way he could.

Gloria walked in through the front door to begin her shift.
With a start, Jamie wondered if she was aware of the gossip, or
if she knew the truth. If she didn't know, should he tell her? At
least perhaps he should mention that there was some talk going
round. Surely it was better coming from him than from one of
the nosey bitches that lived around here?

*

It had turned into a busy morning for Diana. She'd only
planned on a quick walk up to the high street first thing to get a
bit of shopping; trying to avoid the supermarket and Lou until
she'd had a chance to quietly apologise to her. She bitterly
regretted the things she had said on Sunday and had hoped
they'd have been able to clear the air last night; but there was no
answer at Lou's apartment when Diana knocked. She hoped
Lou wasn't avoiding her. She wanted and needed their
friendship in her life.

As she'd walked past the post office that morning she'd
spotted Jamie coming out of the butchers on the opposite side of
the road. She'd waved over at him but he'd seemed lost in
thought and hadn't notice her. A few more yards up the high
street and she'd bumped into Muriel outside the card shop.
Everyone was up and about early today, it seemed. Diana was
shocked to hear that her friend knew all about Lou's pregnancy.

"I don't think that should be spread about," she'd advised
Muriel, "I don't think Lou is ready for the world to know."

The chat had then moved on to Joyce's plans for a new

387

committee. From what Muriel said it sounded to Diana like Joyce wanted to go back to her original plans for 'helping' the youth of the area with curfews and bans.

"I'm really sorry you resigned," Muriel had told her, "I know I'm not meant to mention it, but I was surprised when I heard."

"I didn't resign," Diana had replied, "You wanted me gone."

"I didn't. I don't."

"Not you personally, but the rest of the committee did."

Muriel had looked puzzled.

"No one said that to my knowledge."

"Then why…?"

Several thoughts had raced through Diana's head at once, how quiet Joyce had been at recent meetings, which was unusual for her; how the problems with using the village hall only come to light after an application had been put in. Joyce was a trustee; wouldn't she have known about any problems beforehand? Then there was the caretaker who had refused to help up at the school. Hadn't someone said he was a friend or an acquaintance of Joyce's?

Diana had made her excuses to Muriel and then spent the next couple of hours walking around the town, tackling the vicar, the school caretaker and then Tess Andrews down at the doctor's surgery. Now she was heading back up the high street again to the charity shop; fuming.

There were several customers milling around when Diana entered. Handwritten signs had been pinned up declaring a sale. As Norman had told Diana when she'd phoned the house, Joyce was here working an extra shift. She was standing behind the counter looking a little flustered.

"Oh Diana," she called over, in a relieved sounding voice, "Am I glad to see you. You haven't got a spare hour have you to help out? This sale has gone crazy. Mrs Whittaker and I are rushed off our feet. I've not been able to get hold of Moo."

Diana looked at the shop's four customers. This was busy? If Lou was here right now she'd have laughed at the absurdity of Joyce's statement.

"I haven't got the time," she replied, turning back to face Joyce, "In fact I won't ever have any time to help you out again."

"Diana? What's wrong?"

Joyce's face appeared to show genuine concern and Diana had to take a deep breath and remember what she had found out.

"You ask me what's wrong," she said, "I don't know how you've got the nerve to stand there and say that."

Joyce leaned over to the woman beside her.

"Mrs Whittaker," she said, brightly, "Would you be a dear and go out the back and start unpacking those boxes of new stock?"

"But we were going to clear what's out here first," Mrs Whittaker replied, sensing the tension in the air. She didn't want to miss out on a decent bit of gossip.

"Now; if you don't mind," Joyce told her, forcefully, a very pained smile on her face, "Diana and I can cope out here. Off you go."

Once Mrs Whittaker had resignedly gone out the back, Joyce turned her attention back to her friend, the smile no longer visible.

"What did you just say?" she asked.

"I thought you were my friend but you've spent the last few weeks purposely ruining my plans, haven't you."

A customer walked up to a display near the counter.

"Diana, dear," Joyce said, trying to maintain a lightness in her voice, "You appear a little hysterical."

The customer moved away.

"What are you talking about?" Joyce hissed.

"You know damn well," Diana whispered back, angrily, "I can't believe what a bitch you've been."

"Diana!"

"You can't tell me you haven't. I've spent the morning unravelling all of your evil. I can't begin to imagine the time and effort you've put into it. The vicar told me that there is no covenant on the village hall so there would be no problem with a playgroup; but you knew that already, didn't you."

Joyce looked down at the counter.

"We don't want children causing havoc in the hall," she mumbled, "Or running about shouting on the road outside."

"The road that runs beside your own house you mean," Diana said, "And then there was the school. I spoke with the caretaker today. You blackmailed him to not let us use it as an after school club."

Joyce's head whipped back up.

"I don't use blackmail."

"Oh really? You threatened to tell the caretaker's wife about his affair with the lollipop lady. What else would you call it?"

Joyce didn't respond. She turned her head towards the book display to avoid Diana's gaze. A customer was flicking through a book.

"We're not a library service," Joyce shouted over at him, "Either buy it or get lost."

The man left empty handed.

"And then there was the premises at the harbour," Diana continued, "I have to admit, you were clever with that. You were the one who came up with the idea of expanding the surgery, not Dr Bryant. You got Tess Andrews to suggest it to him. God knows why he agreed to it. My goodness, Joyce, do you really hate me that much?"

"I don't hate you," Joyce told her, "But I hate what you've become. All of these radical ideas and views aren't yours. They come from that slut you've become friends with."

Mrs Whittaker popped her head round the corner.

"Would either of you like a nice cup of…"

Joyce span round.

"No!" she shouted, "Now bugger off, you nosey old, cow."

"Why are you still going on about Lou?" Diana asked, once Mrs Whittaker had tearfully disappeared from view.

A hard, triumphant look appeared on Joyce's face.

"I see she's having another bastard," she said.

"What?"

"Pregnant again. Who knows who the father is this time?"

"I don't know how you find these things out."

"I have my ways."

Diana's face darkened.

"My God; you are a witch. Lou was right; our little social group should be called the coven. You don't really do anything to help the community of our town do you; you just help yourself."

A lady came up to the counter to purchase a blouse and cardigan.

"Not now," Joyce told her.

"But I have an appointment to get to."

"Fine, take these with you;" Joyce screwed the garments up into a ball and handed them back to the woman, "They're free."

The woman's eyes lit up.

"That's great," she said, "Could I have them wrapped?"

391

"Just get out!"

Joyce grabbed the balled items and threw them across the room towards the door, the lady in hot pursuit.

"How can you say I don't help the community," Joyce said, turning back to Diana, "I do nothing but help this town. Who wants noisy teenagers shouting abuse up and down the high street while knocking back alcohol and drugs? Who wants annoying tourists crowding our town and big, noisy coaches clogging up our streets?"

"So that was why you campaigned to get the smuggler tunnels closed off," Diana replied, "It wasn't for health and safety at all, it was to make the road outside your house quieter. Lou was right. She was right about it all."

"What do you mean?"

Diana leaned across the counter.

"I haven't always seen eye to eye with Lou," she said, "Yes she was an annoying teenager but the woman is thirty years old now. She is raising a child mostly on her own and doing it beautifully. She's hard-working and she knows a lot more about this town than you do."

Joyce sniffed.

"And I'll tell you another thing," Diana continued, "She's a darn sight better mother than you ever were."

This caused a reaction. Joyce stood up straighter.

"What did you say?"

"When was the last time you saw your son?" Diana asked.

"He's a very busy man."

"Yes, busy coming up with reasons not to visit. You've always been an over-bearing woman who wouldn't let him lead his own life. He didn't leave home at eighteen for university, he escaped."

392

"How dare you!"

"You ruined his childhood, you ruin your poor husband's existence and now you've ruined our friendship. Is that why you scuppered my plans? You've ruined so much of your own life that you don't want to see anyone else happy?"

"Get out of my shop," Joyce said, tears forming in her eyes.

"This isn't your shop, this isn't your town. You need to start understanding that," Diana told her, "I've been a complete idiot. Do you know I've even defended you to Lou? I've messed up everything."

Diana turned to leave but then remembered something.

"By the way," she said, turning back, "I've not just spoken with the vicar and the caretaker today. I've also spoken to several committee members who seemed very surprised to learn they'd taken a dislike to me. Good luck with your next meeting, Joyce. You might find it lonely, sitting there all on your own."

Diana turned and walked out of the shop.

*

It all seemed a little weird. Lou had only missed one day of work but coming back into the store today everything appeared different; just…well; weird was definitely the word. Everyone was quieter around her; not always able to meet her eye. She'd caught Precious staring at her twice. Each time, Precious had just smiled at her in an almost pitying way and continued serving her customers. When Lou told Simon she was turning down the place on the management training program he didn't look at all surprised and told her he understood. Lou only realised what had happened when her mother stormed into the shop at ten o'clock.

"You're pregnant?!" she called out, incredulously, in front of the entire store.

393

"Ssh," Lou hissed, pulling her mother over to one corner.

"Oh don't bother trying to keep it quiet;" Gloria told her, "It's all round the town anyway."

Lou looked desperately around the shop. No one was looking their way but she could tell they were all listening in. So that explained the odd behaviour. My God, she thought; is that why Chris phoned in sick this morning?

"I, I don't know how that happened," she whispered.

"Why on earth didn't you tell me?" Gloria continued, "Imagine how I feel; having to find out from Jamie."

"Jamie?"

"Yes, Jamie. He was worried that I didn't know and didn't want me to overhear it from some stranger. Why didn't you tell me, Lou; your own mother?"

"Because it's only just happened," she replied, "Jesus Christ I'm only about a month gone. I didn't want to tell anyone yet. How did that get out? I've only told…"

Lou stopped talking. Diana; how could she? What a bitch, Lou thought; that's just vindictive. She knew exactly what had happened. Diana had told her coven and the news had spread that way. She wouldn't be able to get rid of the baby now even if she wanted to. Diana had taken her choices away from her. Tears sprang to Lou's eyes. Gloria hugged her.

"Don't cry," she said, "I'm sorry I shouted. I was just shocked that's all. I'm here for you, you know that."

"Lou," Simon called out to her, "Why don't you and your mum use my office."

Once inside Lou wiped her eyes.

"I didn't want anyone to know yet," she said, sitting down in Simon's chair, "I wasn't sure what I wanted to do about it."

Gloria's eyes widened. "Oh Lou," she said, dropping into

394

the seat opposite, "You mean you were considering…" She let the sentence hang in the air.

"I don't want another child," Lou confessed, "I'm sorry, but I really don't. I love Maddie to bits but I was just getting to a stage, with her at school full-time, where I could improve my life. I mean, this management course I've just turned down really could have made a difference. If I was a manager of a store I'd have a career; a chance to improve life for me and Maddie. That's what I've always wanted to do. You remember what it was sometimes like when I was young don't you mum?"

Gloria sighed. "Yes I do," she said, "Those times between jobs when we had to hide from the rent man or cadge a few coins off of a neighbour to pay for the gas; having sandwiches for dinner."

Lou nodded. "That's why I've always had this little dream of owning my own place; something that was mine that no one else could take away. I mean I love the apartment and we're settled there, but it's not mine. That's why I don't know what to do."

"But you've just told me you've turned down the management course," Gloria said, "Doesn't that mean you've made the decision to keep it?"

Lou shook her head.

"Not necessarily," she admitted, "There are other options and at the moment I don't know what the future holds. I turned down the place on the training program because it was one less thing to worry about. Who knows, perhaps I will be able to reapply at a later date; perhaps I won't want to. At the moment I don't feel up to it. I need time to decide what I want to do, although now it feels like I'm being forced into keeping the baby if the whole town knows I'm pregnant. How could I get

395

rid of it or put it up for adoption? The whole town will know what I've done. God I can't believe Diana would do this to me."

"Diana?" Gloria questioned.

"She's the only one I've told. We ended up having a bit of an argument. I can't believe she's been so vindictive."

"I can't believe that either," Gloria said, "Maybe someone else found out?"

Lou shook her head and sighed.

"I've played right into this town's impression of me haven't I?"

"What do you mean?"

"Like mother, like daughter; that's what they all say."

Gloria took hold of her daughter's hands across the desk and made her look her in the eye.

"No they don't," she said, "A couple of mean-spirited, busybody bitches do, but it's not the whole town Lou. You haven't believed that all these years have you?"

Lou didn't respond. Gloria let go of her daughter's hands and threw herself back into the chair.

"Do you think I would have come back here to live if I thought a whole town disliked me?" she said, "I know that Joyce Pendleton woman likes to put her nose into everything but she doesn't run this town. She likes to think she does but she doesn't. Do you remember when the smuggler tunnels were closed? Joyce lets everyone believe she got them closed but the council were already thinking of doing it anyway."

"Really?"

"Of course. Her little campaign did nothing. My friend, Gillian, used to work in that department at the time. The council already had health and safety worries about the place.

They don't pay any attention to Joyce up at the Town Hall.
She's just the local busybody. So don't you pay any attention
to her either. You can't trust Joyce Pendleton as far as you
could throw her. Honestly, you should hear some of the things
she's called behind her back. Don't ever let her or anyone else
make you feel bad. Do you know what I do when I see her?"

Lou shrugged her shoulders.

"Two fingers?"

Gloria smiled. "No," she said, "That would play into her
hands. I smile or wave and always make the effort to call out,
'Hello.'"

"What does she say?"

"Nothing. But it really gets to her, I can tell; especially
when she is with other people from her social circle. I reckon
she gets worried that they think we're friends. It's the best way
to be, love; honestly. Don't fight them."

"You're right," Lou said, "I've been trying to fight them ever
since I moved here. I mean I know I'm no saint and I wasn't
always easy to like, but I'm not the person the Joyce Pendletons
of this town see. I thought Diana was different but I'm starting
to think I was wrong about her. Honestly mum, you should
meet her boyfriend. He really fits in with that group. I've
hardly seen her since he came on the scene."

Gloria stood up and laughed.

"That's not surprising is it," she said, "Don't you think if
things were the other way around, Diana would be seeing less
of you if you'd just got a new man in your life?"

Gloria stopped talking.

"Oh my God," she said, "Who's the father? Please not that
gob shite Chris. Oh God, please tell me you didn't…"

"I'll discuss the father with you once I've spoken with him,"

Lou replied, desperate not to get into that conversation right now.

"Okay. Well, I guess I should be getting back to the pub," Gloria said, "Unless you want me to stay with you?"

Lou shook her head.

"No, I'll be fine. Head down and get on with work; just like I do every day."

Gloria smiled. "That's what we all do," she said.

As she made to open the door Lou called out to her.

"Mum," she said, "Did you ever…you know; consider getting rid of me when you were pregnant?"

"Never once," Gloria told her, "I know I've not always been the best mother in the world but as soon as I found out I was pregnant I knew I wanted you and would love you forever. And I do."

Lou smiled, but as her mother left the office she realised she still didn't feel that way about the little life growing inside of her.

*

Tears were streaming down Diana's face on the bus but she didn't care if anyone stared. After confronting Joyce at the charity shop she'd desperately needed someone to talk to. Muriel would probably have been at home but Diana wanted to speak to Lou. Perhaps if she went and apologised to her, they could bury the hatchet and Lou would listen to what had just taken place and tell Diana she'd done the right thing. Aside from Muriel, Lou was now the only true friend she had.

Diana had made her way down to the supermarket to make peace but was met with a tirade of abuse she wasn't prepared for. She'd never seen Lou so angry and upset. She was too stunned to take in everything but it seemed that Lou was

398

accusing her of telling everyone she was pregnant.

"I've told no one," she tried to say, but Lou was having none of it. The vitriol only stopped when the manager dragged Lou into his office and Diana had fled the shop in tears.

Now she was on the bus to Tenham. She needed Keith. She needed his arms around her. She needed to hear someone tell her everything was going to be okay. Diana had tried calling him from the payphone beside the bus stop but he wasn't answering his mobile.

She knew the office building where he worked. Once in town she would try calling his mobile again from one of the public phones inside the shopping centre and if he still didn't answer then she would go straight to his office. She had to see him.

The bus seemed to take forever to arrive but eventually it pulled up into the large bus bay by the mall. Diana made her way to the Ladies in one of the department stores and almost jumped when she saw her reflection in the mirror; all puffy eyed and smudged mascara. She took a good twenty minutes to put everything right before calling Keith's mobile again. He still didn't answer so she made her way to the office block.

She felt nervous entering the reception area. Would Keith be annoyed to see her here? She couldn't help that now. Diana walked up to the main desk.

"Hello," she said, to the young girl behind it, "Would you be able to call up Keith McArthur for me please?"

The girl pulled a face.

"I can try," she said, "But I'm new and the phone system keeps getting the better of me."

Diana smiled politely at her. The girl picked up the phone but then put it back down again.

"I guess it would help if I looked up his extension first wouldn't it," she said.

She began typing on the computer.

"Now that's Keith with a K is it?"

"Erm, yes it is."

"Right. Now, what was that surname again?"

"McArthur."

The girl tutted and smiled.

"He couldn't have a name that was easy to spell, could he."

Diana thought that if she had trouble with 'Keith' the girl would probably struggle with most names. She spelt it out for her.

"Oh God, I pressed escape rather than enter. Sorry, I won't keep you a moment. I'll just have to type that in again. Honestly, I'm always like this when I get my period."

There was no response to that.

"Ah, there we go, you beauty," the girl said, "We have a number."

She grinned at Diana as she dialled it.

"Oh hello," she said, "Is Arthur McKeith there?"

"Keith McArthur," Diana whispered at her.

The girl nodded.

"Sorry, I meant…oh you realised. Yes that's right, this is Charlotte. Oh hello you. Yes, I've missed you too."

Charlotte giggled into the phone. There was a gap while whoever was at the other end spoke and then she giggled again, twirling the end of her auburn hair around her index finger while she did.

"Has anyone ever told you, you're a naughty boy and need a good spanking?"

She laughed loudly but then saw the look on Diana's face.

400

"Anyway," she said, "Is Arthur McKeith not there? No? Yes, Ok, right; thanks."

She laughed out loud.

"Bye big boy," she said, "Keep it warm for me."

The smile dropped from her face as she replaced the receiver and tried to become more business-like.

"I'm afraid he's at an external meeting at the moment," she told Diana.

"Do you know where?"

"I'm afraid not. Would you like me to call upstairs again?"

"Er, no; thank you," Diana said. She could do without listening to another flirtatious call, "Perhaps I could wait here for him?"

"Oh certainly," Charlotte told her, indicating the two sofas over by the front window, "Please, go take a load off."

Diana assumed that meant, 'Please go and sit down', so she did.

Being an insurance company there were only magazines relating to that industry available on the table. Diana picked one up and pretended to read. Each time the door opened her head shot up to see if it was Keith. Every so often, Charlotte called over to her.

"I had cheese in my sandwiches at lunchtime."

"Did you?"

"Bit naughty really."

"I suppose."

"I also had a big bag of crisps and a five hundred gram bar of chocolate as well. I probably shouldn't have eaten those either. I'm meant to be on a diet for my holiday next week."

"You don't need to lose any weight," Diana informed her.

"Ah, isn't that a lovely thing to say. I'm filling up, really I am. That's so nice. I've got a sausage roll in my handbag. Perhaps I'll have that with a cup of tea a bit later on."

Diana nodded and returned to the magazine; which she realised she was holding upside down. Charlotte saw her turn it the right way up and laughed.

"I'm always doing that," she said, "Thought I'd gone dyslexic the other day."

Diana really hoped Keith wouldn't be long.

"Sorry, I forgot to ask," Charlotte continued, "Are you Keith's wife?"

"No," Diana said, "No I'm…" she felt too old to say girlfriend, "I'm…a friend. Keith's widowed."

"Is he? That was sudden."

"Sorry?"

"Well I thought I heard him say he was about to celebrate a wedding anniversary."

"You must have got him mixed up with someone else," Diana said, adding under her breath, "Arthur McKeith perhaps."

"Probably," Charlotte replied, "I am new. Oh, but that's him now, isn't it?"

Diana's head whipped round to where Charlotte was looking. Her heart skipped as she saw Keith standing outside the window. He was smiling at someone up the street, just out of vision from where Diana sat. Suddenly a slim, blonde woman appeared. From the brief glance she got Diana thought she looked to be in her forties but she ran giggling into Keith's arms like a teenager. They laughed while they hugged. They broke apart for a second and then kissed each other; a long lingering kiss that told Diana this wasn't just a business acquaintance.

"Ah," she heard Charlotte say behind her, "That's sweet isn't it."

402

Keith and the blonde finally broke apart. They grinned at each other and then had another quick kiss to say goodbye. The woman walked off in the same direction she had come from and Keith walked into the reception area, whistling. He walked straight up to the desk.

"Hello there, gorgeous," he said, "Thought anymore about that dirty weekend away?"

Charlotte laughed. "Get away, cheeky," she said, "Your friend is waiting for you."

She indicated the sofas. Keith turned round and his face fell. Diana was stood there, staring back at him; tears once again falling down her face.

"Ah, look," said Charlotte; "Isn't that lovely? She's so pleased to see you."

Chapter 22

Lou's nerves were almost getting the better of her as she walked up the path to Chris's mum's house. He'd been off work all week and Lou wasn't sure whether that was genuine illness or if he'd heard the gossip and was just trying to avoid her. Each day that he'd phoned in sick she'd felt relief but knew she couldn't put off facing him and having this conversation about her pregnancy. At least with the eating competition starting in half an hour she had the perfect excuse to escape afterwards. Maddie was out at yet another birthday party for the whole afternoon so Lou didn't have to worry about her. Mind you all these birthday presents for school friends were starting to get a bit expensive.

She rang the doorbell and fought the urge to flee. Lou felt this conversation would be slightly easier than the one she would have to have with Tony. Fortunately his mother didn't venture into Ryan Harbour too often so neither of them should have heard the gossip; yet. Chris opened the door, blowing his nose into a wet-looking handkerchief.

"Hi babes," he said, "Probably not looking my best at the moment. Do you want to come in?"

"If that's okay."

Chris gave his gummy grin; but hadn't quite finished cleaning his nose.

Morning sickness on its way, Lou thought, her stomach beginning to churn.

She followed him into the lounge where he, fortunately, continued to wipe.

"Sorry I've not made it into work. I've had a shocking

cold."

Chris coughed and spat the contents into the same handkerchief he'd just been using.

"I'll come straight to the point," Lou said, trying not to gag, "Do you remember that night a few weeks ago; when I stayed over after 'Pete Crick Day' at the supermarket? That's why I'm here now. I had to see you again, alone."

Chris grinned. "Well it's a nice idea, sweetheart," he told her, "And I appreciate you driving all the way over to have another try but it won't be that great. I'm still pretty phlegmy."

"What?"

"But I'm game if you are."

"Oh God, I didn't mean that," Lou said, wrinkling her nose in disgust, "Do you really think that's why I came over here; to sleep with you?"

Chris shrugged his shoulders in a, 'what else could you mean' manner.

"Look," she continued, "I had a lot to drink that night."

"Don't I know it? You did your party trick of turning your knickers into a hat."

Lou groaned inwardly.

"Yes, well anyway; I had a lot to drink that night and I wasn't...well I wasn't really in control of my actions."

Chris was laughing.

"I thought you had great control of my tongue in your mouth."

Lou willed herself not to be sick.

"It's just a shame you passed out really," he added.

"Sorry? What was that?" she asked.

"I said it's a shame you passed out," Chris repeated, "Right on the doorstep. I had to carry you upstairs."

Lou was incredulous. "Are you telling me you forced yourself on me while I was unconscious?"

"Eh? No, of course I didn't," Chris replied, looking shocked, "Big Chris and his two bald-headed boys didn't service you that night. When a chick is with me, she always remembers it."

Yes, because of the flatulence after the main event, Lou thought. Then she remembered.

"If you didn't sleep with me, why was there that usual stale fart smell in the morning? You know you only let rip after you…you know."

Chris sniffed. "Hey, I undressed you and put you to bed. Just because you were out for the count didn't mean I couldn't still knock one out on my own."

Lou supposed she couldn't really argue with that.

"And I even gave you a quick wipe over with the flannel afterwards."

"Sorry?"

Chris looked sheepish.

"Well, I did make a bit of a splash, if you know what I mean," he confessed.

Lou leapt out of her seat.

"I really need to use your toilet," she said, and ran from the room.

She just about made it into the downstairs bathroom before being sick. When she re-emerged Chris looked concerned.

"You okay, babes?" he asked, "You look peaky. Hope you're not coming down with anything."

Lou almost told him the truth but stopped.

"I'm fine," she said, "I have to go now though."

"What was is you wanted to tell me?"

Lou shook her head.

"It doesn't matter now," she told him, "I hope you feel better soon."

"I'll be back at work on Monday, babes; standing to attention and ready for anything."

When Lou got back into her car she took a deep breath and leant her head against the steering wheel before slowly exhaling. She'd hoped for a feeling of relief but it didn't come. If Chris wasn't the father then Tony definitely was. What on earth was he going to say about that?

*

Jamie really hoped today was going to go well. He'd planned everything down to the last detail and had been busy in the kitchen all week. It had meant Gloria being out front in the bar on her own but it's not like they were exactly rushed off their feet. Even Old Joe was taking a few days off from the pub. Gloria had been in a very snappy mood anyway and Jamie was glad he'd had a reason to keep out of her way in the kitchens. She was probably just worried about her daughter and he could understand that. Jamie hadn't had a chance to speak to Lou about the pregnancy yet and hoped she didn't blame him for telling her mother in the first place. He'd see her soon anyway. She was coming to the pub to support the eating competition.

Today's event was very much stylised on one of those American 'all you can eat' challenges which Jamie had seen on various television shows. The contestants would each be given a tray with different sized plates and bowls on it, containing portions of everything on Jamie's new menu. This included a range of deep-filled sandwiches, three large jacket potatoes with an assortment of various fillings on the side; a cheeseboard and a huge pile of chips.

Jamie felt exhausted after a morning of preparation but everything was set up and ready to go and there was the largest group of people in the pub that he had seen for a long time. He took the first of the trays out to the eight contestants. Four of them were big guys from the local rugby club who looked like they would beat most of the competition but Jamie's money was definitely on Mrs Bryant, the doctor's wife. She was sat at the head of the competitors' table, which gave her plenty of elbow room. Of the other three only the butcher's assistant did he recognise.

A small trophy had been purchased for the winner and the local paper had sent a reporter and photographer so the champion would also appear in next week's edition. As he brought out the final trays Jamie noticed Lou had arrived and had stepped behind the bar to help her mother serve. The place was heaving. He smiled and winked at her and, although she grinned back; he thought she looked rather tired and pale. He'd try and take over from her as soon as he could.

Jamie put the last two trays down onto the table. He was a bit worried about the hot food getting cold but perhaps that would make the contest more of a challenge. He hoped the spectators would like the look of the food and come in another time for something to eat.

The photographer started snapping away again. She'd already taken a few pictures of the interior and exterior of the pub and the reporter who'd interviewed Jamie had seemed interested in his plans for the future.

"Okay Ladies and Gentlemen," Jamie called, "The rules are very simple. The first one to finish their plate is the winner. If, after twenty minutes, no one has managed to clear their tray then the person judged to have got the farthest will be the victor. Contestants, are you ready?"

There was a general shout of, "yeah."

"Right then; three, two, one, go."

All eight dived into the food. It was pretty disgusting to watch. Mrs Bryant sucked the potato out of the jackets before filling the skins with the cheese and stuffing them into her mouth. She got a bit carried away halfway through the competition and after emptying the bowl of chips, threw it over her shoulder where it smashed against the back wall. Aside from that; all seemed to go well.

"What do you think?" Jamie asked Lou, while there was a lull at the bar.

"Apart from the sight making me feel queasy, I have to say, it's pretty impressive and very professionally executed. I've never seen so many people in here before."

"Wow, a complement Miss Turner. Is that the hormones talking?"

Jamie's question was greeted with a punch to the arm.

It only took Mrs Bryant twelve and a half minutes to complete the challenge. Most of the other contestants hadn't managed to get halfway through their trays. She was declared the winner and Jamie presented her with the trophy. He didn't think his internal organs would ever return to their normal positions again after Mrs Bryant hugged him while the winner's photograph was being taken for the newspaper. Still, the competition had been a success and a lot of people stayed around for drinks afterwards and had a browse through the new menus that Jamie was going live with on Monday.

He took all of the leftovers and piled the plates and dishes up in the kitchen. He left them for later and went back to take over bar duties to give Gloria and Lou a break. He felt so happy. Finally an event had gone right for him. Surely this was the start of great things to come for The Smugglers Inn. It was ten minutes later he heard the scream.

*

Lou was feeling a little odd. It wasn't tiredness exactly and it wasn't sickness either, although if she thought about Chris and his cold symptoms her stomach did begin to churn. She was glad he wasn't the father of her baby but that meant a very difficult phone call to London in the morning. Still, she'd forget about that for now and try and enjoy the eating competition.

She'd never seen The Smugglers this busy before. When she'd walked in Jamie was nowhere to be seen and her mother was running up and down the bar trying to serve everyone. There was none of her usual friendly banter with the customers. Despite how she was feeling Lou stepped behind the bar and began serving.

Watching the contestants shovelling in the food once the competition had started brought back the nausea but there was a real buzz to the atmosphere of the bar. Seeing Jamie grinning made Lou feel happy and proud.

Once the competition was over and Jamie had cleared the tables he stepped behind the bar and insisted the two women took a break. Lou didn't know where his energy came from. It felt marvellous to sit down and relax. She watched him as he served the customers that had hung around after the competition and smiled.

He really is the nicest guy, she thought, and once again imagined how much easier and happier it would be telling Jamie he was the father of her child. Lou swallowed the lump

410

that rose into her throat.

"Oh my God that's so much better," Gloria said, removing her shoes and stretching her feet out in front of her, "My feet are killing me."

Lou took a closer look at her mother. She looked tired too. Gloria pushed her feet back into her shoes.

"I'm not sure the old pins could have stood much more today."

"I'm not surprised," Lou said, glancing under the table, "Look at the size of heel you're wearing. Why don't you wear flats when you're here?"

"Well for one thing I wouldn't be able to reach the glasses above the bar," Gloria told her, "But when was the last time you saw me in a pair of flat shoes anyway?"

Lou thought back. "Never," she said.

"Exactly. Gloria Turner doesn't do flat shoes."

"Or loose clothing."

"Oi, cheeky."

Lou's grin disappeared. "I have to say though, mum; you do look tired."

"I feel it," Gloria sighed, "I know we're never busy in here but what with running back and forth to the kitchen being taste tester for His Nibs over there this past week, I feel like I've been running a marathon."

"Then tell him how you feel," Lou said, "Jamie's a great guy, he'll understand. The hours you've spent working here for him lately you deserve a break."

Gloria leaned in closer to her daughter.

"To be honest," she said, quietly, "I'm a bit fed up with bar work anyway. I really need a change. I'm tired Lou and not just because of work."

411

"What do you mean?"

"I'm tired of my life. I mean I love having you and Maddie in it, but all I'm doing at the moment is working and then going home. I don't go out like I used to. I don't have much of a social life because I don't want to meet up with friends in a bar when I've been working in one all day. And I'm tired of this grotty, little town."

"Mum!"

"Well I am. The way the gossip spread about your predicament. It's disgusting. That sort of thing should be private until you choose otherwise. I'm sick of it all."

"Are you thinking of leaving?"

Gloria was silent for a while before saying,

"I don't know, Lou; I really don't. I feel I need to make some changes, you know how it is; but I also don't want to be away from you and Maddie; especially now with you…" she indicated Lou's belly.

"I'm pregnant, mum. You can say the word. Besides, don't think about me in this. If I've learned anything these past weeks I've learned that you need to be happy in your life, and if you're not; change it. You've got to do what's right for you."

"But you're going to need help…"

"Perhaps, but if I do then I'll sort it. I don't want to be a burden on you. I'm not expecting you to look after my children for me just so I can go to work. I want you to be their grandmother, not their guardian and carer. You're meant to spoil your grandchildren, not raise them yourself. If you want to go off somewhere, I'm not going to stop you; just so long as you're happy."

Gloria smiled. "Thanks, baby," she said, "And I hope you're going to be happy too. You've been so down lately. I guess that's the pregnancy but, well; since you and Diana started on her list, you've really seemed to come alive. Where is she today, by the way? I thought she'd have been here."

Lou sighed. "I haven't got around to apologising to her yet. I had a real go at her in the supermarket that day you found out I was pregnant. I thought she'd spread the gossip."

"Oh Lou! Why would you think that? Diana's lovely, she wouldn't hurt you."

"I know, I know. I think we'd just allowed some tension to build up between us that exploded that day. She'd been worried about me getting along with her new boyfriend while I was upset she hadn't introduced me to him. If only we'd had a chat about it and been honest with each other we could have avoided the row. Anyway, with a bit of help I managed to work out that the news of my pregnancy came from the doctor's surgery. It must have been that cow of a receptionist but I haven't got enough proof to put in a complaint. I will go and apologise to Diana; I've just had a few other things on my mind. Besides I've not seen her around for the last few days."

Gloria sniggered. "Perhaps she's run off with Old Joe," she said.

Lou raised her eyebrows, questioningly.

"Old Joe," she asked, "What do you mean?"

"Well," said Gloria, getting up, "He's not been seen either. Two people disappear at the same time; maybe they're together. Anyway, I'm going to go and start on the washing up while Jamie's at the bar. Are you staying?"

"No," Lou replied, standing up as well, "No, I think I'll go home."

She walked slowly out of the bar, turning things over in her mind. So caught up in her own thoughts was she that Lou didn't hear her mother scream.

When was the last time she'd seen Old Joe? She usually spotted him somewhere during the day, either walking up to the shops on the high street or strolling along the harbour front to look at the new apartments. Why hadn't she noticed before now that he was missing?

Lou's tiredness went up a notch as she entered the hallway of her apartment block and she took the lift up to her floor instead of using the stairs. She walked through the fire door and out onto the landing, passing by her own and Diana's front doors and onto Old Joe's, opposite Grace and Robert's. She'd never been inside his place before or even knocked at the door. She almost felt nervous as she rang the bell. Lou waited for what felt like five minutes but was probably only one. She rang again, twice this time. There was no answer. She leaned down and lifted up the letterbox. Lou never knew why these apartments had letterboxes seeing as all mail was delivered to individual boxes downstairs.

An indescribable smell hit her as she lifted the flap, making her throw her head back and gag. She really had to force herself to look through the gap again. The door into the main bedroom was open but the curtains were drawn, making the room dark. As Lou's eyes became accustomed to it she was able to make out a shape crumpled on the floor by the bed.

*

We've definitely got it right this time, Robert thought confidently, as he buttoned up the frock coat. He and Grace had spent a lot of time discussing fantasy people before they'd hired their costumes for today. Mind you there had been several arguments as well. Grace had an obsessive fixation with that gas meter reader in Robert's opinion. He was getting

414

mentioned every time the fantasy costume subject came up.
And Robert was none too pleased when Grace said she'd had a
naughty dream about Diana's new boyfriend.

"He was a doctor and I was a nurse," Grace told him, going
into detail, "He'd just saved my sister's life and I took him to a
private room in the hospital to thank him."

"And where was I while all this was going on?" Robert
asked, clearly miffed.

"Well actually, you were in the main ward having a boil
lanced."

But anyway, here they were at last. Robert pulled the coat
straighter and looked in the mirror, turning to the side and then
face-on again.

"Not bad for sixty-five, Robert," he said, aloud.

He was quite glad Grace had finally settled on Mr Darcy
from her favourite book, Pride & Prejudice. The outfit was
smart and remarkably slimming.

"Grace, are you ready?" he called out. She was dressing in
the spare bedroom so that they wouldn't see each other until
fully in costume.

"I suppose so," she replied, sullenly.

"I'll meet you in the lounge in two minutes," he called again.

Robert was really starting to feel excited. He had high hopes
for how Grace was going to look for him. It was a secret
fantasy he'd had for years. After two minutes he made his way
down to the lounge.

"Well, what do you think, Miss Bennett?" he said, spinning
around, "Will I do as your Darcy?"

"I can't see you," Grace told him.

Robert stopped turning and faced his wife. It wasn't quite
the image he'd dreamt up. Grace was standing slouched in the

415

middle of the room, clearly embarrassed. The white calf-length boots and tight, pink miniskirt left a lot of veiny leg on show. The matching pink, sparkly jacket reflected up onto her face, giving Grace a blotchy complexion. The tall white hat was a little on the large side and had slipped down over her eyes. Grace had to tip her head back to look out. She picked up her baton.

"Well?" she said, glumly, "Is this doing it for you?"

"Oh Grace," Robert moaned, "You're dressed as a majorette, not a cheerleader."

"What's the difference?"

"Well you shouldn't be twirling a baton for a start. Careful with that, you'll have someone's eye out. You should be shaking your pompoms."

"Not in this bra I can't. Oh this is so unfair," she sighed, "You get to wear a nice suit and I've got on this monstrosity."

"No, you look great, love," Robert lied, "Really great. Erm; weren't you going to see Dr Bryant about that vein on your leg?"

"I haven't got around to it yet."

Grace sighed again and sat down on the sofa.

"I feel ridiculous," she said.

"It's just a costume," Robert told her, "We can always change it next time and…"

"It's not just the outfit," Grace interrupted, "It's this whole thing."

"What thing?"

"This sexual experimentation thing. It's been a disaster from start to finish."

"Don't say that love," Robert said, sitting down beside her.

"How else can I describe it?" she told him, "I've been stuck

416

in a lift with no bra, walked back from the harbour front without my knickers on and flashed the regatta in a see-through negligee. I've seen strippers finish a routine showing less flesh than I have lately."

"You're exaggerating."

"Not by much. And you've suffered too. You managed to put your back out while trying to bend over backwards and then you spent a week walking about like John Wayne after your testicle swelled up. The bruising has only just faded away. "

"Yes but…"

"No buts, Robert," Grace said, standing up again, and straightening her hat, "I'm done with this."

Robert didn't get a chance to reply. The doorbell rang several times in quick succession, followed by frantic knocking on their front door.

"Robert, Grace; are you there? Please open up."

"That's Lou," Grace said, "What does she want?"

"I'll go and find out."

"Robert, no," Grace hissed, "You can't answer the door while we're dressed like this."

"Robert, Grace, please."

"Look," he said, "She obviously needs us. We've got to go and answer the door."

*

Lou had panicked after seeing Old Joe on the floor. She couldn't handle this situation on her own and needed some assistance. She hammered on Robert and Grace's door. It took an eternity for it to open. As Robert and Grace appeared so Diana opened her front door.

"What's all the noise?" she said, coming over, "What's happened? What's wrong? What the hell are you two

417

wearing?"

"I told you not to open the door," Grace whispered.

Robert bit his lip to stop himself saying something he'd later regret.

"What is it for, a fancy dress party?" Diana asked, "Your costume is great Robert but you might need to rethink yours, Grace."

"What do you mean?" Grace said, sounding affronted.

"Well I'm sorry but, you do rather resemble a drunken majorette with measles."

"There's no call for that. What do you think you'd look like in a short miniskirt at your age?"

"I'm only two years older than you."

"Not to look at!"

"Guys!" Lou interjected.

The two ladies stopped arguing, remembering why they had all come out of their apartments in the first place.

"What's happened?" Diana asked.

"It's Old Joe," Lou whispered, "He's dead."

Four sets of eyes turned to Joe's front door.

"Are you sure?" Diana asked.

Lou nodded. "Mum mentioned she'd not seen him for a few days and I realised I hadn't either. Oh God; why didn't I notice before now? I could have checked in on him days ago instead of waiting until it was too late and seeing him now through the letterbox."

"Shall I check as well?" Robert said, walking over to Joe's door.

He lifted the flap of the letterbox and his head snapped back as Lou's had done. He looked in again.

"Joe," he called, "Joe, can you hear me; it's Robert from

across the hall."

He waited a few moments and then stood up.

"He's definitely dead in there. I don't know why I called through really."

He walked back to the ladies and Grace rubbed his arm, consolingly.

"Poor Joe," Robert whispered.

All four fell silent for a moment.

"What should we do now?" Lou asked.

"I think we need to call the police," Diana told her, "They'll have to break in."

"I'll do it," Robert offered, and headed back down his hallway.

"Why don't you both come inside too," Grace said, "I'll put the kettle on."

Diana moved to follow Grace but Lou stayed where she was.

"Lou?" Diana said, quietly, "Are you coming in?"

Lou looked back at Joe's door again.

"No. It would feel like we were leaving him on his own. I'm going to stay out here until the police arrive."

Diana smiled. "I'll wait with you."

They both sat down on the floor on either side of Joe's door.

"I hate to think of him lying in there on his own. He must have been there for days," Lou said, "It's horrible. Why didn't we realise?"

"You know Joe," Diana told her, "He always preferred his own company. Have you ever seen anyone enter that apartment before?"

Lou shook her head.

"I wonder how old he was."

"I don't know. He's always looked the same; ever since I

first saw him after moving here. In his eighties I'd guess."

Tears were making their way slowly down Lou's face.

"I don't even know his surname," she whispered, "Isn't that terrible?"

"I think we were all as close to Joe as he allowed us to be," Diana told her, "He preferred it that way."

"I suppose," Lou replied, wiping her eyes.

The two women remained silent for a minute, both remembering times in their lives when Joe was there in the background.

"I owe you a big apology, by the way," Diana finally said, "For that argument we had in your apartment. I was horrible to you. I didn't mean what I said; it was just the heat of the moment. I don't think badly about you or your mother; you're both lovely people."

"I'm sorry too," Lou replied, "I should never have thought that it was you who had spread the rumour about my pregnancy."

"I was shocked when I found out Muriel and Joyce both knew," Diana told her, "I don't know how that happened. I had a big row with Joyce."

"Not about that I hope."

"No, it was about…well everything really. She's been scuppering my plans for the youth club left, right and centre and tried to turn the committee against me."

"I wish I could say I was surprised," Lou said.

Diana leant her head back against the wall.

"I really don't like arguments," she admitted, "But I told Joyce a few home truths. I can't believe after all these years of friendship that she would turn on me like that."

"Jealousy is a powerful emotion."

420

"I think I saw, for the first time, what you see," Diana told Lou, "She's really not a very nice person. Mind you I do feel a little guilty. I informed the rest of the committee about what had happened."

"Good for you."

"Do you think so?" Diana asked, "Joyce lives for her committee work. I may have destroyed her."

"I doubt that."

Diana mused. "Well I assume a few of the group will rally round her," she said, "People like Celia and Tess Andrews. And Muriel is friends with everybody."

Lou looked over at her.

"What are you going to do now?" she asked.

Diana let out a long sigh.

"I'm not making up with her, that's for sure; but I don't know. I really felt I was making a difference with the youth club idea."

"Then carry on with it," Lou said, "Go back to your plans, start a new committee with some of the old members and a few new faces."

A smile appeared on Diana's face.

"I did like the idea of the club being on the harbour front. But it's no good if Dr Bryant is expanding the surgery."

"Is he?"

Diana nodded. "Yes," she said, "Expanding into the premises next door; the one we'd hoped to use."

"Well then, it's a good time to go and speak to him about it," Lou told her, "Ask him what his plans are. He may want the space for some kind of clinic; you know, like a big room for group meetings. If so, perhaps he would be open to you using it for the local kids at certain times too. He already has a play area in reception."

"That's a great idea," Diana said, her eyes shining, "Do you want to join a new committee?"

Lou laughed. "I think I'm going to be a bit busy," she indicated her belly, "But maybe ask my mum. She's looking for something new."

Grace reappeared with two cups of tea. She was still in her majorette outfit but had removed the hat.

"Here you go," she said, "A hot cup of tea. I've put sugar in. That's good for shock."

She dropped a cushion onto the floor from under her arm.

"Here," she told Lou, "You shouldn't be sitting on a hard floor in your condition. Use this."

"Thanks Grace."

"The police are on their way," she told them, and returned to the apartment.

Both ladies took a sip of their tea before the conversation moved on.

"How are you and Keith getting on?" Lou asked, "I'm sorry I didn't really give him a proper chance."

Diana's smile fell from her face.

"You were right about him," she said, and told Lou the story about her trip to Tenham.

"What a bastard," Lou said, after Diana had finished, "I'm starting to wonder if all men are like that."

"What do you mean?"

Lou sighed. "I've got a bit of a story to tell you myself."

She told Diana about her night with Tony.

"I really felt like he used me. I thought he'd started to see me in a different light; just like I had when I looked at myself in the mirror in that red dress. I saw a confident woman who knew where she was going in life and had some self-worth. I was taking care of myself through healthy eating and exercise, I took an interest in my home and kept it clean and tidy for me and my daughter and I had a chance to further my career. He noticed those things but they didn't actually matter to him. He still only saw the old me. Good, old Lou; she'll enjoy a meaningless fun night because she doesn't care about anything; especially herself."

"You deserve better," Diana said.

"I didn't feel like it after that," Lou confessed, "I felt like the coven's view of me was right. Their opinion was obviously shared by Tony. I lost all the confidence I'd gained. And then I had a disastrous day with Pete Crick where everything went wrong so that didn't help either."

"Yes I did hear a few stories about what went on. Didn't the actor get hit?"

Lou nodded and told her why.

"My goodness," Diana said, shocked, "I'm so sorry I wasn't there. I was wasting my time at home, preparing myself all day for that first date with Keith. You were right about the person I became with him. I did hang around at home in case he called. I was behaving as I had with Richard; being the little woman on a man's arm, rather than being an actual person first and foremost."

She sighed.

"Do you know, I've just realised he was only using me for sex as well. I mean, we did have some lovely dates but once our relationship moved into the bedroom, it was difficult to get Keith out of there. Do you suppose that's what he wanted all along? When he met me that night in The Smugglers, is that the sort of woman he saw?"

"Welcome to my world," Lou said.

Both ladies looked at each other and smiled, dejectedly.

"I feel so used," Diana admitted, "And so stupid. I thought I was too old to be taken in by a cheat."

"I don't think it matters what age you are," Lou replied.

She sighed and continued on with her story about Pete Crick.

"I felt utterly worthless after he attacked me," she said, "So much so that I got hopelessly drunk at the nightclub and woke up the next morning in bed with Chris."

"Oh dear God."

"I know. I felt terrible. I'd slept with two different men in the space of twenty four hours and a third had also thought me an easy lay. I saw it as a sign. I was getting too cocky about myself. At the singles night I'd practically told Jamie he was a terrible landlord and he should buck his ideas up. What the hell do I know about business or running a pub? When I discovered I was pregnant and realised I didn't know who the father was I felt I was being punished."

Lou shook her head, sadly.

"Anyway, I found out today that Chris and I hadn't actually slept together."

"So Tony is the father then."

Lou nodded.

"Does he know?"

She shook her head.

"No, not yet. I'll have to tell him but to be honest…Oh Diana; I don't want to have this baby," Lou confessed, "How cruel must that sound, especially to you? You must think me heartless after all your struggles to have a child; but I don't want it."

Diana crawled over to Lou and placed her hand on Lou's

arm.

"It's so difficult admitting that out loud," Lou continued, "And so selfish of me, but I can't help feeling that way."

Diana couldn't think of anything to say to comfort her friend.

"I'd started making and creating plans for the future but now they've all gone. I feel like there's no future left for me."

As Lou began to cry, Diana placed her arms around her friend. A moment later Lou leaned forwards, groaning and grabbing her belly. Inside her apartment, Grace had just emerged from the bedroom after changing. She didn't want to have to explain her outfit to the police. She heard Diana call out,

"Someone phone for an ambulance."

Chapter 23

Dr's Case Notes – Wednesday 18 November

My heart is broken. Dr Moore is definitely leaving. I've been given an official six month notice period. I wish now that I had declared my love when I said I would. I got as far as opening the surgery door that day after my last diary entry but Dr Moore was having a consultation with Mrs O'Brien after the unfortunate mistake the private clinic made when filling her lips with collagen for a better pout. Surely any sane person would have realised that she was talking about the lips on her face and not on her…the poor woman squeaks like a balloon every time she takes a step. Camel-toe; it's more like the whole foot down there.

There's no point saying how I feel now anyway. Dr Moore's mind is all made up and I see such happiness and excitement in that beautiful face every time I'm told stories about the rural practice and the picturesque village it's in. I can't stop this happening as much as I would like to. This is Dr Moore's dream and I want that dream to come true.

The Lake District is so far away though. How am I going to cope? Has Ryan Harbour and its residents been cursed? Recently it feels like it has. An old man in one of the apartments above the surgery who wanders up and down the harbour front died and wasn't discovered for several days. I don't know if he had an illness, he was never one of my patients. Poor Lou Turner found him, about ten days ago now, and then suffered a miscarriage. That was the same day that Mrs Bryant and I were caught up in a fire at The Smugglers pub after her victorious win in the eating competition.

Some old, faulty wiring in the kitchen caused the fire I believe. It was lucky that the barmaid went in there when she did and raised the alarm otherwise it could have spread into the bar area where we all were. Mind you that didn't stop Mrs Bryant throwing me over her shoulder and running outside to safety. She's not a bad, old stick really. The firefighters fought the flames from the back entrance by the car park but initially had trouble getting the doors open. Mrs Bryant was able to rip them off their hinges, no bother at all; bless her. The inside of the kitchen is pretty much destroyed so I hear. Mind you the insurance will pay out so it's not too bad. Not as devastating as the loss of my lover.

Okay, so Dr Moore and I have never officially been lovers; not in real life so to speak. Mind you, the fantasies that still rage through my imagination are certainly hot. I must still love Mrs Bryant too as there's actually one fantasy that includes both Dr Moore **and** Mrs Bryant satisfying me at the same time. It's a very passionate threesome but the only problem is that I can't quite imagine the huge bed we would need and so we're all stuck together in a standard sized double. It starts off quite enjoyably but then we have to keep stopping to replace the fitted sheet that has come up at the corner. It's always the person on top who has to do that. You would think I could make sure that Mrs Bryant never gets up there, the size that she is, but she always demands to take a turn. The fantasy usually ends then, although one time she somehow managed to break Dr Moore's arm and so I had to imagine a rush to the hospital to make sure it was set properly before I could leave the fantasy that day. I do like things settled. Mind you, it did make me late for my house calls.

Anyway, what can I do about Dr Moore? Either I'm going

to have to just get over it and advertise for another doctor or I need to move up North too. I'd have to take Mrs Bryant with me. I don't think she'd allow me to leave her. We'd just have to make the best of things. I'm sure she'd fit in up there. She enjoys lake swimming, although that time at Loch Ness caused a few rumours. Still, someone thinking they spotted Nessie wearing a pink and blue striped two-piece must have been good for tourism. That was a great trip. I tried haggis and Mrs Bryant went caber tossing.

Speaking of tossing, I've just got enough time for that threesome fantasy before morning surgery starts. I must remember to lock the door first this time. It's difficult coming up with an excuse as to what you're doing with your feet up on the desk and your trousers around your ankles when a patient walks in on you. I had to tell Mrs Whittaker I was practicing some physiotherapy stretches. She said she was pleased as that explained what her fourteen year old grandson was doing when she walked into his bedroom one time unannounced.

*

Gloria was on her way to Diana's to pick up Maddie. Lou was back home and fighting fit, physically but she was obviously still upset about the miscarriage. It wasn't fair on Maddie to keep seeing her mother cry without really understanding why and so Gloria and Diana had stepped in to help over the past ten days with school runs and meals.

Lou was blaming herself, Gloria knew that. Her daughter had told her she didn't want the baby and felt it somehow knew. In her mind she had killed it and nothing Gloria said could sway that opinion. It was worrying but hopefully, with time; things would get better.

She had a lot of free time at present to look after Maddie

anyway. Jamie was another person she couldn't cheer up. Not that she could blame him either. Just when the pub was about to be popular with a new food menu, the kitchen was destroyed. The insurance were willing to pay out and Gloria couldn't understand why Jamie was still so depressed. The bar area could still be opened but he hadn't been bothering.

"We only had one regular left," he'd told her, "And he's dead now so there's no point."

Gloria sighed as she took the lift to the second floor. At least she and Diana were both cheerful enough. They'd had a long chat about men and relationships after Gloria found out about Keith and she thought she'd managed to keep Diana positive about future dating.

As she pressed the doorbell, Gloria realised that she had never been inside Diana's apartment before. She looked at her watch. There'd probably be time to have a cup of tea.

*

Diana enjoyed having Maddie over that morning. Even though she was off school with a cold, she was really well-behaved and didn't moan or go crashing around the apartment. Diana smiled as she pictured the scene Gloria had probably had with her granddaughter before she came over.

"Now listen," she would have said, her face pressed right up against Maddie's, "When you go in there, you don't touch anything. Do you hear me?"

She'd let Maddie feed Charlie and they'd watched him swim around the bowl for a while but a five year old soon gets bored with that. They'd made some rock cakes together (Maddie's tray turning out a lot better than Diana's) and were watching one of Maddie's favourite television programmes when Gloria rang the doorbell.

429

"How's she been?" Gloria asked; making sure she took in all the décor as she was led down to the lounge.

"Fine," Diana replied, "We've been baking."

"Successfully?" Gloria questioned; a twinkle in her eye.

Diana laughed. "One of us has her mother's talents in that area," she said, "Do you have time for a cup of tea? Lou's got a doctor's appointment hasn't she?"

"She has, yes," Gloria replied, having a good look round the lounge and dining area, "I'm taking Maddie back to mine for lunch but I do have time for…"

She stopped mid-sentence. Diana looked over from the sink, kettle in hand. Gloria was staring at the wall. She looked a little horrified; scared even.

"Are you okay?" Diana asked.

"Erm; you know what," Gloria said, not taking her eyes off of the wall, "I won't stay for tea. I'm afraid I have to go. I've just remembered something I need to do on the way home. Come on Maddie; thank Auntie Diana for looking after you."

"Aw. My programme's still on."

"Will you come on!"

Maddie and Diana were both taken aback by Gloria's sudden abruptness. Maddie got up from the sofa and glumly gave Diana a hug. Gloria grabbed her granddaughter's hand and practically dragged her out of the room.

"Thanks again," she called back, over her shoulder.

Diana walked over to where Gloria had been standing. What was it that she had seen to spook her like that? As she looked at the wall Diana saw a large spider just beside the photographs of her parents and her wedding day. She smiled as she rolled up a magazine,

"Is that all it was?" she said.

Dr Bryant had just told Lou she was perfectly fine but she didn't feel it. She'd tried to explain to him why the miscarriage was affecting her so much, emotionally. She'd said she was happy being a mother to Maddie but it really hurt that their twosome wasn't about to become a threesome. Dr Bryant went very red in the face at that point and quickly ended the appointment.

She came out of the surgery into a beautiful, bright day; the harbour bathed in glorious, autumn sunlight. She walked across to the slipway and sat down on the harbour steps beside it. The fishing boats bobbed gently on the water. Lou bowed her head; the idyllic scene in front of her too painful to look at. It was full of so much beauty and happiness and she couldn't allow herself to feel those emotions.

Jamie came and sat down beside her. He looked as rough as she felt; unshaven and his hair on end like he'd just very quickly run his hands through it. He didn't say anything. Eventually Lou rested her head on his shoulder and they continued to sit that way for a few minutes more.

"Life's shit; isn't it," he eventually said.

Lou murmured in agreement.

"Do you want to enter a competition to see which one of us feels the worst?" he asked.

"Aren't you afraid I'd win," Lou replied.

Jamie's laugh was more of a snort.

"I'll run you a close second," he told her.

The silence resumed until Jamie said,

"I'm sorry Lou, for your loss."

Tears sprang to her eyes. Jamie placed his arm around her.

"I'm sorry I had to tell your mum about the pregnancy but I

didn't want her to hear the gossip," Jamie continued, "There are times when I really hate this town."

Lou sat up and looked into his eyes.

"You're not thinking of leaving are you?"

He couldn't hold her gaze.

"I don't know," he said.

"Please don't," Lou told him, overwhelmed with a sudden rush of emotion, "I don't want to lose anything else, I couldn't bear it."

Jamie felt a lump in his throat as he stared down into her face.

"Couldn't you?" he asked.

Lou shook her head.

"You know, when I found out you were pregnant," Jamie confessed, "I had an overwhelming feeling of jealousy; about the father."

"Did you?"

"I realised I wanted it to be me."

Lou's bottom lip trembled.

"I wish it had been yours too," she whispered.

They both flung their arms around one another and cried; neither caring who saw them, both letting their built up emotions overwhelm them. When they eventually untangled themselves, both wiping their eyes, they managed to smile shyly at each other.

"Well I know why I needed to cry like that," Lou said, "I'm not sure I quite understand why you did."

Jamie sighed. "It's finished," he said.

"What is?"

"The pub. I can't afford to run it anymore."

"But isn't the insurance going to pay out for a new kitchen?

I thought everything was okay."

Jamie put his head in his hands.

"I've no money left to run the pub until the insurance comes through," he said, "I threw everything into the new menus and meals. That's what was going to save the pub, but I can't do the food without a kitchen. The article in the paper that was meant to advertise the new menus turned into an article about the fire. They only mentioned that a competition was running at the time. There was no reference to the range of foods on offer at all. No one's going to come to the pub now. Even my last regular has died. I've received a letter from a solicitor in Tenham who wants to see me tomorrow and I bet that's going to be bad news as well; I have some loans outstanding. It's hopeless."

"Don't say that," Lou told him, placing her hand on his shoulder, "There's got to be something else. You'll think of it; you always do."

Jamie shrugged Lou's hand away and stood up.

"There's nothing left," he said, "I'm finally facing facts. I blew it. I tried my best but it just wasn't good enough. **I'm** not good enough."

"This is so unlike you."

Jamie looked down at Lou.

"What do you expect me to say? Pretend it's all okay? Pretend I'll bounce back? I've been pretending for far too long. You saw that yourself. You were the only one who did. I've not been breaking even since I started running the pub. I lied about that. I've been using all my savings and credit cards trying to make this place work. I really thought I was going to, but look at me; I'm useless."

Lou stood up and walked away.

"Where are you going?" Jamie asked.

"I'm not going to sit here and listen to a load of self-pity," she informed him.

"What?"

"You've lost nothing," she said, turning to face him, "Look over there; your pub is still standing and functioning as it should. Maybe if you hadn't felt sorry for yourself and opened up the day after the fire, people might have come in to check you were okay or just to have a nose around. I don't know; maybe you could have let them have a peek through the kitchen doors to see the mess, just so long as they bought a drink. You could have kept the bar open and milked the fire for all it was worth. You could have got the reporter back for a follow up interview, telling him how you were facing adversity by opening the next day. But no, you'd rather sit back and wallow in self-pity. I think you'll find that I win your competition about who feels worse hands down. I actually did lose something; I lost a child. It may not have been fully formed but it was a baby that I kept saying I didn't want. Perhaps it heard me."

Lou's tears had returned and were streaming down her face.

"Now I'm free again to have the life I'd started planning for myself but do you know what? I would give up everything for the chance to give birth to that child and raise it. What's the point in living my life if I've taken my own child's away?"

Lou crumpled onto the floor. In three strides Jamie was beside her; hugging her to him.

"I'm sorry," he said, "I'm so sorry."

He lifted Lou's face up to his and kissed away her tears. Lou stopped crying and kissed Jamie on the lips. It felt like the first proper kiss either of them had ever had. It felt right.

"I've wanted that to happen for such a long time," Jamie confessed, once they'd stood up again.

"What; see me in a crumpled heap on the floor?"

"Of course; what else?"

They both managed to laugh.

"God, that's the first time I've allowed myself to do that in a while," Lou said.

"You shouldn't deny the feeling," Jamie told her, gently running his fingers through her hair, "There's nothing wrong with being happy. You've got to live your life. Your loss is not your fault. These things happen. It's awful but they happen. You just told me I should have focussed on the positives after the fire; that goes for you too. You have a beautiful daughter who needs you. You have friends and family around who just want to love and help you."

After a second he added,

"And you've got me too, Lou; if you want."

Lou smiled. "I do want," she told him.

The smile fell away from her face.

"What you just said makes sense," she told him, "My head knows that, but my heart won't accept it; not yet."

"I can understand that. But just remember, this wasn't your fault. There are lots of reasons why a miscarriage occurs but wishing a baby wasn't there isn't one of them."

Lou looked back out to sea while Jamie spoke.

"Perhaps the baby wasn't forming as it should. Perhaps if he or she had been born they wouldn't have had any quality of life; we just don't know. Just because you hadn't planned another child didn't mean you wouldn't have loved it as much as you do Maddie. You're a mother, Lou; a great mother. You would have made all the right decisions. Don't blame yourself for what happened."

Lou continued to stare out at the harbour.

"Do you know what's odd," she said, "I'm grieving for someone I never got to meet. When I found out I was pregnant I tried desperately to think of it as a collection of cells and not as a fully formed person; but I couldn't. It was a baby; my baby. And you're right, I didn't plan it but I was going to have it. I faced the decision of abortion and decided I couldn't go through with it. I still couldn't say I actually wanted the baby, but then I lost it anyway. It's gone and there isn't a body to mourn. There hasn't been a funeral. A funeral gives closure doesn't it? You say goodbye and then surround yourself in the memories. I don't have memories, but I do need to be able to say goodbye. I need to set myself and the baby free."

Jamie walked over to the harbour wall and picked up a large pebble that someone had left there. It was perfectly round and a beautiful shade of blue.

"Here," he said, calling Lou over, "Why not use this as representing your lost child."

He placed the pebble gently in Lou's hand.

"Now, what would you like to do with it; keep it, bury it; what?"

Lou stared at the pebble for what felt like an eternity. She thought about Maddie and all the times they had shared these past five years. She thought about the lost child and how they weren't going to be able to share anything like that. She lifted her hands and gently kissed the stone.

"Goodbye my little one," she whispered, "You'll never be forgotten."

Lou looked out beyond the boats to the horizon. She threw the pebble as far as she could into the water.

"Be free."

*

Diana was watering the plant outside her front door when Lou walked through the fire door from the lift. She looked brighter than she had in a long time. She indicated the plant.

"You know you're the only one who likes that thing."

"It's staying," Diana told her, smiling.

Lou laughed. "Do you fancy a glass of wine?" she asked, "I know it's only lunchtime but I've not had a drink in ages and I'm gagging for one. Mum will be back with Maddie in about an hour and she can join us too. Think of it as a very small way of saying thank you for all your help this past week."

Diana smiled, put down the watering can and followed Lou into her apartment.

It was nice to be sitting together and laughing again, Diana thought, as her glass was topped up. Lou had just told her about kissing Jamie.

"It's about time," Diana replied, "I think the two of you are so well suited. It was Muriel who made me realise that; on the day of the treasure hunt in The Smugglers."

"Doesn't that seem like such a long time ago," Lou said, "The treasure hunt, the regatta; writing your list?"

Diana smiled. "I think that's the best thing I ever did," she said, "I was pretty useless at the individual items on it but overall it did the job I wanted it to; it has changed my life for the better."

"I wouldn't say you were useless at all the items on it," Lou told her.

Diana raised her eyebrows.

"Really?" she said, "I was the worst driver to ever get behind the wheel of a car, I couldn't make a sponge to save my life, I

437

split my trousers at my first keep fit class, I still jump at anything that flutters near me and I dated a cheater."

"Okay maybe I would say you were useless," Lou grinned, "But still, there are plenty of other things you can have a go at. That list has boosted your confidence enough to try anything. You've got your committee up and running, so I hear."

Diana nodded. "Yes, and I'm meeting with Dr Bryant on Monday regarding using his premises for some after school clubs."

"It's all happening."

"Thanks to you."

"Thanks to your sister, really," Lou said, "She was your inspiration."

Diana nodded. "That's very true," she held up her glass, "To Frances."

Lou held hers up too. "To Frances."

They both took a sip of wine.

"Anyway," Lou continued, a sparkle in her eye, "The list isn't quite completed yet, is it."

"Isn't it?"

"Broaden horizons."

Diana smiled. "Oh yes, the cruise. Should I get some brochures?"

"I can't see why not now," Lou told her, "What the hell, let's drink to that too."

Diana laughed. "I will once I've used your toilet."

"Oh, use the en suite," Lou told her, as Diana got up, "Maddie somehow managed to break the flush in the main bathroom this morning. I'll have to get someone in."

After washing her hands Diana took a bit of the hand cream that Lou kept beside the basin. She rubbed it in as she emerged from the en suite. It smelled lovely and she made a mental note to ask Lou where she'd bought it from. She heard the front door open and then Maddie's voice and footsteps as she ran down to the lounge.

"Why don't you play in your bedroom for five minutes," she heard Gloria say, "Nanny needs a word with Mummy."

Diana walked out into the hallway, just as Maddie disappeared into her bedroom. It sounded like Gloria had something private she wanted to tell her daughter. Perhaps it was best if she left them to it. She'd just pop into the lounge and say her goodbyes.

"What's wrong?" Lou said, before Diana could reach the lounge.

"Oh God, I've seen your father," Gloria replied.

Diana stopped in her tracks.

"What do you mean?" Lou said, "You told me he was dead. How could you..."

"I saw him in a photograph," Gloria said.

There was a momentary silence.

"Mum, you're not making any sense."

"Oh God this is awful. I saw the man who was your father in a photograph at Diana's house...and he was marrying her."

The hallway began to swirl in front of Diana and she leaned against the wall. Surely she hadn't heard correctly.

"I knew he was married but I didn't know who to; I swear it," Gloria said.

Diana turned to leave but the room still wasn't in focus. She stumbled up to the front door and heard something fall off of the hall table as she passed by it. Her name was being called behind her but she didn't stop. She wrenched open the front door and fled.

Robert entered his apartment.

"Hello love; had a good day."

"Mmm."

Robert walked into the bedroom and stopped. Why hadn't Grace continued to talk on as she usually did? It was Wednesday. Surely she'd forgotten the lamb chops again. He walked back out and down to the lounge. Grace was sat at the dining table with a bottle of Chablis and two glasses but nothing else.

"Sit down, love," she said, and poured the wine.

Robert did as he was told.

"Now then," she said, "Tell me what's going on."

"Eh? Nothing's going on."

"Oh really? You've been miserable and moody since that day with the costumes."

Robert picked up his glass and took a swig.

"Well, you said we weren't going to try anything else," he mumbled.

"And I ask my question again; tell me what's going on? What is happening inside that brain of yours?" she tapped her index finger against Robert's forehead, "What's all this really about?"

"I don't understand, Grace."

"Neither do I," she said, "I mean; what was it that put all this stuff into your head in the first place? You told me you were bored with life. I can understand that part. You're retiring soon and obviously you're going to worry about what you're going to find to do all day, but why all this sex stuff?"

Robert felt embarrassed; like a naughty child in front of the headmistress. He found he couldn't look his wife in the face.

He took another swig of wine.

"It's just one aspect," he said, quietly.

Grace sighed and sat back in her chair.

"We used to make love once a month," she told him, "Now if that wasn't enough for you then you could have come and told me about it. Instead you've had the pair of us involved in all the weird and wonderful and do you know what; we haven't made love once since all this happened. Had you realised that?"

Robert hadn't.

"All we've done is bicker. That's never been us, Robert. We don't argue."

"But everything is the same all the time," Robert blurted out, standing up and pacing the floor, "We have exactly the same routine, day in and day out. You always cook the same thing on the same day…"

"Fine. You tell me what you want and I'll cook it for you. You can try and come up with ideas for dinner each night because I tell you, it's not that easy. I tried making a Chicken Kiev for you once but you didn't like it."

"That's because you got cloves and bulbs mixed up in your head. The whole block complained about the smell."

"But you never wanted me to try it again. 'Don't bother with that, Grace,' you said, 'Stick with the chops on a Wednesday.'"

Robert sat back down again.

"Did I really say that?" he asked.

"Yes, you did. You know, routine makes things easier; that's all. Do you think I like cooking every day? Don't you think I'd like a break from it? When was the last time you said, 'Forget dinner, let's eat out tonight?'"

"I can't remember," Robert admitted, sheepishly.

"That's the point," Grace continued, "I'm all for making

441

changes to our lives Robert but why can't it be something like we eat out once or twice a week? Maybe we could take in a film at the cinema every now and then or have a picnic in the park on a nice day? I don't get this fixation you've had with sex."

"All the guys at work go on about it all the time," Robert confessed.

"Sorry?"

"All the blokes I work with," he continued, "They're always going on about what they do with their girlfriends or wives or mistresses. I can never join in that conversation. They're all younger than me and I think they just assume that, at my age, I don't do it anymore. I don't want that."

Grace sighed and shook her head.

"Oh Robert," she said, "Is that it? My God, those guys are probably talking about it because they're **not** doing it very often."

Robert looked into his wife's eyes.

"How would you know that?" he asked.

"I'm a woman. I talk to other women. We know what men are like," Grace smiled, "I'm not saying all men are liars but really; think about it; are all those guys really doing what they say they are or are they just trying to outdo one another with their stories? Who are these guys anyway? Is it Don and Martin?"

"They're part of it."

"Well, I know their wives and I can promise you; those two are definitely lying."

Robert sighed. "I feel so old, Grace," he said, "Old and stupid. You're right, I'm scared of retirement. It's a nail in the coffin."

"Robert! That's not the way to look at it. We can't any of us stop the aging process. It's just another part of life. All we can do is focus on the positives. Look at us; we're both in good health, we still enjoy spending time together. Do you know how much I'm looking forward to having you home each day when you retire next month? I can't wait."

Robert smiled. "Really?" he asked.

"Of course."

"I've been a fool, Grace," he told her, "A damned fool."

"Now, don't beat yourself up about it," she told him, rubbing his knee, "I'll be honest with you; when I look back at some of the things we've tried I can't help laughing. We've got ourselves into some funny situations. Maybe if we hadn't tried those things we wouldn't be sitting here now having this conversation."

Robert smiled. "Perhaps," he told her, "But you're right about our sex life. We haven't managed to make love in ages."

Grace stood up.

"Well," she said, taking Robert's hand in hers, "We can change that right now."

He stood up as well and Grace began leading him down the hallway.

"But it isn't my birthday," he said.

"Pretend it is."

She opened the door to their bedroom.

"What about the chops for dinner?" Robert asked.

"Sod the chops."

"Grace! Ooh; that was kind of hot."

Grace giggled and pulled her husband into the bedroom. Robert closed the door behind them.

Chapter 24

Lou waited until the next day before attempting to talk to Diana. She'd obviously heard what her mother had said the way she stumbled out of the apartment. What a way to find out your husband had cheated on you and so soon after learning your recent boyfriend had been doing the same thing. Lou thought it best to give her a bit of time to get over the initial shock but wasn't going to let the situation fester. She didn't want Diana and her mother having a nasty argument like Diana and she had had.

Maddie was feeling well enough for school so Lou dropped her there first thing and decided to pop into the supermarket to get some supplies before tackling Diana. She hadn't been back to work since the miscarriage but was going to tell Simon she'd return on Monday. Chris was standing at the front door when she entered. He looked exhausted with dark circles around his eyes but he was grinning away.

"Are you alright, Chris?" Lou asked.

"I'm fantastic, babes."

"Right; good. I thought you looked a little tired, that's all."

Chris began laughing.

"Oh yeah, I'm tired alright, babes," he said, and winked.

Lou decided not to probe him further; she'd probably end up regretting it. She grabbed a basket and made her way over to the fruit and veg area. She glanced back and saw Chris was still standing motionless by the front door, grinning away in a world of his own. Lou shook her head and began looking at the fruit. She heard the familiar click of the public address system being switched on and Terry's voice came through the speakers.

"Today only ladies," he said, "I can offer you something big in the underwear department."

Lou dropped her shopping basket.

"Seventy per cent off of panties and bras on the last day of our clothing range clear-out sale."

Lou retrieved the basket and made a mental note to spend some time with Terry next week going over his announcements. Simon's lessons obviously weren't helping.

Once she'd filled her basket Lou walked across to the checkout. Precious was staring dreamily into space and jumped when she realised a customer was there. She grinned widely when she saw who it was.

"How are you, darling?" she asked, as she put Lou's items through the scanner, "I've missed you, babes."

Babes?

"I'm doing okay," Lou said, "I'm coming back to work next Monday."

"That's great."

Precious suddenly giggled and waved at someone over Lou's shoulder. When she turned round she saw Chris, who had one hand behind his neck and one on his crotch. He was thrusting towards them.

"I take it you've still got your crush then," Lou said.

"Oh babes, it's more than that," Precious replied, "We've been seeing each other every night this week. My God, he's really funny."

"Yeah I've always thought him a bit strange."

Precious tapped Lou playfully on the arm.

"You," she said, "I mean it though; I can't get enough of him."

She leaned forwards in her seat.

445

"We're doing it every night too," she whispered, "Last night it was three times."

She winked. Lou felt like her morning sickness was coming back.

"He's an animal," Precious continued, "Like a horny badger."

No wonder he looked so knackered.

"But how are you handling the…," Lou tried to think how she could phrase her sentence delicately, "You know. The wind problem, every time he…"

Precious waved her hand dismissively.

"To be honest I don't have much sense of smell," she said, "I think it's the cigarettes."

"Right," Lou replied, as she finished packing up her goods, "I never thought I'd say this to someone but I don't think you should give them up."

Precious grinned.

Lou left her blowing kisses to Chris while she went over to Simon's office. He was pleased to see her.

"It's not the same without you," he told her, pulling out a chair.

"Well I thought I'd come back next Monday if that's okay."

Simon's face brightened.

"Wonderful. But only if you're ready."

"I'm ready. It was good of you to give me so much time off."

"Well I want my best member of staff to be at the top of her game. I've relied on you a lot these last nine months," Simon's face lost its smile, "I must mention that I wasn't able to get you back onto the management trainee course."

"I didn't expect you to even try."

"I'm going to get you made up to assistant manager here anyway, but that's just between us at the moment."

Lou grinned. "That's really nice of you," she said.

"It's no more than you deserve. Besides, I want the next manager to realise what a necessity you are to us."

"The next manager; are you leaving?"

Simon's smile returned.

"I shouldn't say anything but I'm being offered a promotion. Head Office is really impressed with our sales figures for their clothing range. Most stores had trouble selling it, I can't think why. They want me to run the large store over in Cunden Lingus."

"Congratulations."

As Lou left the supermarket and walked back to the apartment with her shopping she realised she was genuinely happy for Simon. Although the design of the clothing display had been down to her really, she'd not exactly made any extra effort to sell the old tat afterwards. Simon didn't appear to do much on the shop floor but he had recognised her potential and pushed her forwards. Maybe that was the best quality a manager could have. And he was giving her a promotion too. Perhaps her career aspirations were still possible after all, just on a slower path.

After dropping her shopping off at home, Lou knocked at Diana's door. She wasn't sure what sort of welcome she was going to receive. Diana smiled when she opened the door but exhaustion and shock showed on her face. Lou guessed she hadn't slept all night.

"Would you like some tea?" Diana asked, as they walked down to the living area.

She stopped suddenly and sighed.

447

"Oh God," she said, "That's so English. Whatever the crisis; make tea."

"Why don't I make some for both of us," Lou suggested, "You go and sit down."

Diana sniffed. "Maybe I'll just go and splash some water on my face."

She disappeared off to her bedroom and Lou went into the kitchen to switch on the kettle and put some bread into the toaster. She doubted Diana had eaten anything since lunchtime yesterday. When she came back into the room, Diana looked a little more refreshed and had changed into a new outfit. Lou saw her cast an eye up at the wall and when she looked herself she saw the wedding photograph. It hit her like a bolt from the blue. That was her father looking back at her. She dropped the teacup she was holding. Diana jumped at the sound of breaking crockery and swung round to look at Lou.

"Oh God," she said, "I'm sorry; this must be just as awful for you too."

Lou was still staring at the photograph and it took some effort for her to turn away.

"No, it's fine," she said.

"I was so caught up in myself I forgot how this affected you," Diana told her.

The two ladies sat down at the dining table, tea and toast forgotten.

"What can I say to help," Diana asked, "I really can't imagine how you are feeling right now."

"We'll worry about me later," Lou told her, "Right now I'd like to help sort this mess out between you and mum. I mean, I was always aware of her reputation. I saw it; I resented it; but she is still my mother. I've never seen her as upset as I saw her yesterday. She feels terrible. Do you hate her?"

Diana sighed. "A big part of me wants to," she admitted, "I keep going through so many emotions; anger, upset, fear. Mostly I'm still in shock. I can't take it in."

"I think it would help if you spoke to her," Lou said, "You obviously can't speak to your husband about it but mum can tell you what happened. She stayed the night at my place and is still there now. I can go and get her."

"Oh I don't know about that."

Lou took her friend's hand in hers.

"Diana," she said, "Mum was the woman you heard about; the one who sat with Richard when he died."

Diana's other hand shot up to her mouth and tears sprang to her eyes.

"She told me everything last night," Lou continued, "She's never opened up that much to me before. It was lovely, in a way. I think it would be good for you to hear the story too. What do you think?"

Diana took a moment but then nodded her head. Lou went off to fetch her mother. When she came back Diana had just finished sweeping up the broken cup. Gloria hadn't slept last night either. Her eyes were still red and puffy from crying. She looked terrified to be in Diana's presence.

"Let's sit down," Lou said.

In silence the three women sat down at the dining table.

"Mum, why don't you start?"

Gloria was staring down at the table. Finally she looked up and met Diana's eye.

"I'm so sorry," she blurted out, "I never knew you and he were together, I…"

"Just tell your story," Diana interrupted.

449

Gloria pulled a tissue out of her sleeve and wiped her nose. She took a deep breath before speaking.

"Okay," she said, "Right, well; it was thirty years ago during my first stint working at The Smugglers. It was a busy place back then as there weren't the number of pubs in the high street that there are now. I was always a…a loud kind of barmaid. You had to be, in that environment. If a man made some sort of comment I always gave back as good as I could get. It was still a time when a man thought a pat on the bum was a compliment to a woman. I always made a joke of it and took it in good faith but well, being called 'Good Time Gloria' wasn't the nicest thing to be known as."

"Is there a point to this biography?" Diana asked, crossly.

Gloria looked down again, obviously embarrassed. Lou touched her hand and she continued.

"I just wanted you to know what it was like back then so that you could see why, one day, I noticed a man sat at the bar in a very decent suit," A slight smile appeared on Gloria's face as she recalled the event, "He ordered a pint of bitter, saying please and thank you; rather than the usual, 'Oi, over here, knockers; I'm gagging for it.' I noticed his clean, tidy fingernails and he addressed me as Miss. He was such a gentleman."

Gloria stopped talking, still smiling away to herself. Lou loudly cleared her throat. Startled, she continued the story.

"Richard became a bit of a regular and always sat up at the bar. We seemed to get on well and enjoyed chatting to each other about nothing in particular. This went on for a while and then one day, he asked me out for a meal. I'd seen the wedding ring on his finger. He didn't try to hide the fact. I had a rule not to date married men but he was so…so charming and before

I knew it, I'd said yes."

Lou looked across at Diana. She was staring passed Gloria, down the hallway; but she was obviously listening to every word.

"I don't think Richard was a serial cheater or anything like that," Gloria said, "I don't think he ever looked at another woman."

Diana's eyes came back to focus on her.

"Apart from the two of us?" she said, sarcastically.

Gloria bit her lip.

"I wasn't counting myself in that," she mumbled, "It was only ever you he loved. He never mentioned you by name; he just used to say, 'the wife.' I think you were having a few arguments at that time because of the problems with trying for a baby. When he came into the pub I was there being happy Gloria for the customers; that's all. He used to call me his 'breath of fresh air.' When I think of that now, I don't really see it as a complement."

Gloria sighed.

"Anyway, I very quickly became pregnant, which was a shock to both of us. After the initial surprise I told Richard I was keeping the baby but didn't expect anything from him. He said he would like to help out. I left Ryan Harbour for Tenham and he gave me a little money for rent when I could no longer work. Once the baby was born Richard would visit when he could. He set up a payment for Lou each month and I made sure that money was only ever spent on her, never me. After a while I got a couple of part-time barmaid jobs and I started to go out on the occasional date. I was lonely at home all day with a baby. Richard's visits were often sporadic. Sometimes it was a couple of months before we saw him. I think he expected me to be waiting at home for him. He didn't like it that I was out dating. Not that we had a relationship then; that had stopped when I fell pregnant; I swear to you. Anyway, I got angry and told him that who I was dating was none of his business. I wasn't his wife."

Gloria stopped as she realised what she had just said. She looked across at Diana but there was no anger on her face. There was no emotion at all. Gloria continued.

"I think that's why I went a little crazy on the dating scene after that," she said, "To try and show him that he didn't own me. Richard's visits became rarer and when Lou turned three I received a letter from him. He said that he felt it was best that he didn't come to see me anymore. He told me, in no uncertain terms, what he thought of my lifestyle. He said he would continue to send money each month until Lou was eighteen. And that was the last contact I had. Lou told me last night that she thinks that was about the time you had your last pregnancy, where you almost died too."

Gloria stopped talking and took a deep breath. The silence that entered the room was almost palpable.

"And what about when he died," Diana asked, eventually.

Fresh tears sprang to Gloria's eyes.

"Lou and I weren't getting along," she began, "Her teenage years were a bit of a nightmare and I didn't handle things well. I'd never been a strict mother but started to be when she was fifteen. I didn't want her life going the same way mine had. Of course a strict parent is the last thing a teenager wants. We lived together in the same apartment but hardly a word was spoken between us, except when we argued."

Lou squirmed in her seat as she recalled those past years.

"When she moved out, just before her eighteenth birthday,

she came to Ryan Harbour; not that I knew that at the time. Richard heard Muriel talking about her new lodger; a young woman named Louise Turner. He got hold of my address and came to see me at the small apartment I was renting along the high road in Tenham. He was frantic with worry. He thought I'd sent her there to find him. He was scared about the past being raked up. He didn't want his wife to know; they'd been so happy together, he told me.

I got angry. He'd just turned up at my house, out of the blue and had a go at me. No 'how are you' or anything. I told him Lou was none of his business and she could go wherever she wanted. She was a grown woman now, not that he would have realised that. He said of course he realised it. He knew she was about to turn eighteen as he was about to stop the monthly payments to my bank account. Well that didn't help my anger and I told him a few home truths about the cost of raising a child and the paltry amount he used to send me that he hadn't increased in eighteen years. I accused him of not understanding what being a parent meant and of not knowing what love was. He told me of course he knew what love was. He'd felt it as soon as he'd clapped eyes on his beautiful daughter coming out of Muriel's house one day. Well, that knocked the wind out of my sails, I can tell you. I didn't know he'd actually seen her."

Lou's cheeks were covered in tears.

"We sat down and talked properly," Gloria told them, "I got out some photograph albums and he got to see his daughter grow up through the pages. By the time he left my apartment Richard was telling me that he wasn't going to approach Lou, but if she ever did want to contact him, he'd be willing to see her."

Gloria reached into her sleeve for another tissue.

"I walked him downstairs to the street. His car was in the car park across the road. If only I hadn't gone down. He stopped halfway across the road to wave. The car, it was so quick. I wasn't sure what had happened at first. Richard was there and then he wasn't. When I saw him in the road I ran over. So many people were around us. He was still breathing but wasn't conscious. I took his hand and kept talking to him. I can't remember now what I said. It didn't take long for the breathing to stop. I kissed the side of his cheek and then disappeared into the crowd as the ambulance arrived. I couldn't stay there and risk being a witness. I couldn't let his wife find out about me...and now she has. Oh Diana; I'm so sorry."

Gloria pressed the fresh tissue into her eyes as her tears flowed freely.

"I feel terrible."

Diana shook her head.

"Bastard!" she spat.

"I know; I'm sorry."

"Not you, Gloria; him!"

Shocked, both Lou and Gloria stopped crying and stared at Diana.

"What did you say?" Lou asked.

"Richard. How could he just have abandoned you like that?"

"Oh," Lou was taken aback, "I suppose because he thought he was having a legitimate child with his wife at the time. Besides he did send money."

Diana huffed.

"Money," she said, standing up and going over to the photographs on the wall. She took down her wedding photo and stared at it, "He thought that would solve all problems. If I ever told him I was unhappy he'd give me money and say,

454

'Here, go buy yourself something nice' as if that would make everything okay. What a bastard."

She threw the photo down hard onto the mahogany armrest of the sofa where the glass smashed and the frame fell apart. Lou and Gloria both jumped.

"Diana, please; calm down," Lou said.

It was scary to witness her friend so angry and distraught.

"But he is a bastard," Diana replied, turning round to face the two women, "If he wanted a child so badly, why didn't he see you? You weren't far away. After I lost our last one, our little boy; why didn't he resume actual contact? I can't help wondering if he just wanted children to be able to show off. 'Look everybody, I have a big house, a wife and I've been able to produce all of these children. How much of a man am I?' Is that the real reason he wanted them?"

"I can't answer that."

"But don't you see," Diana said, coming over and sitting back down again, "I've thought myself a failure because I couldn't give my husband what he wanted. I've punished myself all these years and yet he had a child all that time but he abandoned her. While we eventually managed to live happily and very comfortably just the two of us, there was a little girl close by, growing up without her father. I've been punishing myself when it's him that's been the failure."

Diana stopped talking and burst into tears. It was Gloria who got up and ran round the table to cradle her in her arms.

*

Jamie didn't know who the solicitor was or what he wanted.

Am I being sued, he thought, as he sat in the waiting room; perhaps one of the contestants from the eating competition got food poisoning. Well, they can sue me for every penny if they

455

want. It won't add up to much.

Jamie wasn't in the best of moods. He'd texted Lou this morning but she hadn't replied yet. She wasn't back at work so what else was she doing? She hadn't got cold feet about them and their relationship, had she?

"Mr Taylor; Mr Rodgers will see you now."

Jamie was led into a very plush-looking room. It was nothing like the office of the solicitor that he normally used, where you had difficulty trying to find a space to sit between the piles of paper. Mr Rodgers was a short but very dapper looking man in a three-piece, expensive, grey suit. He came round from behind his desk to shake Jamie's hand.

"Please," he said, returning to his seat and indicating the chair opposite.

"Look," Jamie told him, once he had sat down, "I'm not sure who's contacted you, but if it's about the eating competition then I can promise you that food was cooked properly."

Mr Rodgers held up his hands in a 'calm down' gesture.

"Mr Taylor," he said, "This has nothing to do with any kind of complaint. This is about the will of Mr Joseph Johnson."

"Who's that?" Jamie asked.

"Joseph Johnson," Mr Rodgers repeated, as if everyone should know the name, "He used to frequent your bar I believe," he looked at his notes, "The Smugglers Inn?"

Jamie frowned. "I don't know anyone called...oh; you mean Old Joe."

Mr Rodger's looked a little shocked to hear his client described that way but he quickly regained his composure.

"Erm, yes; I suppose so," he said, "Anyway, Mr Johnson has left you something in his will."

"Has he? That's kind of him, but, really; what did he have to leave?"

"Five hundred thousand pounds."

"What?"

Jamie was up and out of his seat. Mr Rodger's looked up calmly from his notes.

"He's left you five hundred thousand pounds. Plus the apartment he used to live in."

Jamie fell back into the chair.

"But, but, but…why? How? I don't understand. Joe was, well; he was an old man struggling to get by on his pension, wasn't he? You must have him mixed up with this other Mr Johnson."

Mr Rodgers smiled. "I don't make mistakes, Mr Taylor, I assure you. Mr Johnson's apartment is in Ryan Harbour, is it not?"

"Well, yes; but…"

"Then we have the right person," Mr Rodgers took off his glasses, "Mr Johnson was a very wealthy man, Mr Taylor. He owned quite a bit of property and land in various areas of Tenhamshire, including a large chunk of the harbour front in Ryan Harbour; which he sold for a substantial sum many years ago to developers. He kept a small part back which I believe he kindly allowed his ex-wife, Selina, to run some amusement arcades on; even though they had been estranged for over forty years. When she died he sold that as well; to the same developers."

Jamie was having trouble taking all of this information in.

"But why leave it all to me."

"Oh he hasn't left all of it to you, far from it," Mr Rodgers chuckled, "No, the bulk of his estate has been split amongst various charities but he made a special request recently that you

457

receive the sum I already mentioned."

The solicitor put his glasses back on and read from the papers in front of him.

"It's due to the kindness you have always shown him each day since you became landlord of his favourite public house."

"But all I ever did was let him have the odd free pint and cigar."

Mr Rodgers looked up at Jamie and smiled.

"And those gestures and a kind word were something Mr Johnson very much appreciated. Look Mr Taylor, I've known my client for a number of years. He was a very shy but very kind and observant man. He liked the simple things in life, a pint of bitter, a smoke; he had no need for vast sums of money. He lived his life as he wanted and knew that it was coming to an end. I believe your pub is going through some problems at present. Mr Johnson was well aware of that and admired your determination to make things better. He told me that this sum of money should be enough for you to make the changes you need and his apartment will give you somewhere to live while these alterations are being made. It's very simple."

Simple? That's not the word Jamie would have used. Magical seemed more appropriate. He left the solicitor's office in a daze. As he climbed back into his car he switched his mobile back on and saw a text from Lou. He phoned her straight away.

*

Dr's Case Notes – Tuesday 24 November

I'm turning into a wreck. I can't get Dr Moore's departure out of my mind. What am I going to do? What state am I going to be in six months from now? I'm already losing concentration at the most inopportune time. It's not nice for a patient during a prostate exam to hear the doctor exclaim, 'Oh my God, am I in too deep?'

I'm getting very snappy with everyone. I sacked Mrs Andrews yesterday. Well there have been a lot of rumours about confidential information being leaked and I caught her with a pad and pen, writing out patients' information from the details on the computer. If I'm honest I was probably more worried about her finding these 'case notes.' Anyway, she's gone. Fortunately Diana Carlton had come in to see me regarding the surgery expansion and she offered to step in and help me out for a while until I find someone else, so that's okay. I must say, she's picking things up very quickly.

Mrs Bryant has definitely noticed the change in me. She brought it up last night while she had the angle grinder out, giving herself a pedicure. She told me I was being inattentive, moody and should buck up. I told her she could go fuck herself. Apparently I was out cold for twenty minutes.

But let's face it; she is right. I do need to buck up. Dr Moore's leaving and I can't do anything about it. Perhaps if I had been braver sooner and taken a chance on showing my true feelings, things might have been different. Oh well Cedric, you'll never know now. Stop moping and start concentrating on your Practice. I've got an interview with a possible replacement doctor in half an hour. Not that I could ever replace Dr Moore.

Oh my God! It's an hour later and I've just had an interview with the most beautiful person I've ever seen. Dr Sanderson is breathtaking. I think I'm in love.

Chapter 25

Lou looked at the 'Bon Voyage' banner hanging up above the ground floor bar area. Had it really taken six months to finally complete the last item on Diana's list, 'Broaden Horizons?' Still, there had been a lot going on in that time. Where Lou was standing now was the biggest change; no longer in the empty, rather small Smugglers Inn but the newly expanded and popular Old Joe's Bar and Restaurant.

Jamie had done what Lou suggested back on singles night and bought Celia's old tearoom next door and knocked through. It was a blessing that the old buildings on this side of the harbour had never been listed. With Old Joe's money Jamie had transformed the ground, first and some of the second floors of both buildings to create a beautiful new restaurant which the town had flocked to. He'd retained the look of The Smugglers and the theme of the décor was very much boat and pirate related, with lots of polished wood and brass on show. It looked fantastic and the newly employed chef had created a terrific menu.

Lou had done her bit by helping with the design and the style of seating and lighting. She'd also written a weekly blog on the town's community website as the work was being done; keeping the local residents up-to-date and interested in the project until its grand opening last month. She'd been so busy she hadn't had time to miss the supermarket. Lou hadn't taken the assistant manager promotion and only returned to serve her notice period. She and Jamie had decided to make a go of things and became partners in both business and pleasure.

So many things had changed at the supermarket anyway.

Simon had moved on to his new store, taking Terry with him (Lou still wasn't sure why). After Precious had given up smoking she and Chris drifted apart. Wanting a fresh start away from the shop, Diana had shown her the ropes at the surgery and she'd taken over as receptionist; freeing up Diana to finally go on this cruise. Chris had managed to retain his job as security guard but as he was now having an affair with the new manager, Lou felt he wasn't going to be there much longer.

She walked away from the bar area in search of Diana who had disappeared. She'd been getting quite nervous about the trip these past few days and Lou hoped she hadn't bailed on her. Grace and Robert were sat at a corner table and Grace reached out and tapped Lou as she was about to pass them.

"I can't get over how wonderful this place is," she said, "Robert and I come in here at least once a week now."

"I've noticed," Lou replied, "Retirement is suiting both of you; you're never at home."

The couple both smiled.

"Yes, we're off out once we've finished these drinks," Robert said, "I've got a little mystery tour planned for Grace this afternoon."

Grace giggled.

"Not that it's as exciting as going down to Southampton to get on a cruise ship mind you," he added.

"Yes," Lou said, "Have you seen Diana by the way? I've lost her."

They both shook their heads. Lou stepped away from the table and made a quick scan of the back of the restaurant. Unable to spot her friend, she turned to go back the way she had just come from and collided with Dr Moore.

"Oh I'm sorry," she said.

"My fault," Dr Moore replied.

"Aren't you off today as well," Lou asked.

Dr Moore smiled. "Yes, your banner suits me too."

"I hope everything goes well at your father's old practice. It was good of you to give such a long notice period and to help Dr Bryant with the surgery expansion. I'm sure he's going to miss you."

"Oh I don't think he'll miss me that much," Dr Moore replied, stroking his beard. He indicated another table with his head, "Not now he's got Dr Sanderson to stare at."

Lou looked over at the table where the Bryants were sitting. She saw Dr Bryant making furtive glances across the table to where the young Dr Sanderson and his wife were seated.

"I used to be on the receiving end of those little looks," Dr Moore told Lou.

"Really?"

"Oh yes. I don't think I imagined it."

He shrugged his shoulders.

"Still, it's too late now. He is quite a sweetie in his way and I have always preferred the older man."

This seemed a very surreal conversation to Lou.

"I think the poor guy just really needs a change in his life," Dr Moore continued, "A bit of excitement. It's a shame he didn't take a chance and tell me how he felt. He's not going to get anywhere with Dr Sanderson."

Dr Moore sighed and looked at his watch.

"Oh well," he said, "Life goes on. I guess I'd better have a drink with them all before I leave."

He smiled and nodded at Lou before heading off to the bar. Lou shook away the thoughts that had entered her head and made her way out to the front entrance. She scanned the harbour front; spotting Diana standing by the slipway, looking out at the boats. She walked over to her.

"There you are," Lou said, "I thought you'd done a runner."

Diana gave a rather melancholic smile.

"I've just come from the cemetery," she replied, "It would have been Richard's seventieth birthday today."

"Oh right. Sorry, I didn't realise."

"I didn't know whether to mention it or not," Diana said, "I decided to go see him and say goodbye."

"Goodbye?"

"Well, again I mean. After I found out about the affair I felt there was a part of him I didn't know. It's taken me these past six months to properly acknowledge that side of his life; and to forgive him. It's that part I'm saying goodbye to now. I've finished mourning the man once and for all. Today seemed to be the right day to do it; now that I'm taking such a big step forward."

"It's only a holiday, Diana; you're not emigrating."

"It's a big step for me," she said, "My first time abroad. I'm still not sure I'm doing the right thing."

Lou patted her reassuringly on the arm.

"It's going to be wonderful," she told her.

Diana smiled and then she frowned as she looked at her friend.

"I've just realised something," she said, "You've got Richard's father's nose. I was looking at some old photographs last night."

"Have I?" Lou asked, absently touching her own nose.

"Yes. I didn't know him that well but he always seemed a rather kind and generous man."

"Right."

Diana reached down and took Lou's hand.

"When you feel ready," she said, "I can show you all the photographs I have and tell you all about Richard and his family. But only if you want me to, of course."

Lou sighed. "I've been putting it off, I know I have," she confessed, "I've used the alterations to the pub as an excuse really, but Jamie and I have been getting along so well and everything has been happy and exciting, I didn't want to think about anything that may cause some upset; like getting to know my father."

"I understand," Diana said, "There's no rush."

The two ladies stood looking out at the boats.

"There you are," a voice behind them called out.

Turning, they saw Gloria standing in the doorway to the restaurant, champagne glass in hand.

"What are you doing out there? Come on; Diana and I have got to get going soon."

Diana sighed as the two of them made their way back over to the restaurant.

"I still can't believe I'm going on a three week cruise with your mother," she said.

"Yes," Lou replied, "I'm glad I'm not going on a three week cruise with her."

She smiled at Diana's haughty expression and then laughed.

"I'm joking," she said, "You're both going to have a marvellous time."

They reached the door. Gloria was grinning. It obviously wasn't her first glass of champagne.

"Come on in here you two and have a drink to celebrate," she said, "I still can't believe I'm going on a cruise. I feel as giddy as a teenager. It's going to be great; good food, delicious wine and lots of rich men to have our pick of. We're not going to share one again are we?"

Gloria elbowed Diana in the ribs. She laughed loudly and tottered off to the bar. Diana raised her eyebrows at Lou.

"You're both going to have a marvellous time," Lou repeated.

Jamie walked through from the kitchen as Diana headed off to join Gloria. He came up behind Lou and placed his arms around her waist.

"Hey you," he said, kissing her on the neck, "Where have you been hiding?"

"I was making sure Diana hadn't done a bunk," she replied, turning round.

"Well you couldn't blame her. I love your mother but probably not after three solid weeks together."

"It will be the making of them," Lou said.

"Are you trying to convince me or yourself?"

"A bit of both really. What have you done with Maddie? I thought she'd want to be out here."

"She's putting swirly lines of raspberry sauce onto plates in the kitchen and then I'm adding the slices of cheesecake. She's not half bad actually; very neat and precise."

"I think that's called child labour."

"Only if I was paying her anything," Jamie told her, "At the moment it's just slavery."

Lou laughed and then waved at Muriel whom she'd just spotted rushing in through the door.

"Oh good," Muriel panted, as she came to a stop beside them, "I thought I was going to miss it."

"Have you been chasing the paperboy again?" Jamie teased, "I've told you, he's too young for you."

Muriel chuckled. "No, I was just packing up a few more boxes and lost track of time."

"I told you there's no rush, Muriel," Lou said, as Jamie returned to the kitchen, "We'll move into your house only once you're ready to move into Old Joe's apartment."

"Oh I'm ready," Muriel said, "I'm really looking forward to it. I can't believe it after all these years; my own little apartment; no more taking in lodgers. And it will be nice to be so close to Diana as well."

"Well I've loved living in it these past six months. It took a while to clear out all of Old Joe's clutter and give the place a fresh lick of paint, but I hope it will be a happy place for you."

Muriel nodded. "I don't know how you found the time to do all that and get the restaurant up and running."

"Neither do I, if I'm honest," Lou told her, "It has been a busy six months. Still, we're up and running now. Hopefully once we're in your house we'll get some time over the summer to enjoy having a garden. Maddie's really looking forward to it, she can't wait."

"And I can't wait to see what you do to the house."

"I won't do too much, Muriel," Lou said, sounding a little embarrassed, "It's the house you grew up in. I'll feel bad if we start knocking down walls and changing things."

"Oh my dear, you must change it," Muriel told her, "It's tired, I'll admit that. No, you bash down any walls you like. I'm sure you'll make it look stunning. I'm so happy you're moving in there."

"How does Joyce feel about it?" Lou asked.

Muriel pulled a face. "She's not happy that I've managed to sell and she hasn't. Over six months her place has been on the market now. She's going to have to drop the price. It's on for

466

far too much."

Lou smiled. "It'll be worth even less when the likes of me moves up the hill."

Muriel's eyes twinkled. "I must admit it wasn't a pleasant experience when I told her who had bought my house, but still; I'm happy. The apartment is just what I want and it's so convenient for when I run the kiddies art group at the surgery."

Diana walked over to greet her friend.

"Muriel, thought you weren't coming," she said, and grinned.

Muriel laughed. "I was just talking about the kiddies' art group and how easy it will be for me to get to when I move into the apartment."

"Oh yes," Diana said, remembering something, "Now, I've given Mrs Brownlow my key to the clinic room at the surgery. She's going to let the teenage writing group in on Wednesdays and the drama group on Saturday morning. Dr Bryant mentioned changing the well woman clinic to Wednesdays but he didn't say when."

"Don't worry, I've sorted that with Precious," Muriel told her, "You just enjoy your trip."

Lou laughed. "Listen to you two," she said, "Talking matter-of-factly about the youth groups. Six months ago you didn't think you were going to pull it off."

Diana and Muriel smiled at each other.

"I do feel quite proud," Diana admitted, "And we've got other ideas on the go as well. The old art shop next door to here has agreed to display all of the children's artwork in their gallery."

"That sounds like fun."

"Yes, I'm excited about it," Diana said, "Muriel, you haven't got a drink. Let's get you one."

Diana turned to go to the bar but Muriel didn't move.

"What wrong?"

"Oh nothing; I was just thinking over the past year," Muriel told them, "Realising how much has changed, and all for the better. It's due to you two really."

"Why us two?" Lou asked.

"Well, ever since you became friends and created that list, everything else seems to have improved."

Lou and Diana both grinned at each other.

"Of course I wasn't sure it was a good idea at first," Muriel continued, "Especially when I saw you up on the balcony that day of the regatta with your bosoms out. I hope you're not going to give a repeat performance this summer."

Muriel walked off to get a drink, leaving behind two very red-faced women.

Half an hour later the taxi arrived to take Diana and Gloria down to Southampton. There were lots of goodbyes and hugs and kisses. Lou felt a lump in her throat, even though they were only going away for three weeks. As the car left and people waved, Lou found herself at the back of the crowd. Jamie made his way through it with Maddie. She ran up to her mother and gave her a hug.

"Auntie Diana looked scared," she said.

"Did she?"

Maddie nodded. "Why is that?" she asked.

"Well she's never been abroad before," Lou told her, "It's a new experience."

"Why do something if it scares you?" Maddie asked.

"Sometimes you have to, sweetheart," Jamie said, "But it usually turns out okay in the end."

This seemed to satisfy her. Lou looked at Jamie and he winked and smiled at her before placing his arm around her shoulder.

"Do you think they're going to survive the trip or end up killing each other?" he whispered.

Lou giggled. She slipped her arm around his waist.

"No, everything is going to be fine," she said, stroking her emerging baby bump with the other hand, "Everything is going to be just fine."

Driven to Distraction

By

Stuart Bone

Derek Noble wishes now that he'd read the small print in the holiday brochure before booking the luxury coach trip to rural Tenhamshire. Apparently it's fine for Scrimshaw Travel to make last minute amendments to the holiday without incurring any penalties or reducing the price in any way. That's what the indifferent courier tells him on day one of the tour as she arrives in a clapped-out, old coach driven by a partially-sighted driver.

With the spa hotel replaced by a rundown guest house, staffed by a menopausal manager, decrepit waitress and under-sexed, Italian waiter; there doesn't appear to be much of the brochure-described holiday left.

Thank goodness for Angela, the rather lovely woman Derek pals up with on the journey down. She might just make the trip bearable. If only the other members of the group would leave them alone long enough to get to know each other. But Derek has always had the ability to attract the eccentric characters to him and he can't escape them. Still, perhaps they'll surprise him as he learns about their lives and secrets as they move from one hilarious excursion to another. And maybe Angela will provide one or two surprises herself.

'Driven to Distraction is definitely high on the humour quotient and a delightful recommendation for everyone who is up for a good laugh.' – *SeriousReading.com*

Printed in Great Britain
by Amazon